William Jesse

The Life of George Brummell

William Jesse

The Life of George Brummell

ISBN/EAN: 9783744662765

Printed in Europe, USA, Canada, Australia, Japan

Cover: Foto ©Raphael Reischuk / pixelio.de

More available books at **www.hansebooks.com**

THE LIFE

OF

GEORGE BRUMMELL, Esq.

COMMONLY CALLED

BEAU BRUMMELL

BY

CAPTAIN JESSE
Unattached

Revised and Annotated Edition from the Author's
own Interleaved Copy

With Forty Portraits in Colour of Brummell and his Contemporaries

IN TWO VOLUMES

VOLUME THE FIRST

LONDON
JOHN C. NIMMO
14, KING WILLIAM STREET, STRAND, W.C.
1886

PREFACE

TO THE NEW EDITION.

" The Life of George Brummell, commonly called Beau Brummell," by the late Captain Jesse, has been a scarce book for a long time. It is now reprinted, and a large quantity of new matter has been introduced, which had been collected by the author, but which it was not deemed prudent or delicate to insert in former editions. Many notes have also been added.

please is not, however, always attended with success, for the very
simple reason, that it is impossible
to please everybody; and those
who expect to find in the Life of
George Brummell a delightful dish
of scandal, will, no doubt, exclaim,
" His shot has gone very wide of
the mark!" I could, it is true,
have served up one so hot, that it
would have shrivelled up the ears
of the most inveterate lovers of
it; but, to repeat the anecdotes I
have heard the Beau relate, of the
orgies of Carlton House, of tip-
pling Dowagers, doating Ex-chan-
cellors, shy Generals, and borrowed

Jewels,[1] &c., &c., forms no part of my intention; and, even if it were desirable that Brummell's gossip on such subjects should be repeated, it would be impossible

[1] It was reported that a lady of high rank, whose name Brummell mentioned to me, requested a certain noble duke, with whom she was very intimately acquainted, to lend her the family diamonds, either to wear at Court or at some grand ball of the day. His Grace could, of course, refuse her nothing; he immediately acceded to her wishes, and gave her an order on his jeweller for them, imagining, no doubt, that his fair friend would return them to his tradesman when the occasion for which they were borrowed had passed over. The duke, however, reckoned too much upon her honesty, for after his death, which took place a few months later, his brother, who succeeded to the title, found on applying to the family jeweller that Lady —— had never returned the diamonds into his custody, nor were they, according to the *on dit*, ever recovered.

About the year 1842, it was also hinted about in society that a certain noble countess had borrowed some jewels from a lady of high rank—her intimate friend—without the latter's permission or knowledge, but in this case the missing articles were restored.

to vouch for its authenticity; for no one so delighted in mystifying and hoaxing people as he did, or could so readily find imaginary, and very plausible, proofs, when the truth of his fictions was assailed.

That he wrote some detached papers in the shape of reminiscences, there can be no doubt: many passages in his letters prove this. In the centre of his diminutive garden, under the ramparts at Calais, which he frequented a good deal during the summer months, there was a small pavilion; and here, when the heat obliged him to lay aside his hoe or rake, he amused himself with his pen. The common-place book in which he inserted these memoranda was secured by a lock, and one of his great friends, who, in his way through Calais, occasionally spent a portion of the day with him in his retreat, informed me, that Brummell once drew his attention to the manuscript—calling it, "his book of life," and saying, as he turned carelessly over the leaves, " Here is a chapter on Carlton House; here one on Mrs. Fitz-herbert and the Prince; this is devoted to Lady H——," &c.

This book was in his possession at Caen, and, as it lay on his table, he sometimes pointed it out to his visitors, remarking, that it contained recollections of his own life, and descriptions of the gay world he had formerly lived in. Indeed, it appeared almost as if he kept a diary, for, dining one day at Mr. Villiers's, he said to the lady of the house, " Mrs. Villiers, I was looking at my journal yester-- day, and I see, that it was on this very day two years that I had the pleasure of making your acquaint-ance." These, and many other reasons, render it more than pro-

bable that Brummell not only recorded the events of his past life,
but also of each day, or perhaps
week. Nothing, however, has been
heard of these papers since his
death ; perhaps they were destroyed by him when imbecility
had set the seal of unconscious-
ness upon his actions, or he may
have delivered them up, for a
pecuniary consideration, to those
who were most interested in obtaining possession of them. It
is, however, a highly honourable
trait in his character, that he did
not, amidst all his troubles and
difficulties, publish them for his

own benefit. When in jail at
Caen for debt, he said to Monsieur Godefroi, one of his fellow-
prisoners, " I have letters of the
Royal family, of Lord Byron, and
others, the sale of which would
produce me more than sufficient
to pay my debts; but I will not
part with them, for I should com-
promise several families." Mr.
Leleux, his landlord at Calais,
also informed me, that a London
publisher had offered his lodger a
thousand pounds if he would give
up his memoirs. " When this pro-
position was made to Mr. Brummell," said Mr. Leleux, " he was

in great distress, and I frequently asked him why he did not accept it? To this he usually made some frivolous excuse; but on one occasion, when pressed hard for his real reason, he said, 'I promised the Duchess of York that I would not publish any notes of mine during the life-time of George the Fourth or his brothers; and I am under so many obligations to her, and have such a deep respect for her generous and amiable conduct to me in our early friendship, and since, that I would rather go to jail than forfeit my word. She is the only link that binds me in this matter.'" At Brummell's death several packets of letters, tied up with different coloured ribbons, and carefully numbered, a minia- ture, a silver shaving-dish, a gold ring, and a few silver spoons, were found in a trunk at the hotel. The miniature and letters were taken possession of by the vice- consul, and the remaining effects by the landlord, in liquidation of an account which had only been partially cancelled. This person said, that in the same parcel with the letters was another containing a great many locks of hair. They were each of them in a separate

envelope, and, on the outside of
one, in Brummell's hand-writing,
was the following remark:—" Lady
W——, la femme la plus coquette
du monde." From the foregoing
remarks, therefore, the reader will
understand that, with the exception of his letters, and the poetry
taken from his album, I was not
assisted in the compilation of this
memoir by any papers left by
Brummell, nor by any obtained
from his family (to whom I applied),
for they had none to give me, but
by information which I collected
from various sources. Amongst
the numerous attempts that have

been made in the novels of the day to delineate Brummell's character, Trebeck, in Granby, was the only one that he considered successful. I once heard him say, " Lister must have known those who were intimate with me :" from this clever and entertaining book I have made one or two extracts. The principal portion of the materials, however, from which the sketch of his early career has been drawn, was procured from friends who were intimate with him. The description of the last years of his life is the result of my own observations, and that of

those who were constantly about
him. To them, and to those noblemen and gentlemen who were kind
enough to reply to my inquiries,
I beg to return my acknowledg-
ments; and in conclusion I have
merely to add, that whatever im-
perfections the work may have,
whether as to the choice of subject, the style, or execution, I
have carefully refrained from any
attempt to enliven it by the introduction of anecdotes, which,
though witty and amusing, would
have wounded the feelings of
others. In this, at least, I trust
I have not failed.

CONTENTS OF VOL. I.

CHAPTER I.

CHAPTER II.

CHAPTER III.

CHAPTER VIII.

CHAPTER IX.

CHAPTER X.

CHAPTER XI.

CHAPTER XXIV.

CHAPTER XXV.

CHAPTER XXVI.

CHAPTER XXVII.

LIST OF ILLUSTRATIONS.

VOL. I.

———+·———

LIST OF ILLUSTRATIONS.

THE LIFE

OF

BEAU BRUMMELL.

CHAPTER I.

*Early Distinctions in Dress—Milton's Eve—The Roman Exquisite—
The Native Princes of Britain—Hotspur's Fop—The Beaux in
the Reign of Charles the Second—Beau Hewitt—Beau Wilson—
Beau Fielding—Beau Edgeworth—Beau Nash—Petrarch—Lord
Byron—The Abbé Delille—Prince Kaunitz—English Fops.*

THOSE who yet remain of his generation, but who
were not acquainted with the subject of these
memoirs, will, no doubt, be astonished that any one
should have taken the trouble to be his biographer,
and much wonder what there can possibly be to say
about Beau Brummell—unless, indeed, it were to
give the impertinent witticisms currently reported
of him. But of those contemporaries who knew
him intimately and still survive, few will be surprised that I have found some amusement in col-

lecting the scattered reminiscences of so singular a character.

The term Beau is now very nearly obsolete, and Brummell, to whom the term in its popular sense was erroneously applied, will, in all probability, be one of the last persons distinguished by that sobriquet; but, before entering upon this memoir, perhaps a few words respecting the most notorious of the species so denominated may not be out of place. From the earliest ages there have always been individuals vain enough to be completely absorbed in the study of dress, yet this can hardly be matter of astonishment, for every one must allow that vanity in the abstract is coeval with humanity; and it was, possibly, under this conviction that even Milton suffered himself to accuse Eve of contemplating her beautiful form in the looking-glass of Nature.

> That day I oft remember, when from sleep
> I first awaked, and found myself reposed
> Under a shade on flowers, much wondering where
> And what I was, whence thither brought, and how.
> Not distant far from thence a murmuring sound
> Of waters issued from a cave, and spread
> Into a liquid plain, then stood unmoved
> Pure as th' expanse of Heaven; I thither went
> With inexperienced thought, and laid me down
> On the green bank, to look into the clear
> Smooth lake, that to me seem'd another sky.
> As I went down to look, just opposite,
> A shape within the wat'ry gleam appear'd
> Bending to look on me: I started back,
> It started back; but pleased I soon return'd,
> Pleased it return'd as soon with answering looks

Of sympathy and love : there I had fix'd
Mine eyes till now, and pined with vain desire,
Had not, &c. &c.

Paradise Lost, book iv.

Distinctions in dress, it may be inferred, were at
a very remote period highly prized, or the venerable
patriarch Jacob would not, in the indulgence of his
parental vanity, have selected "a coat of many
colours," as the most gratifying gift he could bestow
upon his youngest and favourite son ; a gift which
was probably valued by Joseph, not only as a proof
of his father's affection for him, but also on account
of its being a garment of peculiar beauty, and
superior to those worn by his brethren. The hope
expressed by Sisera's mother, that her son would
find amongst the spoil of Barak's camp "a prey
of divers colours of needlework on both sides," has
also been adduced as an evidence that the princes
and great men of Israel were fond of arraying themselves in glorious apparel, and far from indifferent
to the decoration of their persons.

Of the toilette of the Hebrew beau or belle,
however, few details have been preserved ; but no
such blank exists in the history of the last conquerors of their nation ; of *their* dandyism many
and amusing particulars have been handed down to
us in those works which treat of their domestic
manners, after riches and luxury had increased in
Rome, and corruption had stamped the character
of her citizens with effeminacy and voluptuousness.

The tunic of the Roman exquisite was often of green silk; he painted, rouged, and curled his hair, wore a great number and variety of rings, light or heavy, according to the season; and the most superlatively finished fops had the hairs, even of their legs, plucked out by the roots with small tweezers, called *volsellæ*. In this state of things, it was very natural that the dress of the women, which had been, till then, modest and simple, should become the chief object of their attention; and so completely was this the case, that a lady's toilette and ornaments were called her world, *mundus muliebris*.

But a refined state of society, however it may excite personal vanity, is certainly not necessary to its development: it is exhibited by the savage, in the taste he displays in the choice of his beads, shells, and feathers, and the variety and elegance shown in the designs of his tattooing; and it is highly probable, that when Julius Cæsar landed in Britain, he found some of our native princes much better painted than others, and their blue tints of a brighter hue. Perhaps the iron age of chivalry, when women's hearts were won in coats of mail, not in silk tunics, was more free from dandyism than any other. In the days of the Crusades men thought but little of themselves, and, excepting in the splendour of their armour, and a gay plume or scarf, still less of their outsides. The gallant Hotspur's indignant description of the finical fop, "who shone so bright and smelt so sweet, and talked so like a waiting gentle-

woman," is one of the earliest, best, and most
entertaining given in our language. In the reign of
Elizabeth, the distinguished men whom her vigorous
mind induced her to select for her companions and
advisers, were remarkable for the bravery of their
attire, for they were obliged to fall in with the
taste of their imperious mistress, who devoted much
time to the adornment of her person : it was, however, reserved for the court of that luxurious monarch,
Louis the Fourteenth, who never permitted even his
own valet to see him without his full-bottomed wig,
to give effect to that spirit of coxcombality, which was
introduced into England at the Restoration, by the
rakish and rollicking cavaliers who formed the unprin-
cipled suite of Charles the Second. His reign produced a host of *beaux*, at which time the term appears
to have been first used, and amongst others was applied
more particularly to Hewitt, Wilson, and Fielding.

The first of these worthies, Sir George Hewitt,
afterwards an Irish Viscount, which peerage seems
to have died with him, had the credit of being the
individual from whom "gentle George Etheredge,"
though himself the involuntary original, is said to
have drawn the character of Sir Fopling Flutter,
in the "Man of Mode"—the prototype of all the
fops in comedy. The Viscount appears, also, to
have been one of the first persons who reduced the
robuster "damn me" of the preceding age to the
modern "dammee;" since become the consumptive
"demmee" of our own. In Sir Walter Scott's

edition of Dryden, we have, in Rochester's farewell, an example of this mincing innovation of Beau Hewitt's :—

> Had it not better been than thus to roam,
> To stay, and tie the cravat-string at home ;
> To strut, look big, shake pantaloon, and swear,
> With Hewitt, " Damme, there's no action here?"

Wilson, too, another Beau of that day, is described by Grainger as a most mysterious person. He was the younger son of a respectable family, and entered the army, from which, after a short service in Flanders, he was dismissed for cowardice, when he returned to England with forty shillings, borrowed from a friend. Here, to the astonishment of every one, he in a short time appeared the brightest star in the hemisphere of fashion ; his dress, table, equipages, and stud, being perfect, and his hospitality profuse. As he seldom played, and was not known to have any intrigues, it soon became matter of lively speculation, how he contrived to support all this state ; many of his friends tried to worm out his secret, but without success ; for, though his conduct and conversation were apparently perfectly open, he was in reality so guarded even in his convivial moments, that no expression ever escaped him that could give a clue to the source of his wealth. Some said that he possessed the *grand secret* of converting meaner metals into gold, and others that he had robbed a Dutch mail of a package of rough diamonds. But a more natural solution of the mystery attached to Mr. Wilson's proceedings, is given in some intercepted letters appended to a work published in 1708, entitled "Memoirs of the Court of England, in the Reign of Charles the Second;" and which seems to have been much read at the time, for it went through several editions. In one of these epistles, it is stated that Beau Wilson's ability to pursue his extravagant career was owing to the liberality of the beautiful Duchess of Cleveland, with whom he intrigued; but the details of the story are so singular and minute, that the authenticity of some of them may fairly be doubted. Mr. Wilson was killed in a duel by that Prince of schemers, Mississippi Law, who it is said ran him through the body before he could draw his sword in his own defence.

Beau Fielding, who stands on record as the best-looking of the beaux, and is mentioned by Swift, as one of those "who made mean figures upon some remarkable occasions," was of a good family in War-wickshire. Being intended for the bar, he was sent to London early in life, but, giving way to the temptations of fashionable vices, soon abandoned that profession. His person was exceedingly beautiful, and he took infinite pains to set it off. Charles the Second was so struck with his figure when he first saw him at court, that he called him the "handsome Fielding." From that moment, he became the most conceited of all fops, and was not only vain and expensive in his own dress, but fantastical in that of his lacqueys, who

usually wore yellow liveries, with black sashes, and
black feathers in their hats.   His courage was of the
same quality as that of his contemporary, Mr. Wilson,
his greatest piece of heroism having been to run a
helpless linkboy through the body in St. Martin's Lane.
One evening, however, in pushing forward, to show
off his dress and figure, at the theatre in Lincoln's Inn
Fields, he trod upon the foot of a lawyer named Full-
wood, who thereupon instantly challenged, and wounded
him, but who, singularly enough, was killed in a duel
with a Captain Cusack the same night.   Fielding also
received a severe caning from, and was subsequently
wounded by, a Welsh gentleman of the name of Price.
His excesses and extravagance at length consumed
his patrimony, after which, he subsisted upon his
gallantries and the supplies that he obtained at the
gaming table, where he was generally successful.   To
repair his shattered fortunes he eventually married a
connexion of Dean Swift's, the only daughter and
heiress of Lord Carlingford.   By this lady, a zealous
Roman Catholic, he was converted to her faith, and
probably induced to attach himself to the cause of
James the Second, for whose service he raised a regiment in his own county, and whom he afterwards
accompanied to France, where he lived handsomely
on his wife's remittances.

When this lady died, being again in difficulties,
Fielding once more had recourse to matrimony for a
subsistence, but this time he was completely taken in
by a certain Mary Wadsworth, who had assumed the

name and character of Madame Delaune,[1] a person of great wealth. Discovering the fraud he soon forsook her, and subsequently espoused, when in her sixty-first year, Barbara Villiers, Duchess of Cleveland, the reputed mistress of his predecessor, whom he treated with insolence and brutality. This occasioned a prosecution, and on the 4th of December, 1706, a year after this marriage, he was tried and found guilty of bigamy at the Old Bailey; but, when sentence was passed upon him that he should be burnt in the hand, he craved the benefit of clergy, produced the Queen's warrant for suspending execution, and was admitted to bail. After this he became reconciled to his false Mary, and styles her, in his will, his dear and loving wife. Beau Fielding was the Orlando of the Tatler, and died of a fever at his house in Scotland Yard, in 1712, at the age of sixty-one.

The next on the list is a member of that family which, through the talents of both father and daughter, has become so distinguished in this century—Beau Edgeworth. It is to him that Steele, also fond of dress in his younger days, and called a coxcomb by his libellers, alludes, in the two-hundred and forty-sixth number of the Tatler, as, "a very handsome well-shaped youth, that frequents the coffee-houses about Charing-Cross, and ties a very pretty ribbon, with a cross of jewels, to his breast:" in a note to Goldney's edition he is called the "prince of puppies." Colonel

---

[1] Sir John Suckling speaks of Van Dyck being paid £80 "for copying a Mrs. Delanae's picture."

Ambrose Edgeworth died in the Bridewell of Dublin, having been out of his mind some time previously to his death.

Beau Nash, who was usually styled the " King of Bath," follows next. " His prosperity," says Butler, in his Chronological Exercises, " was of long duration ; and if a man who supported himself by gambling and intrigues can be said to deserve prosperity, it was justly due to this celebrated character ; but at length age and infirmities approached ; and though Horace says, we should preserve consistency to the last, it appeared ridiculous to see grey hairs and decrepitude aping the gaiety and hilarity of youth."

His Life has been written by no less eminent a hand than that of Dr. Goldsmith, whilst his tailors' bills have been printed by Mr. Prior, and his dress and appearance have been described in Boswell's biography of Dr. Johnson. Nash could be very rude at times, even to ladies, and as master of the ceremonies took a great deal of trouble to bring his code of dancing discipline and ball-room order to perfection. His picture was to be seen at full length in the ball-room of the Bath Assembly Rooms, between the busts of Sir Isaac Newton and Pope. The witty Lord Chesterfield wrote the following epigram on it :—

> Immortal Newton never spoke
>   More truth than here you'll find ;
> Nor Pope himself ne'er penned a joke,
>   More cruel on mankind.

The picture placed the busts between,
Gives Satire all her streng*h ;
Wisdom and Wit are little seen,
But Folly at full length.

Beau Nash was buried in the Abbey Church at Bath, on the 3rd February, 1761, having lived to the great age of eighty-eight : his funeral obsequies were conducted with much parade and solemnity, and at the expense of the corporation.

There were, no doubt, during this period, many other eminent fops besides these ; but it is observable, that, a man was never distinguished by the title of Beau, if he had anything in him superior to it ; that is, assuming that the epithet means a fop, which, in the words of Roscommon, is, "a man of small understanding and much ostentation." Still, and inconsistent as it may appear, very superior and clever men have bestowed far more than necessary attention upon their dress. Petrarch, in writing to his brother, says, "Recollect the time when we wore white habits, on which the least spot, or a plait ill-placed, would have been a subject of grief, and when our shoes were so tight, that we suffered martyrdom." Lord Byron avows that he had "a touch of dandyism in his minority," and "had retained enough of *it* to conciliate the great ones, at four-and-twenty." The Abbé Delille, who, besides being a priest, was also a poet, and, perhaps, the ugliest man of his day, lost so little of his personal vanity, that even in mature age, he invariably had his hair dressed with powder *couleur de rose;* and Prince Kaunitz, who wore satin stays, passed a portion of every morning in walking up and down a room in which four valets puffed a cloud of scented powder, but each of a different colour, in order that it might fall and amalgamate into the exact *nuance* that best suited their master's taste. "Ils étaient," observes a French writer, "des dévots à l'élégance, et en cela ils méritent nos respects; mais étaient-ils élégants? Voilà la question." Upon Rafaelle, the most spiritual of painters, has the epithet, "coxcomb," been irreverently bestowed. Nelson, who wrote the Companion to the Fasts and Festivals, and who is supposed to have been the author of The Whole Duty of Man, was a splendid dresser: it was from him that Richardson drew his character of Sir Charles Grandison. Charles Fox also, who, late in life, was one of the most unostentatious, not to say slovenly, men about town, was a macaroni in his youth, and, with his friends Lords Carlisle and Essex, wore red-heeled shoes! At this period the coxcombality of dress was necessarily great, for muffs, velvets, ruffles, gold lace, and perfumed powder, were then the usual appendages of male attire. We might, and with reason, imagine it was a woman, and not the Earl of March, a great sporting character, who, writing to George Selwyn, at Paris, in 1766, says, "The muff you sent me, by the Duke of Richmond, I liked prodigiously, vastly better than if it had been *tigré*, or of any glaring colour—several are now making after it:" and again, in 1776, he remarks, "pray bring me two or three bottles of

perfume to put amongst powder, and some patterns
for velvets that are new and pretty." But perhaps the
most remarkable instance that can be cited in proof of
the fact that a feeling of dandyism sometimes forms a
component part of a great mind, is that of the late
Marquis Wellesley; to whom, almost to the last moment of his life, and when still in the full possession
of those vigorous and intellectual faculties, the evidence of which forms one of the most brilliant historical pictures in the public annals of this and the
latter part of the last century,—a piece of rich waist-
coating was as much an object of attraction and delight
as to his handsome and youthful secretary. Indeed
it is said that this nobleman frequently sat alone *en
grande toilette*, decorated with his blue ribbon and the
garter, as if intending to appear at a royal levee, or a
chapter of the order. But to return to the period at
which the macaronies flourished (who, according to
the testimony of Horace Walpole, were travelled young
men who wore long curls and spying-glasses), the
adoption of broad cloth made sad havoc with the tastes
of such men as the Duke of Queensberry; and the
beaux who came in when muffs and velvets went out,
were of a very different description. One of the most
notorious was the late Lord Harewood, called, from
the singular *penchant* he had for imitating the Prince
of Wales in his dress, Prince Lascelles. Of this mania
he was cured by Fox, Sheridan, and Wyndham, who
persuaded His Royal Highness to allow his queue
(which it was then the fashion to wear) to be concealed

by the collar of his coat. He readily consented, and
during dinner, for they were all dining with the Prince,
one of the three called Lascelles's attention to the fact,
who, completely tricked into the idea that the queue
was cut off, appeared the next day, to the amusement
of the conspirators, without his own. Colonel Mont-
gomery, also a friend of the Prince of Wales's, and
the unsuccessful principal in the duel with Captain
Macnamara, was in the habit of dressing like the
Duke of Hamilton, and thus received the sobriquet
of the Duke of Hamilton's *double.* Another fop of
this century was a Colonel Matthews, who being extremely distressed at the loss of one of his front teeth,
determined upon having it replaced by one drawn from
another person's jaw, trusting perhaps to that jargon
of the doctors called " healing by second intention."
He was fitted accordingly, but, horrible to relate, the
saliva, or something adhering to the tooth, inoculating
the system, brought on a cancer in the mouth, of
which he died.

Though many others might be enumerated besides
those I have mentioned, I will close the list with the
name of the venerable patriarch of the Beaux, Sir
Lumley Skeffington, who was still alive when these
volumes first appeared, and was some connection of
the Massareene family. He is said to have been entitled to the enviable denomination of the most amiable
of the genus *beau;* and a distinguished author, who
allowed his pen to dwell briefly on these matters some
years ago, says, " that under all his double-breasted

coats and waistcoats he never had any other than a single-hearted soul."

Having brought this sketch of the principal Beaux upon record to a close, I will now enter upon the life of him who Lord Byron said was one of the three great men of the nineteenth century, placing himself third, Napoleon second, and Brummell first. To this postulate it is not my intention to offer any support; but I think there is sufficient evidence to show that he ought not to be classed with the Beaux, if, as I have before remarked, a beau is a fop, and a fop a man of small understanding. But if I prove my own assertion, what then? Does it at all signify whether his reputation remains as it is or not? No. Then "Le jeu, vaut-il la chandelle?" Yes, if the first portion of this biography amuses the reader, and the last pages excite reflection. Some indeed will smile at the moral Brummell's life conveys : others may perhaps agree with me in the views I have taken of it.

CHAPTER II.

Brummell's Origin—The Death of his Grandfather—Lord Liverpool patronises his Father, and subsequently introduces him to Lord North—Made Private Secretary to that Nobleman—The Richardson Family—George and his Aunt Brawn—Lord North's Regard for Brummell's Father—Instructions for a Prince and for the Representatives of the People—Mr. Brummell's retirement from Public Life—Donnington—Sheridan and Miss White—Death of Mr. and Mrs. Brummell.

BRUMMELL's origin, like that of many greater men than himself, was humble. A French journalist, who wrote a biographical notice of him a few months after his death, says that " his grandfather, the first of the Brummells and the founder of the family, was originally a Treasury porter, a situation which he obtained through the patronage of Lord North, and that prudence and industry enabled him to give his son a good education ; " also, " that he succeeded, through the kindness of the same nobleman, in procuring him employment in that office." A writer in a late periodical has asserted that Beau Brummell was the son of a confectioner ; and others have described his father as having been in Lord Bute's household. But these accounts are all, or nearly all, equally incorrect. George Brummell's grandfather was in business in Bury Street, St. James's, and might have been a confectioner, though I have no evidence of the fact; he was buried in St. James's Churchyard, in a corner of which his tombstone may still be seen, and on it the following inscription : "Here lies the body of Mr. William Brummell, who departed this life the 31st of March, 1770, aged 61 years." His wife's death is likewise recorded thus : "Also the remains of Mrs. Jane Brummell, who departed this life on the 27th of July, 1788, aged 73 years." An uncle of the Beau's, Benjamin Brummell, of the Treasury, who died in February, 1816, is likewise buried in the same vault. Within a few feet of Mr. Brummell's grave is that of the celebrated Tom Durfey, a tablet to whose memory is inserted in the wall of the church itself, facing the west entrance.

Not being in affluent circumstances, Mr. Brummell, like many persons in business in the present day, let a portion of his house, and, fortunately for him and his family, not only "the spirit of Jenky arose," but Jenky himself; or, in words less Ossianic than those of the song of Scrutina,[1] his lodgings were taken by Charles Jenkinson, afterwards the first Lord Liverpool; and it is said, I know not with what truth, that his distinguished lodger was attracted to

---

[1] *The Song of Scrutina*, a poetical squib on the Westminster scrutiny, when, in 1784, Fox, elected a member of Parliament, defeated the Government candidates, was written by the late Sir Robert Adair, under the pseudonym of Macpherson. It will be found among the "Probationary Odes for the Laureateship," published with the *Rolliad*.

the house by the perfect penmanship of the *affiche*, "Apartments to let," written in his son's, the Beau's father's, best hand.

Mr. Jenkinson, as is well known, was not only clever, but remarkably laborious; and though one of that administration contemptuously spoken of as "all the hacks," in contradistinction to the one yclept "all the talents,"[1] it should be remembered that hacks are more useful than race-horses; and that his lordship, instead of closing his career like the high-mettled racer, in a kennel, died in ermine trappings, and left a very comfortable *écurie* to his successors, while the "talents" hardly left a shed to theirs.

Brummell's father was but a boy when Mr. Jenkinson came to lodge in Bury Street, but his active disposition soon attracted that gentleman's attention, and, pleased with his quickness, he made him his amanuensis, and, when joint secretary of the Treasury, in 1763, he obtained for him a clerkship in that

[1] About 1807 a satirical poem published by Stockdale, called "All the Talents," went through several editions and'was a most violent tirade against the Whigs. The author of this squib took the very appropriate name of Polypus, and it was dedicated "to the Emperor of China." The "All the Talents" ministry, said to be formed without regard to party distinction, came into office in 1806, and was composed of the following members: Lord Erskine, Lord Chancellor; Earl Fitzwilliam, President of the Council; Viscount Sidmouth, Lord Privy Seal; Lord Grenville, First Lord of the Treasury; Lord Hawick, First Lord of the Admiralty; Earl Moira, Master General of the Ordnance; Earl Spencer, Secretary of State for Home Affairs; Mr. Fox, Foreign Affairs; Mr. Windham, Secretary at War; Lord Henry Petty, Chancellor of the Exchequer, and Lord Ellenborough, Chief Justice, with a seat in the Cabinet.

office. In this subordinate situation young Brummell remained for some time; but fortune is generally the friend of industry, and his unremitting attention to business and strict integrity, together with Mr. Jenkinson's recommendation, who was a Lord of the Treasury in 1767, induced his successor, Lord North, to appoint him his private secretary. This nobleman honoured him with his friendship, and continued him in this confidential post during his administration; that is, from 1770 to 1782, when the Marquis of Rockingham took office. It is rather curious that clergymen at this period sometimes held the situation of secretary to the First Lord of the Treasury; the Rev. Mr. Walker had that appointment under the Marquis, and the Rev. Mr. King under the Duke of Portland.

Advanced thus, in all probability beyond his most sanguine expectations, Mr. Brummell's shrewdness and intelligence were constantly exerted; and he not only succeeded in obtaining emoluments under his new patron, but drew a prize in the lottery-office of Mr. Richardson, by marrying his youngest daughter. She is said to have been one of the prettiest women of her day, and not erroneously, if the artist who executed the miniature of her, now existing, was not a Lawrence, or a rival of Mr. Brummell. But though this marriage must have been a very eligible one for the young lady, it does not appear that the connection exactly suited the ideas of the Richardson family, who were fond of

pedigree, and claimed to be descended from no less
a personage than Sir W. Richardson, Chief Justice
in the reign of James I. The shield of the Chief
Justice is still to be seen in the painted window
of Lincoln's Inn ; and his monument, which is in
Westminster Abbey, is near to that of the celebrated
Dr. Busby, who wielded the birch so vigorously and
successfully, during the fifty-five years that he was
master of Westminster School. Mr. Richardson's
objections, however, were probably softened afterwards ; for another daughter was not so fortunate,
and married Mr. Vernon, an actor ; a third sister
espoused a Mr. Hughes, a very respectable person
in the City ; and the fourth married a gentleman of
the name of Brawn, who had a farm near Lilbourn.

George Brummell occasionally paid a visit to his
aunt Brawn ; and one of the earliest episodes remembered of his childhood is, that he was one day guilty
of crying most bitterly, because he could not eat any
more of her ample damson tart. The eldest son of
Mr. Richardson, who succeeded to the lottery-office
at his father's death, was a great friend of the late
Mr. Coutts, the banker, and an expensive man about
town ; he died early. The second brother was in the
navy, and sailed in the *Alarm* frigate, the first in the
service that was coppered ; he was also on board the
Centurion, the ship in which Lord Anson circum-
navigated the globe. At his brother's death he
replaced him in the lottery-office.

How very highly Lord North appreciated the

services of Mr. Brummell, is satisfactorily proved by
the lucrative appointments which that minister con-
ferred upon him ; for, at his decease, he held those of
Receiver of the Duties on Uninhabited Houses in
London and Middlesex, Comptroller of the Hawkers'
and Pedlars' Office, and Agent and Paymaster to the
Out-pensioners of Chelsea Hospital, the net salaries of
which amounted to two thousand five hundred pounds
per annum. As Mr. Brummell enjoyed such a handsome share of the good things in the gift of Lord
North, called by the pamphleteers of the day " the
God of Emolument," it was not only natural but fair,
that he should occupy a prominent position in the
squibs so frequently launched forth against his master,
and with justice too ; for perhaps no country with free
institutions ever suffered so much from the obstinate
" honesty," perhaps his admirers will exclaim, as
England did from the colonial policy of that minister.

In one of the pamphlets I have alluded to, entitled
" Instructions for a Prince, with State Maxims and
interesting Papers, found in the Cabinet of the King
of Lunaria," the author gives the following letter from
a certain secretary to a newly elected member of the
House of Commons ;—that secretary was Brummell's
father ; and the note is supposed to have been written
by order of Lord North.

" SIR,—Permit me to congratulate you on the
honourable seat which you have lately obtained in so
honourable a manner. I inclose you, by order of my

master, Lord N——, a copy of instructions drawn up by himself for the use of *his* members.—I have the honour to be, Sir,—&c., &c., &c.,

" WILLIAM BRUMMELL."

The instructions to the representatives of the people were as follows :—

" 1st. You are to use your best endeavours in bringing over the opposition.

" 2nd. You are never to play the orator, lest you should stumble on unseasonable truths (applicable to some cases in the present day) ; an Aye or No, judiciously employed, is infinitely preferable to the finest rhetorical flourish.

" 3rd. You are not to be absent from duty on any pretence whatever.

" 4th. Good posts will be provided for your relatives and friends ; but, if they cannot be immediately given, you are not to murmur, or threaten, or even talk of conscience.

" Lastly. You are to pay implicit obedience to the will of the minister."

The expenditure of secret-service money is thus humorously made out by the same author ; the initials only of the names of some were given in the original —I have filled them up.

" To my dearly beloved cousin the Earl of Bute, the Mazarin of Lunaria, for his care of me in my nonage, £20,000 per annum.

"To the Earl of Mansfield, the Solon of the age, as a reward for his assiduity in new-modelling the laws, £5000 per annum.

"To the Poet Laureat, Mr. William Whitehead, exclusive of his salary, for making me the paragon of princes and humbling my enemies in the birthday odes, £500 per annum.

"To sundry posts and pensions in the Lords and Commons, in order to secure a majority in both houses, value £300,000.

"To several of the poorer and more noisy patriots, £30,000 per annum.

"(*N.B.* We are making daily converts.)

"To a common-councilman of Lunaria, for his speeches at the halls, and endeavouring to persuade the liverymen of London that they have no will of their own, £500.

"To a lord of the Admiralty (probably Charles Fox), to enable him to purchase a new suit, and that he may appear at Court with clean linen, £100.

"To Lord North, he having a very large family, seven children, and a very small income (only £20,000 per annum), for his assistance in raising Lunaria to her present height and prosperity, a douceur, £50,000.

"To Edward Gibbon, Esq., for 'An Essay on the Art of Sinking in Politics ; or, Rules for the Ruin of a State,' £500.

"To the commissioners, cash to bribe Congress, £100,000.

"To Oberea, queen of Otaheite, my sole, yet

powerful [1] ally, for dolls, beads, ribbons, &c., value
£2000.

"To divers new writers for puff and panegyric,
£10,000 per annum."

These were indeed glorious days for the writers
of "puff and panegyric." Major Topham, the editor
of the *World*, actually succeeded to David Hume's
pension.[2]

After Lord North's resignation, Mr. Brummell
retired to the country, and in the year 1788 served
the office of high sheriff for Berkshire. In the
immediate vicinity of his seat, the Grove, near Donnington Castle, a place famous for having been the
residence of Chaucer, and for its spirited resistance
to the Parliamentarian army in the civil wars, he was
eminently distinguished by his private virtues, particularly in his exertions on behalf of the infant poor,
many of whom he benevolently rescued from ignorance
and destitution; and by them his loss was truly
deplored—for it was felt. Nor was he forgetful of
the duties of hospitality to his affluent friends; the

---

[1] As the *powerful* may by many be thought somewhat questionable,
the following extract from Captain Cook's voyage is submitted to the
reader : "The fleet of Otaheite, which I then saw, consisted of 210
vessels, besides smaller ones to serve as transports, &c. ; and it appears
from an accurate calculation, that the whole island can furnish for immediate service 68,000 able men." No despicable assistance to Lunaria
in her *present despicable* situation.

[2] Major Topham died at Doncaster on the 20th April, 1820 : he was
known to the lovers of the drama by the many prologues and epilogues
which proceeded from his pen ; also by several minor theatrical pieces.
He likewise wrote a Biography of the celebrated and eccentric John
Elwes, Esq.

hall-door, though it hung upon an old-fashioned hinge, yielded easily to the touch of his numerous visitors, and the Grove was universally acknowledged to be one of the most agreeable houses in the neighbourhood. That such should have been the case was not extraordinary. Mr. Brummell had for twelve years been in habits of intimacy with perhaps the most delightful of companions, who, whatever might be his political obstinacy or manœuvring to retain office, was possessed of more *bonhomie* and powers of pleasing all that came within reach of his conversation, than any other of the great public men of his time.

The society which Mr. Brummell received at Donnington was of the best and most talented description ; both Fox and Sheridan visited there, and tradition has still preserved the remembrance of one - of the practical jokes, in which the latter was so fond of indulging. It was played off on a Miss White, a spinster, who had passed her grand climacteric, but whose vanity was so little tempered by age, that Sheridan, in one of his frolicsome and persuasive moments, succeeded in inducing her to believe that Mr. Henry Harris, the proprietor of Covent Garden Theatre, and a guest at Donnington, was in love with her. "My dear Miss White," said Sheridan, "my friend is endowed with great sensibility ;—only touch him on that point, and he is yours :" and the lady, instigated by the mischievous wit, and hoping to attract the admiration of Mr. Harris, dressed herself in the

costume of one of those pastoral beauties immortalised
in Chelsea china; and attired in a stiff dress of prim-
rose brocade and gipsy hat, with pale blue ribbons,
sat by the side of a pond, in the grounds, with a
fishing-rod in her hand, the best part of a broiling
summer's day, nervously expecting her Colin—it is
needless to add, in vain.

Under the influence of these examples, Master
George Brummell doubtless cultivated his natural
penchant for fun; but in the early part of the year 1793,
the sounds of festivity were hushed at the Grove; death
left Mr. Brummell a widower; and exactly one year
and a day after his wife's burial, he was himself carried
to the family vault at St. Martin's-in-the-Fields, and
laid beside her. This event took place the 17th of
March, 1794. Mr. Brummell died, leaving two sons,
and a daughter; William, the eldest, married in May,
1800, Miss Daniel (whose sister was married to a
brother of Lord Gwydyr), and the daughter became
the wife of a Captain Blackshaw, who resided in a
cottage near the Grove.

Mr. Brummell's youngest son, George Bryan Brummell, the subject of the present memoir, had not quite
completed his sixteenth year at the time of his father's
death, having been born on the 7th of June, 1778, and
baptized on the 2nd of July, at St. Margaret's, Westminster. I am ignorant who on this occasion promised
to answer for his anticipated misdeeds, but his second
Christian name would seem to imply, that the shade
of the old Irish hero came back from the world of

spirits to do him honour. A very handsome provision was left, at Mr. Brummell's death, for his three children, proving that he not only knew how to acquire money, but how to keep it; a virtue which in this, as in the generality of cases with fortunes rapidly made, did not descend,—at least to his youngest son. The sum of £65,000, which Mr. Brummell died possessed of, was placed in the hands of trustees, to be equally divided amongst his children, on their attaining their majority. The amount is so large, more particularly when it is remembered that Mr. Brummell was given to acts of hospitality, that it leads to the supposition that he speculated successfully; probably like his patron, Lord North, in the funds.

Such was the origin of the Beau's family, and such the details I have been able to collect respecting it. He seldom touched upon the subject of his genealogical tree—never in conversation; but, in one of his notes to a lady hereafter given,[1] he appears to allude to it when he says in the commencement, " I swear to you by those humble ancestors who sleep in their parish churchyards ; "—humble they were, but respectable; and it is a pity that Brummell did not content himself with the position in society their industry and better judgment had secured for him, and this he was probably brought to think by the sufferings and reverses of his later life.

---

[1] See volume II., chapter VII.

CHAPTER III.

Buck Brummell at Eton—His gentlemanly deportment—The Windsor
Bargeman—The sporting High Sheriff—His novel estimate of
Character—Dame Young—Description of George by the Captain of
her house—His great dexterity in Toasting Cheese—His Peccadilloes
—Dr. L.—Brummell enters at Oriel College, Oxford—His Con-
sumption of Midnight Oil there—Leaves the University—Is Gazetted
to a Cornetcy in the Tenth—Introduced to the Prince of Wales—In
attendance on His Royal Highness at his Marriage—The Blue Nose
—Reasons for disliking the Army—Retires from the Service.

AT Eton, to which his father sent him in 1790, at
least he appears in the list of the lower school for that
year, George Brummell was remarkable for his quiet
gentlemanly manners and ready wit, as well as for the
excessive neatness of his personal appearance. At
that time the term "dandy" was not the vogue:
"bucks," and "macaronies," were then the nick-
names of such as affected peculiar elegance in their
dress; and, according to one authority formerly living
at Eton, he was distinguished from his fellows by the
sobriquet of "Buck Brummell." The anxiety with
which he eschewed the dirty streets on a rainy day,
his white stock with a bright gold buckle behind, and
the measured dignity of his step, were remembered
by his contemporaries; his language, dress, and

deportment, were in this respect always in perfect keeping.

It frequently happened that a contest took place between the boys and the Windsor bargemen, and on one of these occasions, an unhappy bargee fell into the hands of the exasperated lads, who having been in a former row very roughly handled by these Jacob Faithfuls, gave momentary way to passion, and were literally contemplating throwing him over the bridge into the Thames. In the midst of the uproar and hauling about, fifty pulling him one way and fifty the other, Buck Brummell came over the bridge, and probably from a goodnatured motive, he, in the quietest tones of remonstrance, addressed his incensed companions as follows : " My good fellows, don't send him into the river ; the man is evidently in a high state of perspiration, and it almost amounts to a certainty that he will catch cold." A finer instance of bathos seldom occurs—from drowning to catching cold ! but to be sure, either might have happened, even to a bargee. This appeal of George Brummell's was irresistible ; the boys took it, and in an ebullition of laughter, projected the bargeman along the road, who took to his heels and was out of sight in an instant.

Little, however, is now remembered of Brummell at Eton ; old Sukey, the purveyor of tarts and apples, died an inmate of the almshouse, but her mind was too enfeebled by age for her to recollect whether he patronised her, and if he was ever so vulgarly happy

as to enjoy cranberries, bull's-eyes, or the classical
elecampane; neither have I been able to ascertain,
whether like other boys he hacked his desk, or cut his
name on the walls.   In the upper school-room, where
upwards of three thousand names are cut on the oak
panelling, numbering among them those of Charles
Fox, and scores of others of our young nobility and
commoners scarcely less distinguished in the senate,
or the field—that of George Brummell does not
appear.

I was dining one day with the high sheriff of a
county contiguous to the metropolis, a Nestor of
Nimrods, and accidentally hearing him remark that he
was at Eton in the latter part of the last century, I
asked him whether he recollected Brummell there.
The rough, but good humoured, old fox-hunter immediately acknowledged the acquaintance.   " I knew him
well, Sir," said the veteran sportsman; " he was
never flogged; and a man, Sir, is not worth a d—n
who was never flogged through the school." Here
the conversation, to my great regret, was cut short by
the under sheriff hopping into the room and announcing to his chief, who was doing the honours most admirably, that " in the great tithe cause, Smith *versus*
Jones, a verdict had just been recorded in favour of
the plaintiff."   This brought on a perfect typhoon
from the high sheriff, mangel wurzel, fat beasts, and
the sliding-scale.   I made a waiting race of it, but it
was of no use; the whole of the squires present went
off at score, I could never get old Hubert to hark

back to the Beau, and the evening passed without my being able to take advantage of this rencontre with a brother Etonian of my hero.

Indeed I had some time previously completely given up all hopes of obtaining anything more relating to Brummell's school-boy days, when, through the kindness of a friend, I received a communication on the subject from a gentleman, whose name it is not necessary to mention, but from whose courteous letter I now quote the following passage: " I was three years at Eton with my old friend Brummell. We were at Dame Young's, and I was the Captain of her house, in which there were forty boys. All these three most happy years George was my fag. He was a far livelier lad than his handsome brother William ; indeed no one at the school was so full of animation, fun, and wit. He was a general favourite. Our dame, his tutor, and my tutor (the father of Dr. Hawtrey), and Dr. Goodall, all petted him. You ask me whether he was pugnacious; I do not remember that he ever fought or quarrelled with any one : indeed it was impossible for any one to be more good-natured than he was. With George, afterwards General Leigh, and Lord Lake, and Jack Musters, who were all in the same house with us, and Berkeley Craven, a great pickle in his boyish days, and living at Dr. Foster's, and with all his other intimate companions, I never heard of his having a single disagreement. Like them also he was not in the least studious, but a very clever and a very idle boy, and very frank ;

and then, whatever he became afterwards, not in
the least conceited, though Nature seemed to have
supplied him with a quadruple portion of amusing
repartee.

"I recollect nothing about his fondness for athletic
exercises, boating, cricket, &c., but I really believe no
young Etonian was ever more popular with all his
companions than George Brummell, not even excepting
his celebrated namesake, George Canning. As head
of the house I had two suppers of cold meat and
pastry, and a double portion of bread and cheese.
No toaster of bread and cheese ever surpassed or even
equalled George Brummell; and I can speak from
experience, as he nightly toasted mine most delicately
for three years. When the toasting was over he
divided it into two as equal parts as he could, and
I choose mine first. When I divided what he had
toasted, he always had the first choice.

"About two years after he had been at Eton, his
father having been informed of some peccadillo he had
committed, sent his butler from Donnington with a
paternal letter to his eldest son, which began, 'My
dear William,' and another to the Beau, commencing,
'George.' George's letter was in other respects a
most disagreeable one, intimating as it did the order
for his immediate return, with all his clothes; his
father having determined not to allow him to return
again to Eton. Hearing of his trouble I went to his
room, and found him with the two letters before him :
they were wet with tears, which, *parvis componere*

magna, fell, if not like the Falls of Niagara, like those
of the Clyde ;—such a stream of tears I never saw,
and have never seen since. ' George,' said I, ' what's
the matter?' He could not speak ; but, sobbing,
pointed first to—' My dear William,' and then to the
monosyllable ' George.' I give you this anecdote as a
trait of his being possessed, at least at this time, of a
warm heart. His father's relented also, for after the
next holidays George reappeared amongst his companions, the most manly boy of them all."

The only person who appears to have been unfa-
vourably disposed towards the young Etonian was
Dr. Langford, one of the masters of the Lower School,
who frequently forwarded a true and particular
account of his delinquencies to the Grove ; but it does
not appear that he was himself immaculate. Abraham
Moore wittily remarked of this reverend gentleman,
when he was elected to a vacant fellowship, that his
success proved the truth of the poet's observation,
that " *worth* makes the man—the want of it a fellow ! "
Brummell was in the fifth form in 1793, the year he
left Eton, and though he took very good care that
none of his companions should impute to him the
intention of succeeding the head master, he left the
college a gentlemanly scholar ; and also with an ample
share of that precocious worldliness, of which a public
school generally imparts some to the dullest com-
prehension. It was this, together with the originality
of his character, his good humour, vivacity, and ready
address, that gave him an ascendancy over his school-

fellows ; a position which his classical attainments or superior physical power never would have procured him.

From Eton he went to Oxford, and entered at Oriel College. Here, according to Mr. Lister, in Granby,[1] " he rapidly progressed in the exclusive habits to which he had shown himself predisposed, the little that remained of schoolboy frankness was quickly thrown aside in his violent desire to be perfectly correct ; and, to gratify this taste, he cut one of his brother Etonians, because he entered at a junior college ; and discontinued visiting another, because he had invited him to meet two men of —— Hall. The plan which he acted upon was to make intimacies with men of high rank and connections : he was a consummate tuft-hunter ; and to the preservation of an embryo baronet or earl, he fancied it necessary to sacrifice a friend a term.

" He consumed a considerable quantity of midnight oil ; but very little of it over his books : and it was not so much from a meritorious motive, as a wish to do something that nobody thought he could or would do, that he wrote for the Newdigate prize.[2] It is true he was not successful ; but his copy was considered the second best, and he contrived to make people believe that he would have been, if he had

---

[1] A novel, written by T. W. Lister, which produced a great sensation, was published in 1826, and was said to contain in Trebeck a portrait of Brummell, drawn to the life.

[2] The Newdigate prize for English poetry, established in 1719 by Sir Robert Newdigate.

taken sufficient pains; for his friends asserted that his failure was mainly owing to his indolence, in having neglected to count his verses. He was more celebrated, however, for his systematic violation of college rules than for his stanzas; he always ordered his horse at hall-time, was the author of half the squibs that appeared on the screen, turned a tame jackdaw, with a pair of bands on, into the quadrangle, to parody the master, and treated all proctors' and other penalties with contempt."

This account of Brummell's college career is probably correct as far as relates to his studies : he, no doubt, gave himself very little trouble about lectures, and, like the generality of under-graduates, was wise enough not to importune his tutor for instruction ; but the accusation of cutting an old schoolfellow, and a friend a term, may fairly be doubted, for it does not at all accord with the character given of him by his captain at Eton, nor by those of his contemporaries at Oriel, with whom the author is acquainted. It seems, indeed, as if Mr. Lister had imagined this college sketch, to make it correspond with the habits and disposition of Trebeck in after-life.

But although he did not devote himself to study, he gained from a fellow Oxonian some useful information in the line that he intended to take : this gentleman, a Mr. E——, was famous for his comic songs and good stories, and many of these he imparted to Brummell, who afterwards gave them with such good effect at the wine-parties of his

friends, that he left the university with a better reputation for wit and fun than his instructor. Having
added these qualifications to the many he possessed
when he arrived at this seat of learning, he took an
early leave of Alma Mater, and three months after
his father's death, viz., on the 17th of June, 1794,
was gazetted to a cornetcy in the Tenth Hussars,
at this time commanded by the Prince of Wales.

According to Brummell's own statement, he had
been presented to the heir-apparent on the Terrace
at Windsor, when a boy at Eton; and he used to
say that his subsequent intimacy with His Royal
Highness grew out of the slight notice with which
he was then favoured. A contemporary and friend
of his told me that, on his arrival in London, some
of the caterers for the Prince's amusement informed
him that the young Etonian had grown up a second
Selwyn, upon which His Royal Highness intimated
a desire to see him again. A party was accordingly
made for this purpose, and George, not being embar-
rassed by any real modesty, as many similarly
situated would have been, acquitted himself so much
to the Prince's satisfaction, that the fortunate result
was the gift of the cornetcy already spoken of.

Adorned with the rich uniform of the Tenth, which
his slight but handsome figure was well calculated to
show off, and brought forward under the auspices
of his royal patron, Brummell found himself at once
in the highest society in the country,—in a position
that in all probability he had never dreamed of

attaining, even in his most sanguine and ambitious moments. The intimacies also, which he formed with several of his brother officers, no doubt contributed to facilitate his reception in families of the highest rank and fashion; for amongst them were Lord Petersham, Lords R. E. Somerset, Charles Ker, Charles and Robert Manners, and the Honourables Bligh and Lumley.

Though Brummell was only sixteen years of age, a mere boy, when he entered the Tenth, and the Prince was then two-and-thirty, his partiality for the young cornet did not surprise those who were about His Royal Highness, for he was well known to have a strong predilection for companions who had any marked peculiarities of character about them; hence his former intimacy with Lord Barrymore, George Hanger, and several others. George Brummell was an original too, and a genius in his way; for how could his wit, assurance, and agreeable manners have been acquired at that early age? Many were the marks of royal favour bestowed upon him; and with that precipitation of preference which characterised His Royal Highness's conduct towards his favourites, he was soon placed on a footing of intimacy wholly inconsistent with their relative positions in life.

The Tenth were almost always either at Brighton or in London; and on the arrival of the Princess Caroline of Brunswick to celebrate her marriage with the heir-apparent, a party of the regiment, commanded by Lord Edward Somerset, escorted her

from Greenwich to St. James's. At the august
ceremony Brummell was in personal attendance upon
the Prince as a kind of *chevalier d'honneur;* he also
went down with the happy couple to Windsor, and
his description of the honeymoon was in strong
contrast to the one given by the Princess herself
in the "Diary illustrative of the Times of George the
Fourth."

Brummell's account of these espousals must, however, have been tolerably authentic, as he went the
next morning to take the Prince's orders while His
Royal Highness was still at his toilet, when he
certainly received no unfavourable impression from
the conversation that took place. When I heard
him relate the circumstances, it was years after he
left England ; and he certainly had no lingering
admiration, at that time, for his former friend. He
said that nothing could go off better ; that "the
young couple appeared perfectly satisfied with each
other, particularly the Princess : she was then a very
handsome and desirable-looking woman ;" and it was
only, according to Brummell's version of the story,
when the intrigues of some old ladies about the court
began to take effect, that any disagreement between
them became apparent.

Once included in the brilliant circle that surrounded
the Prince of Wales, he rapidly established a reputation for wit and refinement, and soon became a great
favourite with the fair sex. The following anecdote
will illustrate this remark :—At a ball given by a great

law lord in the neighbourhood of Russell Square, at
which, amongst a very numerous assemblage of the
beau monde, a Miss J——, afterwards Lady G——
H——, was present, a circumstance occurred which
proved that he understood the difficult art of making
himself agreeable to a proud woman.

Miss J—— was a magnificent creature, and of
course the greatest attention was paid her; but though
surrounded by ardent admirers, not one of them had
sufficient influence to induce her to dance.   Like a
spoiled beauty as she was, she declined the offers of
one and all of them.   Quite late in the evening, however, Cornet Brummell was announced, and he had
scarcely made his bow to her, when this *difficile* lady,
who had probably been waiting for him, rose from her
chair, and giving her hand to the new arrival, was
soon seen figuring away amongst a crowd of the discarded who had sought that hand in vain.   As the
Beau approached one of them, my informant, he inquired, with an air of great curiosity, who the ugly
man near the chimney-piece might be ?   " Why surely,
my good fellow, you know him," said his acquaintance ;
" that is the master of the house ! "   " No," replied
the unconscious cornet, " how should I ?   I was never
invited."

When Brummell was with his regiment he was the
life and soul of the mess, for his original wit and collection of good stories were inexhaustible ; and at the
dinner-table he always kept his brother officers in
roars of laughter.   As to duty, he did little or none ;

and when late for parade, which was very often the case, he would ride up to the commanding officer and disarm him with some queer apology, half-impudence half-excuse, which was generally accepted, for he was popular, and the colonel good-natured. But he was so much about the Prince that he was seldom present with the corps; and the gallant Tenth did not therefore benefit much by his services. When, unfortunately for the country, he was with them, it is said that he did not actually know his own troop ; but happily for him, one of his front-rank men had a very large blue nose : this feature was Brummell's beacon ; and when coming on parade, which, as I have said before, was frequently ten minutes too late, he galloped along the line, or between the squadrons, until he arrived at the nose. Here he reined up and took his place in the front or rear, as the case might be.

On one occasion, however, some recruits having joined the ranks from drill, a transfer of men was made, and several were drawn from the front rank of his troop and sent to another. At the next parade that he attended, and several days after this alteration, he found the regiment already in line, and ignorant of course of all the arrangements that had been made at the barracks in the meantime, he rode up and down as usual, and at length stopped opposite his nose—his blue nose. "How now, Mr. Brummell !" vociferated the colonel, "you are with. the wrong troop." "No, no," muttered the Beau, turning round in his saddle, and looking confidently first at his invaluable nose, and then at the colonel, adding, in a suppressed tone, "I know better than that; a pretty thing indeed if I did not know my own troop!"

One of his brother officers humorously told me, that he attended to his duty infinitely better after he had left the regiment than he did when he belonged to it; for he seldom passed within twenty miles of their quarters, without turning out of his road, and paying them a visit. On one of these itinerant calls, he drove into the barrackyard at Canterbury in his carriage, with four posters. "Halloo, George!" said a friend from the mess-room window, "when did you take to four horses?"—"Only since my valet gave me warning for making him travel with a pair." This was Brummell's usual mode of reply, ever ready with some droll excuse for his follies or extravagance.

Rapid as was his promotion, for he commanded a troop in less than three years after he entered the service, having been promoted to the rank of captain, on the 1st of June 1796; and little as he was inconvenienced by his military duties, he did not care to put up with any further interference with his independence; for as soon as the novelty of the thing wore off, he began to think of retiring. This he did, in the very early part of 1798; the disturbed state of Europe, the wailings of the anti-Jacobin, and the splendid declamations of Burke, in the cause of suffering humanity, having failed to induce him to seek "a reputation at the cannon's mouth!"

With such brilliant prospects of advancement as

Captain Brummell had before him, it is difficult to say what was his reason for taking so unwise a step; perhaps it was his anxiety to exchange his *club* for White's, or emancipate his head from hair-powder, which was still worn in the army.

This absurd fashion of powdering the hair originated in the whim of a French mountebank at a fair, who, to get an extra laugh out of his audience, greased his head, dredged it with flour, and then grinned horribly.[1] But though powder was still worn in the army when Brummell left the service, it had been gradually falling into disuse in society in England, since the tax had been laid upon it by Mr. Pitt three years before; to evade this impost, many speculators brought forward powder made of other materials than flour; amongst them was Lord William Murray, a son of the Duke of Atholl, who took out a patent, in 1796, for making starch from horse-chestnuts.

. The fatal blow, however, was given to this custom by Francis Duke of Bedford and his friends, who, in order more effectually to disappoint Mr. Pitt of the revenue that he very reasonably hoped to realise, from

---

[1] An acquaintance accuses me of having mistaken the origin of wearing hair-powder, and certainly gives a more probable reason for the adoption of it amongst the mountebanks. "Hair powder," he observes, "was worn by French ladies in the reign of Louis XIV. (see a portrait in one of the bedrooms at Cassiobury), and was first patronised by women whose beauty was on the wane to enable them to conceal their gray hairs. How could a grinning mountebank induce the fine ladies of Versailles to copy *his* head? These buffoons covered their heads with powder, or rather flour, to laugh at a practice which the ladies at Court had adopted, and to satirise, and make fun of them." (See also Notes and Queries, January—June 1884, pp. 90, 137, 178, 232.)

an article so intimately connected with the vanities and fashions of the day, entered into an engagement to forfeit a certain sum of money, if any of them wore their hair tied or powdered, within a certain period. Accordingly, in the September of 1795, a general cropping, washing, and combing-out of hair took place at Woburn Abbey—probably in the powdering room ; an apartment dedicated to the powder-puff, in the houses of most gentlemen in those days. Amongst the Absaloms present on this startling occasion, this anti-pigtail plot, were the Marquis of Anglesea, Lord Jersey, and Sir Harry Featherstone ; Lord William Russell, Mr. Lambton, the father of the late Lord Durham ; and Messrs. Anthony and Robert Lee, Trevers, Dutton, Day, and Vernon.[1]

[1] The following extracts from the *Times* newspaper, Sept. 25 and 29 for the year 1795, taken from Ashton's "Old Times," will illustrate this still better :—

"The following noblemen and gentlemen were of the party with the Duke of Bedford at Woburn Abbey, when a general cropping and combing-out of hair-powder took place : Lord W. Russell, Lord Villiers, Lord Paget, &c. &c. They entered into an engagement to forfeit a sum of money if any of them wore their hair tied, or powdered, within a certain period. Many noblemen and gentlemen in the county of Bedford have since followed the example : it has become general with the gentry in Hampshire, and the ladies have left off wearing powder."

"THE BEDFORD CROPS.—Something has at last fallen from this party to entertain the public. We hope they will find their heads cooler for this salutary operation. Dr. Willis (a physician for the insane) is of opinion, that more than one of them ought to have been *shaved.* If the *Shavees* think by publishing their names they will gain proselytes, till their absurdity is lost in the crowd, they are mistaken. Can it be supposed that a few drunken persons in a frolic will be followed by the sober part of the people of England ?

"The new Crop is called the *Bedford Level.*"

But, in spite of this opposition on the part of the leading Whigs, there stilled remained energetic supporters of powder and the minister; amongst these were to be numbered all the elderly ladies, who naturally enough patronised a habit that made the young and old appear equally gray. Their exertions, however, were fruitless; and the Treasury was amusingly charged with entertaining the idea of taxing the substitute which eventually replaced their powder, and, to make up for the unlooked-for deficiency in the tax, it was proposed that a return should be made of false hair, whether worn in scratches or fronts; but the perruquiers defied Nature, and the plan, if ever contemplated, was relinquished.

But at the time Brummell left the Tenth, it was highly desirable that the use of powder should be countermanded in the army; for a scarcity of corn was seriously felt, and the following calculation, made when the powder-tax was first imposed, shows how much of this invaluable article of food was uselessly consumed in that service alone. The military force of the United Kingdom and our Colonies at this period, including foot, horse, militia, and fencibles, amounted to two hundred and fifty thousand men; each of whom was supposed to use a pound of flour per week: this made no less a sum than six thousand five hundred tons weight a year; a quantity sufficient to make three millions, fifty-nine thousand, three hundred and fifty-three quartern loaves, and to supply fifty thousand persons with bread for that period. The scarcity

two years after Brummell's retirement, viz., in July
1800, was so great, that the consumption of flour for
pastry was prohibited in the Royal Household, rice
being used instead ; the distillers left off malting,
hackney-coach fares were raised twenty-five per
cent., and Wedgewood made dishes to represent
pie-crust.

But to return to Brummell, though probably he
was sufficiently annoyed at being obliged to wear
powder when it was going out of fashion, his principal reason for leaving the profession was, his objection to being quartered in a manufacturing town ; at
all events, it was the one that he chose to assign.   It
appears his regiment was at Brighton when they suddenly and unexpectedly received an order to march
for Manchester.   The news arrived late one evening,
and early the next morning Brummell, according to
the account he gave me, made his way to the Prince,
who expressed some surprise that he should be
favoured with a visit from *him* at such an unusual
hour, when the Beau, after due apology, said—"Why
the fact is, your Royal Highness, I have heard that
we are ordered to Manchester.   Now you must be
aware, how disagreeable this would be to me ; I really
could not go—think, your Royal Highness, Manchester !   Besides," and here was an instance of his
tact, "you would not be there.   I have, therefore,
with your Royal Highness's permission, determined to
sell out."—"Oh ! by all means, Brummell," said the
Prince, "do as you please, do as you please."   And

accordingly he resigned with the most perfect indifference, and before he was of age, his troop in the Tenth—at that time the most dashing regiment in the army ! [1]

[1] " This conversation about Manchester," observes Brummell's friend Jack Robinson, " is utterly unworthy of him and impossible ; he was incapable of it." All I can say is that Brummell told the anecdote to my friend Wells and other persons at Caen. But it is possible his reason for leaving the Tenth was that the expense exceeded his means, and that he wanted the money with which he purchased his commissions.

CHAPTER IV.

Brummell attains his Majority, though not in the Tenth—Establishes himself in Chesterfield Street—His Figure and Countenance—His Style of Dress—A French Author's Opinion of him—The Dandies, English and Indian—Wraxall's description of Dress in 1794—Brummell's Cravat—His method of tying it—His Condemnation of the Duke of Bedford's Coat—The Beau's Tailors—"Superfine" and "Bath Coating"—The Prince of Wales's Wardrobe—Brummell's Dress at the cover side.

BUT the profession of arms was decidedly not Brummell's proper vocation, and the service did not suffer severely by his resignation; the least restraint or compulsory exertion was perfectly repugnant to his nature, and the trifling inconveniences of a soldier's life, even in England, were in the last degree unlikely to suit a young man who seemed created on purpose to personify elegant idleness. A year after he left the army he came into possession of his fortune, which having accumulated during his minority, amounted to thirty thousand pounds.

Being now master of his time as well as of his money, he determined to devote himself to a life of pleasure, and the first step he took towards the accomplishment of his design, was to establish himself, with all the means and appliances of comfort, in

No. 4 Chesterfield Street, May Fair ; in which street, by the by, George Selwyn also resided. There, with the assistance of a man-cook, who formed one item in his small but *recherché ménage*, he gave some excellent little dinners ; his guests were congenial spirits, and on the authority of a noble duke, I can say, that even the Prince honoured them with his presence.

But while he preserved all the appearances necessary to support the position he had acquired in society, there was nothing outrageously extravagant in his general routine of expenditure : at this time, he was wise enough not to play, and his stud consisted only of a couple of horses to enable him to air himself in the Park.

It has already been observed, that Brummell's figure was well set off by his hussar uniform, but it should be clearly understood that it derived no other advantage from it ; the reverse of which is the case with so many young men who hide a bad one under the attractive shelter of regimentals. Nature had indeed been most liberal to him in this respect ; he was about the same height as the Apollo, and the just proportions of his form were remarkable ; his hand was particularly well-shaped, and, had he been inclined to *earn* his livelihood after his flight from London, he would readily have found an engagement as a life-sitter to an artist, or got well paid to perambulate France from fair to fair, to personate the statuary of the ancients.

His face was rather long, and complexion fair; his whiskers inclined to sandy, and hair light brown.[1] His features were neither plain nor handsome, but his head was well-shaped, the forehead being unusually high; showing, according to phrenological development, more of the mental than the animal passions—the bump of self-esteem was very prominent. His countenance indicated that he possessed considerable intelligence, and his mouth betrayed a strong disposition to indulge in sarcastic humour; this was predominant in every feature, the nose excepted, the natural regularity of which, though it had been broken by a fall from his charger, preserved his countenance from degenerating into comicality. His eyebrows were equally expressive with his mouth, and while the latter was giving utterance to something very good-humoured or polite, the former, and the eyes themselves, which were gray and full of oddity, could assume an expression that made the sincerity of his words very doubtful.

This flexibility of feature enabled Brummell to give additional point to his humorous or satirical remarks; his whole physiognomy giving the idea that, had he devoted himself to dramatic composition, he would have written in a tone far more resembling that of the "School for Scandal" than the "Gamester," or any plot developing reflection and deep feeling. His voice was very pleasing.

---

[1] Hulse, the court page, told me that his hair was thin and light, and that Robinson, his valet, turned it with the irons, when it looked very nice.

Having described his person, it is high time to advert to the point in Brummell's character which procured him the sobriquet of Beau—his taste in dress and great attention to it. On this subject, he has been much misrepresented; and it is strange how very few persons there are out of the class with whom he associated, who appear to be aware that he possessed a single idea that did not originate in his glass or his wardrobe. By the majority, he is considered to have been an overdressed and finical puppy; and he is represented by a journalist of modern days, to have worn a dove-coloured coat and white satin inexpressibles, with an artificial scented clove carnation in his button-hole.

"This the early period of his life, and not the least important part of it," says the *Revue de Paris*, "was signalised by the famous pair of gloves, to ensure the perfection of which two glovers were employed; one being charged exclusively with the making of the thumbs, the other, the fingers and the rest of the hand;" in accordance, I suppose, with the grand principle of the subdivision of labour. The author of " Pelham " has improved upon this, and assigns three as the number of glovers employed in this achievement.

"At this time," says the same *feuilletoniste*, "three coiffeurs were engaged to dress his hair, one for the temples, one for the front, and the third for his occiput : his boots were *cirées au vin de Champagne*, and the ties of his cravats designed by the first portrait painter in London, who only became the rage when

Brummell had entrusted him with this delicate and
sacred task." In other words, the author of this
pamphlet would have his readers believe that he was
an *incroyable.* In this light he is always viewed by
foreigners, and Alfred de Musset, in "Les Contes
d'Espagne et d'Italie," thus alludes to him in apostro-
phising the Muses :—

> "Muses! depuis le jour où John Bull en silence
> Vit jadis par Brummell, en dépit de la France,
> (Exemple monstrueux) traîner les pantalons
> Jusqu'à," &c. &c.

Another witty Frenchman,[1] anxious for information
on the subject of the English Beau, wrote me the
following characteristic letter, in which he evidently
asks for the most minute details of Brummell's life :—

"Quelles ont été les relations de Brummell avec
Sheridan, Fox, Erskine? Etaient-ce plus que des
relations de monde? Brummell avait-il des passions?
Qu' étaient elles? Etait-il joueur, ivrogne, libertin, etc.?
Etait-il marié? a-t-il pu vivre avec sa femme? Avait-
il des maîtresses en pied? Lui a-t-on connu des
maîtresses publiques. Je ne parle pas des bonnes
fortunes. . . A-t-il eu une femme étiquetée à son
nom, et quelle était cette femme?—détails sur ce
point. Quel était son tempérament? sait-on l'emploi
de sa journée? était-il capricieux dans la distribution
et l'occupation de ses heures ou routinier? . . . a-t-il

---

[1] This witty Frenchman, here alluded to, is Mons. J. Barbey d'Aure-
villy, who has made for himself a name in literature, and also written
a small book *Du Dandysme et de Georges Brummell,* which has gone
through several editions.

laissé des mémoranda ?   Il a laissé des aphorismes.
Ne pourrai-je en avoir quelques uns ?   Je suis moins
curieux de ses vers : des aphorismes me serviraient
bien davantage ; les vers d'un homme montrent plus
ou moins de talent, mais un homme est tout entier
dans ses idées générales.   A-t-il servi dans le 10ᵉ de
dragons ? Quel était son grade ?   L'aventure du 'nez
cassé' et celle du 'pavillon de Brighton' sont-elles
authentiques ?   La mesure exacte de ses rapports avec
le prince de Galles ? Son portrait physique et quelques
anecdotes ? J'y tiens moins qu' aux aphorismes, mais
les aphorismes j'y tiens beaucoup, parce que l'homme
entier est là. . . . .   Encore une question.   Pitt portait
d'ordinaire   un   habit   bleu   et   un   gilet chamois ;
Brummell affectait-il une certaine couleur aussi, ou les
portait-il   toutes   avec   une   même   souveraineté ?   En
somme, autant de détails extérieurs que possible ?
Quand il s' agit de Brummell, la manière dont il cou-
pait ses ongles est important.   *L'âme se mêle à tout,*
dit Madᵉ. de Stael."

Our own great lyric poet seems also to have entertained a similar opinion of him, when he makes Mr.
Bob Fudge remark to his friend—

"There goes a French dandy : ah ! Dick, unlike some ones
 We 've seen about White's, the Mounseers are but rum ones.
 Such hats ! fit for monkeys : I'd back Mrs. Draper
 To cut better weather-boards out of brown paper ;
 And coats, how I wish, if it would not distress 'em,
 They'd club for old Brummell from Calais to dress 'em !"

Yet these lines will bear a more liberal construction ;

and perhaps the poet brings him forward more in
reference to his good taste on this subject, and with a
view to the correction of dandyism in others, than as
a culprit in foppishness himself. It is surely in irony
that, in his description of a great fête at Carlton
House, he makes Brummell so interested in a pea-
green coat! and says—

> "Come to our fête, and show again
> That pea-green coat, thou pink of men,
> Which charm'd all eyes that last survey'd it,
> When Brummell's self inquired 'Who made it?'"

It would be unjust indeed to Brummell's memory if
I neglected to show the impropriety of calling him a
"dandy:" the few associations connected with the
term all teem with vulgarity; the tap-room measure
of that name is not an example of refinement, and
in Johnson the nearest approach to the word is the
Dandelion, a vulgar flower! But, if in the true
etymological style we divide the word, with the hope
of improving its credit, what does the first syllable
bring to mind? Somebody quite as notorious as
Brummell, but whose follies have been far more mischievous; whose eloquence is great, but certainly not
always refined: and to whose health many a dandy
of whisky has been tossed off.[1] The thing, the

---

[1] In the *Dublin Review*, for Sept. 1844, appeared a sharp criticism on the first edition of this book, in which, amongst other things,
it is said that—" Captain Jesse . . . . has had the bad taste to insert
the following (above) impertinent and irrelevant piece of personality in
his book. Now, Captain Jesse knows that the individual against whom
he has directed his pointless shaft, and who, in addition to his trans-

"dandy," however, still exists, and will do so to the
end of time ; but the term is nearly obsolete, and has
been replaced by the "tiger" in England, and, oddly
enough, by the "*lion*" in France.

The only "dandies" I ever knew that do in any
way relieve the just imputation of egregious folly attached to that *outré* character, are those the traveller
meets with in Hindustan—beings half fish, half men—
the boatmen of the Ganges ; and good reason have I
to remember them, for they ran away one day from our
budgerow, because, when walking on the bank, my
shadow had passed over their cooking-pot, and they
vowed that I had thereby spoiled their dinner.   Vishnu
alone knows whether this was true or false ; all I can
say is, they made a terrible commotion, and left me
and my brother subaltern on the shore to mourn their
departure.

"The bark was still there, but the '*Dandies*' were gone."

I was then inexperienced in the enlightened doctrines
of Bramah ; but after I had been a short time in the
country, I found it was really necessary to look after
my shadow, not only out of respect to "civil and
religious liberty all over the world," but out of regard
to my own convenience, which was of much more consequence ; and often when landing from my boat, after

cendant merit as a statesman, orator, and philanthropist, is also a
distinguished literary man, was, when his book appeared, the inmate of
a prison.   The feelings of a gentleman, therefore, and of a British
officer, should have induced him to have repressed this silly and malignant attempt at pleasantry."

the day's tracking was over, and the bank was crowded
with cooking-pots, for these boatmen never cook on
board, I would gladly have been like Peter Schlemihl.[1]
There was certainly something very peculiar in the
dress of these Dandies; it was simply a rag round
their waists, and not generally very clean; but our
countrywomen in India look upon Nature thus primi-
tively draped with the utmost composure : never, to the
best of my recollection, have I seen a blush mantle the
cheek of a new arrival; far be it from me, however,
to insinuate that a want of modesty was the cause of
this—the Dandies are black !

If, as I apprehend, glaring extravaganzas in dress
—such, for instance, as excessive padding, trousers
containing cloth enough for a coat besides, shirt-collars
sawing off the wearer's ears and the corners threatening
to put out his eyes, wristbands intruding upon his
plate, or an expansive shirt-front like a miniature
bleachgreen, &c., &c.—constitute dandyism, Brummell
most assuredly was no dandy.

He was a *beau*, but not a beau of the Sir Fopling
Flutter [2] or Fielding school ; nor would he, like Charles
James Fox, have been guilty of wearing red-heeled
shoes ! He was a beau in the literal sense of the
word,—" fine, handsome." As an auxiliary to his
success in society, he determined to be the best-dressed

---

[1] Peter Schlemihl, the hero of a popular German legend, sells his
shadow to the devil, and is a prototype of people who make foolish
bargains.

[2] The chief character of Sir George Etherege's comedy, "The Man
of Mode."

man in London, and, in the commencement of his
career, he, perhaps, varied his dress too frequently; the
whim, however, was of short duration, and, scorning
to share his fame with his tailor, he soon shunned all
external peculiarity, and trusted alone to that ease
and grace of manner which he possessed in a remarkable degree.

His chief aim was to avoid anything marked; one
of his aphorisms being, that the severest mortification
a gentleman could incur was, to attract observation
in the street by his outward appearance. He exercised
the most correct taste in the selection of each article
of apparel, of a form and colour harmonious with all
the rest, for the purpose of producing a perfectly elegant general effect ; and no doubt he spent much time
and pains in the attainment of his object.

According to Wraxall, dress at this period had
become exceedingly slovenly. "That costume," he
observes, "which is now confined to the levee or
drawing-room, was then worn by persons of condition,
with few exceptions, everywhere and every day. Mr.
Fox and his friends, who might be said to dictate to
the town, affecting a style of neglect about their persons,
and manifesting a contempt of all the usages hitherto
established, first threw a sort of discredit on dress.
From the House of Commons, and the clubs in St.
James's Street, it spread through the private assemblies of London. But, though gradually undermined,
and insensibly perishing of an atrophy, dress never
fell till the era of Jacobinism and of Equality, in 1793

and 1794. It was then that pantaloons, cropped hair, and shoe-strings, as well as the total abolition of buckles and ruffles, together with the disuse of hair-powder, characterised the men; while ladies (having cut off those tresses, which had done so much execution, and one lock of which purloined, gave rise to the finest model of mock-heroic poetry which our own, or any other, language can boast), exhibited heads rounded '*à la victime, et à la guillotine,*' as if ready for the stroke of the axe."

About the beginning of this century the late Lord Jersey's servant was the first to introduce the common blacking now in use. It was, of course, much sought after, particularly by the members of the Melton hunt, many of whom paid this gentleman's gentleman five guineas for the receipt, so that he made a small fortune. Fashion, about the year 1800, was infinitely more tyrannical than it is now. At that time nothing could exceed the *outré* character of ladies' dresses or their extreme indelicacy. Public decency, as evinced by the drama, was certainly improved, but the beauties of Charles the Second's time looked like *sœurs de charité* when compared with the uncovered come-and-look-at-me ladies of this period. "While fashion," says a morning journalist, "strips the beauty of St. James's of the encumbrance of dress, the beauty of St. Giles's is hurried into nakedness in spite of the weather by insurance in the Lottery[1] and visits to the gin-shop. The muslin draperies of the former reminded the

---

[1] The first Lottery was drawn in England in the year 1569; it was abolished by Act, 4 Geo. IV. c. 60, 1823.

spectator of one of those elegant dishes of Weltje's,[1] in which a fish or a bird is seen (the latter of course without its plumage), through a covering of jelly, neither exposed or concealed." An old lawyer at the opera observed that in a little time there would not be a *femme couverte*[2] in the nation, and another critic, fond of statistics, calculated, that owing to this fashion of wearing muslin, eighteen ladies caught fire, and eighteen thousand caught cold. Hair-powder had, it is true, thanks to the Duke of Bedford, been shaken off, and the Grecian style introduced from the court of the First Consul[3] into that of our own ; *toupets* had also been abandoned, and hoops were almost matters of history ; but, with all this reform, female dress continued extremely singular and devoid of taste. The short waist must have looked abominable, nor could the habit of picking up the train and pulling it through the pocket hole, before dancing, have had a very elegant appearance. In the article of female attire the "Aerial" appears to have been the most popular dress. It was made of white muslin, the body plain, and trimmed round the bosom with lace, whilst the sleeves were of lace and muslin ; the drapery went over the left shoulder, and

---

[1] Weltje was a fashionable pastry-cook of that time. I have a strong suspicion his original name was Gualtier.

[2] A *femme couverte*, or in law a "feme-covert," is a married woman who is under "covert" of her husband, and cannot sue or be sued for money.

[3] Napoleon Bonaparte was appointed First Consul on the 10th of November 1799, and two other consuls were selected to rule with him, namely, Sieyès and Roger Ducos. On the 2nd of August 1802, he was nominated First Consul for life, and assumed the title of Emperor on the 18th of May 1804.

was fastened in different parts with gold and silver
sliders, or diamonds, and had silver trimmings round
the bottom. White ostrich feathers fixed at the back
of the head fell over the front, and an "indispensable"
was the favourite jewel, whilst gold chains and neck-
laces had also to be worn by a lady in full dress.
Another dress was the Russian robe of velvet trimmed
all round with silver; the bottom of the train was also
trimmed with the same material. The cap called the
"Amanthis" was of white spangled crape, with a
wreath of flowers on the left side. Velvet was
generally worn both as a trimming and in the headdress. The hair was in braid and curls, and, with a
solitary exception, without powder and ornamented
with plumes and birds of Paradise feathers. Silver
and gold flowers, and ornaments of all kinds with
crape and velvet netting, plain, spangled, beaded and
bugled, were much introduced into caps and bonnets.
To match the spangled nets, a beautiful flower, the
lily of the valley, with corresponding wreaths, was
made. The feathers, usually worn, were those of
the Argus pheasant, the Indian macaw, the argilla, the
flat and porcupine ostrich and the Scringapatam plume.
Diamonds were the rage, as indeed they have always
been with women, since they were first discovered;
and, though pastry was forbidden at the Palace in
consequence of the great scarcity of corn, *paste* was
worn by those whose jewels were at their jeweller's
or the fashionable pawnbroker's. Earrings were
short instead of long; some were in single drops,

others in clusters, and some were of a circular ring shape. Bandeaux of various kinds, with precious stones of different colours, were made in patterns of oak and laurel leaf. At the birthday ball of the late Queen Charlotte, in 1800, the Duchess of York was dressed in a petticoat richly embroidered in purple and gold wheat ears, terminating at the bottom with a border of geranium leaves entwined with gold. Over the petticoat was a magnificent Indian sash, looped up at the left side by a rich cord and tassels, whilst the body and train were of white satin embroidered with gold and ornamented with purple to correspond. The full dress in the month of July of this year was a black muslin over pink sarsnet, satin ribbands, black elastic velvet and antique gems and chains. Surely there was in all this enough to throw Lord Ogleby[1] into a more profuse perspiration than " hot rolls and butter." The walking dress must have done so to the wearer, if not to his lordship. It consisted of a silk pelisse trimmed with broad black lace, hat of purple chip or willow, with a bow behind and white roses on the left side, also a " silver bear muff"—in the dog days ! ! Leghorn hats were then from thirty-five shillings to two guineas a piece, and it was these prices that brought in the simple English straws. The vehicles were as low as the dresses ; a tall footman might very

---

[1] In Colman and Garrick's comedy, "The Clandestine Marriage," Lord Ogleby is represented as an old and vain but good-natured fop, and a slave to the fair sex, even at the age of seventy. He needed "brushing, oiling, screwing, and winding up before he appeared in public " to make love to Fanny Sterling, already privately married.

easily have set astride on the top of a fashionable
carriage, if it were not for fear of splashing his stockings. The most superb equipages were launched on
the queen's birthday alluded to above ; those of the
Marquis and Marchioness of Donegal particularly
attracted attention, for exclusiveness was then so much
the vogue that man and wife were separated when
going to court, the *vis à vis* of the Marquis on this
occasion preceding her ladyship's carriage, whilst two
tall footmen stood behind each of them, in magnificent
liveries and miniature greenhouses on their breasts,
so that although carrying only one person inside,
these vehicles were constructed for and actually did
carry three out. This custom might have arisen in
the days of hoops, but there were no hoops at this
time. Minuets also were rather on the decline, and
were danced only at this birthday ball by two dukes,
an English prince and two other nobles of high rank,
whilst ten couples stood up for country dances, and
the company separated at eleven !

In Paris the fashion changed as rapidly as politics,
and the Parisians of 1800, emerging from the accumulated horrors of the Revolution, made, with the characteristic *légèreté* of the nation, of that city one vast
ballet. Dancing came into fashion with the celebrated
Vestris, and every one was on tiptoe. The cutting
off of heads ended in the cutting of capers, and
politics which had hitherto absorbed every mind, were
voted, by universal consent, disgusting. *Ma foi*, a
lady is reputed to have said, *c'est une chose assez*

*ennuyeuse que la politique ! on se sert toujours des mêmes
mots, des mêmes idées ; il n'y a point de variété. Il est
assez cruel*—this was the climax—*d'avoir un mari
toujours à nos côtés au bal masqué de l'Opéra.* Still the
French continued to originate and provide us with the
externals of dress, and hardly ever adopted or copied
one of our fashions, though they would willingly
have received the materials for some of the dresses as
well as certain articles of toilette. Talleyrand begged
hard that one of his couriers might be permitted to bring
over four razors from England, and the Empress José-
phine condescended to petition our Government for six
pair of cotton stockings which were forwarded to her
Majesty agreeably to the pattern sent.

Brummell was one of the first who revived and
improved a taste for dress amongst gentlemen ; and
his great innovation was effected upon neckcloths :
they were then worn without stiffening of any kind, and
bagged out in front, rucking up to the chin in a roll ;
to remedy this obvious awkwardness and inconvenience,
he used to have his slightly starched ; and a reasoning
mind must allow, that there is not much to object to
in this reform.

He did not, however, like the dandies, test their
fitness for use, by trying if he could raise three parts
of their length by one corner without their bending ;
yet it appears, that if the cravat was not properly tied
at the first effort, or inspiring impulse, it was always
rejected : his valet was coming down stairs one day
with a quantity of tumbled neckcloths under his arm,

and being interrogated on the subject, solemnly replied, " Oh, they are *our* failures." Practice like this of course made him perfect ; and his tie soon became a model that was imitated, but never equalled.

The method by which this most important result was attained, was communicated to me by a friend of his, who had frequently been an eye-witness of the amusing operation.

The collar, which was always fixed to his shirt, was so large that, before being folded down, it completely hid his head and face, and the white neckcloth was at least a foot in height. The first *coup d'archet* was made with the shirt collar, which he folded down to its proper size ; and Brummell then standing before the glass, with his chin poked up to the ceiling, by the gentle and gradual declension of his lower jaw, creased the cravat to reasonable dimensions, the form of each succeeding crease being perfected with the shirt which he had just discarded.

His morning dress was similar to that of every other gentleman—Hessians and pantaloons, or top-boots and buckskins, with a blue coat, and a light or buff-coloured waistcoat ; of course fitting to admiration, on the best figure in England. His dress of an evening was a blue coat and white waistcoat, black pantaloons which buttoned tight to the ankle, striped silk stockings, and opera-hat ; in fact, he was always carefully dressed, but never the slave of fashion. Still he criticised severely the dress of others, more particularly when there was a want of neatness in it.

A nobleman now living told me, that when he was a young man, Brummell not only noticed him a good deal, but from the way in which he patronised him, evidently appeared to think that he was doing him a great kindness. They were walking together arm-in-arm one day up St. James's Street, when Brummell suddenly stopped, and asked Lord ——— what he called those things on his feet ? " Why, shoes," he replied. " Shoes, are they ? " said Brummell doubt-fully, and stooping to look at them, " I thought they were slippers."

On another occasion, the Duke of Bedford asked him for an opinion on his new coat. Brummell exa-mined him from head to foot with as much attention as an adjutant of the Life Guards would the sentries on a drawing-room day. " Turn round," said the Beau : his Grace did so, and the examination was continued in front. When it was concluded Brummell stepped forward, and feeling the lappel delicately with his thumb and finger, said, in a most earnest and amusing manner, " Bedford, do you call this thing a coat ? " The following reply to a question addressed to him by one amongst a knot of loungers at White's, was given in the same spirit of *badinage*. " Brummell, your brother William is in town ; is he not coming here ? "—" Yes, in a day or two ; but I have recom-mended him to walk the back streets till his new clothes come home."

Brummell's tailors were Schweitzer and Davidson, in Cork Street, Weston, and a German of the name of

Meyer, who lived in Conduit Street. The Stultzes, Nugees, &c., did, I believe, exist in those days, but they were not then held in the same estimation as their more fortunate brethren of the shears. Schweitzer and Meyer worked for the Prince ; and the latter had a page's livery, and on great occasions superintended the adornment of His Royal Highness's person. The trouser, which opened at the bottom of the leg, and was closed by buttons and loops, was invented either by Meyer or Brummell : the Beau at any rate was the first who wore them, and they immediately became quite the fashion, and continued so for some years.

A good-humoured baronet, and brother Etonian of his, who followed him at a humble distance in his dress, told me that he went to Schweitzer's one morning to get properly rigged out, and that while this talented purveyor of habiliments was measuring him, he asked him what cloth he recommended ? "Why, sir," said the *artiste,* "the Prince wears superfine, and Mr. Brummell the Bath coating ; but it is immaterial which you choose, Sir John, you must be right ; suppose, sir, we say Bath coating,—I think Mr. Brummell has a trifle the preference."

Brummell's good taste in dress was not his least recommendation in the eyes of the Prince of Wales, by whom his advice on this important subject was constantly sought, and, for a long time, studiously followed. Mr. Thomas Raikes says, in his " France," [1]

---

[1] " France since 1830," London, 1841, vol. ii. p. 377.

that His Royal Highness would go of a morning to
Chesterfield Street to watch the progress of his
friend's toilet, and remain till so late an hour that he
sometimes sent away his horses, and insisted on
Brummell's giving him a quiet dinner, which generally
ended in a deep potation.

After their quarrel, however, the Prince spoke of
his former friend as a mere block, which a tailor
might use with advantage to show off the particular
cut of a coat; and this speech went some way to
confirm the notion of the nonentity of Brummell's
character. But there is good reason for asserting
that an extravagant devotion to dress might, with
far more justice, be charged against his royal patron;
especially when corpulence, that sad annihilator of
elegance, made it difficult for him to get into leathers
of the dimensions he was anxious to wear. It was
this that gave rise to the caricature in which a pair
is represented lashed up between the bed-posts, and
their owner, having been lifted into them, is seen
struggling desperately to get his royal legs satisfactorily encased; leaving the imagination to picture the horizontal hauling that must have taken
place, after the perpendicular object had been effected,
to make the waistband meet.

In fact the Prince, not Brummell, was the Mecænas
of tailors; and perhaps no king of England ever
devoted so much time to the details of his own dress,
or devising alterations in that of his troops. On this
point, whatever attention he gave to it, he displayed

little judgment, as the chin of many a Life Guardsman
in a windy day attested. The extent to which he
indulged his passion for dress is seen in the proceeds
of the sale of his wardrobe, which amounted to the
enormous sum of fifteen thousand pounds ; and if we
are to judge by the price of a cloak purchased by
Lord Chesterfield for two hundred and twenty, the
sable lining alone having originally cost eight hundred,
it is scarcely straining the point to suppose that this
collection of royal garments had cost little less than one
hundred thousand. A list of the articles was given
in the *Athenæum* of the day, which, after expressing
its astonishment at the prodigious accumulation of
apparel, says, that " Wealth had done wonders, taste
not much."

But the best evidence that I can offer in support
of the opinion that the word Beau ought not to be
applied to Brummell in an offensive sense, is the
following extract from a very kind and courteous
letter which I received from the Rev. G. Crabbe, to
whom I had written, having observed Brummell's
name mentioned in his Life of his talented and
amiable father.

" I am sorry that I can give you no other information respecting the communication between Mr.
Brummell and my father at Belvoir, than the short
and trifling remark in the Memoir, as I never heard
my father mention him except when he made that
remark ; but short as it was, it entirely accords with
the impression which I believe was general in that

neighbourhood, viz., that Mr. Brummell was a sensible
man and a finished gentleman; the term 'Beau,'
which the world has offered to him, might be more
applicable perhaps in his earlier years; but when my
father met him at Belvoir, he was, I conceive, about
forty, and certainly did not, either in manners or
appearance, exhibit that compound of coxcombry in
dress, and vulgar assiduity of address, which marks
the 'Beau' (that is the dandy); I remember being
struck with the misapplication of this title when I
saw him one day in the Belvoir hunt. He was
dressed as plain as any man in the field, and the
manly, and even dignified, expression of his countenance ill accorded with the implication the sobriquet
conveyed." And yet Jack Robinson, an acquaintance
of his early life, observes—"Brummell's carriage was
never at any time graceful; perfect gentleman as he
was, there was something of a slang air about him."
I have heard it stated that Sir Henry Mildmay made
the same remark. I cannot, however, agree with
either of them; he might have been ungraceful and
have had something unusual in his manner in early
life; but, when I knew him at Caen in his old age,
Brummell was eminently graceful and distinguished-
looking, and was considered so by French ladies, no
mean judges.

CHAPTER V.

Brummell's Extreme Neatness—Lord Byron's Opinion of his Outward Appearance—Leigh Hunt's—The Beau's Cleanliness—His Precautions to ensure it—Why Country Gentlemen were Disqualified for becoming Members of Watier's—Mr. Pitt's Opinion of them— Brummell's Manners and Tastes—Lord Chesterfield's Gentleman— Lord Petersham's Snuff-cellar—The ex-Garde-du-Corps—The Gentleman of the Old School—Innovations not Improvements—The Minuet and Cotillons—American Manners.

THERE was, in fact, nothing extreme about Brummell's personal appearance but his extreme cleanliness and neatness, and whatever time and attention he devoted to his dress, the result was perfect; no perfumes, he used to say, but very fine linen, plenty of it, and country washing. With regard to perfumery, his taste perfectly coincided with that of the Champion of England. "I remember," says Lord Byron, in his letter on Bowles' Strictures on Pope, "(and do you remember, reader, that it was in my earliest youth, 'Consule Planco')—on the morning of the great battle (the second) between Gully and Gregson, —Cribb, who was matched against Horton, for the second fight, on the same memorable day awaking me (a lodger at the inn in the next room), by a loud

remonstrance to the waiter against the abomination of
his towels, which had been laid in lavender!"   Mr.
Leigh Hunt in a note, in which he kindly referred me
to some anecdotes of Brummell, says, "I remember
that Lord Byron once described him to me, as having
nothing remarkable in his style of dress, except a
'certain exquisite propriety,'"—and that gentleman,
in a sketch which he gave of the Beau at an early
period of his life, observes, when speaking of his
superior judgment on this point, "that the poet's
hyperbole about the lady might be applied to his
coat, 'You might almost say the body thought.'"—It
did think; and, had Montesquieu known Brummell,
he would never have said, "Le goût est un je ne
sçais quoi."

Cleanliness, however, rather than taste, was the
touchstone upon which his acquaintances were invariably tried; to detect in them any deviation from
that virtue, which has by common consent been
placed next to godliness, was a sufficient reason for
his declining any further intercourse with them.
One of his friends, curious to know something of a
family that he had passed a day with in the country,
inquired of him, what sort of people they were:
"Don't ask me, my good fellow," replied Brummell;
"you may imagine, when I tell you, that I actually
found a cobweb in my ——— !"   The anecdote is,
perhaps, true; and it was probably this that induced
him to keep a travelling one, for one of these
indispensable articles of bed-room furniture is de-

scribed in the catalogue of the sale of his effects as such, "in a folding mahogany case, with an external carpet case for the same." It is said, that he objected to country gentlemen being admitted to Watier's, assigning as a sufficient reason for their exclusion, that their boots stunk of horse-dung and bad blacking. If this had been true, many would have been of the same opinion, but his jocose remark was very probably made against some individual candidate. His objection to one of the prevailing tastes of his day—excessive devotion to stables, dog-kennels, and coachmanship — appears to have been strong; and he gives a proof of this by having taken the trouble to insert some very severe lines against the Whip-club in his album.

But though ridicule, false or true, is often more keenly felt than just censure, the Squire Westerns must have been far more indignant with Mr. Pitt, who, after all the support they had given him, did in his convivial hours forget his official circumspection and suffer his real opinion of them to escape him. A diplomatist of my acquaintance, now living, was present when the flattering expressions I allude to were uttered at Lord Mulgrave's table, that nobleman being, at the time, First Lord of the Admiralty.

My gossip was then a young man, and the day on which he was so fortunate as to meet the Prime Minister at dinner, was remarkable for being the one on which the First Lord was to examine a boat,

constructed by Sir Sidney Smith, in 1805, for the
purpose of acting against the Boulogne flotilla. This
vessel, which was in fact nothing more than two
boats fastened together like those of the Pacific
islanders, was navigated by the proper officers to
Putney, and there, under the Admiral's orders, put
through all the manœuvres which could in any way
explain her use and capabilities : she was called
the *Gemini*, and as it was a subject of some
importance, Mr. Pitt and a large party had been
invited to Lord Mulgrave's, whose house was on
the banks of the Thames, to see the trial. Accordingly before dinner they went on the lawn to see
the boat, and afterwards returned to the house,
where Sir Sidney having joined the party, which
consisted of about twelve persons, they sat down to
table : there was every prospect of the dinner being
an agreeable one, and so it turned out; Mr. Pitt
was in great spirits, and amused those near him
exceedingly, conversing with them on a .variety of
subjects, politics apparently never entering his head,
and he was no flincher at his wine.

But after the cloth was removed the conversation
became less general, and was carried on by two or
three persons, who had each their little knot of listeners ; one of the speakers being Colonel, afterwards
Lord Dillon, who was holding forth on the good old
times of Sir Robert Walpole, and the great utility
of that noble class, the country gentlemen. " What's
that you say, Colonel," said Pitt, " of the good old

times ?" The Colonel repeated his eulogium, finishing of course with a still more splendid peroration. " Ah," replied Pitt, in his deep sepulchral voice, " ah, Colonel Dillon, those were indeed the good old times, —for they were days when country gentlemen were even more ignorant and more obstinate than they are at present ! "

" Imagine my astonishment, however," said the diplomatist, " on hearing Mr. Pitt in the House of Commons, two months after, when he had some tax which he was anxious to saddle upon these ' ignorant and obstinate gentlemen,' make the most laboured panegyric in their praise ; and particularly addressing Colonel Stanley, the late Earl of Derby's uncle (for the House was in Committee at the time), instance him as one of the finest examples of this class ! "

Brummell's great external characteristic was the elegance of his manners ; they were the gift of nature, not the conventional ones usually acquired, in greater or less perfection, in the class of society that he frequented. There was no affectation or pretension about him ; but if any peculiarity could be observed, it was a tinge of the graceful formality generally described as " of the old school." His carriage was noble, all his movements were gentle and dignified, but never gave the impression that they were studied ; and his deportment was so peculiarly striking, that in walking down St. James's Street, he attracted the attention of the passers-by as much as the Prince of Wales himself. To admire whatever was elegant was natural to him, and his living in the midst of every description of refinement, in palaces, or in mansions hardly, if in fact at all, inferior, fully accounts for the taste and judgment which he possessed in buhl, china, and other objects of *virtù;* he was very curious in snuff-boxes, and had a collection of great beauty and value : as also of canes.

Here, however, panegyric on his judgment must stop; for it is doubtful whether his mind was so keenly alive to the sublime beauties of the Italian school of painting, or the sculpture of the ancients. His small library was stored with standard works, and though by no means comprising the extent of his reading, as he could at any time avail himself of superior ones, and constantly did so, showed the same good taste.

Being thus habitually, as well as naturally, elegant and refined, he of course had an antipathy to vulgarity of any sort, especially in manners; but his sarcastic allusions to it were directed, generally speaking, against those whom he considered ought to have known better.

But it would be difficult indeed to fix the precise standard of manners that constitutes the finished gentleman, and many and amusing are the dicta of some, who have undertaken to supply rules for the guidance of such as are anxious to excel in that rare and difficult character. Amongst the prohibitory ones is Lord Chesterfield's declaration that a gentle-

Lord Petersham

man ought not to play on the violin. Would it
not have been more sensible had he said, a gentleman ought not to take snuff? that most nasty operation, the only deviation from the practice of personal
purity in which Brummell indulged. Happily for
the fair sex, it has long fallen into general disuse
as a fashionable habit, which it was in his day.
The Prince of Wales took snuff, a sufficient reason
for the almost universal adoption of the custom.
But even this Brummell did in an elegant manner,
scarcely inferior to that of His Royal Highness :
like him, he opened his box with peculiar grace,
and with one hand only, the left. One of the great
amateurs of this nasal pastime, and a friend of
Brummell's, was Lord Petersham, whose cellar of
snuff—not wine—was said by the tobacconists to be
worth three thousand pounds.[1]

But to return to the consideration of gentlemanly
demeanour. A good many years ago, a friend of mine,
a young clergyman, whose manners were peculiarly
pleasing and correct, was out shooting, in Norfolk,
with an elderly gentleman of his acquaintance. It was
a bright burning day in September, and they had
walked over miles of stubble and turnips with pretty

[1] Lord Petersham, who afterwards became Earl of Harrington, was
as choice in his selection of teas as he was in snuff and snuff-boxes, of
which boxes it was said he had one for every day of the year. He
was tall, and in his countenance resembled somewhat Henri IV. of
France ; he patronised tailors, and gave his name to a great-coat as well
as to a particular snuff-mixture ; he also cut his own clothes and made
his own blacking. His horses, carriages, and the coats of his servants,
were always of a brown colour.

good success, when, stopping in the middle of a field for a momentary rest, the young clergyman took his handkerchief from his hat, and, passing it across his brow, said to his companion, "Oh! how thirsty I am!"—"What!" exclaimed the old sportsman in a tone of unfeigned surprise, "thirsty? a gentleman, young man, is never thirsty;" and, taking a dried camomile flower out of his pocket and placing it in his mouth, he shouldered his gun, recommending my friend, as they renewed their walk, to carry a similar antidote with him in future.

Such was the feeling of the "old school" with regard to propriety of manners, though, perhaps, a little exaggerated in this instance, and certainly in that of Lord Chesterfield; for with that nobleman it was a mere affectation of refinement, but with the old gentleman it was a real feeling of propriety.

A ci-devant garde-du-corps of Charles the Tenth's, who formed one of the society of Caen when Brummell was residing in that town, was also an example of stoicism similar to that required of a gentleman by this venerable critic. He had only his half-pay, seven hundred and fifty francs a-year, and his wardrobe, as might naturally be expected, was rather deficient on such an income. It was little enough for a man who might be sans home, sans shirt, sans everything,—whose salon is the wretched cabaret at the corner of the street; but for a legitimist, supporting the character of a well-dressed man, and a ruined cause, it was positive starvation. Fortunately

his affluent friends of the same political opinions
sometimes assisted him with a coat, and occasionally
with a pair of inexpressibles, or a dinner; but never
did their friendly donations extend to a cloak or a
great-coat, and in the most bitter weather, no matter
whether it was sleeting or snowing, he was never
seen in the street habited in anything of the kind.

One keen winter afternoon, an Englishman, who
was making his way to his dinner at the hotel as
rapidly as he could, to his infinite amazement met
Monsieur de Z—— with his surtout open, and
looking the very emblem of the season. Boldly
erect, however, with his hat on one side, he appeared
to defy the elements, and stalked towards him as
magnanimously *insouciant* as if he had been clad in
sables. The Englishman, with his cloak thrown up
to his very eyes, like a true Hidalgo, struck with
the transparent appearance of the garde-du-corps,
asked him, in a really compassionate tone, if he did
not feel the cold? "Froid, monsieur!" said the
haughty Carlist, "un homme comme il faut n'a jamais
froid."

Though there may be two opinions as to whether
it is necessary that a gentleman should never be
either thirsty, or cold, or play the violin, few will
deny that "the gentleman of the old school" is now
a *rara avis*, and that, in doing away with the for-
malities by which society was regulated in days gone
by, we have lost much of the polish that distinguished
him. Had the old sportsman, of whom I have been

speaking, written The Adventures of a Gentleman,[1] he would scarcely have allowed his hero to set dogs to fight in a house,—in one, too, in which he was a perfect stranger!

May we not question whether society has gained by the extent to which the relaxation of its forms has been carried, though some was desirable? The intercourse between a father and his son had in the last generation much of formality in it; but the restrictions which then existed were useful, and tended strongly to preserve that consideration and respect which are too often broken through in the present day. In writing to his father, the son then addressed him as " My dear sir; " in conversation, " Sir." A complete upsetting, instead of the modification of such forms as these, has not created a warmer affection between the two; while it has certainly given rise to a familiarity that frequently terminates in impertinence, and, finally, in a total want of filial respect. Many an under-graduate, or incipient field-marshal, in penning a letter home for a fresh supply of funds, now commences his epistle with " My dear Governor," who at his wine-party designates his father by the still more elegant denomination of the " old boy," or the " old cock." The use of such coarse language, in speaking of a parent, cannot fail in time to breed contempt; and, in truth, it does so.

[1] " Pelham; or, The Adventures of a Gentleman," by the late Lord Lytton, was first published in the year 1827.

But manners, as well as dress, will of course vary, as they ever have done, with each succeeding generation ; a hoop did not make a lady, nor gold lace a gentleman ; neither of these appendages is a loss, but the minuet contributed far more to make them elegant, than the gallopade ; and Sir Roger de Coverley was a better style of Christmas revel, than the dance termed a Polonaise, into which is introduced a promenade through the bedrooms and down the corridors of our country mansions ; on the walls of which the venerable ancestors of the family are shaking—yes, shaking with indignation at such hoydenish proceedings. What would be the feelings of the youthful and stately beauties of preceding generations—and beauties they were, in spite of pearl-powder and pomatum—if they could be resuscitated, and (placed against a truncated column of gas sent from London, to light the ball-room) see their great grand-daughters dancing the Coquette, or some of the other cotillons ? I venture to assert, that they would have no necessity for rouge that night.

The comparative merits of different forms of government is a prolific subject of discussion, and none is more worthy of attention, or more deeply interesting ; but it is astonishing how much opinions upon abstract principles are modified, by the influence which the manners and customs of different countries exercise upon them.

CHAPTER VI.

Brummell's Accomplishments—In London during the Month of November—His Friend the Duke of Bedford—Visits to Woburn, Belvoir, &c. &c.—Fête on the Duke of Rutland's Coming of Age—Brummell is Mistaken for the Prince of Wales—His Indifference to Field Sports —Nimroa's Opinion of his Riding—Thomas Asheton Smith—His Reason for Riding at an Impossibility—The Major of the Belvoir Volunteers—The Regular and the Irregular—Brummell's Stud— The late Duchess of Rutland—The Beau's Friends and Associates at Belvoir.

BRUMMELL's manner and address, which made him so acceptable, and enabled him to take such a leading position in society, were not his only recommendations ; he was a charming companion, and was possessed of the best of all claims to popularity—good humour. He drew well, and was not ignorant of music, and his voice was very agreeable in singing as well as speaking ; he also wrote *vers de société*, one of the accomplishments in vogue in his day, with facility, and his dancing was perfect.

Though these qualifications, and the quiet unassuming manner which distinguished him, were more likely to make him a favourite with the fair sex than his own, he was as much liked by the men, and became most intimate at a very early period of his life with some of the first families in the country ; the intervals between his seasons in London being varied by visits to the Prince at Brighton, or to Belvoir, Chatsworth, Woburn, &c. &c. Nevertheless the following note will show that he positively was once in town during the month of November ; but his friend Beauvais was probably an *émigré*, and he was good-naturedly showing him the lions.

"Woburn Abbey, November 10.

" MY DEAR BRUMMELL,—By some accident, which I am unable to account for, your letter of Wednesday did not reach me till yesterday. I make it a rule never to *lend* my box, but you have the *entrée libre* whenever you wish to go there, as I informed the box-keeper last year.

" I hope Beauvais and you will do great execution at Up-Park.[1] I shall probably be there shortly after you.—Ever yours sincerely,

" BEDFORD."

At Belvoir he was *l'ami de la famille*, and at Cheveley, another seat of the Duke of Rutland's, his rooms were as sacred as the Duke of York's, who was a frequent visitor there ; and if any gentleman happened to be occupying them when he arrived unexpectedly, he was obliged to turn out.

On the Duke of Rutland's coming of age, in January

---

[1] The seat of Sir Henry Featherstonhaugh, Bart.

1799, great rejoicings took place at Belvoir, and Brummell was one of the distinguished party that assembled there, amongst whom were the Prince of Wales, the late Duke of Argyle, his eldest son the Marquis of Lorne, the sixth Lord Jersey, &c., and all the neighbouring gentry.

The festivities on this occasion lasted for three weeks, and were conducted on a truly ducal scale. Fireworks of the most splendid description were let off in front of the Castle, one bullock was roasted whole on the bowling-green of the quadrangle, and another at the bottom of the hill on which the noble pile of building stands; but such was the severity of the weather, that while one side was roasting the other was freezing. This, however, did not deter the peasantry from making their way in hundreds to the Duke's kitchen and servants' hall, where the table groaned with substantial fare, and the " brown October " was not only " drunk on the premises," but carried away in pailsful. This unrivalled example of baronial magnificence and hospitality is still remembered in the vale of Belvoir; a circumstance not very extraordinary, for this proof of the warmth and generosity of the young and noble duke's disposition is said to have cost him sixty thousand pounds.

The weather being severe, there was of course no hunting, so skating was the order of the day; and Brummell, in going down the hill to the ice, clad in a pelisse of fur, was one morning mistaken by the people, who had assembled in great numbers, for the

Duke of Argyle

Prince of Wales, and was loudly cheered. This little incident will give some idea of the elegance and dignity of his carriage. It was indeed nearly as remarkable as that of His Royal Highness, who, in spite of the opinion retailed by a modern novelist, that " in the zenith of his popularity and personal advantages, he seemed positively vulgar by the side of the Count d'Artois," was allowed by his greatest enemies to be the most distinguished-looking man of his day.

Though I had the preceding anecdote from the very best authority, I did not hear whether Brummell, when he arrived at the ice, " made a star" upon it, or rivalled the former Marquis of Lorne, a perfect skater, by engraving his cipher. Certain it is that he hated personal exertion in any way, and it was difficult to make him give up his book and shoulder his gun, to join in a scramble over hedgerows and ditches. He was not much of a shot, and looked upon a battue only as an excellent opportunity for letting off his fun.

In those primeval days, there was no such thing as patent wadding ; and punched cards, if known, were not general ; at any rate he did not choose to adopt them, and used to excite a laugh among the sportsmen by appearing at the breakfast table with fifty or sixty pieces of paper like spills, attached with a large whistle to the button-hole of his jacket.

One of his greatest feats with his gun, was perpetrated at Cheveley, where he had just returned from a grand day, on which three hundred head of game had been slaughtered : the rest of the party were contemplating the fruit of their success, as it lay upon the lawn ; but Brummell, who took little interest in the deceased, having accidentally caught sight of two tame pigeons which had lovingly perched upon one of the chimnies, tempted by a standing shot, carefully raised his gun, and brought them both down. His satisfaction, however, was very transient, for a general exclamation from the bystanders followed, and he soon learnt they were the pets of one of the upper servants; great was then his regret, and many the apologies he made to the owner. But this unfortunate chance was not quite so serious in its results as that of the Duke of York, who, while shooting at Cheveley, during a Newmarket October Meeting, mistook a favourite liver-coloured pointer of the Duke's for a hare, and shot her dead. Poor Venus was a beautiful bitch, one of the finest dogs in the kingdom, and His Royal Highness was even more hurt than his friend, who valued her very highly.

Though Brummell was so much at Belvoir, and kept a stud of horses there, he was never a " Melton man ; " and his friends, as well as every one else, were amazingly astonished when he joined in the pleasures of the chase ; for, like many other gentlemen, he did not like it ; it did not suit his habits, and his servant could never get him up in time to join the hounds, if it was a distant meet : but even if the meet was near, and they found quickly, he only rode a few fields, and

then shaped his course in an opposite direction, or
paid a visit to the nearest farm-house, to satisfy
his enormous appetite for bread and cheese. I have
heard him, but many years after, laugh amazingly over
these incidents of his Melton days, and say in his
usual droll way, that he " could not bear to have his
tops and leathers splashed by the greasy galloping
farmers."

The truth was, he preferred returning at two o'clock
to lunch with the Duchess and her female guests : he
was to them a most sociable, cheerful, and amusing
companion ; and yet very much liked by the fox-
hunters, farmers as well as gentlemen, for he had
always a merry word to say to them, and the late Mr.
Apperley assured me, that when he chose to ride, he
rode respectably : but he did not say that he ever
heard of his having been in at the death, after the
famous run from Billesden Coplow, immortalised in
verse by a clergyman, the son of a bishop : neither
did he say, that he ever rode, like Tom Smith, at a
Croxton Park paling, with a hurdle on the top of it.
It was on this occasion that Mr. Smith, being taken
up half-stunned, and asked what on earth could tempt
him to go at a fence impossible to clear ? replied, " I
had a lead, and if I had not gone at it *somebody else
might have tried."*

But, many years after this period, when, at Caen,
Brummell used sometimes to revert to the pleasurable
recollections of times past, he once spoke of an
occasion on which he was obliged to exercise his best

powers across country; and the anecdote, as it was
repeated to me, was so amusing, that though I cannot
authenticate the fact on which it depends, I cannot
refrain from inserting it.

It appears that after he retired from the Tenth,
he was tempted to accept a majority in the Belvoir
Volunteers, raised by the Duke of Rutland after the
short peace of 1803, and that while he was in this
responsible and complimentary situation, a General
Officer was sent down by the Horse Guards to inspect
the corps : the official notifications had been given and
received, the time and place named, and General Binks
(for such shall be his incognito) arrived punctual to the
minute. The men were there, the officers also ; the
drums and colours,—not a halberd was missing,—but
Major Brummell,—where was he at this critical juncture ? nobody knew.

The indignant regular waited and waited, the
charger snorted, the General snorted, and at length,
both being equally exasperated at the unreasonable
delay, the gallant officer commenced the performance
of his now unpleasant duty ; this was terminating, of
course not much to his satisfaction, when the truant
Major was descried in a scarlet coat in the distance,
coming at speed across the country, occasionally craning
on his way, and then with renewed energy making
play over the flat. A few minutes, and the Beau was
cap in hand to General Binks, who suddenly halted
the line, which then much resembled that formed by
a patriotic Volunteer corps, when reviewed in the

Phœnix Park, and for the serpentine character of which, their learned commander so drolly apologised to the Lord Lieutenant, by saying, " Your Excellency, we are Lawyers, as this indenture witnesseth." But in this case, the commanding officer had to make an apology for himself, not for his corps, and he entered upon a series of explanatory speeches commencing with, Having left Belvoir quite early,—fully thought he should have been home in time, for the meet was close at hand, but the favourite horse failed and landed him in a ditch,—was dreadfully shook, and had been lying there an hour,—which the state of his pink amply testified.

Excuses, however, were vain ; General Binks was a martinet *enragé :* he remained inexorable, and raising himself in his stirrups, addressed the delinquent in the following pompous and inflated style : " Sir, this conduct is wholly inexcusable ; if I remember right, sir, you once had the honour of holding a Captain's commission under His Royal Highness the Prince of Wales, the heir-apparent, himself, sir ! Now, sir, I tell you, I tell you, sir, that I should be wanting in a proper zeal for the honour of the service ; I should be wanting in my duty, sir, if I did not, this very evening, report this disgraceful neglect of orders to the Commander-in-Chief, as well as the state in which you present yourself in front of your regiment : and this shall be done, sir. You may retire, sir."

The Beau bowed low and in silence, and did retire ;

but he had scarcely walked his horse five paces from
the spot, when he returned and said in a subdued
tone, " Excuse me, General Binks, but in my anxiety
to explain this most unfortunate business, I forgot to
deliver a message which the Duke of Rutland desired
me to give you when I left Belvoir this morning : it
was to request the honour of your company at dinner."
It would be difficult to say which gave the oddest
grin, the culprit or the disciplinarian ; the latter
coughed, and at length cleared his throat sufficiently
to express his thanks in these words :   " Ah : why,
really I feel, and am, very much obliged to his Grace ;
pray, Major Brummell, tell the Duke, I shall be most
happy ; and,"—melodiously raising his voice, for the
Beau had already turned his horse once more towards
Belvoir, " Major Brummell, as to this little affair, I am
sure, no man can regret it more than you do.   Assure
his Grace, that I shall have great pleasure in accepting
his very kind invitation."   And they parted, amidst a
shower of smiles.

But Brummell was as yet only half out of his difficulties ; the invitation he had so readily given to the
General was coined on the spot, was his own invention, to save himself from the consequences of his
neglect of duty, and he had to ride for his life to the
Castle to prepare his friend the Duke for an unexpected
visitor, the distinguished Binks.   This anecdote does
not tell well on paper, but let the reader imagine
Brummell giving his own account of the scene, taking
off the graceful and submissive bow with which he

acknowledged the reproof, and the arch twist of his eyebrows as he described himself giving the invitation, that acted as such an efficient anodyne to the General's indignation.

Another anecdote is also related of the Beau at Belvoir Castle. In a certain part of this noble seat is a large hall round which runs a gallery that communicates with the sleeping apartments. In this corridor is suspended the rope of the great bell used only in case of fire. It appears, however, that one night about half an hour after Brummell and a numerous company had retired to their rooms, the iron tongue of this giant communicator was heard speaking in no very gentle tones to the inmates of the castle, and those in the houses of the neighbourhood. The effect upon the household, as may be readily imagined, was electrical, and in a very few seconds after the first note had been struck, the hall was crowded with masters, mistresses, and servants in every variety of male and female nocturnal costume. No symptom of fire could, however, be detected, and they were wondering what could have induced any one to toll the bell, when the Beau came forward to the edge of the gallery, and said with one of his most placid smiles : " Really, my good people, I regret having disturbed you, but the fact is my valet forgot to bring my hot water."

Brummell always appeared at the coverside admirably dressed, in a white cravat and white tops, which latter, either he or Robinson, his valet, introduced, and which eventually superseded the brown ones ; his horses were always in as high condition as himself, their coats looking like silk. They stood at the Peacock at the bottom of the hill, near Belvoir, and were under the care of a person of the name of Fryatt, who perfectly understood his business; indeed he was more an agent than a groom, for he purchased, when and what he thought proper, without much, if ever, consulting his master, who had too much sense to interfere with him.

The truth was, Fryatt was an excellent rider, a capital judge of horses, and sometimes put money into Brummell's pocket, besides mounting him well; he also took care of himself, and at his death left eight or ten thousand pounds behind him, made out of horse-flesh: the inn which he kept at Melton for one or two years, was not so profitable a concern. After a few seasons, Brummell's stud was removed to Knipton, on account of some misunderstanding with Shipton, the landlord of the Peacock; in 1807, his horses stood at Grantham.

Knipton is a very beautiful village about a mile and a half from Belvoir Castle, and near it is a lake, of two hundred acres in extent; the spot is richly wooded, and the late Duchess took great pains to improve it, particularly in the drives, which are laid out with much judgment; the Castle, also, will long remain a magnificent memorial of her architectural taste, for the plan of it was her own selection. Her love of landscape-gardening probably originated in her talent for drawing, which was considerable, as the collection at

Belvoir of her own doing affords ample and pleasing evidence. Brummell's capability of appreciating this accomplishment, and his own proficiency in it, combined with his other acquirements, and his indifference to field-sports, naturally made him a very welcome guest in the drawing-room at Belvoir, and led to greater intimacy with his noble hostess than he might otherwise have aspired to.

He appears to have taken a pleasure in applying his talent for drawing, to the not unamiable object of preserving the memory of some of the distinguished women, that he was fortunate enough to be able to number among his friends. These sketches are from miniatures or pictures. One, of Georgiana, Duchess of Devonshire, was taken from a portrait by Sir Joshua Reynolds, and is now, or was, in the possession of Lady Granville; two others, those of the late Duchesses of Beaufort and Rutland, are now in the author's hands. The former is in water-colours, the latter in pencil: though not highly finished, both are very creditably executed for an amateur.

In a letter of Brummell's, subsequently given, written many years after the death of the Duchess of Rutland, he feelingly alludes to her in terms that would confirm the most delightful impression of her disposition. But, however the society in which she moved might have regretted her Grace's premature death, inasmuch as it removed one of the brightest and most fascinating ornaments from their gay circle, yet her loss was far more sincerely deplored by the

poorer classes of her own neighbourhood, in whose
welfare and happiness she had always manifested a
most lively interest, and who assembled in vast crowds
at her funeral, to pay the last tribute of a sincere
respect to their benefactress.

In concluding this chapter, the principal part of
which relates to Brummell's intimacy with a family in
which he for many years passed much of his time, it
may not be altogether uninteresting to mention some
of the guests with whom he was frequently associated,
and with the majority of whom, now like himself in
their graves, he was on the most friendly footing; as
it will give the reader an idea how deeply he must
have felt the alteration in his circumstances, and the
change he had to encounter in society, during his long
and compulsory residence abroad—from Belvoir to
Calais! Amongst these were the Dukes of York and
Cambridge; the Dukes of Beaufort, Manchester,
Dorset, and Argyle; the Earls of Westmoreland and
Chatham (William Pitt's brother, and the great
friend of the Duke of Rutland on the turf); the
Lords Delamere, Apsley, Forester, F. Bentinck, and
Robert Manners; the Honourables W. Howard, Irby,
and Henry Pierrepoint (Lord Manvers's brother, and
one of the leaders at Watier's); Chig Chester (a
great whist-player, sportsman, and good fellow); Sir
Watkin Wynne, Sir John Thoroton; Colonel F.,
and the Rev. P. Thoroton; Colonel G. Cornwall,
Parson Grosvenor, Mr. Delmé Ratcliffe, and John
Douglas.

Lord Manners.

There were also present, Lords Jersey, Alvanley, Willoughby d'Eresby, and Charles Manners; who, as well as Lord Robert, was with Brummell in the Tenth. A few commoners were likewise there; namely, Richard Norman, the Duke of Rutland's brother-in-law, Culling Smith, Sloane Stanley, General Grosvenor, and General Upton.

CHAPTER VII.

Brummell's Influence in Society—Proofs of it—The young Débutante at Almack's—The Hogshead of Martinique—Brummell's Assurance— Mr. Lister's Elucidation of that Subject—Mrs. Johnson Thompson— Brummell and Wyndham—The Dinner at Mr. R.'s, and the Ride to Lady Jersey's—The Horrid Discovery—The Double Distress.

BRUMMELL's intimacy with the Prince of Wales, and also with so many families of distinction, in addition to his social qualifications and perfect manners, soon made him sought and courted in society, and he was at length the vogue—no party was complete without him ; and the morning papers, in giving the details of a rout, always placed his name first on the list of untitled guests.   But his ambition was, not only to shine in the fashionable world, but to be its dictator, and, to effect this object, he saw that he must be formidable ; like Sylla, he must be feared.   A quick perception of the folly and gullibility of many of its members, enabled him to shape his course accordingly ; and, being fully aware of the power of ridicule, and not inconvenienced by any undue proportion of feeling for the crowd, he used it freely.   His disposition to satirise was, no doubt, unamiable ; but there was an essential difference between exercising his sarcastic vein upon people who were perfectly indifferent to him, and making an ill-natured use of it in private circles. In cutting up individuals with whom he had no feelings in common, which was pretty often the case, he did no more than hundreds of others; but, having a most perfect tact in all matters appertaining to mien and conduct in society, he made the witty, satirical, and cynical points of his character tell with much more effect than they did theirs.

How well he eventually succeeded in making his opinion valued or dreaded, the following anecdote will give an idea. "Do you see that gentleman near the door?" said an experienced chaperon to her daughter, whom she had brought, for the first time, into the arena of Almacks, "he is now speaking to Lord ———." "Yes, I see him," replied the light-hearted, and as yet unsophisticated girl; "who is he?" "A person, my dear, who will probably come and speak to us; and if he enters into conversation, be careful to give him a favourable impression of you, for," and she sunk her voice to a whisper, "he is the celebrated Mr. Brummell."

This is no fiction; the young Lady Louisa was the daughter of a duke, and her rank, wealth, and personal attractions might well have been thought sufficient to secure her against the criticisms of any man. This doubtless was her mother's opinion; but such was Brummell's influence, and such his supposed ill-nature in the use of his powers of detraction, that she was obliged to warn her young débutante not unthinkingly to expose herself to them. It has been asserted that even Madame de Staël was haunted by a dread of his disapprobation, and that she considered her having failed to please him, as the greatest " malheur " that she experienced during her residence in London ; the next—that the Prince of Wales did not call upon her. The following is an extract from the Aurora Borealis of periodicals, which proves that it also acknowledged the existence of his extraordinary influence :—" Every one has heard the story of the man who, when Pitt inquired what could be done to forward his interest, simply requested the Prime Minister to bow to him in public. There was some sense and knowledge of the world in this request ; nor was it altogether an unmeaning affectation in Brummell when, in reply to a nobleman of the highest rank, who accused him of inveigling his son into a disreputable gambling transaction, he exclaimed, ' Really I did my best for the young man : I once gave him my arm all the way from White's to Watier's.' " [1] Brummell was so far right ; for had the young man possessed any sense, and profited by his example, he would at least have gamed amongst gentlemen ; and in losing his money would not have lost caste also, as it is to be presumed the transaction occurred at some low hell, and not at either of these clubs : unless indeed the opinion of the commentator on Lord Byron's works is correct, namely, "that a ' hell ' is a gaming-house so called, where you risk

[1] "Edinburgh Review," Feb. 1843.

little and are cheated a good deal, and a 'club' a pleasant purgatory, where you lose more, and are not supposed to be cheated at all.' "

Mr. Benson Hill, in his "A Pinch of Snuff,"[1] likewise relates the following anecdote, as a proof that Brummell's opinion was above appeal in the world of fashion; it shows also that he turned his power to some account: " Fribourg and Treyer had received an anxiously expected supply of the veritable Martinique—the list of applicants for this highly prized article had long been filled up. The hogshead was opened in the presence of the Arbiter, who, after taking a few pinches, gravely pronounced it 'a detestable compound, and not at all the style of thing that any man, with the slightest pretensions to correct taste, could possibly patronise.' This astounding announcement, which must soon spread among the candidates, petrified the purveyors : they had procured the snuff at a heavy outlay, and it was now likely to remain on their hands. The companions of the Dictator left him to discuss the matter with the proprietors ; no sooner were they gone than Brummell said,—' By some oversight I did not put my name down on your Martinique list, and I must have allowed the thing to be dispensed to others, who know not its value as I do. Since the hogshead has been condemned, you will not object to my having three jars full of it : that fact once known, there is

---

[1] This booklet the author published under the pseudonym of Dean Snift of Brazen-nose, in 1840.

little doubt that the remainder will find a speedy demand.'

" The Messrs. Fribourg gladly yielded to the *ruse* of the exquisite, and in a few days it having become known that *he* had absolutely bought, and positively paid for, the quantity above-named, not a grain was left."

But many were the steps by which Brummell arrived at this culminating point, and incalculable pains did he devote to his object before his opinion weighed with the *élite* of Almacks—before he could arrogate to himself the power of assigning the limits of gentility, and deciding who were " *bon ou mauvais ton ;* " before he dared to permit himself to exercise his wit at the cost of an insult to his future sovereign, even though they had quarrelled—an insult that he would never, under any circumstances, have addressed to an equal. The recollection of the anecdote to which I allude leads me to the consideration of another feature in Brummell's character, and one which mainly assisted him in attaining his singular eminence : I mean his indescribable assurance, which, without scandalising his memory, was not trifling.

" No one," says the author of " Granby," " could talk down his superiors, whether in rank or talent, with more imposing confidence than Trebeck could ; his denunciations were always couched in a witty form ; and when it was needless or dangerous to define a fault, he could check applause with an incredulous smile, or depress pretension by the raising of an eyebrow. He observed, with derision, how those who were delighted and amused, vainly thought themselves confidentially treated, and exulted in the mistaken idea of being exempted from his cutting criticisms. No keeper of a menagerie could better show off a monkey than he did an original : on these occasions he always contrived to make the unconscious object of his experiments place his absurdities in the best point of view, concealing his own intentions under the blandest cajolery.

"In the art of *cutting* he shone unrivalled; he knew the 'when,' and the 'where,' and the 'how :' without affecting useless short-sightedness, he could assume that calm, but wandering gaze, which veers as if unconsciously around the proscribed individual, neither fixing nor being fixed ; that indefinable look which excuses you, perhaps, to the person *cut*, and at any rate prevents him from accosting you."

In searching for materials for this work, I happened one day to stumble, and as I thought, very fortunately, upon a duodecimo volume, entitled "Anecdotes of Impudence." Here, thought I, something is surely to be gleaned ; but I was disappointed, and not only that, but surprised, for there was not a word about Brummell in the book ; and the frontispiece, which on the impulse of the moment I hoped was a portrait of the Beau, proved to be one of the late Joseph Hume, Esq., M.P. Why Mr. Hume was selected by the author as the best type of the impudence of our times, it is not for me to say ; but I think few will deny that it was very hard upon poor Brummell.

Cool and impertinent, indeed, were the speeches that he often made, and the tricks that he played, especially if he had been affronted, or in self-defence : and then, whether his impudent remarks were levelled at a shoeblack or the Prince of Wales, was perfectly immaterial to him ; for, however unjustifiable his jokes might sometimes be, at least he was never a court sycophant or a parasite. His sarcasms were generally launched at those moving in the same society as himself, at toadies, and rich and assuming *parvenus* who were endeavouring to force themselves into notice ; not at people whose habits were unobtrusive, or who belonged to a more retired sphere of life. But the following well-known anecdote is the most inexcusable instance of his wanton impudence ; for the person whom he made his butt had given him no just cause of offence ; moreover, she was a woman.

It appears that there were two dashing ladies in London, whose patronymics were similar, and who gave great parties. One of them, a Mrs. Thompson, residing in the neighbourhood of Grosvenor Square ; the other, a Mrs. Johnson, living near Finsbury Square. It appears, too, that sometime after Brummell's quarrel with the Prince of Wales, the former lady gave a splendid ball, at which His Royal Highness had signified his intention of being present ; it is therefore scarcely necessary to add, that Brummell

was not included in the list of invitations. On the
evening of the entertainment, however, while Mrs.
Thompson was waiting in her ante-room, supported
by a bevy of intimate friends, in momentary expectation of the arrival of her royal guest, and exulting in
the completeness of all her preparations—the Beau,
to her ineffable surprise and disgust, made his
appearance, and his best bow. Justly indignant
at this outrage, she informed him, with as much
coolness as she could command, that he was not
invited. "Not invited, Madam! not invited!" said
Brummell, in his blandest tones, "surely there must
be some mistake," and leisurely feeling in all his
pockets to prolong the chance of the Prince's arrival,
and therefore her misery, he at last drew forth an
invitation card, and presented it to the incensed lady.
She took it, and saw at a glance it was not her own
card, but that of her rival in the East, and haughtily
throwing it from her, in a climax of vexation and
anxiety to get rid of him, said, "That card, sir, is a
Mrs. Johnson's; my name is Thompson." "Is it,
indeed?" replied Brummell, perfectly cool, and affecting the most innocent surprise, "Dear me, how very
unfortunate!—really, Mrs. Johns—Thompson, I mean,
I am very sorry for this mistake; but you know,
Johnson and Thompson—and Thompson and Johnson, are really so much the same kind of thing.—
Mrs. Thompson, I wish you a very good evening;"
and making a profound bow, he slowly retired from
the room amidst the suppressed anger of the bevy of

intimates, the titter of his own friends, and the undisguised wrath of the lady.

Though Brummell cultivated much the society of women, and his deference to those with whom he associated on intimate terms was great, he had not any very sincere respect for the sex, as the impertinent manner in which he so ill-naturedly harassed this poor lady evidently shows. On that point, as on all others of substantial merit, he was immeasurably below his justly admired contemporary, Wyndham. Brummell's refinement of manners could stand no comparison with his refinement of feeling, and sensitive delicacy towards women, of which the following is a most striking instance:—He was once dining in the country, at the house of a very wealthy but not very polished acquaintance, when the conversation happening to turn upon the subject of female beauty, the gentleman in the course of the discussion said, " But, Mr. Wyndham, what do you think of my wife's eyes?" " Sir," replied the disgusted Crichton, " I never took the liberty of looking at Mrs. F——'s eyes." " Haven't you? well then, take her to the window," said the vulgar hound, quite misunderstanding the reproof, and much in the same tone as, had he been in his farmyard, he would have desired his visitor to examine a favourite Alderney.

The anecdote of Mrs. Johnson-Thompson is no novelty, it has been worn threadbare, but it is, I believe, perfectly authentic, and like some others of the same nature, which may or may not be so, ought not to be omitted in a chapter upon his impudent facetiæ. It is said, that on one occasion when Brummell was dining at a gentleman's house in Hampshire, where the champagne was very far from being good, he waited for a pause in the conversation, and then condemned it by raising his glass, and saying loud enough to be heard by every one at the table, " John, give me some more of that cider."

But although guilty of impertinences of this kind, he was seldom premeditatedly ill-natured or ill-tempered, and, amongst his own set, his impudence was not only permitted, but expected; and no one thought of noticing it any more than they would have done that of a court jester. The following are cases in point :—" Brummell, you were not here yesterday," said one of his club friends; " where did you dine ? " " Dine ! why with a person of the name of R——s. I believe he wishes me to notice him, hence the dinner; but, to give him his due, he desired that I would make up the party myself, so I asked Alvanley, Mills, Pierrepoint, and a few others, and I assure you, the affair turned out quite unique ; there was every delicacy in or out of season ; the Sillery was perfect, and not a wish remained ungratified ; but, my dear fellow, conceive my astonishment when I tell you, that Mr. R——s had the assurance to sit down, and dine with us ! "

On another occasion, a wealthy young gentleman then commencing life, and who afterwards became a member for an eastern borough, being very anxious to be well placed in Brummell's world, asked him and a large party to dine; the Beau went, and a few minutes before they separated, he, addressing the company, requested to know, who was to have the honour of taking him to Lady Jersey's that evening ? " I will," said his host, delighted at the prospect of being seen to enter her ladyship's drawing-room in his company; "wait till my guests are gone, and my carriage is quite at your service." "Thank you exceedingly," replied Brummell, pretending to take the offer in a literal sense, "very kind of you, indeed ! But D——k," and he assumed an air of great gravity, " pray how are you to go ? you surely would not like to get up behind ?   No, that would not be right, and yet it will scarcely do for *me* to be seen in the same carriage with *you*." There was an involuntary roar from all present, in which Mr. D——k, with great good-nature, joined heartily.

But Brummell could not always procure a cast in a friend's carriage, particularly if the friend had to call for him ; and one night being disappointed of a chance that he had calculated upon, when it was too late to send for a glass coach, he was unwillingly obliged to despatch his servant to the nearest stand, with many injunctions as to the selection he should make.   In a few minutes, No. 1803 was at his door, and soon after Brummell, who had alighted a little distance from the house, found himself ascending Lady Dungannon's staircase; he had in fact reached the summit, and was on the eve of entering her splendid drawing-room already filled with guests, when a servant touched him gently on the arm, and to his horror and amazement, for he thought he had effected his purpose undiscovered, said, " Beg pardon, sir, perhaps you are not aware of it, but there is a straw in your shoe."

While we have Brummell's name in connexion with hackney coaches, it may not be *mal-à-propos* to introduce a rather amusing puff, which was inserted some years ago in a weekly paper, by a man who wished to recommend a patent carriage step. To effect his object, he calls the Beau's influence to aid his manœuvre, and gives a very glowing description of his locomotive comforts, not a little in contrast with the preceding anecdote. The article commences with the following axiom :—

" ' There is an art in everything, and whatever is worthy of being learnt, cannot be unworthy of a teacher.' Such was the logical argument of the professor of the Art of Stepping in and out of a Carriage, who represented himself as much patronised by the sublime Beau Brummell, whose deprecation of those horrid coach steps he would repeat with great delight. ' Mr. Brummell,' he used to say, ' considered the sedan was the only vehicle for a gentleman, it having no steps ;—and he invariably had his own chair, which was lined with white satin quilted, had down squabs, and a white sheepskin rug at the bottom, brought to the door of his dressing-room, on that account, always on the ground floor,' from whence it was transferred with its owner to the foot of the staircase of the house that he condescended to visit. Mr. Brummell has told me, continued the professor, that to enter a coach was torture to him. ' Conceive,' said he, ' the horror of sitting in a carriage with an iron apparatus, afflicted with the dreadful thought, the cruel apprehension, of having one's leg crushed by the machinery! Why are not the steps made to fold *outside?* The only detraction from the luxury of a vis-a-vis, is the double distress! for *both* legs—excruciating idea ! ' "

CHAPTER VIII.

Practical Jokes.—The Emigré—Mr. Snodgrass—The Beau's Canine Friend—Affectation—J. W. C——r, and Bloomsbury Square—Brummell's Mots—A Travelled Bore—Vegetable Diet—A Limping Lounger—A New Way of accounting for a Cold—A Bad Summer—The Advantages of Civility—Prince Boothby and Mrs. Clopton Parthericke—Sheridan's Bet.

IN the commencement of the last chapter I alluded to the tricks that Brummell played, meaning thereby practical jokes,—a species of frolic highly amusing to the bystanders, until it is their turn to suffer,—and in which he excelled. His predecessor, George Selwyn, and his contemporary, Sheridan, who loved one another as cordially as wits generally do, were also adepts in puerilities of this kind. Mr. Moore, in his Life of Sheridan, says that he once induced Tickell to run after him into a dark passage, which he had covered with plates, having, however, taken good care to leave a path for himself. Tickell was much cut ; but, when Lord John Townshend came to condole with him, after a little show of indignation against his friend, he could not help exclaiming, " But how amazingly well it was done ! " Brummell's jokes in this way were well done also; and, as is frequently the case, were practised upon those who could not retaliate.

In one instance his victim was an old *émigré*, whom he met on a visit at Woburn or Chatsworth, into whose powder he managed, in concert with a certain noble friend, to introduce some finely-powdered sugar; and the next morning Monsieur le Marquis, in perfect ignorance of the trick, after having been " bien *sucré*," descended as usual to the breakfast-table. He had, however, scarcely made his bow, and inserted his knife into the Périgord-pie before him, when the flies (for the heat was extreme) already attracted to the table by the marmalade and honeycomb, began to transfer their attentions to his head; and before the segment of pie was finally detached, every fly at the table had settled on it. The carving-knife was relinquished, to drive them away with his pocket-handkerchief, but the attempt was futile; they rose for a second, but resettled instantly; a few, indeed, winged their way to the distant parts of the room, but only to return with a reinforcement of their friends, who were vainly seeking a livelihood on the windows.

Murmurs of astonishment escaped from the company, as this new batch assailed Monsieur le Marquis; he fanned his head, but it was of no use; he shook it vehemently, but with no better success; at length, the sugar becoming dissolved by the heat, trickled in saccharine rivulets over his forehead,

which was soon covered by his tormentors, buzzing
and tickling so dreadfully, that even old régime
impassibilité could stand it no longer. The unfortunate Frenchman started to his feet, and violently
clasping his head with both his hands, rushed from
the room, enveloped in a cloud of powder and flies ;
his tormentors, and the echoes of an uncontrollable
burst of laughter, following him up the staircase.
When he was gone, Brummell and his confederate,
of course, expressed more surprise than any one else,
that the flies should have taken such a violent fancy
to the Frenchman's powder and pomatum.

Another gentleman, who suffered by his pranks,
was a Mr. Snodgrass, I believe an F.R.S., and very
fond of scientific pursuits ; probably the reason why
he was singled out by Brummell as a fit and proper
object for his fun. Accompanied by several friends,
he once knocked up this *savant*, at three o'clock on a
fine frosty morning ; and when, under the impression
of his house being on fire, he protruded his body *en
chemise*, and his head in a nightcap, from the window,
the Beau put the following very interesting question
to him :—" Pray, sir, is your name Snodgrass ? "
" Yes, sir," said he, very anxiously, " my name is
Snodgrass." " Snodgrass — Snodgrass," repeated
Brummell, " a very odd name that, upon my soul ; a
very odd name indeed ! But, sir, is your name really
Snodgrass ? " Here the philosopher, with the thermo-
meter below freezing point, naturally got into a towering passion, and threatened to call the watch ; where-

upon Brummell walked off, with—" Good morning to you, Mr. Snodgrass."

Such were the absurd tricks in which Brummell indulged ; and though he was not a wit in the literal sense of the word, like Lord Erskine, Sheridan, or Jekyll, he had a happy facility in placing the most ordinary circumstances in a ridiculous point of view, and never refrained, when opportunity offered, from indulging his taste for exciting the risible muscles even of those who, very probably, thought but little of his talent in this way.   He had, also, a singular power of giving an agreeable effect to a word or action, that in any one else would have been perhaps unnoticed ; or, if noticed—condemned : but his happy hardihood generally carried him through the difficulties into which his fearless love of originality sometimes plunged him. It was, I believe, from one of his odd speeches that a certain gentleman, well known in the world, received the sobriquet of Poodle Byng.   It seems that Mr. Byng had in his youth very beautiful hair, which curled naturally, and it was his practice, not an unusual one in the days of curricles, to be accompanied in his by his French dog.   One day Brummell, who was on horseback, met them quietly driving together in the park, and hailed his friend with, " Ah, Byng, how do you do ?—a family vehicle, I see ! "

His affectation, which was principally assumed for the purpose of amusing those about him, was another characteristic of his wit.   He pretended to look upon the City as a terra incognita ; and when some great

Mr Byng.

merchant requested the honour of his company at dinner, he replied, " With pleasure, if you will promise faithfully not to tell." But a certain ex-secretary of the Admiralty, of graver parts and great political and literary talents, has, since his time, carried on the joke to Bloomsbury, or some other square in that direction ; for, it is related of him, that, when invited to dine in that remote region, he piquantly inquired where he was to change horses ? a *mot* which has, no doubt inadvertently, wandered into Pelham. The following are some of the Beau's *jeux d'esprit* that were at one time in general circulation, and a few of which have already been in print.

An acquaintance having, in a morning call, bored him dreadfully about some tour he had made in the North of England, enquired with great pertinacity of his impatient listener which of the lakes he preferred ? when Brummell, quite tired of the man's tedious raptures, turned his head imploringly towards his valet, who was arranging something in the room, and said, " Robinson." " Sir." " Which of the lakes do I admire ? " " Windermere, sir," replied that distinguished individual. " Ah, yes, — Windermere," repeated Brummell, " so it is, — Windermere." A lady at dinner, observing that he did not take any vegetables, asked him whether such was his general habit, and if he never ate any ? He replied, " Yes, madam, I once ate a pea."

One day a friend, meeting him limping in Bond Street, asked him what was the matter ? He replied, he had hurt his leg, and the worst of it was, " It was his favourite leg." Having been asked by a sympathising friend how he happened to get such a severe cold ? His reply was, " Why, do you know, I left my carriage yesterday evening, on my way to town from the Pavilion, and the infidel of a landlord put me into a room with a damp stranger."

On being asked by one of his acquaintance, during a very unseasonable summer, if he had ever seen such a one ? He replied, " Yes, last winter." Having fancied himself invited to some one's country seat, and being given to understand, after one night's lodging, that he was in error, he told an unconscious friend in town, who asked him what sort of a place it was ? " that it was an exceedingly good house for stopping one night in."

At an Ascot meeting, and early in the day, Brummell walked his horse up to Lady ——'s carriage, when she expressed her surprise at his throwing away his time on her, or thinking of running the risk of being seen talking to such a very quiet and unfashionable person. " My dear Lady ——," he replied, " pray don't mention it ; there is no one near us."

The principal portion of this chapter has been devoted to the consideration of Brummell's most unamiable qualities, to his powers of detraction, his satirical remarks, and practical jokes ; but let not the reader imagine they preponderated to the exclusion of better ones. No one possessed the art of pleasing to a greater degree, or exercised it with greater effect, when he was in the society of those he liked, whatever might be their age or station; had he been the superlatively insolent character he is generally represented, he would have been universally cut, instead of sought after—the absurdity of the notion is its most complete refutation. Well do I remember the lecture on good manners that he gave a young gentleman at Caen, who had justly laid himself open to censure, by the thoughtless omission of an act of courtesy, that Brummell considered due to a lady near whom the youth was standing.

"Civility, my good fellow," observed the Beau, "may truly be said to cost nothing; if it does not meet with a due return, it at least leaves you in the most creditable position. When I was young, I was acquainted with a striking example of what may sometimes be gained by it, though my friend on this occasion did not, I assure you, expect to benefit by his politeness. In leaving the Opera one evening, a short time previous to the fall of the curtain, he overtook in the lobby an elderly lady, making her way out to avoid the crowd; she was dressed in a most peculiar manner, with hoop and brocade, and a pyramid of hair; in fact, she was at least a century behind the rest of the world in her costume: so singular an apparition had attracted the attention of half a dozen 'Lord Dukes,' and 'Sir Harrys,' sitting in the lobby, and as she slowly moved towards the box entrance, they amused themselves by making impertinent remarks on her extraordinary dress and infirm gait.

"Directly my friend caught sight of them, and saw what they were after, he went to her assistance, threatened to give them in charge to a Bow Street officer, and with his best bow offered her his arm. She accepted it, and on the stairs he enquired whether she had a chair or a carriage? at the same time intimating his willingness to go for one. 'Thank you, sir, I have my chair,' replied the old lady, 'if you will only be good enough to remain with me until it arrives:' as she was speaking, her servants came up with it, and making the cavalier a very stately curtsy, she requested to know to whom she had the honour of being indebted for so much attention? 'My name, madam,' replied the stranger, as he handed her to her chair, 'is Boothby, but I am usually called Prince Boothby;' upon which the antiquated lady thanked him once more, and left. Well, from that hour Boothby never saw her again, and did not even hear of her till her death, which took place a few years after; when he received a letter from her lawyer, announcing to him the agreeable intelligence of her having left him heir to several thousands a year! Now, my good sir," said Brummel to the abashed but youthful delinquent, "for the future, pray remember Prince Boothby."

John Skrimshire Boothby, was one of the most celebrated of the fine gentlemen of his day, the great peculiarity of whose dress was the shape of his hat,

which he never changed. He is supposed to be the
person alluded to by Foote in one of his farces, as
distinguished by his partiality for people of high rank,
and ready at any time to leave a baronet to walk with
a baron,—"to be genteelly damned beside a duke,
rather than saved in vulgar company." Moore, in
allusion to him, or his double, says,

> " Beside him place the god of wit,
>   Before him beauty's rosiest girls,
>   Apollo for a star he'd quit,
>   And Love's own sister for an Earl's."

Boothby was well bred, intelligent, and amiable, but
extremely eccentric, and he ended his career at his
house in Clarges Street by his own hand, in July
1800. His servants at the inquest bore the strongest
testimony to his character as a good master, and a
kind-hearted man. He had been possessed of three
large estates; the first was his own inheritance,
which he dissipated; the second came to him from
a distant family connection; and the third was the
gift of the ancient lady in the lobby, whose name was
Clopton, which he afterwards added to his own.
Boothby was a great friend of the fifth Duke of
Rutland, Lords Carlisle and Derby, and Charles
Fox; and was brother-in-law to that fox-hunting
centaur, the late Hugo Meynell. He was also a
member of the clubs in St. James Street, where he
used to play very high; and he is mentioned in
Moore's Life of Sheridan as having made a bet with

the orator of five hundred guineas, that there would not be a reform in the representation of the people of England, within three years from the date of the bet, the 29th of January 1793.   Mr. Moore does not say that Sheridan paid.

CHAPTER IX.

Brummell's Softer Moments—His Numerous Offers—His Honesty in Love Affairs—The Intended Mrs. Brummell—His Flirtations and Love Letters—His Great Popularity with the Fair Sex—His Good-Nature—Miss Seymour's Letter to him—Brummell's regard for her.

THOUGH I have already alluded to Brummell's predilection for female society, I have not yet spoken of those moments, perhaps the most interesting of a man's life, at least to himself—his moments of *tendresse.* Brummell had his; but the organ of love in his cranium was only faintly developed. His temperament was elephantine; still it was scarcely possible for him to be constantly in the society of the most beautiful and accomplished girls in Europe,—and who will deny that the daughters of our aristocracy are so ?—without having a preference for one of them, or perhaps half a dozen ; and this was the case ; for he never attained any degree of intimacy with a pretty woman of rank that he did not make her an offer, not with any idea of being accepted, but because he thought it was paying the lady a great compliment, and procured her an unusual degree of *éclat* in the fashionable world. His original view of the subject appears to have been generally understood and acted upon by his friends. One of his idols, however, seemed inclined to take him at his word, Lady W——; and often have I heard him rave about her.

But Brummell's vanity and honesty in love affairs were equally extraordinary. It is related of him that he came one morning into the library of a noble friend, at whose house he was a frequent visitor, and told him, with much warmth and sincerity of manner, that he was very sorry, very sorry indeed, but he must positively leave —— Park that morning. " Why, you were not to go till next month ! " said the hospitable peer. " True, true," replied Brummell anxiously, "but I must be off." " But what for ? " " Why the fact is—I am in love with your countess." " Well, my dear fellow, never mind that, so was I twenty years ago—is she in love with you ? " The Beau hesitated, and after scrutinising for a few seconds the white sheep-skin rug, said faintly, " I—believe she is." " Oh ! that alters the case entirely," replied the earl ; " I will send for your post-horses immediately." Once, however, though not with a lady of rank, he did very nearly " his quietus make with a gold ring ; " for he interested the demoiselle sufficiently to induce her to consent to elope with him. The most favourable opportunity that presented itself for so doing, was at a ball in the neighbourhood of Grosvenor Square ; but his measures on the occasion were so badly taken, that he and the intended Mrs. Brummell

were caught at the corner of the next street, a
servant having turned mother's evidence. It is said
that when a friend rallied him on his evident want
of success in another matrimonial speculation, and
pressed him for the reason of his failure, Brummell
replied with a smile, " Why, what could I do, my
good fellow, but cut the connection ? I discovered
that Lady Mary actually ate cabbage ! "

But all this tells very little either for his judgment or his feeling ; and it was rather extraordinary
that, with all the advantages and opportunities he
enjoyed, he did not select one lovely flower from the
parterre of rank, fashion, and wealth, and wear it
for life. However, independently of his deficiency
in warmth and perseverance, he had too much self-
love ever to be really in love ; had Cupid's arrow
been a cloth-yard long, and had he drawn it to the
head like the stout archer in Chevy Chase, it would
scarcely have reached the Beau's heart, or if it had
would merely have tickled, not wounded it. He
was a thorough flirt, his love was as light and as
elegant as everything else about him, and, in none of
his disappointments was he likely to have recourse
to a pan of charcoal, or the Serpentine ; it was the
transitory sentiment which, in a subsequent letter,
he says, is " so often and so easily expressed with
a crow-quill, and its feigned regret by tears, made
with a sponge and rose-water, upon perfumed paper."
In this trifling with the god of love he through life
delighted to indulge ; and the following laughable

and amusing letters are specimens of his style in conducting a correspondence of the kind :—

" MY DEAR LADY JANE,—With the miniature it seems I am not to be trusted, even for two pitiful hours ; my own memory must be, then, my only disconsolate expedient to obtain a resemblance.

" As I am unwilling to merit the imputation of committing myself, by too flagrant a liberty, in retaining your glove, which you charitably sent at my head yesterday, as you would have extended an eleemosynary sixpence to the supplicating hat of a mendicant, I restore it to you ; and allow me to assure you, that I have too much regard and respect for you, and too little practical vanity myself (whatever appearances may be against me), to have entertained, for one treacherous instant, the impertinent intention to defraud you of it. You are angry, perhaps irreparably incensed against me, for this petty larceny. I have no defence to offer in mitigation, but that of frenzy. But we know that you are an angel visiting these sublunary spheres, and therefore your first quality should be that of mercy ; yet you are sometimes wayward and volatile in your seraphic disposition—though you have no wings, still you have weapons ; and these are, resentment and estrangement from me. With sentiments of the deepest compunction, I am always, your miserable slave,　　　GEORGE BRUMMELL.

" The Lady Jane ——, Harley Street."

"DEAR MISS ——,—When I wrote to you a century ago, in plaintive strains, and with 'all Hackman's sorrows[1] and all Werther's woes,' you told me, with pen dipped in oblivion's ink from Lethe's stream, that I must desist from my vagaries, because I was trespassing on consecrated ground ; but you offered me instead, your *friendship*, as a relic—by way of a bone to pick, among all my refined and elegant sensibilities ! Well, I struggled hard to bring myself to this meagre abnegation, and my efforts promised to be propitious. I kissed the rod, cherished the relic, and enveloped myself in austerity and sackcloth. I then, by way of initiating myself to penance, inscribed you : missive, in appropriate terms of mortification, presuming, too, that it was the privilege, if not the duty, of my vocation, to mortify you, also, as a votary, with a little congenial castigation. I dare say I wrote to you in a most absurd and recriminating manner, for I was excited by the pious enthusiasm of my recent apostasy ; and I was anxious to impress upon your more favourable opinion, the exemplary and salutary progress I had made in my new school. You are, it seems, displeased at it, though my heresy from my first delightful faith was your own work. I know not now where to turn for another belief.

"I will tell you the truth in plain unmystical language, for I have not yet learnt to renounce *that;* I was irritated because I thought you had cut me dead in

[1] See Chapter XV.'

the morning; and when I was *tête-à-tête* with my
solitary lamp in the evening, a thousand threatening
phantoms assailed me. I imagined that you had
abandoned me; in short, a cohort of blue devils got
the better of me, and I am now all compunction and
anguish. Pray be once more an amiable and compassionate being, and do not contract your lovely eyebrows any more (I wish to Heaven I could see them
at this instance!) in sullenness at all my numberless
incongruities and sins. Be the same Samaritan saint
you have already been to me: you shall never more
repent it. Whatever I may have said in a frenical
moment of exasperation was *unsaid* and *unthought* an
hour afterwards, when I sought my couch, and prof-
fered my honest prayers for forgiveness from above,
and profanely from you who are upon earth. I am
more than conscious of all my derelictions—of all
my faults, but indeed they shall be in future corrected,
if you are still a friend to me. I had vaunted, in the
vanity of my chivalrous spirit, that I had at length
proved one in myself; but it was empty ostentation,
for I find that I cannot exist but in amity with you.
—Your unfortunate supplicant,

"GEORGE BRUMMELL."

Love, indeed, but of this harmless character, formed
one of the Beau's distractions in exile; and the following letter, which, like all the others, I beg to
assure the reader is perfectly authentic, is an amusing
proof, not only how sensitive he was on the subject,

even in mature age, but also how he succeeded in
awakening an interest for him in the minds of those
who were both young and beautiful.   The reader will
remember, the mind—not the heart.

"RUE ROYALE, ——, Wednesday.

"Yesterday morning I was subdued almost to insanity, but your note in the evening restored me to
peace and equanimity, and, as if I had been redeemed
from earthly purgatory, placed me in heaven.   Thank
you, thank you, dearest of beings ; how can I retri-
bute all this benevolent open-heartedness, this delightful proof and avowal of my not being indifferent to
you ?   I cannot, by inanimate words, represent the
excess of my feelings towards you : take, then, with
indulgent admission and forbearance, the simple boon
and sacred pledge of my heart's deepest affections for
you ; they are rooted in my very soul and existence ;
they will never deviate ; they will never die away.
By the glimmering light that was remaining I per-
ceived something in white at your *porte-cochère.*   It
was evident that I was recognised, and the figure
advanced with your *billet.*   In an instant I seized
the hand of your faithful and intelligent messenger,
compressed it forcibly, and had she been as for-
bidding as the old dowager Duchess of ——, I
should have saluted her, if I had not fancied at the
instant that I heard some one coming up the street.
We parted, and I returned to my solitary chamber.
There I lacerated the letter with impatience, and

then the light of love and of joy, and the refreshing
breath of evening stole through the open window
over my entranced senses. After that I sought
another stroll on the ramparts, and again returned
home contented with you, with myself, and with
the world.

> ' I slept the slumbers of a saint forgiven,
> And mild as opening dreams of promised heaven.'

"I have known few that could equal, none that
could excel you ; yet they possessed not your charm
of countenance, your form, your heart, in my estimation.   Certainly they did not possess that unaffected
and fervent homage, which in my constant memory,—
in my heart's life-blood,—and in my devoted soul I
bear to you.—Ever most affectionately yours,

" GEORGE BRUMMELL."

Such were the pathetic appeals that he addressed
to single women—in warm weather ; for his heart
seldom thawed to this extent before the middle of
June, and probably the first frost that nipped the
dahlias crisped it up again till the following summer ;
at least sufficiently so to prevent him from shivering
and shaking near his lady love's *porte-cochère*, in
expectation of a note : he could write hundreds by
his fireside at all seasons. As regards his London
life, however, he generally preferred the society of
married women, whose greater acquaintance with the
world made them far more amusing companions than

single ones; and without any pretensions to *bonnes fortunes*, he was the idol of all those who took any lead in high life : happy was she in whose opera-box he would pass an hour, whose assembly he would attend, or at whose table he would dine. He had also a strong partiality for two or three widows, whose names, however, I should be very sorry to disclose to the present generation ; and I leave Brummell's contemporaries to fix upon any peeress they may think proper, as the one to whom the following letter was addressed :—

"Chesterfield Street.

" DEAR LADY ——,—I am almost inclined to believe that you have forgotten me in the protracted space of five days, and that you have amused your leisure hours with something or somebody more interesting to you. You are too overtly severe with Lord L——; he has effrontery enough to persuade himself that you are piqued with him, and he will interpret that into a latent interest for him : what can it possibly be to you, whether he goes to Brighthelmstone or not? Affront him, but with dexterity, and his own consummate and mistaken vanity will be his speediest drawback ; but never make an enemy of a man whose physiognomy has been ravaged by the small-pox,—for whom Jenner has lived in vain !

" Attar-Gul [1] (for Mr. ——— has adopted that name, in deference to his having inherited some

---

[1] Ottar of roses. The Persian is considered the finest.

ostrich's eggs, glass beads, cockatoo's feathers, and a few shells from an aunt, a sort of vagrant Zingarella, who died recently at Aleppo of the leprosy) has not perceptibly touched a bristle of his raven crown since you saw, or rather turned away your eyes from him. In submission to your desire, I have minutely scrutinised his head. He had the effrontery, the other day, to be irritated because I asked him to lend me his brush of a sconce to assist at the morning toilette of my boots! The monster! Do not forget your parasol in this inflammatory weather.—Yours devoutly,

"George Brummell.

"The Lady ———, Brighthelmstone."

But though his own affections seem never to have been very deeply engaged, the following letter shows that he possessed considerable sense and good feeling, when those of others, in whose welfare he took a real interest, were concerned. It was written by Miss Seymour, and is introduced here as a striking and authentic proof of Brummell's good-nature. It is unnecessary to refer to the actual circumstances alluded to by the amiable and lovely writer: I will merely observe, that the information he gave her was of the utmost value, and that it is highly probable it would never have come to her knowledge but for his disinterested kindness.

"Wednesday morning.

"I am more obliged to you than I can express for your note: be assured that your approbation of my conduct has given me very sincere pleasure: this is the only means I have of telling you so; for I am in such disgrace, that I do not know if I shall be taken to the play;—in any case, I shall be watched; therefore accept my most cordial thanks, and believe that I shall remember your good-nature to me on this occasion, with gratitude, to the end of my life.

"—— does not know how unkindly I have been treated, but is more affectionate than ever, because he sees I am unhappy. We did not arrive in town till seven last night, therefore no play; to-morrow they go to Covent Garden:—perhaps I may be allowed to be of the party.

"Pray don't neglect my drawing; you would make me very happy by lending me the yellow book again; the other I don't ask for, much as I wish for it. Adieu! I shall be steady in my opinion of you, and always remain, yours, very sincerely,

"GEORGIANA A. F. SEYMOUR."

"This beautiful creature is dead!" was the remark Brummell had written at the bottom of the letter, which he kept as a memento of her friendship for him till within four years of his death; he then parted with it, but only to a very intimate friend, who wished for the autograph.

CHAPTER X.

OTHER lady correspondents Brummell had also ; and the subject of the next letter does not, from a motive of delicacy, render any mystery about it necessary. It is from that very erratic being, Lady Hester Stanhope, and was written to inquire the character of a groom, who had been in his service : it bears the Cheltenham postmark.

"August 30th, 1803.

" If you are as conceited as formerly, I shall stand accused of taking your groom, to give me an opportunity of writing to you for his character. All the inquiry I wish to make upon this subject is, to be informed whether you were as well satisfied with

James Ell when you parted with him, as when he
had Stiletto under his care. If so, I shall despatch
him at the end of next week, with my new purchases
to Walmer,[1] where I am going very shortly. You
may imagine I am not a little happy, in having it in
my power to scamper upon British ground, although
I was extremely pleased with my tour, and charmed
with Italy.

" I saw a good deal of your friend Capel at Naples ;
if he fights the battles of his country by sea as well
as he fights yours by land, he certainly is one of our
first commanders. But of him you must have heard
so full an account from Lord Althorp,[2] for they were
inseparable, that I will only add he was as yet unsuccessful in the important research after a perfect snuff-
box, when I left Italy.[3] What news the last despatch
may have brought upon this subject I am ignorant
of, but take it for granted you are not ; as in all
probability the *Phœbe* was by your interest appointed
to the Mediterranean station for three years, to accom-
plish this grand and useful discovery. Should it
prove a successful one, Capel, on his return, will of
course be made Admiral of the White, for the signal
services he has rendered to coxcombality.[4]

[1] The official residence of Mr. Pitt, as Warden of the Cinque
Ports.

[2] Lord Althorp, who died in 1845, and was then in his twenty-first
year, was the uncle of the present Earl Spencer.

[3] See Chapter XXIV.

[4] The Honourable Sir Thomas Bladen Capel, K.C.B., &c.,
youngest son of the fourth Earl of Essex, was born on the 28th of
August 1776. This distinguished officer had the honour of being the

" I met with a rival of yours in affectation upon
the Continent, William Hill !¹ I fear it will be
long ere this country will again witness his airs,
as he is now a prisoner ;—this, perhaps, you are
glad of, as the society of statues and pictures has
infinitely improved him in this wonted qualification,
and therefore rendered him a still more formidable
competitor.

" Hester L. Stanhope."

That Lady Hester knew the Beau well is evident
from the first paragraph in her letter.   In it she
disarms him at the onset ; and in her fearless
disposition, makes no difficulty of lashing him and
his friends, with a keenness and dexterity quite
equal to his own, and, apparently, with as much
pleasure : of course she had an advantage in the
lady's privilege, of saying what she pleased ; but
there is every reason to suppose, that, when Brummell returned her a compendium of James Ell's

signal-lieutenant of Nelson's ship, the *Vanguard*, at the battle of the
Nile, and was promoted for his conduct on that day.   He also
rendered important services to the fleet when in command of the
Phœbe, after Trafalgar.   Sir Bladen likewise commanded the *Endymion*, at the passage of the Dardanelles, in 1807, and was actively
employed in the Hogue on the coast of America, from 1812 to the conclusion of the war.   It was while serving on this station that his ship was
nearly blown up by a petard.   The admiral entered the navy at the
early age of six years, and died in 1853, when he was seventy-seven
years old.

¹ William Noel Hill, second son of the first Lord Berwick, who
succeeded to that title on the death of his brother.   He was at one
time ambassador to the court of Turin, and died on the 4th of August,
1842.

qualifications in stable affairs, he did not conclude his billet, without responding to the gossip and raillery that pervaded hers.

After perusing this amusing letter, one is tempted to think what a pity it was, for her friends and society, that Lady Hester emigrated to the mountains of Lebanon, on which the cedars would have grown just as well without her ; but the letter affords some indication of the independent disposition that she afterwards displayed to such an unusual degree, and in a manner so perfectly original ; for it must be admitted, that it was, at least, a slight deviation from ordinary custom, for a young lady to write to a gentleman on such a subject.

Independence like her ladyship's could hardly be accounted for by her education, singular as it must have been under the direction of " Citizen Stanhope ; " much less by an early introduction to men's society at her uncle's table ; though there may, perchance, have been occasionally an adventurous spirit amongst the philo-politicals at Mr. Pitt's parliamentary dinners, of which she so gracefully did the honours.—But, in whatever cause this feeling originated, it is difficult to reconcile Lady Hester's long residence in the mountains of Lebanon, associating only with the wild Arab, or living in the most complete seclusion, with the love of her father-land shown in that part of her letter, in which she expresses her delight " to scamper on British ground ; "

and the pleasure which it may be supposed she
enjoyed in the society with which she was familiar,
the most *recherché* of her own class.   Why did
Lady Hester thus expatriate herself?—was it for
love?   If so, for whom, or what—her uncle's
memory, or Beau Brummell?   Certain it is, that in
her solitude the latter was still remembered by her,
even as late as the year 1830.

A friend of the author's, then serving in the
Mediterranean, having obtained leave of absence
for a few months, spent a portion of that year in
wandering through Palestine and the adjacent countries, and in his travels he paid a visit to the "old
Lady of the Mountain," who received him most
graciously, for he was the bearer of a letter from an
old friend of hers ; and Lady Hester signified her
willingness to grant him an interview, the day after
he had made her aware of his arrival by sending her
his credentials—these were highly necessary, for she
was not in the habit of so favouring travellers in
general.

At the hour named, therefore, my friend, full of
anxiety to see and converse with such a singular
character, made his way to her house : he was
admitted by a little black female slave, possibly a
mute, for it was in perfect silence that she ushered
him into an apartment, so dark, that he could with
difficulty discover the ottoman, on which a voice at
the other end of it desired him to be seated ; he had

scarcely obeyed, when a very small latticed window near him was suddenly opened by some invisible means, and the light thrown full upon his countenance, without, however, having any, or but little effect in relieving the obscurity, which reigned complete at the opposite end of the long room.

When his eyes had become somewhat accustomed to the glare, he saw a female figure sitting *à l'orientale* on a carpet, dressed in the Eastern style, and by her side the black slave who had been his guide. Lady Hester, for it was his hostess who now addressed him, enquired first after the Duke of Wellington, and then after George Brummell; these two being apparently the only individuals of her own, or any other European nation, for whom she seemed to entertain the smallest interest, as, during the remainder of his audience, she adverted only to events that were passing in the country of her adoption. It would have been extraordinary, indeed, had Lady Hester not been anxious for intelligence respecting the hero of her younger days, the victor of Assaye; with whom she had probably been acquainted before she left England, and the details of whose subsequent career had been the theme of admiration, even of the rude mountaineers that surrounded her,—but that she should have been interested in obtaining tidings of the Beau was rather remarkable.

Let not the reader imagine, however, I was serious, in insinuating that her ladyship entertained any tender sentiments for Brummell. Lady Hester is said to have mourned one of a very different mould—he who was by his gallant soldiers, buried

——————"darkly at dead of night,
The sod with their bayonets turning ;
By the struggling moonbeams' misty light,
And the lantern dimly burning."

This rumour was, I believe, entirely without foundation, though dates and circumstances gave some appearance of truth to it. Sir John Moore fell on the 16th of January 1809, and Lady Hester left England in deep mourning and for ever early in the spring of the following year : her Ladyship's half-brother, Major Stanhope, was also slain at the battle of Corunna. It was of this officer, and the hero of Meanee, while leading on the Fiftieth Regiment, that Sir John Moore said, " Well done, my Majors ! " Such was the imperfect recollection I retained of the fireside narrative my friend gave me, some years ago, of his interesting visit to Lady Hester ; and I was regretting his absence, as he could have made my sketch so much more worthy of the reader's perusal, when he opportunely arrived in England. Of course I immediately availed myself of this fortunate circumstance, and the following letter contains his own striking and animated description of herself and her wild retreat ; which he forwarded to me with a kindness and promptitude, that proved, how little his friendship or his memory was impaired by the time that had elapsed since we met.

"Many years have passed since I was in Syria; but, as you desire it, I will endeavour to describe my visit to Lady Hester Stanhope, as well as my memory permits. I was furnished with a letter of introduction from Lord ———, which I sent from Sidon; a knowledge of her disinclination to receive Englishmen generally, having prevented my delivering it personally when passing near her abode on my way from Damascus. Her ladyship, however, acknowledged the letter most politely, invited me and my companion to visit her for as long a time as we found it convenient, and sent two fine Arabian horses to convey us to her residence, which was formerly a convent, and crowns the summit of a hill about eight miles from Sidon.

"The ascent to Mar Elias (for so the convent is called) was steep, and the approach to it more like that of a crusading baron's castle than of the residence of a solitary lady, whose education had been finished, and early habits formed, amongst the most refined and intellectual of the English nobility. A strong guard of Albanians protected the gate, and numbers of armed men, of the same nation, were idling about, as if time was a heavy burthen on their hands. We were conducted to a kiosk or summer-house, outside the main building, and there an Italian, dressed like an Arab, received us and provided dinner in the European fashion; this last appeared to be a matter of some difficulty, as her Ladyship conformed to the Eastern habits, in eating, dress, and other matters, and some time had elapsed since plates and forks had been called into requisition. During dinner, an Arab, who spoke French most volubly, made his appearance and told us he was her Ladyship's astrologer, and enlarged upon her good fortune in possessing so talented a wizard as himself.

"Soon after, Lady Hester sent to say, she would be happy to receive us; and we were accordingly ushered through several apartments, by various attendants, until we reached a small and rather dark room, in which sat her Ladyship, dressed as an Arab sheick, and looking more like a young man than an elderly lady. She sat with her back to the light, which streamed in through a small window full on our faces; this she afterwards told me was arranged on purpose to give her a fair scrutiny of the faces of her visitors : chibouques (the long cherry-stick pipe) were introduced, and in a short time she became most agreeably communicative.

"Her conversation was more than ordinarily eloquent, though tinctured with somewhat of the strangeness that pervaded her whole life and character : her thorough knowledge of the language, habits, and customs of the East, combined with the ease with which she expressed her ideas, enabled her to draw the most vivid pictures of those countries, and convey her information in a very agreeable manner. Nor was her conversation by any means confined to these subjects ; for when trifling circumstances recalled her thoughts to the days of her youth, when

she presided at Mr. Pitt's table, she described those
scenes, and the persons of such as were admitted to
the circle of her uncle's society, as faithfully and
minutely as if the memory of them had not been
overlaid, by the eight-and-twenty years she had
passed amidst the exciting events of her later life.

"Beau Brummell, who was in her youthful days
the friend of the Prince of Wales, and envied and
admired by both beaux and belles of all ranks of
society, appeared to have been an especial favourite
of hers ; and though I am unable to repeat the
description as she gave it, I can even now fancy
that I see him riding up to her in the Park in a
suit of plum-coloured clothes, to give her a stick of
perfume of his own manufacture; a peculiar mark
of favour, granted only on condition that she promised faithfully not to give a morsel to the Prince,
who was dying to get some.

"I hinted at Brummell's eccentricities; but she
replied, that he was an exceedingly clever man,
always suiting his conversation to his hearers, and
that he almost always paid her the compliment of
talking very sensibly. She added, that she had once
rebuked him for some folly or other, and inquired
why so clever a person as he was did not devote
his talents to a higher purpose than he did ? To
which Brummell replied, that he knew human nature
well, and that he had adopted the only course which
could place him in a prominent light, and enable him
to separate himself from the society of the ordinary

herd of men, whom he held in considerable contempt.
These conversations, with the attendant chibouque,
which her Ladyship smoked as determinedly as the
longest-bearded Mussulman in the land, were generally prolonged until near daylight, when we retired
to rest.

" During the day we were left to amuse ourselves,
and did not see our kind hostess until after a late
dinner.   On one occasion, however, she showed
us her garden, which, though very small, was laid
out with great taste, and in the Eastern style, and
contained many very beautiful and rare flowers.
Trellises and lattice-work, covered with creepers,
were so arranged, that, when lit with lamps, and
viewed from the convent windows, the garden would
look exactly like a scene in the opera.

" Lady Hester had acquired considerable influence
amongst the Arab tribes, with whom she passed
much time during the earlier period of her residence in Syria : this she obtained, partly because,
though she professed a partial belief in the Koran,
and conformed to most of their customs and pre-
judices, her life and habits were beyond their com-
prehension ; and her morality being unquestioned,
they looked upon her somewhat in the light of a
supernatural being—a belief that she was inclined
to encourage, rather than undeceive.   Having tried
her courage, which was indomitable, and experienced
her hospitality, and the readiness with which her
purse was opened to every call of distress, some of

the tribes near Palmyra endeavoured to persuade her to permit herself to be called "Sovereign of the Desert;" and, as she assured me, prepared a sort of ceremony for her installation at Palmyra;—an honour, however, which she prudently declined. She believed in all kinds of astrology, and some of the wildest of the Eastern legends; especially in that which alludes to the Thirteenth Imaum, whom she called the Saviour, and for whom she kept a horse that had the natural mark of a saddle on its back, which she said had never been mounted by man or woman.[1]

"She also told me, that her astrologer had been closely observing us, during our first dinner, and had been able to assure her, that we were not born under a hostile planet, nor had either of us red hair, or foreheads 'villanously low;' for, had such

---

[1] Mussulmen reckon, I think, twelve Imaums, commencing with Moussa (Moses), Ibrahim (Abraham), and Husrut Esau (Jesus Christ), the Healer of the Lame and Blind, and their own prophet Mahomet, &c. The word is also applied to the principal sects, as Ali, the Imaum of the Persians, or the sect of the Shiaites; Abu-Beker the Imaum of the Sunnites, the sect of the Turks; and Safi, of another sect, &c.

The Mahometans look for the advent or reappearance of another Imaum, who will convert the whole world to the faith of Islam, and reign on earth for a time in great glory and happiness: the end of this period and of the world will be simultaneous. The Mussulmen of India and Affghanistan expected the advent alluded to in A.D. 1842, and thought their successes at Cabul a prelude to it. A Belooch chief, when consulting a friend of the writer of this note, as to the advantage of his surrendering on certain terms, observed that if he could but hold out a little longer, his surrender would be rendered unnecessary by the appearance of the Thirteenth Imaum, whose arrival in that year was predicted by all the learned Faquirs in India.

been the case, she would have been unable to have admitted us to her presence; and this precaution she always took, with those who were favoured by a reception at her house. Being aware of a prophecy believed by the Mussulmen of Damascus, which declares that the Turkish Empire will crumble to pieces in a certain number of years, after the day on which a Christian or Jew shall first ride on horseback through the holy gate which leads to Mecca—she rode up to the guard stationed there with her suite (always numerous and formidably armed), spurred her horse, dashed through it, and went straight to the durbar of the Pacha, to acquaint him with her exploit.

"In the course of conversation, during the last night we remained at Mar Elias, she inquired whether we had seen the Emir Beschir, and on our replying in the negative, she clapped her hands, and the little black slave, who appeared, with hands crossed over her bosom, to answer the summons, was directed to call the scribe, to whom she dictated an epistle, which was despatched on the instant to the emir; saying, that two friends of hers would visit him next day, and desiring a suitable reception. Soon after daylight the messenger returned, though the emir's residence was some miles distant, bringing a cordial invitation, which we accepted.

"It was not without a feeling of great sadness that I took leave of Lady Hester; but when I ventured to hint at the possibility of her return to Europe, she cut the conversation short, by asking me if I thought she could make up her mind to knit or sew like an Englishwoman, after having spent her life amid the stirring scenes she had been constantly engaged in? I then alluded to her forlorn situation, among men upon whose consciences the blood of a lone woman would have scarce weighed heavily; but her eyes flashed fire, as she replied, drawing a dagger from her breast, 'Who would be the first to venture on the wild cat in her den?' Her reply to the consul at Cairo, who addressed her by desire of Ibrahim Pacha, then Governor of Syria, was highly characteristic of herself; without deigning to enter upon the subject of his letter, she directed her secretary to write—'Consuls are for trade, not for the nobility.' The above meagre account will convey but a faint idea of this extraordinary woman, whose whole life was one continued romance; but it is all my memory enables me to give; and therefore, my dear Jesse, I must beg you to accept the will for the deed."

In a subsequent letter, a reply to one in which I had requested a more exact description of Lady Hester's personal appearance, my kind correspondent says, "Her ladyship must have been a tall woman, but her male attire took off from her height; she was slight, well formed, and carried herself exceedingly well. The folds of her turban concealed her grey hairs; and the fairness of her complexion, the absence of beard, the brightness of her eye, and the vivacity of her expression, gave her the appearance of a young man, until a strong light betrayed the wrinkles which

time never fails to engrave on the fairest face. Her
enunciation was rapid and fluent ; and when excited,
her whole countenance seemed to light up, and she
used her chibouque much in the same way that a
Spanish lady would her fan—except that her gestures
were more often those of command than entreaty.
She rode as a man, and was always well armed."

Such was my friend's clever outline of this singular
woman, whose martial spirit and independent bearing
remind us of those heroic ladies who, in ancient days,
inhabited the banks of the Thermodon.[1]

---

[1] Those "heroic ladies" were the Amazons, a tribe of warlike
women, who dwelt in Pontus, on the banks of the river Thermodon,
and are said to have cut or burnt off their right breasts, and to have
killed all their male children.

CHAPTER XI.

Brummell's Album—His Letter presenting it to a Friend—Georgina Duchess of Devonshire—Lines on the Death of Hare—Wraxall's Description of her Grace—Her Fascinating Manners and Love of Dress and Dissipation—Lord Carlisle's Apology for her Plume—Her Friend Charles Fox—His Lines on the Death of her Favourite Spaniel —A Scale of the Beauties of 1793*—Mrs. Bouverie and Charles Fox.*

HAVING been able to collect only a few letters, written or received by Brummell before he left England, the most interesting substitute that I can offer in place of such materials is, extracts from his Album of the unpublished poetry of several of the most eminent characters of his time; indeed all the poetry subsequently given, is from that collection. This volume is a ponderous quarto, of plain vellum paper, and, though totally devoid of interior decoration, is, nevertheless, an example of his taste and extravagance; for the corners and clasps are of massive embossed silver gilt, like those on old missals, and the binding is dark-blue velvet.

The velvet has long been faded, and the gilding is much worn, as if he had often meditated after his reverses over its well-stored pages; and though several blank leaves remain, it contains no fewer than two hundred and twenty-six pieces of poetry: the choice of the subjects, and the manner in which they are treated, are not at all consistent with a worldly and selfish disposition ; many of them are descriptive of the characteristics of childhood, in which certainly no one would suspect Beau Brummell of ever having interested himself ; nor is the fact of the volume being such as he could with perfect propriety present to a lady, any trivial proof of his good taste.

The whole seem to have been kept as they were sent to him, either in notes, or on loose scraps of paper, and carefully copied in at different periods ; for they are arranged so exactly as to avoid turning over a page in any one of them, that did not require it on account of its length. This album is a little monument of industry, the poetry is all inserted with his own hand, and the writing is remarkably neat ; it might, indeed, challenge comparison with any lady's for elegance and regularity, with the advantage over modern penmanship, that it is as legible as printing.

About six years before his death he presented this collection to her, whom he deemed most worthy of possessing his treasured memorial of times past,—a young lady from whose family he had received the greatest attention at Caen, and who had, by her wit and amiability, won the then old gentleman's heart.[1]   The following note accompanied it.

" Wednesday, April 1834.

" If you are fond of poetry, and you have not any-

---

[1] See vol. ii. Chapter X.-Chapter XV.

thing more dull to read, you may, perhaps, find something in my old Album to yawn over, if it does not
actually close your eyes ; what it contains was written
in other and happier days, and most of them were
given to me by the authors *themselves*, long before
their minor productions had assumed any other form
than that of manuscript : such as the Duchess of
Devonshire, poor Byron, Sheridan, and Lords Erskine
and John Townshend—all now peacefully sleeping in
their graves ! The principal part of those verses that
are not recommended by the name being attached to
them, are the namby-pamby compositions of an unfortunate person who shall be nameless, but whom you
cut dead during the last several evenings, and who,
in desperate consequence, has been measured for a
winding-sheet this morning.—Always devoutly yours,

"GEORGE BRUMMELL."

By the Duchess of Devonshire, the first person to
whom Brummell makes allusion in this letter, he seems
to have been far more than tolerated,—he must have
been liked ; for it is scarcely probable that her Grace
would have presented her own poetry to a person
whom she did not think worthy of the compliment,
and capable of appreciating it. But previously to
laying the extracts I have selected before the reader,
the following imperfect sketch of her character may
not be altogether superfluous. Her Grace, the
daughter of John, first Earl Spencer, was born on the
9th of June 1757. Of her father's virtues we have

had sterling evidence in the tenor of his life, and the general esteem in which he was held; and these virtues the duke, his son-in-law, has feelingly commemorated in his epitaph, which

" Records the debt by love and duty paid."

From her cradle Lady Georgiana Spencer gave promise of being unusually intellectual and beautiful; and her sensible and excellent mother, who was a daughter of Stephen Poyntz, Esq., bestowed the greatest care, and exercised the greatest judgment, on the cultivation of every principle and attainment that could improve either mind or body. Her success was complete as regarded the elegance of both; but her daughter's mind was by nature deficient in the strength and dignity on which such a woman would have wished to see her character based. She was enthusiastic, but excessively volatile, and the combined temptations of rank, wealth, and beauty were too great not to have a ruinous effect; for when released from her mother's guidance, by her marriage with William, Duke of Devonshire, on the 6th of June 1774, at which time, observes Horace Walpole, " she was a lovely girl, natural, and full of grace," she was rapidly drawn headlong into the vortex of fashionable life.

In palliation of this want of firmness, however, it should not be forgotten that she was but seventeen years of age, and, by an indulgent husband, placed in possession of the means of gratifying not only her wishes, but her whims. She thus became speedily

the authority for every idle fashion ; her name was attached to every novelty in dress that she chose to adopt ; and even the colour of her carriage was known, for some years after her death, as the " Devonshire brown." Her beauty and the brilliancy of her career soon attracted crowds of flatterers, besides the admiration of the very superior men that her husband's political influence and opinions, good taste and hospitality, induced him to receive almost as constant visitors at Devonshire House. Distinguished among them, and distinguished indeed they were, compared with the wits and politicians of our days, were Fox, Wyndham, Burke, Tickell, Lord J. Townshend, Fitzpatrick, Sheridan, and others. The kind, the courted, and the witty Hare,—" the Hare of many friends," [1] from whom a bow at the opera was considered a greater compliment than from the Prince of Wales, was also at the feet of the young and lovely duchess ; and it was in concert with the duke that she thus lamented the death of this, their mutual friend in 1804.

" Hark ! 'twas the knell of death—what spirit fled,
    And burst the shackles man is doom'd to bear ?
Can it be true, and 'midst the senseless dead,
    Must sorrowing thousands count the loss of Hare ?

Shall not his genius life's short date prolong,
    (Pure as the ether of its kindred sky),
Shall wit enchant no longer from his tongue,
    And beam in vivid flashes from his eye ?

---

[1] Mr. Hare, who died in 1804, was the son of a chemist at Winchester, and at Eton and Oxford the companion of Mr. Fox and his intimates, with whom he maintained till the close of his life an indissoluble friendship. He was considered one of the most accomplished and wittiest men of the day, and sate in parliament for Knaresborough until the time of his death.

Oh no !—that mind, for every purpose fit,
    Has met, alas ! the universal doom ;
Unrivall'd fancy, judgment, sense, and wit,
    Were his, and only left him at the tomb.

Rest, spirit, rest ! for gentle was thy course :
    Thy rays, like temper'd suns, no venom knew ;
For still benevolence allay'd the force
    Of the keen darts thy matchless satire threw.

Yet not alone thy genius I deplore,
    Nor o'er thy various talents drop the tear ;
But weep to think I shall behold no more
    A loved companion and a friend sincere."

Amongst such men as those I have mentioned, there must have been some who would never have been fascinated by a mere woman of fashion ; no, it was the extent and variety of the Duchess of Devonshire's intellectual acquirements, so far exceeding those of the generality of women in her time, that won their attentions. She was well read in the belles-lettres, and in the history and polity of most countries ; she was also perfect mistress of the French and Italian languages, had both skill and taste in poetry, and could play upon the lyre. Indeed her mind, if we are to believe Wraxall,[1] was far more gracefully modelled

[1] Sir Nathaniel William Wraxall, "Historical Memoirs of my own Time, 1815." We have already spoken of this gentleman in Chapter IV., and, when we quote him, have to add, "if we are to believe him," for his character for veracity was far from established. Thus the "Edinburgh Review," vol. xxx., in an article on these Memoirs, denies them all credit, and gives even the following epitaph of their author, written by a "young gentleman of Oxford : "

        " Men, Measures, scenes and facts, all
            Misquoting, mistating,
            Misplacing, misdating,
        Here lies Sir Nathaniel Wraxall."

Lord Macaulay, in his essay "On Barrère," also states : " Among the

than her person. He says, "The personal charms of the Duchess of Devonshire constituted her smallest pretension to universal admiration ; nor did her beauty consist, like that of the Gunnings, in regularity of features, and faultless formation of limbs and shape ; it lay in the amenity and graces of her deportment, in her irresistible manners, and the seduction of her society. Her hair was not without a tinge of red, and her face, though pleasing, yet had it not been illuminated by her mind, might have been considered as an ordinary countenance. Descended in the fourth degree, lineally, from Sarah Jennings, the wife of John Churchill, Duke of Marlborough, she resembled the portraits of that beautiful woman."

As, however, the Duchess was generally called then, and is so in our generation, "the beautiful duchess," it is scarcely possible to believe that her face, under any circumstances, could have been "considered an ordinary countenance ;" nor does the splendid portrait of her by Sir Joshua Reynolds give that impression : but, beautiful or not, she bewitched every one into believing that she was so, and speedily captivated a society so perfectly capable of appreciating her, as that by which she was surrounded.

numerous classes which make up the great genus *Mendacium*, the *Mendacium Vasconicum*, or Gascon lie, has during some centuries been highly esteemed as peculiarly circumstantial and peculiarly impudent ; and among the *Mendacia Vasconica*, the *Mendacium Barerianum* is, without doubt, the finest species. It is indeed a superb variety, and quite throws into the shade some *Mendacia* which we were used to regard with admiration. The *Mendacium Wraxallanium*, though by no means to be despised, will not sustain the comparison for a moment."

In doing the honours of her noble mansion, which was characterised by a splendour far greater than that of the court, her unusual accomplishments told with double effect; and their value to her guests was so enhanced by the natural fascination of her manners, that they soon looked with leniency upon her foibles. Tickell, in the " Wreath of Fashion," which had reached its sixth edition in 1780, wrote stanzas in honour of her petticoat; and Lord Carlisle, "a Rhapsody on seeing her Grace in full dress: " he also undertook to justify her caprices in the following lines :—

" Wit is a feather, this we all admit,
But sure each feather in your cap is wit ;
'Tis the best flight of genius—to improve
The smiles of beauty and the bliss of love.
Like beams around the sun your feathers shine,
And raise the splendour of your charms divine ;
Such plumes the worth of mighty conquerors show,
For who can conquer hearts so well as you ?
When on your head I see those fluttering things,
I think, that love is there, and claps his wings.
Feathers help'd Jove to fan his amorous flame,
Cupid has feathers, angels wear the same.
Since then from Heaven their origin we trace,
Preserve the fashion—it becomes your Grace."

Indeed there was scarcely a man of eminence in her day, who could write a stanza, that did not address some complimentary verses to her. Dr. Darwin, "that mighty master of unmeaning rhyme," sings her praises in his " Botanic Garden," and her friend, Charles Fox, did not think it beneath him to write some verses on the death of her favourite spaniel : they were in the album.

" ON THE DEATH OF FADDLE, A FAVOURITE SPANIEL OF
   GEORGIANA, DUCHESS OF DEVONSHIRE, WHO DIED AN
   EARLY VICTIM TO LOVE ; HIS FATHER, FADDLE, SENIOR,
   HAVING PERISHED BY A SIMILAR FATE.—C. J. FOX.

" Not Edward, when he saw with courage fell,
   The beaten foe beneath the stripling run,
   And, his career in Cressy's field begun,
   Did the black warrior's future fame foretell—
   Not great Pelides, when in that dark dell
   Of grisly Pluto, from Laertes' son
   He learnt the trophies by his Pyrrhus won,
   And stalk'd away, the proudest ghost in hell,
   More joy'd—than ancient Faddle's shade, when late
   The tidings through the grove of myrtle flew,
   That mighty Love had caused young Faddle's fate :
   Thus mortals, to their follies ever true,
   Of favourite passions would extend the date,
   And, in their offspring, love or fight anew ! "

But all this homage is not surprising. In her
youth the Duchess must have been, in spite of
Wraxall's allusion to red hair, a lovely woman ; for,
when she was about six-and-thirty, two years after
the Doctor *botanised* her, she held no mean position
in the following amusing estimate of the personal
attractions of our then reigning beauties. This
arbitrary mode of estimating the comparative merits
of individuals, was the invention of Akenside, who
first applied it to poets ; and the plan, whether well
or ill executed, in the present instance, is a far more
complete one than Lord Byron's pyramid, or rather
Isosceles' triangle, of which the Pleasures of Memory
form the apex. The point of perfection is twenty :—

	Form.	Elegance.	Grace.	Feature.	Complexion.	Countenance.	Softness.	Expression.	Loveliness.
Princess Mary	15	16	19	16	18	14	18	16	20
Duchess of Devonshire .	16	17	18	14	15	20	17	16	18
Duchess of Rutland . .	17	18	12	19	14	16	14	14	18
Duchess of Montrose . .	16	15	15	12	14	18	18	14	16
Lady Stormont	12	14	13	17	10	16	14	17	15
Lady Anne Fitzroy . . .	17	17	16	17	15	16	17	18	17
Lady Anne Lambton . .	15	14	16	13	11	10	16	12	20
Lady William Russell . .	14	16	15	12	16	14	15	14	17

The Duchess of Gloucester, at this period in her seventeenth year, and perhaps the loveliest girl in England. Her Royal Highness's foot and ankle were faultless; a fact which was frequently divulged to her numerous admirers by the short petticoats worn in 1797.

Georgiana, eldest daughter of John, first Earl Spencer, at this time in her thirty-sixth year. Died, 30th March 1806.

Mary Isabella, daughter of Charles, fourth Duke of Beaufort. Her Grace was an intimate friend of Georgiana, Duchess of Devonshire, and in the thirty-seventh year of her age. Died, 2d September 1831.

Caroline Maria, daughter of George, fourth Duke of Manchester, in her twenty-third year

Louisa, youngest daughter of Charles, ninth Lord Cathcart, afterwards Countess of Mansfield, and subsequently married to the Hon. Fulke Greville. Her ladyship was in her thirty-fifth year. She died in July 1843, aged eighty-three.

Probably afterwards Lady Anne Culling Smith, daughter of the first Earl of Morning-ton, then wife of the Hon. Henry Fitzroy, son of the first Lord Southampton, who died in 1794. Her ladyship was at this time in her twenty-fifth year.

Anne Barbara, second daughter of the fourth Earl of Jersey; married, in 1791, W. Lambton, Esq., and subsequently the Hon. Charles Wyndham, brother of the Earl of Egremont. She was in her twenty-first year. Died, April 1832.

The lady of the late unfortunate Lord W. Russell. She was an elder sister of Lady Anne Lambton's, and was in her twenty-second year. Died in 1808.

	Form.	Elegance.	Grace.	Feature.	Complexion.	Countenance.	Softness.	Expression.	Loveliness.
Lady Erskine St. Clair . .	18	17	16	15	16	18	14	13	17
Lady Webster	16	16	12	12	17	18	14	18	14
Lady Caroline Campbell .	18	16	16	17	19	18	18	12	20
Lady Elizabeth Lambert .	15	14	15	18	20	14	17	18	17
Mrs. Tickell	17	16	18	20	16	20	18	19	20
Mrs. Law	18	16	14	20	15	14	17	17	18
Miss Ogilvie	17	16	17	14	12	15	14	18	16
Pamela	16	18	18	16	14	18	18	18	20

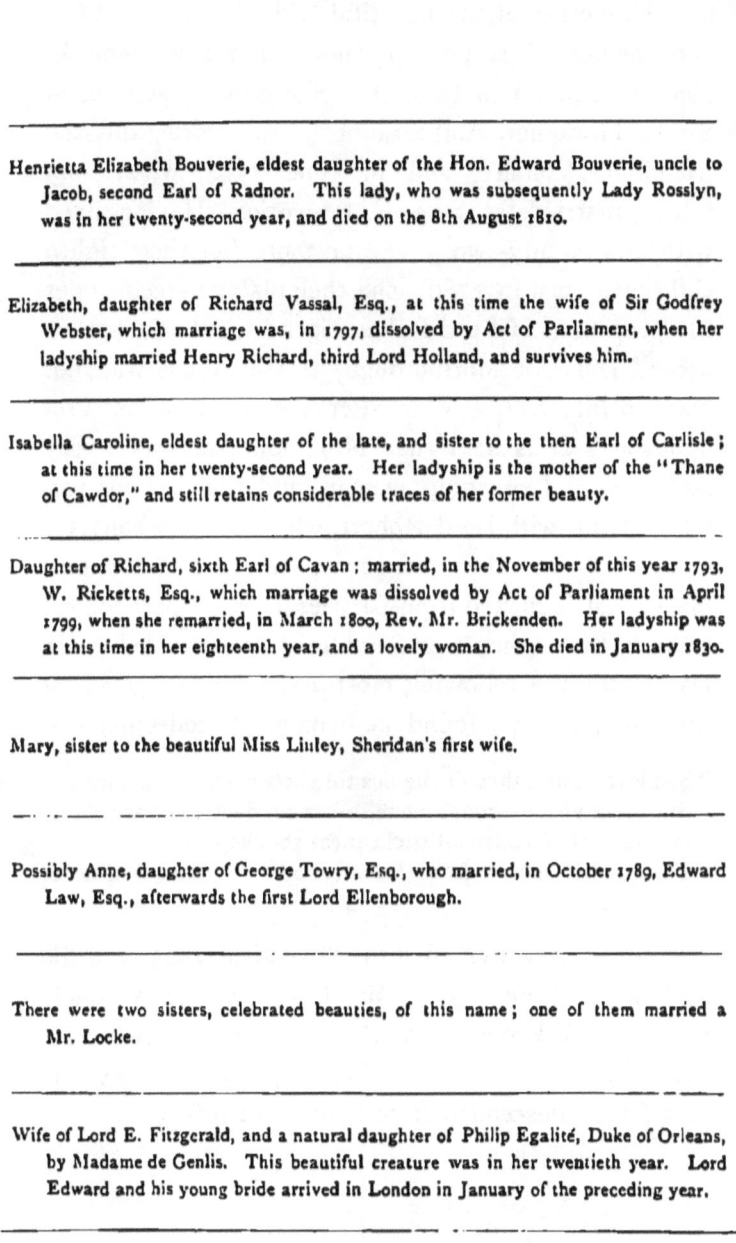

Henrietta Elizabeth Bouverie, eldest daughter of the Hon. Edward Bouverie, uncle to Jacob, second Earl of Radnor. This lady, who was subsequently Lady Rosslyn, was in her twenty-second year, and died on the 8th August 1810.

Elizabeth, daughter of Richard Vassal, Esq., at this time the wife of Sir Godfrey Webster, which marriage was, in 1797, dissolved by Act of Parliament, when her ladyship married Henry Richard, third Lord Holland, and survives him.

Isabella Caroline, eldest daughter of the late, and sister to the then Earl of Carlisle; at this time in her twenty-second year. Her ladyship is the mother of the "Thane of Cawdor," and still retains considerable traces of her former beauty.

Daughter of Richard, sixth Earl of Cavan ; married, in the November of this year 1793, W. Ricketts, Esq., which marriage was dissolved by Act of Parliament in April 1799, when she remarried, in March 1800, Rev. Mr. Brickenden. Her ladyship was at this time in her eighteenth year, and a lovely woman. She died in January 1830.

Mary, sister to the beautiful Miss Linley, Sheridan's first wife.

Possibly Anne, daughter of George Towry, Esq., who married, in October 1789, Edward Law, Esq., afterwards the first Lord Ellenborough.

There were two sisters, celebrated beauties, of this name ; one of them married a Mr. Locke.

Wife of Lord E. Fitzgerald, and a natural daughter of Philip Egalité, Duke of Orleans, by Madame de Genlis. This beautiful creature was in her twentieth year. Lord Edward and his young bride arrived in London in January of the preceding year.

The history of the Hon. Mrs. Bouverie's domestic life, the mother of the beautiful Lady Erskine St. Clair here mentioned, is perhaps one of the most remarkable to be found in Debrett. She was a daughter of Sir E. Fawkener, Ambassador to the Porte, and the friend of Voltaire, and in June 1764, when only fifteen, married the Hon. E. Bouverie. Having lived with him twenty-two years, or more (for their eighth child was born in 1786), she then placed herself under the protection of Lord Robert Spencer, son of Charles, second Duke of Marlborough, to whom she was not married till 1811, a year after the death of her first husband. It is said that Mrs. Bouverie was a very attractive and engaging woman, and that her conduct when living with Lord Robert, who was very constant to her, was in other respects so amiable and exemplary, that it elicited from Charles Fox the paradoxical remark, that " they made adultery respectable." He also wrote the following most extraordinary *quatrain* upon her, which I found in Brummell's collection :—

"She loves truth, though she lies till she's black in the face ;
She loves virtue, though none in her conduct you trace ;
Her delicate feelings all wickedness shocks,
Though her lover's Lord Robert, and her friend is Charles
Fox !"

Lady R. Spencer died in November 1825, and his lordship in June 1831. Mr. Bouverie was an uncle of the well-known Dr. Pusey, whose father first assumed that name : it is curious, but the Doctor is of a family descended from Protestant refugees !

CHAPTER XII.

The Duchess of Devonshire—Her Follies and Infirmities—Taste for Play at this Period—Charles Fox and the Jews—His Lines on the Gaming-table—The Duchess's Kindness of Heart—Her Enthusiasm—The Contest for Westminster in 1784—Anecdotes of and Squibs let off at this Election—The Duchess's Poem of " The Passage of the St. Gothard"—Her Knowledge of French and Italian—Her Translation of one of Petrarch's Sonnets.

In the short space of three years after her marriage, the Duchess of Devonshire's extravagance became the subject of public criticism, and several pamphlets were addressed to her, reflecting severely upon her con-duct ; the motto of one was, " Pleased with a feather, tickled with a straw,"—alluding to Lord Carlisle's verses: that of another was also from Pope, " She sighs, and is no Duchess at her heart," and both of these were very severe. But long after this period, having been fifteen years devoted to pleasure, she was still foremost in every fashionable folly ; and, in 1793, was at the head of the Lady Patronesses of the celebrated pic-nic parties. There is, however, every reason to fear, that her Grace's excessive extravagance was not her worst fault ; not only from traditional report, but from the evidence that may be met with in every auto-

graph collection, we learn that the Duchess was devoted
to faro,[1] the fashionable game of the day, and other
games of chance, which brought her into positions
greatly detrimental to her character, and the dignity
of her high station.   In this she certainly was not
discouraged, either by her male or female friends, and
gaming in private circles was then far more common
than in the present day ; though, unfortunately, the
vice is not extinct, and fashionable women of rank
might now be named, who play as deep as did then
her Grace of Devonshire.

It was, indeed, one of the characteristic follies of
" All the Talents ; " the absorbing passion of several
members of the party who were most intimate at
Devonshire House.   The devotion of Fox to play is
notorious, and he seems to have been scarcely able to
pass forty-eight hours without it.   A gentleman, now
living, informed me, that one evening, when he and
two or three other friends of Mrs. Fox were drinking
tea with her in South Street, the door opened, and
Charles James came skipping into the room, in most
unusual spirits ; they were on the point of inquiring

---

[1] Frao was a game of cards, in which one person held the
bank, and an indefinite number of players staked their money
on one of the fifty-two cards of the pack.   The dealer dealt two cards
for himself from another pack ; one on the right for himself, and one on
the left for the punters ; and, of course, the highest was the winning
card.   Besides this, the dealer had certain advantages.   The name
Faro is said to have been derived from the name of the ancient Kings
of Egypt, a representation of a Pharaoh having been depicted on one
of the cards.   It was first introduced into France by the Venetian
Ambassador in the year 1674.

the cause, but he saved them the trouble, by exclaiming, as he continued his capers, which he cut all round the room, " Great run ! great run ! vingt-et-un ; lucky dog ; to-morrow morning pay the Jews—pay them all ! " Unfortunately for him, and for them too, it was Friday night, which, in the excess of his honesty and happiness, he did not think of. Of course, the next day no Israelite would come for his cash ;—and that night the monies were carried to the Club, and there lost—the love of powerful excitement, and the insatiable cravings of the gamester's heart, overcoming that great man's better feelings, and good but transient resolutions.

But, though a slave to this dreadful passion, and therefore to its degrading consequences, he wrote the following curious description of the gaming-table, in which the political feelings of this constitutional statesman are singularly interwoven with the subject, and in terms that would scarcely be agreeable to, or in accordance with, the opinions of the Whigs, in these days of the march of opinion. The critical powers of Fox, however, on points relating either to history or historians, generally led him to just conclusions ; and his denunciation of Cromwell, though on so trifling an occasion, is made in a spirit as liberal as that of his remark on the partiality of Hume and Gibbon, for their respective and favourite opinions : namely, " that one so loved a king, and the other so hated a priest, that neither of them could be depended upon, when either a priest or a king was concerned."

These lines by Fox were copied from the Beau's album, and I believe have never been published :—

THE GAMING-TABLE.

" A spot there is, say, Traveller, where it lies,
And mark the clime, the limits and the size,
Where grow no trees, nor waves the golden grain,
Nor hills, nor vales, diversify the plain ;
Eternal years without the farmer's toil,
Through all the seasons clothe the favour'd soil ;
Fair pools, in which the finny race abound,
By human hands prepared, enrich the ground—
Not Indian coasts produce an ampler store,
Pearls, ivory, diamonds, gold and silver ore :
Yet, Britons ! envy not these wealthy climes,
Perpetual war distracts and endless crimes
Pollute the soil ; pale Avarice triumphs there,
Hate, Envy, Rage, and heart-destroying Care ;
With Fraud and Fear, and comfortless Despair.
Their government not long remains the same,
Though they, like us, revere a monarch's name ;
Now Cromwell-like, a low and base-born knave,
Nobles, and Kings and Queens presumes to brave :
The nobles fall—the king's a captive slave.
Britons, beware—let Avarice tempt no more—
Spite of its wealth, avoid the fatal shore."

But to return to the Duchess. Though she played high and all her amusements were of an expensive character, and her love of dissipation became so strong that she never deliberately improved her habits of life, yet she constantly gave remarkable instances of generosity and kind feeling ; being in that respect, as she was in everything else, a creature of impulse, she yielded without discrimination to the supplications of

distress, as easily as she did to the temptations of
luxury, and those pleasures, which her success and
influence in society induced. She liberally assisted
literary characters, and especially protected Charlotte
Smith, the novelist,[1] who, at one period of her life,
lived at Devonshire House : but the most pleasing
trait of her domestic character was the example she
set her fashionable friends by nursing her own
children ; thereby discouraging the unnatural practice
prevalent in her time, of sending them into the country
and leaving them to the management and discretion of
ignorant, and sometimes unfeeling nurses. A poet of
the day thus refers to this incident :—

> " So when the mother bending o'er his charms,
> Clasps her fair nursling in delighted arms,
> Throws the thin kerchief from her neck of snow,
> And half unveils the pearly orbs below,—
> With sparkling eye the blameless plunderer owns
> Her soft embraces, and endearing tones ;
> Sucks the salubrious fount with open lips,
> Spreads his inquiring hands, and smiles and sips."

The interest which the Duchess of Devonshire took
in public affairs was far beyond what had ever been
displayed by any of her female contemporaries. When
the American War broke out, she was seen at Tiptree
and Warley Camps, dressed in the regimentals of the
Derby Militia. The consequence was a military fever
amongst the women, which was followed by a naval

---

[1] Charlotte Smith published several poems and novels from the year
1791 until the year 1802, of which a few enjoyed some reputation, but
are now buried in oblivion.

one, when the victories of Howe, Jervis, Duncan, and
Nelson revived the national spirits; and the Egyptian,
Aboukir, and Nelson bonnets, caps, and head-dresses
were all the fashion.   On the declaration of war being
made against France, she set to work with all her
friends to make flannel waistcoats for the troops; and
she showed the same enthusiasm in the cause of her
friend Charles Fox, in his great contest for Westminster in 1784, which appropriately enough commenced on "All Fools' Day;" and, being in the
"good old times," lasted for one month and seventeen
days.

The excitement which this election caused amongst
all grades of society, was never exceeded in the most
turbulent republics.   The most refined ladies quite
forgot all propriety of demeanour, and some of the
highest rank actually pulled the favours from each
other's bosoms in the opera refreshment-rooms, ac-
companying the action with screams of "No Fox! no
Fox!"   Even at Carlton House, election jokes were
permitted, and at the breakfast given by the Prince of
Wales on this occasion, some one pinned a Fox cockade
on the head of Lady Talbot, who was a violent Tory;
for some time her Ladyship did not perceive it, but a
tell-tale mirror at length revealed the affront, when
the favour was removed with no gentle hand, and not
only indignantly thrown at her feet, but stamped upon
—to the great amusement of the bystanders.

But no one was so devoted to the interest of the
popular candidate or the success of his cause as the

Duchess of Devonshire, who was then figuratively called, and is still distinguished by the appellation of, " Fox's Duchess." Accompanied by her sister, Lady Duncannon, and her friend the Duchess of Rutland, she attended continually at the hustings in an elegant equipage with a favour in her hat, and one on her breast, inscribed with the word " Fox,"—and supported by the presence of her scarcely less fascinating sister, she visited the houses and shops of the electors and dazzled and enslaved them by her enchanting manners, her beauty, and the influence of her high rank ; nor did she object to convey the humblest of the electors in her own carriage to the hustings to vote for her friend.

But the most convincing proof of her ardour in his cause, is the well-authenticated story, that rather than lose a plumper for her candidate, she permitted a butcher,—a man probably surrounded at the time with slaughtered beeves and fat southdowns, to kiss her in Newport Market ! Of course, this enthusiasm called forth philippics from the Tories, and the greatest admiration from the Whigs ; but what it called forth from the Duke, her husband, has not transpired. To excuse this kiss one of her party quoted Dean Swift, who says, " that an over-nice man is a man of nasty ideas ; " and another compared her to Cornelia, the wife of Pompey, and daughter of Metellus Scipio. In an account of this memorable election, which filled a thickly printed quarto volume of eight hundred pages, published by Debrett, a few months after, there are one hundred and thirty squibs and pieces of poetry from the wits and versifiers of both sides. The following are specimens of their powers, and the compliments paid to her Grace :—

" Fair Devon all good English hearts must approve,
   And the Waldegraves,[1] God bless their sweet faces !
The Duchess she looks the sweet Queen of Love,
   And they like the three sister Graces.
     Then let each of us say,
     May the D—l take Wray,
   And Charley and Liberty carry the day.

" E'en cobblers she canvass'd, they would not refuse,
   But huzza'd for Fox and ' No wooden shoes.'
She canvass'd the tailors, and ask'd for their votes,
   They all gave her plumpers, and cried, ' No turncoats.'[2]
     Then let each of us say, &c."

But would a canvasser like her Grace be so successful in these degenerate days of "pounds, shillings, and pence," in which the very ghost of chivalry has been hunted from the land? Could she still find in Newport Market a butcher who would prefer a kiss to a ten-pound note? I fear not. It was during the excitement and turmoil of this election that the flattering and well-known exclamation burst spontaneously

---

[1] Elizabeth Laura, at this time Lady Chewton, afterwards Lady Waldegrave ;
Charlotte Maria, afterwards Duchess of Grafton ;
Hannah Horatia, afterwards Lady Hugh Seymour. All three daughters of the 2nd Earl of Waldegrave.
"The Ladies Waldegrave," writes Dr. Warner to George Selwyn, in June 1779, "have been about marrying the whole town, but are not married. Lord Egremont was very near, but he said he should hang himself before the summer was over if he did."
[2] Alluding to Sir Cecil Wray's change of opinion.

from the lips of the impassioned coalheaver, who, roused by her expressive countenance, said, while gazing with admiration upon it, " I could light my pipe at your eyes." This compliment was highly appreciated by the Duchess, and she always admitted it as the most gratifying one that had ever been paid her.

Though this celebrated woman devoted herself heart and soul to politics, and the gaieties and dissipation of the sphere of life in which she moved, she was capable of enjoying pleasures of a very different character; for on her return from Italy, in the autumn of 1793, to which country she had gone with her mother and Lady Bessborough, on account of the delicate health of the latter, the passage of the St. Gothard suggested to her the pleasing little poem of that name, the opening of which is an apostrophe to the lovely land she was leaving. A natural benevolence and warmth of feeling pervade this poem; the stirring points in Swiss history are evidently dwelt upon with energy and admiration; nor is the descriptive part wanting in beauty, simplicity, and strength. Her Grace, with maternal feeling, dedicated it to her children; and perhaps the prettiest quotation to make from it is the concluding stanza, in which she thus addresses them :

" Hope of my life ! dear children of my heart !
    That anxious heart, to each fond feeling true,
  To you still pants each pleasure to impart,
    And more—oh ! transport, reach its home and you."

Soon after this poem was published it was translated into French by the Abbé Delille, a member of the French Academy, and author of "Les Jardins," who was probably an emigrant friend of hers. When the Duchess presented him with this specimen of her poetical powers, she sent with it the following complimentary lines :—

A MONSIEUR l' ABBÉ DELILLE.

Vous dont la lyre enchanteresse
Unit la force à la douceur,
De la nature amant flatteur ;
Vous qui l'embellissez sans cesse,
J'ose vous offrir en tremblant
De l'humble pré la fleur nouvelle ;
Je la voudrais une immortelle,
Si vous acceptez le présent.

GEORGINE DEVONSHIRE.[1]

Though these couplets are in themselves trifling, yet they show that her Grace was, as I have before remarked, a perfect mistress of French ; but the following translation of Petrarch's thirty-fourth sonnet

---

[1] These lines are evidently imitated from the well-known *quatrain* which Desmarets de St. Sorlin wrote for the violet, one of the sixteen flowers constituting the poetical portion of the celebrated *Guirlande de Julie*, painted by the artist Robert, each of which addressed itself in verse by the mouth of various poets to the fair Julie d'Angennes, to whom this garland was offered in 1641 as a homage by her future husband the Duke de Montausier. The *quatrain* of St. Sorlin is as follows :—

" Modeste en ma couleur, modeste en mon séjour,
Franche d'ambition je me cache sous l'herbe ;
Mais si sur votre front je puis me voir un jour,
La plus humble des fleurs sera la plus superbe."

is a far more remarkable instance of her proficiency in the Italian language, an accomplishment which her friend Charles Fox also possessed. This the reader may see in his " Il piacere è il Desire," an imitation of Monk Lewis's poem, " In yonder bower lies Pleasure sleeping," which is printed in the edition of " Dark Musgrave's " poems, published in 1812. The friend who was kind enough to send me a copy of this translation by her Grace, is perhaps better able to appreciate the merits of Italian literature than any Englishman now living. He gave me also some details of the circumstances under which it came into his possession, and I now insert them in his own words.

" My first visit to the Eternal City was in 1822, and it was there that I had the pleasure of making the acquaintance of Elizabeth, Duchess of Devonshire. Knowing that one of my objects was, to investigate certain controverted points in the life of Petrarch, she very kindly assisted me in my researches ; and one morning, whilst we were engaged in discussing the nature of his attachment to Laura, she presented me with the translation of ' Levommi il mio pensier,' as a specimen of the poetical talents of her predecessor Georgiana, and a striking proof of the facility with which the English language, when properly handled, renders the sublimity and tenderness of the great lyrical poet of Italy." As the reader may like to compare it with the Italian, I have given the original with it.

SONNETTO XXXIV.

Dice essersi levato col pensiero infino al cielo, e quivi aver ve-
duto Laura che lo prese per mano e parlogli.   Dice in ultimo
che al suon delle sue parole poco mancò che non morisse di
dolcezza.   Questo si può dir veramente il più bel sonnetto del
Petrarca.

> Levommi il mio pensier in parte, ov'era
> Quella, ch'io cerco e non ritrovo in terra ;
> Ivi fra lor, che'l terzo cerchio [1] serra,
> La rividi più bella, e meno altera.
> Per man mi prese, e disse : 'In questa spera
> Sarai ancor meco, se 'l desir non erra :
> I'son colei che ti diè tanta guerra,
> E compiè mia giornata innanzi sera,
> "Mio ben non cape,[2] in intelletto umano ;
> Te solo aspetto, e quel che tanto amasti,
> E laggiuso è rimaso, il mio bel velo." [3]
> Deh perchè tacque ed allargò la mano ?
> Ch' al suon de' detti, si pietosi e casti,
> Poco mancò, ch'io non rimasi in cielo.

TRANSLATED BY GEORGIANA, DUCHESS OF DEVONSHIRE

> In spirit I had mounted to the sphere
> Where she amidst its gentle inmates beam'd,
> Whom still I fondly seek, but found not here :
> More beautiful and less severe she seem'd.
> She press'd my hand, and said, " In this bright star
> With me, if hope deceive not, thou shalt dwell :
> That maid I am who caused thy live-long war,
> And closed her day of life ere evening fell.

---

[1] *Il terzo cerchio.* Si finge rapito al terzo cielo, luogo assegnato dai.
Poeti agli amanti virtuosi e casti.

[2] *Mio ben non cape*, ac. l' intelletto umano non è capace di com-
prendere la pienezza della mia felicità.

[3] *Te solo aspetto e il mio bel velo* (il corpo), cioè, quello che tu tanto
amasti e ch'è rimaso laggiuso sulla terra.—*Commentator's Note.*

My bliss transcends the reach of human mind :
   Thee only I desire, and what thou prized'st so much,
Those beauteous spoils, I left on earth behind."
Why ceased she, why withdrew the pledge thus given?
   That chaste, that thrilling voice, that holy touch,
Had sure sufficed to keep my soul in heaven !

CHAPTER XIII.

*The Duchess's Fugitive Poetry—The Late Lord Morley—Borino the Brave
—His Feats at Melton described in Verse by George Ellis—Short
Notice of that Gentleman—The Duchess of Devonshire's Lines on a
Bust of Charles James Fox—Her Verses from a Blind Man to his
Wife—Death of her Grace—Anecdote of Lady Bessborough.—
Visit to the Vault of the Cavendishes—Elizabeth, Duchess of
Devonshire—Gibbon in Love—Sketch of her Grace's Character—
Her Patronage of Literature, and Antiquarian Researches.*

No doubt many other examples of Georgiana, Duchess
of Devonshire's, taste and acquirements exist in the
domestic archives of Chatsworth ; but though they
were not accessible to me, I trust I have in some
degree succeeded in my attempt to awaken the reader's
interest in the lovely authoress of the fugitive poetry
that I now transcribe from Brummell's album, and
which, after diligent search, I have not discovered in
print.   The first piece gives ample evidence of her
classical taste, and the richness and elegance of her
imagination.

" Here, in the bower of beauty, newly shorn,
    Let Fancy sit, and sing how Love was born ;
    Wrapt up in roses, Zephyr found the child
    In Flora's cheek, when first the goddess smiled ;
    Nursed on the bosom of the beauteous Spring,
    O'er her white breast he spread his purple wing.

On kisses fed, and silver drops of dew,
The little wanton into Cupid grew ;
Then arm'd his head with glittering sparks of fire,
And tipp'd his shining arrows with desire.
Hence joys arose upon the wings of wind,
And Hope presents the lover always kind ;
Despair creates a rival for our fears,
And tender Pity softens into tears."

The stanzas that follow are not so imaginative, but more natural, and on that account, more pleasing.

" My cherish'd hope, my fondest dream,
    Still, dearest ! rests on thee ;
A blank without thee all would seem,
    And life would lifeless be.

The place thy presence glads to seek
    Is where I'm ever best ;
And when I hear thee kindly speak,
    And speak to *me*, I'm blest.

But should hard fate command it so,
    Still, dearest ! I'm resign'd ;
And if from me thou'rt bent to go,
    Or alter'd, or unkind,—

Unfelt by thee, my silent care
    Shall never claim relief ;
And still I'll wish thou may'st not share
    My solitary grief."

In the next, the Duchess seems to have adopted the metre of Alonzo the Brave and the Fair Imogene, of M. G. Lewis.

The hero of this ballad was Lord Morley, then Lord Boringdon, who was a strong supporter of Mr. Pitt, and when a young man, spoke frequently in the

House of Lords. It is probably to these speeches that her Grace alludes, which no doubt found but little favour in the eyes of such an ardent Foxite as she was. Of the ladies that the youthful Lord Boringdon jilted, the author has no gossiping details to give; but of the one who jilted him the Peerage gives due information, and shows that these verses were written previously to the 24th of June, 1804, on which day he married the Lady Augusta Fane, second daughter of John, tenth Earl of Westmoreland; which marriage was dissolved in 1809, when her ladyship re-married the late Right Honourable Sir Arthur Paget. Lord Morley died on the 14th March 1840.

BORINO THE BRAVE.

" A baron so bold, and of parentage fair,
     Was riding beside the green sea ;
His vizor was up, and his forehead was bare,
His face it was comely, and long was his hair,
     And tall, and full portly was he.

He slowly rode on, 'twas for exercise' sake,
     Nor trotted, nor canter'd did he ;
He mused on the speeches he'd made, and would make,
Of the vows to fair damsels he'd keep or would break,
     And on many a quaint repartee.

Oh ! from him let the barons of England beware
     How their loves and their palfreys they guide ;
Many women may love them, for whom they don't care,
Many horses may stumble, unless they're aware,
     Or if loose in their stirrups they ride.

A Bedlamite Duchess[1] was bathing hard by,
    When she saw the young Paladin pass ;
He bewilder'd her brain, and he dazzled her eye,
Her guides could not stop her, she strove to rush by,
    And swore that she would, ' by the mass ! '

The baron was frighten'd, with reason and truth,
    For her love and her frenzy were strong ;
She turn'd as he turn'd, and with gesture uncouth,
Her arms she elongated straight at the youth,
    And they seem'd to be half a mile long.

He spoke not, he flew not, he only could scream,
    When plump in the water he fell !
And lo ! all this bustle, though strange it may seem,
He found by awaking was only a dream,
    Was a very good story to tell.

And now still at midnight, the supper just o'er,
    Her spirit he seems to behold ;
The story he told, though he told it before,
For each night, as the clock strikes, he tells it once more,
    And forgets it has ever been told ! "

The following ballad is another quiz upon the
same nobleman, for which reason I have placed it
with the preceding one : it was written by George
Ellis, another of Brummell's friends, and is in some
measure a parody on Monk Lewis's ballad of Duran-
darte and Belerma :—

    " Sad and fearful is the story
      Of the Roncesvalles fight."

It was written when Mr. Ellis was on a visit to his
cousin, Baron Seaford. Brooksby Hall is on the
road from Melton to Leicester.

    [1] *Quere*, her Grace of Gordon ?

" Sad and fearful is the story
     Of the hunt in Leicestershire,
On that fatal field of glory
     Met full many a dashing squire.

There fell bold Borino, never
     Horse did such a baron bear,
Thinking he could ride for ever,
     Mounted on so dun a mare.

Scarlet spencer deck'd his shoulders,
     Of his coat the skirts were blue ;
Pantaloons charm'd all beholders,
     Leather, and of yellow hue.

Huge his hat, to put his head in,
     Longer queue was never seen ;
Round his neck his 'kerchief spreading,
     Check'd with faded blue and green.

Leaps he thought were quite delightful,
     Hedge and ditch, what'er might hap,
Even gates were not too frightful,
     Leap he would,—and chose a gap.

O'er the gap the dun mare vaulted,
     Glow'd with joy his noble blood ;
Pass'd the gap, the dun mare halted,—
     Dropp'd the Baron in the mud !

' Although young I fall, believe me,'
     Cried this lord, of noble mind,
' Think not, sirs, a fall would grieve me,
     'Tis to fall before we find :

' Comforts twain my griefs have lighten'd,
     Though your grooms have seen me down ;
First I prove I was not frighten'd,
     Next, the spencer's not my own.'

Laugh'd the grooms, the farmers hearty,
Laugh'd the huntsman till he cried ;
Laugh'd each sportsman of the party,
' Good, my lord, thus ever ride.'

Baron, bolder, wiser, graver,
(Riding'Spanish, sure to fall),
Lord in scarlet spencer, braver
Started ne'er from Brooksby Hall."

Perhaps no one ever better united the character
of a gentleman with that of a man of letters than the
author of this humorous scrap, which is valuable as
the trifle of a very superior man.   Mr. Ellis was a
person of gentle and polished manners, and his mind
was peculiarly formed to feel and inspire others with
the warmest sentiments of friendship.   Mr. Lockhart,
in speaking of the intimacy that existed between this
talented individual and Sir Walter Scott, calls him
the "elegant and amiable Ellis ; " and that he was
amiable there is little reason to doubt, for he was the
friend of the great and good Heber, who introduced
Scott to his acquaintance.   The intimacy thus formed
between Sir Walter and Mr. Ellis lasted for many
years, indeed until the death of the latter ; for besides
the many social qualities which they possessed in
common, their great taste for national antiquarian lore,
and deep knowledge of this particular study, were
subjects of mutual interest ; and when in London the
great novelist always reserved Saturday and Sunday
for a visit to Sunning Hill, the residence of his friend.
Dr. Leyden, Sir Walter Scott's amanuensis and assist-

ant, also paid him a visit there, and thus described
his countenance in a letter to his patron :—

> " His eyen graye as glas ben
> And his looks ben alto kene,
> Loveliche to paramour ;
> Brown as acorn ben his faxe,
> His face is thin as bettel axe,
> That dealeth dintis doure."

This grotesque sketch by the enthusiastic lover of old
English verse does not convey to the mind of the
unlearned any other idea than that of a rusty battle-
axe,—a very moat-drawbridge-and-portcullis cast of
countenance.   In the early part of Mr. Ellis's career
he was, like Burke, a Whig, and contributed his share
of satires to the Rolliad and Probationary Odes ; but
in 1779 he changed his political opinions, a circumstance rather more unusual in those days than in the
present ; and after he became the coadjutor of Canning
and Frere, he wrote as ardently and well, and praised
Mr. Pitt as cleverly, in the Anti-Jacobin, as he had
abused him in the opposition periodicals.

> " Pert without fire, without experience sage,"

was the opening line of one of his gibes against that
minister ; but though engaged in the literary warfare
of the pen in early life, Mr. Ellis was not afflicted
with the odious asperity which frequently results from
that occupation, or from entering actively upon the
arena of politics.

His literary claims to our admiration and respect
rest, however, upon more solid and commendable

grounds than his political versification. His writing has been compared to Addison's for purity, and his Essay on the Formation and Progress of the English Language, his antiquarian knowledge, and contributions to the *Quarterly Review,* of which he was one of the earliest supporters, will remain, and be prized as the evidence of his talent, long after the remembrance of his social accomplishments has passed away. Mr. Ellis also wrote some light poetry, of which he limited the publicity to circulation amongst his intimate friends. In the latter years of this gentleman's life he was much harassed by a painful disease, which he bore with patience and fortitude, and expired at Sunninghill on the 18th of April 1815, in the seventieth year of his age.

There are several other pieces of the Duchess of Devonshire's poetry in Brummell's collection besides the preceding ones ; amongst them are some lines on a bust of Charles J. Fox at Woburn, The battle of Aboukir, and her celebrated Negro Song, " The loud · wind roared, the rain fell fast," which was suggested by a circumstance that befell Mungo Parke during his travels in Africa, and which was set to music many years ago. There is also an excellent specimen of her Grace's wit and domestic satire ; but as the joke on which it turns was taken up by Lord John Townshend, I have placed it with his reply.

The following are her lines on the bust of Charles James Fox at Woburn :—

" Here, 'midst the friends he loved, the man behold,
    In truth unshaken, and in virtue bold ;

Whose patriot zeal and uncorrupted mind
Dared to assert the freedom of mankind :
And, whilst extending desolation far,
Ambition spread the baneful flames of war,
Fearless of blame, and eloquent to save,
'Twas he,—'twas Fox, the warning counsel gave ;
'Midst jarring conflicts stemm'd the tide of blood,
And to the menaced world a landmark stood.
Oh ! had his voice in Mercy's cause prevail'd,
What grateful millions had the statesman hail'd !
Whose wisdom made the broils of nations cease,
And taught the world humanity and peace.
But though he fail'd, succeeding ages here,
The vain yet pious effort shall revere ;
Boast in their annals his illustrious name,
Uphold his greatness, and confirm his fame."

The succeeding stanzas, on account of their peculiar beauty and pathos, I have reserved for the last,
in order that the impression they will naturally make
upon the reader, may not be impaired by any subsequent trifle from the same pen.

" I've known all the blessings of sight,
　　The beauties that nature displays,
And traced in the splendour of light
　　The glories that stream'd in the blaze ;
Yet though darkness its sorrows has spread,
　　I grudge not the pleasures I've known,
Since, reclining, I thus lay my head
　　On a breast that I know is my own.

I have valued the charms of the rose,
　　As I pluck'd it all fresh from the tree ;
I have kiss'd it, and bid it disclose
　　Its sweets, for I meant it for thee.

But memory still has its bliss,
　　Though no longer I gaze on thee now ;
More sweet than the rose is thy kiss,
　　And more fresh and more lovely art thou.

The life of the roebuck was mine,
　　As I bounded o'er valley and lawn,
I watch'd the grey twilight decline,
　　And worshipp'd the day-breaking[1] dawn.
I regret not the freedom of will,
　　Or sigh as uncertain I tread,
I am freer and happier still
　　When by thee I am carefully led.

Ere my sight I was doom'd to resign
　　My heart I surrender'd to thee,
Not a thought or an action was mine,
　　But I saw as thou had'st me to see.
Thy watchful affection I wait,
　　And hang with delight on thy voice ;
And dependence is soften'd by fate,
　　Since dependence on thee was my choice."

These verses speak eloquently for a heart that the
blandishments of fashion beguiled to a lamentable
extent, but could never entirely corrupt. "To her
mother," says Wraxall, "the Duchess of Devonshire
was attached with more than common filial affection,
of which she exhibited pecuniary proofs, rarely given
by a daughter to a parent. Nor did she display less
attachment to her sister, Lady Duncannon." It is
said, that in her last illness, the retrospect of her life
caused the Duchess of Devonshire the deepest regret,
and that she felt acutely the utter insignificance and

---

[1] *Day-breaking*, Qy. "*gay*-breaking."

emptiness of the pleasures which had so constantly
absorbed her mind and energies.   The disorder which
terminated in her death was an abscess in the liver ;
her Grace having experienced the first attack of it
about three months before, while dining at the Marquis of Hertford's ; from that time it increased so
rapidly, as to baffle every attempt made to subdue it,
by the combined talents of Doctors Baillie, Pitcairn,
and others.   Her disease was beyond the aid of
human skill ; and she expired at Devonshire House,
on the morning of the 30th of March 1806, in the forty-
ninth year of her age.

The Prince of Wales had the greatest regard and
respect for her, and expressed a wish to attend her
funeral ; but the honour was declined, as in London
the ceremonials were conducted with great privacy.
This, however, was not the case at Derby, for the
hearse was met three miles from the town by the
nobility and gentry of the county, and the Duke's
tenantry, who accompanied it to the family vault of
the Cavendishes, in All Saints' Church.   Fifteen years
after her sister, the Countess of Bessborough, was, at
her own request, laid in the same vault.   In the zenith
of their beauty and influence, " the rival sisters," as
they were generally called, were tenderly attached to
each other ; and how this feeling survived in Lady
Bessborough's mind, is attested by an affecting anecdote, which Wraxall thus relates :—

" During the month of July 1811, a very short
time before the decease of the late Duke of Devonshire,

I visited the vault in the principal church of Derby, where repose the remains of the Cavendish family. As I stood contemplating the coffin which contained the remains of that admired female, Georgiana, the late Duchess, the woman who accompanied me pointed out the relics of a *bouquet* which lay on the coffin, nearly collapsed into dust. ' That nosegay,' said she, ' was brought here by the Countess of Bessborough, who had designed to place it with her own hands on her sister's coffin ; but overcome by her emotions on approaching the spot, she found herself unable to descend the steps conducting to the vault. In an agony of grief she knelt down on the stones, as nearly over the place occupied by the corpse as I could direct, and there deposited the flowers, enjoining me the performance of an office to which she was un-equal. I fulfilled her wishes.' " When the Prince of Wales was informed of the death of the Duchess of Devonshire, he is said to have exclaimed, " Then we have lost the best-bred woman in England ! " And Fox observed, on the same melancholy occasion, " She had the kindest of human hearts." How characteristic the remarks of the two men !

A few days after the first edition of this work was published (1844), a visit to Breadsall Priory, near Derby, gave me an opportunity of seeing the vault of the Cavendishes in All Saints' Church. The morning prayers on a week day enabled me to enter this edifice, which is of handsome proportions, and, as Wraxall observes, " the principal church ; " but it required

some little persuasion to induce the sexton to allow me
to look on the remains of "the once rival sisters," no
longer so in the dark tomb.   The unwillingness of the
official to do so arose, as he afterwards informed me,
from some restrictions which had been placed upon
him in consequence of his predecessor having habitually stuck his tallow candle on the coffin of the first
Duke, when showing visitors the vault.   The traces
of the guttering dip had been observed by the present
Duke, who gave an order that the keys of the mau-
soleum should for the future be kept at the under-
taker's.   They were procured from his house, which
is in the neighbourhood, and the sexton having lighted
a candle, we descended.   The vault is on the right of·
the chancel, the steps leading to it being in a pew that
is used by the inmates of the Almshouses which were
founded by the celebrated Countess of Devonshire.
This staircase is commodious, and the entrance to it
by the wooden trap-door large enough to admit one
person easily.   The vault itself is divided into two
chambers, which are, as the passage, so well ventilated,
that very little damp was discernible.   Each of these
apartments is divided into a series of oblong cavities,
dug horizontally within the wall, into which the coffins
are laid.   Those in the second chamber, which is
quite full, are the oldest; and some of them not unlike
an Egyptian mummy in form, being in fact nothing
more than a lead covering which was made to take
the shape of the body.   Most of these coffins are in
an extraordinary state of preservation ; one, however,

had a hole in it sufficiently large to show the skull of a
certain Earl of Devonshire who died in 1670; another,
and a much older coffin near it, leaked, but the liquid
which exuded from it had no unpleasant smell, and
was originally probably of an aromatic nature. The
fragments of the external wooden coffins appeared to
have been collected together with great care, and were
piled up in two or three of the uppermost niches.
The coffin of Georgiana, in the chamber near the door,
was easily recognised by the initials G. D. on the
external end. It lay in a direct line with that of her
sister, Lady Bessborough, which is in the inner apartment; so that the extremities of the two coffins would
touch, were it not for the wall between. I understood
that they were placed in this position by Lady
Bessborough's express desire. The faded gilding, the
tattered velvet of rich crimson, and the tinsel ducal
crowns that rested on the coffins of these two bright
spirits of the fashionable world, were mournful but
appropriate illustrations of the perishable and unsatis-
factory character of the pursuits to which they had
been devoted. Lady Bessborough's coffin, evidently
of foreign make, is of enormous size, and in the niche
above is that of the child, for whom she is said to
have grieved even unto death. Close to the entrance
is the body of Elizabeth, Duchess of Devonshire,
subsequently spoken of; the coffin, like that of Lady
Bessborough's, being of an oblong square and of Italian
manufacture. There are at least forty coffins in this
vault. My feelings were subdued when I left it,

particularly so when I recalled to my mind Wraxall's description of Lady Bessborough's visit to her sister's tomb.

In introducing the translation of Petrarch's sonnet, I had occasion to advert to Elizabeth, Duchess of Devonshire, the Duke's second wife, and to allude to the estimation in which she held her friend and pre-decessor's accomplishments. Before concluding this chapter, it may not be irrelevant to speak of her great taste and acquirements; indeed it is impossible to mention one of these celebrated women without think-ing of the other, for the intimacy that existed between them was perfectly Siamese—and after the separation of Lady Elizabeth from Mr. Foster, her first husband, had taken place, she became an inmate of Devonshire House, on the gossip of which I forbear to dwell. The two friends afterwards travelled together on the Con-tinent, and when at Lausanne, in 1787, an incident occurred which proves that she was scarcely less delightfully insinuating, or less talented, than her gifted companion.

The anecdote, charming in itself, is admirably related in a contribution to the *Gentleman's Magazine,* and amusingly displays the consummate vanity of the philosophic Gibbon, who was a fixed resident in that town, and formed a welcome addition to their society. " Beautiful in her person," says this writer, " fascinat-ing in her manner, still under the age of thirty, and wholly unsuspicious of all amorous pretensions from a man of the mature years, ungainly figure, and love-repelling countenance of her learned countryman, she checked not the exuberance of her admiration of his genius : she had unconsciously, however, made a deep impression on his imagination, and one morning, more especially, just as he had terminated his elaborate performance, and felt elated with the achievement, as he so glowingly describes the sensation in his " Life," he invited the seductive lady to breakfast ; when in a bower, fragrant with encircling acacias, he selected for her perusal various attractive passages of the conclud- ing sheets.

" Enchanted with the masterly narrative, her lady- ship complimented him on the completion of his task with a charm of language, and warmth of address, which the author's prurient fancy, much too licentiously indulged, as his writings prove, converted into effusions of tenderer inspiration. Falling on his knees, he gave utterance to an impassioned profession of love, greatly to the surprise of its object, who, recoiling from his contact, entreated him to rise from this humiliating posture. Thus recalled to cooler feeling, but prostrate and helpless from his unwieldy form, he vainly sought to regain his feet, and the delicate female, whose first astonishment soon yielded to irrepressible laughter at the ridiculous scene, was equally powerless in affording relief; until at length, with the aid of two robust women, he was re-seated in his arm-chair, from which it was pretexted he had accidentally slipt. Thus ' solventur risu tabulæ,' a laugh at once dissolves the lover's enchantment, and with it evaporated the lady's

anger, genuine or simulated; for with the Lady Elizabeth, this demonstration of the Promethean puissance
of her charms, which could quicken into vivid emotion
such a mass of seemingly inert matter, was, on reflection, felt rather as a homage than an offence; and
though unfruitful of effect in evoking, as in the opera
of Zèmire and Azor, or, Beauty and the Beast, a re-
sponsive flame, it in no sense interrupted her friendly
intercourse with Gibbon."

This "decline and fall" in the historian's philo-
sophy, and total forgetfulness of the chances of ridicule, certainly gives an exalted idea of the Lady
Elizabeth's charms; but my amiable friend, to whom
she presented the translation of Petrarch's sonnet, and
on whom, unlike Gibbon, time has exercised a soften-
ing influence over the passions, writes even now thus
eloquently in her praise :—" You are much too young
to have known Georgiana, Duchess of Devonshire,
and therefore felt *la belle passion* for her, as every
man did in my day: I had the honour of knowing
both her and her successor, and in spite of the fine
eyes and seductive manners of the former, I preferred
Elizabeth.   I will not, however, draw any comparisons
between them, unless, indeed, it should be between
their literary accomplishments.   Elizabeth did not, as
far as I know, ever dabble in poetry: she did more
than this; she was a zealous patroness of literature
and the fine arts; she was the Duchess who, at her
own expense, caused a machine to be fabricated for
dragging the Tiber, in the vain hope of redeeming

some of the statues which it is well ascertained had
been thrown into it at different periods during the
civil wars, and the first invasion of Clovis. That
praiseworthy attempt, though often repeated, was
utterly fruitless.

" It was she also who caused, at her own expense,
the Æneid to be translated into Italian verse, a
magnificent work which, in point of elegance, fidelity,
and typographical correctness, leaves nothing to be
desired. With that in his hand, the traveller may
trace the progress of Æneas from his first landing in
Italy, to the fatal termination of his combat with
Turnus. Her palace at Rome, as well as her purse,
was open to all men of genius, without distinction of
rank or country : she may be said to have held the
keys of the Vatican and other libraries ; for, owing
to her influence, I obtained admission to them when
they were closed even to the Romans themselves,
in consequence either of repairs or festivals. Though
others may, I have none but pleasing souvenirs
of that charming woman, for I owed many obligations to her kindness during my residence at
Rome.

" One of the most gratifying memorials I possess is
a letter that she wrote to me shortly after her schemes
for dragging the Tiber for antiques had failed, in which
she feelingly deplores the result : it is a curious proof
of fine feeling and affectation, two qualities not very
compatible with each other ; I allude to her mode of

writing merely the initial and final letters of words,
an affectation which often cost me considerable trouble
in guessing at her meaning.   Thus, in referring to her
repeated disappointments on this subject, he writes,
—' My l—t like my f—t at —s have failed!'   Notwithstanding this, I have no hesitation in saying, that
if a woman could be properly termed the Mæcenas
of her age, Elizabeth, Duchess of Devonshire, well
deserved the appellation."   She also published, at
Rome, an edition of her friend and predecessor's
poem, The Passage of the St. Gothard, and the fifth
satire of the First Book of Horace, with illustrations,
several of which were designed and executed by herself.   Her Grace's death, in March 1824, interrupted
the completion of a Dante, which she had also
intended to illustrate with one hundred plates.   She
was the friend of Cardinal Gonsalvi, of Canova,
Cammucini, and Thorwaldsen, and was generally surrounded by eminent artists and men of letters ;
her influence in Rome was great, partly owing to her
classical and literary taste, but still more to a munifi-
cence which scarcely knew a limit, and it was this
influence perhaps, which led the widow of the younger
Pretender (and afterwards of Alfieri) thus to address
the Duchess from her palazzo at Florence, ' Ma belle
amie, on dit ici, que vous régnez à Rome, permettez
moi d'aller vous visiter dans vos états,' &c., &c.   In
the spirit of old Rome a medal of her was struck at
her death, commemorative of her arduous exertions in

the protection and advancement of Italian literature, and her unwearied efforts to preserve or restore to the world any remains of the classical antiquities which she so deeply venerated. Her Grace was a daughter of the fourth Earl of Bristol."

CHAPTER XIV.

Brummell a Whig, but no Politician—General Fitzpatrick—His Con-
tributions to the Beau's Album—His Lines on a Proposed Grant of
Money for the Prosecution of the War—Mrs. Miller of Bath-Easton
—Horace Walpole's Description of her—Castles in the Air—The late
Lord Palmerston—His Epitaph on his Wife—Lord Upper Ossory—
Lady Tyrconnel—Lines addressed to her by that Nobleman—Lady
Upper Ossory.

AT the Duke of Devonshire's, Brummell had many
and agreeable opportunities of improving his acquaintance with the wits, and celebrated men, of the party
of which his Grace was the leader, and his Duchess
such an enthusiastic supporter. But Brummell, though
a staunch Whig, took little active interest in their
political proceedings, and in all probability, his reason
for preferring their society was, that their leisure
hours were more convivially spent than those of the
ministerial one, and the "Pilot who weathered the
storm."

Foremost amongst these wits was General Fitzpatrick, and I shall in this chapter introduce two of
his contributions to the Beau's album, as well as those
of several more of Brummell's friends, whose verses
have likewise escaped the printing press. Richard

Fitzpatrick, the son of John, first Earl of Upper Ossory, was born January 30th, 1747. In his youth he served in the American War, but, having a political turn, he relinquished active service, and entered the senate as member for Tavistock, in 1780. Though he attained the post of Secretary of War, he was far more celebrated as the friend of Fox, and his companion at the gaming-table, and as one of the best political versifiers of his day, than as a statesman, or an orator. The General was the author of some of the happiest pleasantries in the Rolliad, and the Probationary Odes; he wrote the verses on Brooke Watson, those on the Marquis of Graham, and the Liars; he also wrote Dorinda, a town eclogue, and other short pieces. The following specimen of his politico-poetical talents is nearly, if not quite, equal to any squib Swift ever wrote.

WRITTEN ON THE BACK OF A BILL ENTITLED "AN ACT FOR GRANTING TO HIS MAJESTY AN ADDITIONAL CONTRI-- BUTION FOR THE PROSECUTION OF THE WAR!!"

> " Plan, by general confiscation,
> To redeem a ruin'd nation ;
> Plan, through all its parts a blunder,
> Credit to maintain by plunder ;
> Plan, which property protects,
> By the seizure of effects ;
> Plan, securing general comfort ;
> Can we pay too large a sum for't ?
> Which such comforts soon shall bring, as
> Writs of Capias and Distringas—
> Into poor folks' houses breaking,
> E'en the beds they sleep on taking ;

Thus by wives and children starving,
All that's dear to man preserving ;
Virtue, and good morals guarding,
Base informers by rewarding ;
Strengthening all our social ties
By encouraging of spies ;
Setting down in each man's cot,
What he has, and he has not ;
What though gone all Fortune gave him,
No economy can save him.
Base conceit to fight the French meant,
By prohibiting entrenchment ;
Vital Christians, still repining
That religion is declining,
Here in her behalf decree
Premiums upon perjury ;
Friends of due subordination,
Here, 'twixt high and humble station,
Cordial union to secure,
Drive the rich to starve the poor.
Here a clause which needs must please us,
Of superfluous cash to ease us,
Whence the tax, by dexterous shift,
All at once becomes a gift ;
Clause which leaves an option pleasant
To be robbed or make a present ;
For, should you decline the honour
To become a nation's donor,
Shortly to your cost you'll find
There's a process still behind ;
Which, how closely e'er you lock it,
In due time will reach your pocket.
So sham cripples, whom we meet
Asking alms through many a street,
Rob by night (their wooden leg off)
Those they in the morning beg of,
And, as laws are made restraining
Suffering wretches from complaining,

These, to stop poor people's bawling,
Lift their crutch and lay them sprawling.
In this project what can men see
But the rulers in a phrenzy,
Still the desperate course pursuing
Which has brought us all to ruin?
Who 'mongst country lubbers sees one
So absurd and void of reason,
To increase the ass's loads
He has plung'd in miry roads?
British dolts, if 'tis your pleasure
To endure such loads as these are,
Prate no more about your freedom—
Empty boasts! for none will heed 'em.
All your spirit is but vapour,
Magna Charta mere waste-paper;
All your boasted fire but smoke,—
Beasts of burden, bear the yoke!"

Near these lines of the General's were the following
anonymous verses, also humorously referring to the
excessive taxation of the times. The name of Miller,
in the first stanza, made me fear they might have
been printed in a collection of poetry written for a
fantastical lady of that name, who lived at a villa near
Bath, and published in 1775 for charitable purposes,
under the title of The Vase of Bath-Easton; but on
consulting the work I did not find them, and this leads
me to hope that they have never been printed. At
this villa the lady used to receive a large and distinguished circle of friends every Thursday, and the
chief amusement of these *réunions* was to read aloud
the scraps of sentimental and other poetry that had
been composed by them, perhaps in the King's bath,

in the previous week, much of which was in praise
of herself, her villa, and each other. Horace Walpole,
in describing the Bath-Easton vagaries, writes thus to
General Conway :

"Mrs. Miller is returned a beauty, a genius, a
Sappho, a tenth muse, as romantic as Mademoiselle
de Scudéri, and as unsophisticated as Mrs. Vesey.
The captain's fingers are loaded with cameos, his
tongue runs over with virtù; and that both may contribute to the improvement of their own country, they
have introduced *bouts rimés* as a new discovery. They
hold a Parnassus fair every Thursday, give out
rhymes and themes, and all the flux of quality at
Bath contend for the prizes. A Roman vase, dressed
with pink ribbons and myrtles, receives the poetry,
which is drawn out every festival. Six judges of
these Olympic games retire and select the brightest
compositions, which the respective successful acknow-
ledge, kneel to Mrs. Calliope Miller, kiss her fair hand,
and are crowned by it with myrtle, with—I do not
know what. You may think this is a fiction or
exaggeration. Be dumb, unbelievers. The collection
is printed, published. Yes, by my faith, there are
bouts rimés on a buttered muffin, made by her Grace
the Duchess of Northumberland ; recipes to make
them by Corydon the venerable, alias George Pitt ;
others very pretty ·by Lord Palmerston ; some by
Lord Carlisle ; many by Mrs. Miller herself, that have
no fault but wanting metre, and immortality promised
to her without end or measure. In short, since folly,

which never ripens to madness but in this hot climate, ran distracted, there never was anything so entertaining or so dull."

"CASTLES IN THE AIR."

" Were I content on earth to dwell,
  To earth my views confine ;
With rapture, Miller, I'd survey
  This paradise of thine.

I too my willing voice would raise,
  And equal praise bestow,
But that the scene which others praise,
  For me is far too low.

I grant the hills are crown'd with trees
  I grant the fields are fair ;
Yet after all one nothing sees,
  But what is really there.

True taste ideal fancy feigns
  Whilst on poetic wings ;
'Bove earth, and all that earth contains,
  Unbounded fancy springs.

To dwell on earth's gross element,
  Let grovelling spirits bear,
Whilst I on nobler plans intent
  Build castles in the air.

No neighbours there can disagree,
  Or thwart what I design ;
For there not only all I see,
  But all I wish, is mine.

No surly landlord's leave I want,
  To make or pull down fence ;
I build, I furnish, lay out, plant,
  Regardless of expense.

One thing, indeed, excites my fear,
　Nor let it seem surprising,
Since Ministers, from year to year,
　New taxes are devising,

Lest earth being taxed, as soon it may,
　Beyond what earth can bear,
Our Financier a tax should lay
　On castles in the air !

Well with the end the means would suit,
　Did he in these our days,
Ideal plans to execute,
　Ideal taxes raise."

Multifarious, indeed, were the schemes sent in to Government, towards the close of the last century, with a view of raising new taxes. It must have been at this time that the Austrian General exclaimed one day, in the Haymarket, "Good Heavens! you rule the seas, and you give a guinea-and-a-half for a codfish : " a bitter epigram ; for the Imperialist thought that a guinea was laid on by the Government as a tax !

It is impossible, with every proper feeling of veneration for Horace Walpole's taste, to coincide with him in his admiration of Lord Palmerston's poetry, in the Vase of Bath-Easton. Tickell is more correct, when he says, " With chirps of wit, and mutilated lays, see Palmerston fineer his *bouts rimés*." There are also, in the *Gentleman's Magazine*, several specimens of his Lordship's poetry, which are not very felicitous ; but the following epitaph on his first wife,

Miss Poole, which was also in Brummell's collection, might well have softened Tickell's satire. It is
not exaggerated praise to say, that these lines will bear
comparison with those of Mason ; and the composition
was probably influenced by his Lordship's having read
and admired them ; for the Poet's wife died in her
twenty-eighth year, at Bristol Hot-Wells, March 27th,
1767, two years before Lady Palmerston, who also
expired at the same place.

> "Whoe'er, like me, with trembling anguish brings
> His heart's whole treasure to fair Bristol's springs ;
> Whoe'er, like me, to soothe distress and pain,
> Shall court these salutary springs in vain :
> Condemn'd, like me, to hear the faint reply,
> To mark the fading cheek, the sinking eye ;
> From the chill brow to wipe the damps of death,
> And watch, in dumb despair, the shortening breath ;—
> If chance should bring him to this artless line,
> Let the sad mourner know his pangs were mine :
> Ordain'd to lose the partner of my breast,
> Whose beauty warm'd me, and whose virtues bless'd,
> Framed, every tie that binds the heart to prove,
> Her duty, friendship, and her friendship, love ;—
> But yet remembering that the parting sigh
> Appoints the just to slumber—not to die—
> The starting tear I check'd,—I kiss'd the rod—
> And, not to earth resign'd her, but to God ! "

But these poems have interrupted the conclusion of
this short notice of General Fitzpatrick. He had a
very commanding presence and courtly manners, and
possessed an inexhaustible fund of conversation as
well as wit, which qualities, combined with great good-

nature, rendered him an universal favourite ; but, like his friend Fox, and the rest of that party, Fitzpatrick appears to have been sadly deficient in the principle of moderation, the power of regulating his passions and habits, and the steadiness of character and industry which tended so much to the success of their opponents, and to command for them the respect in which they were held, even by those who differed from their political views. Long indulgence in the pleasures of the table impaired, in later life, his bodily as well as mental faculties, and Wraxall gives a painful account of the shattered state of both, shortly before his death. This took place on the 25th April 1813, in the sixty-seventh year of his age.

Lord Upper Ossory, General Fitzpatrick's elder brother, though not so witty or so popular, was a man of much more temperate habits, and highly and deservedly esteemed. Horace Walpole, in writing from Paris to George Selwyn, in 1765, mentions him in favourable terms :—" We have swarms of English ; but most of them know not Joseph, and Joseph desires not to know them. I live with none of them but Crawford and Lord Ossory ; the latter of whom I am extremely sorry is returning to England ; I recommend him to Mr. Williams as one of the properest and most amiable young men I ever knew." At this time Lord Ossory was only twenty years of age, and Walpole seems to have valued his acquaintance, as he was for many years after a frequent visitor at Ampthill.

His Lordship, who was educated at Eton and Oxford, had a poetical turn as well as his brother; and, to judge by the lines addressed to Lady Tyrconnel, now given, this talent was usefully and kindly employed : the warning, however, that his poetry conveyed on this occasion was unheeded ; or, if it caused a temporary check in her thoughtless career, she did not eventually profit by it. This lady, who was a daughter of the famous Marquis of Granby, married George, second Earl of Tyrconnel, and was divorced from him in 1777, being then in her twenty-fourth year : she subsequently married the Honourable Philip Anstruther, according to the Peerage ; but the *Gentleman's Magazine*, in mentioning her death in 1792, says P. Leslie, Esq., once a wine-merchant in France, and second son of Lord Newark of Scotland.

This discrepancy in this gentleman's identity arose from the 'following circumstances : David Leslie, second Lord Newark, a staunch friend of Charles the First, died in 1694, leaving an only daughter, who married Sir A. Anstruther, Bart. : his son claimed the barony of Newark, after his mother's death, when the House of Lords gave a decision in his favour ; but they afterwards retracted their verdict. Philip Anstruther, Esq., would therefore have been his proper denomination, in 1792, though the metre of the lines seems to indicate Leslie, as the name used by Lord Ossory.

ADDRESSED TO LADY TYRCONNEL.

LORD UPPER OSSORY.

" Envy, that loves not merit, ne'er will spare
A form so perfect, and a face so fair ;
Let prudence, then, o'er all your steps preside,
And sage discretion every action guide.
For know (but first I must demand excuse
For the plain bluntness of an honest muse),
Know and reflect, ere yet it is too late,
You stand this moment on the brink of fate.
By fashion blinded, and by folly led,
The path of ruin and of vice you tread ;
Reflect—long years of sorrow must repay
The short-lived pleasures of one fleeting day ;
Lovely and young, and in Tyrconnel blest,
By strangers honour'd and by friends caress'd,
How will they mourn to hear cursed envy tell
From what a glorious height of bliss you fell !
What charms can you in empty Leslie find,
To shake your virtue, or your judgment blind ?
Shun him—not only him, but all the rest
That would plant daggers in thy youthful breast ;
Guard from their arts thy yet unspotted fame,
And spare thy honour'd father's glorious name."

This is a singular subject for Lord Ossory to have
touched upon ; as, about seven years before these
lines were written, he had married the wife of Augus-
tus Henry, third Duke of Grafton, who had been
previously divorced from that notorious libertine.
The Duke's profligate amours, and more especially
his *liaison* with Nancy Parsons, a once beautiful, but
then superannuated courtesan, led to his estrangement
from his accomplished and injured Duchess ; and it

must have been a deep interest in her misfortunes
that tempted Lord Ossory into forming an intimacy
which led to a dissolution of this ill-assorted marriage.
Many and great were the trials this amiable woman
endured, before she consented to take the step which
tarnished her reputation, and deprived her of the
place in society that her virtues adorned.   Gilly
Williams, intending to throw ridicule on her religious
feelings, writes thus in 1765 : " The Duchess of
Grafton goes nowhere but to church."   Horace Walpole, who was, says Mr. Jesse,[1] an ardent admirer
of her beauty, her good sense, and many endearing
qualities, and who, more than once, speaks of her
enthusiastically as " my Duchess," pays her a pleasing compliment, in his poem of " The Three Herons."
Lady Ossory was the only daughter of the first Lord
Ravensworth, and died in February 1804.

[1] John Heneage Jesse, " Memoirs of the Court of England."

CHAPTER XV.

Lord John Townshend—Lady Hunloke—Sir Robert Adair—Poem of Georgiana, Duchess of Devonshire's, supposed to be addressed to Sir Robert Adair, by Lady Hunloke—Sir Robert Adair's Reply to Lady Hunloke, by Lord John Townshend—Sir Gregory Page Turner— Sir G. Osborne Turner—Sir Thomas Tyrwhitt Jones—Mr. Robson, M.P.

AMONGST the names of valued friends mentioned by Brummell, in his letter to the lady to whom he presented his album, is that of Lord John Townshend, son of the first Marquis Townshend so much distinguished at the battles of Dettingen and Fontenoy, and who had the melancholy satisfaction of receiving the keys of Quebec after the death of Wolfe. Lord John was born on the 19th of January 1757, and was a godson of George the Second. He was educated at Eton, and afterwards went to Cambridge, where his career was so brilliant that the University returned him as their member at the age of twenty-three. He had been a candidate the previous year, 1779, when he was defeated by the Solicitor-General Mansfield, but only by twelve votes. It was on this occasion that the Marquis sent a man up to vote against his son, and for Lord Hyde, the third candidate. Lord

John's adherence to the Whig party cost him his seat in 1784, when he was superseded by Mr. Pitt. He was subsequently returned, with Fox as his colleague, for Westminster, and afterwards sat twenty-five years for Knaresborough, at the expiration of which time he retired from Parliament.

"Few men," says Wraxall, "held a higher place in Fox's friendship than the Lord John Townshend; a place to which he was entitled by the elegance of his mind, his various accomplishments, and his adherence to him through life. If party could ever feel regret, it would have been excited by his being excluded from a seat so honourable in itself as that of the University of Cambridge, to which he had attained by unwearied personal exertions." In early life Lord John was conspicuous in society for the grace of his manners, and, as his friend Tickell says, "for his pathetic bow." His poetical productions were admired for their exquisite humour; and, in conjunction with Tickell, he wrote the satire entitled Jekyll. To him we also owe the Probationary Ode for Major Scott, and the playful parody of "Donec gratus eram tibi;" he likewise wrote a severe ode addressed to Lord North, and similarly pungent verses to Lords Barrington, Dartmouth, and George Germaine.

A party at Chatsworth, at which Lord John was present, gave rise to the following pretty piece of scandal in verse by the Duchess of Devonshire. It has been already alluded to, and will introduce a reply by his lordship, who, as I have before observed, was

one of her intimate friends. In this poem the *spiri-
uelle* Georgiana appears to have been amusing herself
not a little at the expense of Lady Hunloke, wife of
Sir Henry Hunloke, Bart., and a sister of the late
Lord Leicester. Her ladyship was one of the
duchess's country neighbours, and stands accused of
having a predilection for Mr., afterwards the Right
Honourable Sir Robert Adair, also one of her Grace's
political friends, and a visitor at Chatsworth.

   This gentleman, son of the celebrated surgeon of
that name by Lady Caroline Keppel, daughter of
William, second Earl of Albemarle, was the *élève* and
friend of Fox, whose memory he defended against
Tomline; and while he sat in parliament, which he
did, first for Appleby, and afterwards for Camelford,
he steadily supported that statesman. In 1789, when
Russia was menaced by England for her policy with
regard to Turkey, Mr. Adair, under Fox's auspices,
visited St. Petersburgh (a fact which the reader must
bear in mind as he peruses the poem), to counteract
Mr. Pitt's measures; and it was after this that the
Empress Catherine requested Fox to sit for his bust,
which she subsequently placed between those of
Demosthenes and Cicero. That Charles Fox should
feel an honest satisfaction in preserving his country
from being embroiled in an unnecessary war, is perfectly comprehensible; but it is difficult to believe
that he attached any value to this hollow compliment
from the great representative of absolute power. In
1806, Mr. Adair was appointed ambassador at Vienna,

and three years after was sent as minister to Constantinople; after which, he retired from public life.

The "dingy home," of which the duchess speaks in the opening lines of this poem, is Wingerworth Hall, the seat of the Hunloke family; and it was probably the iron founderies in the neighbourhood of Chesterfield that suggested the allusion, for Wingerworth is but two or three miles from that town; the Hall is about ten from Chatsworth. Though the Duchess of Devonshire's love of literature was quite sufficient to excite the envious of her day to call her a Blue, she would, by the quiz she thus inflicted upon her contemporary, have completely escaped the more recent denunciation of that *clique* by Trebeck, who observes, "that the Blues seldom condescend to scandal except scandal of the worst kind, such as ripping up old grievances, and speaking shamefully ill of the dead. I met a Blue the other day who was discussing the Suffolk letters, and Walpole's memoirs, and then went on to say paw-paw things of Lady Mary Wortley Montague. Now really this is quite atrocious: to attack a modern reputation is venial in comparison. Thank Heaven, with all my faults, it cannot be said that I ever slandered anybody's great-great-grandmother." Now I venture to hope the reader will not think that I have slandered a great-grandmother (for such would Lady Hunloke be were she now alive) by publishing these lines, as at the period they were written she was in her fifty-first year.　Lady Hunloke is said to have been a merry, talkative, and coquettish lady, and, like her friend the duchess, very fond of play.

TO ROBERT ADAIR, FROM LADY HUNLOKE.

DUCHESS OF DEVONSHIRE.

" Undone and plunder'd, waddling, sad, and slow,
　From Chatsworth to my dingy home I go ;
　The barren heaths and mines of coal I view,
　And turn my back, but not my thoughts from you ;
　The dreary landscape renovates my care,
　Since gloom and cinders but recall Adair.
　What though on all my smiles incessant shone,
　Except when Bessborough[1] the rubber won ;
　Though softest meanings on my accents spoke,
　Save when I cursed Lord Granville Gower's[2] revoke?
　And though soft looks express'd my feelings bland
　Except when squinting into Denman's[3] hand ;
　Yet though on all with varying grace I rose
　Repeating scraps of poetry and prose ;
　My ample learning though I deign'd to show
　And quoted French and Latin *à propos*—
　Yet still on thee my anxious thoughts were bent,
　For thee, the smile, the nod, the wink, were meant.
　And though, at first, I little understood
　The flattering import of thy pensive mood,
　Thy frowning brow, pale cheek, and downcast eye,
　And absent wandering of each set reply ;

---

[1] The third Earl of Bessborough died in his eighty-seventh year, on the 3rd of February 1844, at Canford House, in Dorsetshire, the seat of his second son, Lord de Mauley.

[2] The first Earl Granville, who married the Lady Harriet Cavendish, second daughter of William, fifth Duke of Devonshire, by Georgiana, the noble authoress of this poem.

[3] Probably Lord Denman.

Yet soon I triumph'd in the inflicted smart,
And prized my conquest o'er a statesman's heart,
And, as bright rays, to one fixed focus brought,
Concent'ring there to blazing flames are wrought,
My charms with shafts of fire inflamed thy pond'rous thought.
'Twas rash in me the dangerous sight to view,
Though fat, and red, I caught the infection too :
And, though much courted by the lordling band,
Though e'en Lord Ossulston [1] on tiptoe stand ;
In spite of all the attentive Morpeth [2] spoke,
All Bennet's pedantry, and Townshend's [3] joke,
All Granville's beauty, and Duncannon's [4] youth,
To thee I vow my constancy and truth.
No longer, then, be politics thy care,—
For can a motion with *my* heart compare ?—
No longer strike the Treasury bench with dread,
Nor like Lord Burleigh shake thy meaning head.
E'en Fox will yield the lightning of thy eye,
Thy frown terrific, and thy mute reply ;
For generous Fox can never disapprove,
That public toils should cede to happy love !
Let Buonaparte sway the jarring world,
Be realms, be empires, from their bases hurl'd,
No counter revolutions me shall wait,
No restoration of a monarch's fate ;
For soon as poor Sir Harry breathes no more
I'll fly to meet the lover I adore !
Bucks and Archbishops I'll alike discard,
And thou of all mankind alone regard.
Then take no mission to the Baltic's tide,
To freeze thy soul and pinch thy scanty side ;
To warmer comforts let thy fancy turn,
Nor longer from thee joys connubial spurn.

---

[1] The late Earl of Tankerville.
[2] The father of the present Earl of Carlisle.
[3] The Lord John Townshend.
[4] The late Earl of Bessborough, then in his twentieth year, and the
youngest of the party.

Nor let thy quondam party's tricks prevail—
Tell them their reign is o'er, their maxims stale,
And that thy choice is, pudding, beef, and ale ;
Bid them alone their empty schemes pursue,
A glittering card-purse opens to thy view.
Then doubt no more, but hear thy Hunloke swear,
With thee, her life, her love,—her jointure too, she'll share. "

As Mr. Adair was a poet, for he is said to have
contributed to the Rolliad and Probationary Odes, it
may be supposed, that he was ignorant of the joke
that the party at Chatsworth were carrying on against
him and the comely half-century from Wingerworth,
or he would have seized his own lyre and sung his
own strain—calm or impassioned. But fortunately
for my readers this was not the case, or they would
have lost the following droll and desperate reply that
Lord John obligingly concocted for him, and while
composing which, it is clear he ludicrously kept in
view Pope's poem of Eloisa to Abelard. By the
allusion to the Congress at Luneville, these *vers-de-
société* were evidently written late in the winter of
1800, or very early in the succeeding year, as the
treaty of peace was not signed until the 9th of February 1801. The "starving land," in the second line,
was no exaggerated expression respecting the state
of the country, for about this period the quartern loaf
was sold for half-a-crown.

ROBERT ADAIR'S REPLY TO LADY HUNLOKE.

LORD JOHN TOWNSHEND.

" In times like these, when to St. Stephen's walls
    A starving land the legislature calls !

Now when the patriot band should be prepared,
Nor pamphlets now, nor paragraphs be spared ;
Why rove I here when Parliament is met ?
Why stray my steps beyond thy shop, Debrett ?[1]
What means this stupor in a statesman's breast ?
Fame, virtue, sleeps,—ambition is at rest,—
My long-made maiden speech remember'd not ;
The House of Commons, the Whig-club forgot !
Far other cares thy lover Hunloke, knows !
All Hackman's[2] sorrows, and all Werther's woes !
Lost and extinct, my party zeal I see,
And pity fools that think of aught but thee.
What though, unmatch'd in diplomatic fame,
Beyond the Baltic they revere my name ?
Though now at Luneville the Congress wait
Adair's decision upon Europe's fate ;

---

[1] Debrett's shop opposite Burlington House, was, until lately, occupied by Mr. Pickering the publisher. Mr. Stockdale, who has been succeeded by Mr. Thorpe, bookseller and autograph collector, lived next door. Perhaps Lady Hunloke's house was nearer to the Park, for a former family mansion of Sir Harry's was in Piccadilly ; this house was purchased by Lord Coventry, in 1765, for ten thousand pounds.

[2] The Rev. James Hackman had first been an officer, and became afterwards a clergyman ; he shot Miss Reay, the mistress of Lord Sandwich, as she was coming out of Covent Garden Theatre. Lust and jealousy hurried him to the commission of this deed on the 7th of April 1779, and he was hung on the 19th of the same month at Tyburn. The hangman's cupidity on the occasion was of the most barefaced description ; when the unfortunate culprit flung down his handkerchief as the signal for the cart to move on, instead of instantly whipping the horses he jumped on the other side of him to snatch it up, lest he should lose this perquisite in the crowd ; he then returned to the cart, and, as Lord Carlisle writes to George Selwyn, "with the gesture so faithfully represented by your friend Lord Wentworth, Jehu'd him out of the world." There still exists in a private garden at Hampton Court, a grotto that was constructed by Miss Reay—and with her own hands. She left Lord Sandwich five children, one of whom, Mr. Basil Montagu, became a lawyer of eminence, and died in 1851, in his 82d year.

Should at my feet the mighty Consul fall,
France, Austria, Russia, I would scorn them all.[1]
Not Fox's mission would I deign to carry,
Here let me stay, the rival of Sir Harry !
Thou know'st how first at Chatsworth I was made
Thy hapless victim, as at whist we play'd ;
Each wink, each shrug, each whisper, and each look,
For softest hints my vanity mistook ;
Too soon I found, how rash was my conceit,
All eyes but mine thou couldst contrive to cheat.
Say not for me were meant thy sly regards,
Not me they ogled, but Lord Bessborough's cards ;
Too plain I saw (no wonder in the dumps)
Thy side-long glances leering at his trumps ;
Thou say'st that when Sir Harry leaves thee free,
Thy heart, thy card-purse, shall belong to me ;
Nor beef, nor ale, nor pudding wilt thou grudge,—
All this thou say'st—but all thou say'st is fudge.
Soon as Sir Harry's fatal knell shall toll,
Oh ! that 'twere mine his widow to console ![2]
But ah ! some youth more delicate than I,
Shall hush thy murmurs, and thy tears shall dry.
Some sturdier swain more suited to thy taste,
With keener stomach for the rich repast.
Then fly me, fly—to Wingerworth repair,
Forget, renounce, abjure, the lost Adair !
Yet say, my Hunloke, thou who every part
Of Shakspeare's drama canst repeat by heart,

---

[1] "Should at my feet the world's great master fall,
Himself, his throne, his world, I'd scorn them all.
Not Cæsar's empress would I deign to prove,
No—make me mistress to the man I love."
POPE.—*Eloïsa to Abelard.*

[2] How much unnecessary trouble the Duchess and Lord John gave themselves about the Rt. Hon. diplomatist's love affairs was shown by his marrying, in 1805, Gabrielle Angelica, Countess d'Hagincourt, at which time Lady Hunloke was "a widow," Sir Henry having died on the 15th of November 1804.

Where's the mock envy, or fictitious spleen,
But some similitude in me is seen?
Long nursed and train'd in Melancholy's school,
One sad epitome of every fool.
Oft hast thou heard me sigh, and seen me look,
Like musing Jacques stretch'd by a murmuring brook ;
Seen me its stream augment with many a tear,
And mourn and moralise the passing deer :
Vain of my yellow hue, oft seen me move,
The piteous pageant of Malvolio's love.
Oft, too, like Romeo's, is my woful plight,
Banish'd from thine, as he from Juliet's sight ;
Prostrate the holy priest beheld him fall,
And heard the frantic wretch for poison call ;
From thee exiled, not less I madly rave,
Or ' take the measure of an unmade grave ; '
Not less resolved to play some desperate freak,
And stare, and terrify poor Parson Peeke !
Yet oh, vain cares, not all the fire I've felt,
' That solid, ah ! too solid flesh can melt '—
Vain is my vacant stare, my random talk,
Vain the slow grandeur of my pensive walk ;
Vain is my faded form's pathetic grace,
My hopeless, endless, comfortless disgrace !
My sallow cheek—my sad funereal air,
And deep and hollow groans, that paint the soul's despair.
Then rouse, Adair ! assume a nobler part !
Let fame, let glory, re-inspire thy heart !
Lo ! where St. Stephen's chapel greets thine eyes,
Its proudest triumphs are thine easy prize ;
There anxious ever, ever on the watch,
Each trick of singularity to catch,
To pause and bow, and every gesture ape
That art assumes in senatorial shape ;
Lend me, ye mimic powers ! your aid divine,
Each grace concentrate, and each charm combine.
Teach me, like Grey,[1] to rise, or to sit down ;
To stare like Sheridan, like Tierney frown ;

---

[1] The first Earl, then Mr. Grey.

To stoop like Wyndham, or erect, like Pitt,
Proudly take out my handkerchief, and spit ;
Or rap with all Dundas's force the box,
And shriek and scream, and almost sweat like Fox.
I fly, I fly, impetuous to town,
Pride of the Whigs, and terror of the Crown ;
Rush to the House, and furious to impeach,
Discharge at Pitt my long-projected speech.
Then, not on thee, not on my Hunloke's face,
My ardent gaze is fix'd—but on the mace ; [1]
These eyes, that wont to languish in despair,
Then flash their fire around the Speaker's chair.
And now, both sides attentive homage pay,
Sir Gregory Page [2] and Tyrwhitt Jones [3] give way ;

---

[1] " Not on the cross my eyes were fix'd, but you ;
Not grace, or zeal, love only was my call,
And if I lose thy love I lose my all."

POPE.—*Eloisa to Abelard.*

[2] Sir Gregory Page Turner, third baronet, succeeded his great uncle, Sir G. Page, in August 1795, when he added to his own the name and arms of Page. Sir Gregory was a Tory, and at the general election in 1784 was chosen member for Thirsk, in Yorkshire, which he represented up to the time of his death. He did not, however, add much to the brilliancy of the debates, and when Mr. Grey, in 1797, moved for a reform in the representation of the people, a motion that was seconded by Erskine, and supported by Fox, Sheridan, and others, Sir G. Page Turner gave it his most strenuous opposition, pathetically asserting, "that he always felt for the Constitution, and nothing else, when he got up in the morning, and when he lay down at night." His death is said to have been caused by his chagrin at not succeeding in a trial that he had with a builder, who made an iron bridge over a stream in his garden, the erection of which had been suggested to Lady Turner by a friend, and which cost nine hundred pounds. On examining his secrétaire, his executors found in it sixteen thousand seven hundred guineas. He was succeeded by his eldest son, Gregory Osborne, who had as litigious a disposition as his father, and was defeated in two celebrated trials ; one with a Mr. Stroehling, who had painted a picture for him of Daniel in the lions' den, for the sum of fifteen hundred pounds ; the other, with the Rev. Mr. Beazley, also on the subject of pictures. Sir G. Page Turner died on the 4th January 1805, at his house in Portland Place.

[3] Thomas Tyrwhitt Jones, Chancellor of the Duchy of Cornwall,

I rise, and frowning at the Treasury-bench,
Full in their view my doubled fist I clench.
Loud and more loud the opposition cheer,
Sturt [1] in the van, and Robson [2] in the rear ;
Pitt shrinks, turns pale, and trembles, as I shed
My long-stored vengeance o'er his guilty head.
Then he whose voice now melts in strains of love,
Shall call for papers, for committees move ;
Bill after bill bring in, fresh motions make,
Secure, at least, to keep himself awake ;
Or, should a tasteless audience cough and groan,
Proud to prolong their sufferings not his own ;
Heavens ! in what seas of patriot flame I'm toss'd—
How soon the lover's in the statesman lost !
Vain hopes, deceits—his heart's illusion o'er,
And thou and Wingerworth ne'er thought of more.[3] "

---

and a great friend of the late Prince of Wales. Mr. Jones was member for Bridgenorth, and created a baronet in 1808. In politics he was a Whig, and spoke often.

[1] Charles Sturt, Esq., M.P. for Bridport.

[2] Richard Bateman Robson, M.P. for Honiton, afterwards for Oakhampton ; one of the "noisy patriots" of his day, and who had the satisfaction of proving, before the House of Commons, in February 1802, that the country was insolvent; for that a Mr. Martin, another member of the House, had presented a bill at the Sick and Hurt Office, for nineteen shillings and sevenpence, which had been refused payment. He died at his house in Manchester Square, on the 10th of March 1827.

[3] Lady Hunloke died at her house in Saville Row, on the 22nd of January 1820.

CHAPTER XVI.

Charles Sturt, M.P. for Bridport—His Gallantry in Rescuing some Ship-wrecked Seamen—His Perilous Adventure and Great Presence of Mind—Mr. Sturt in the House of Commons—The young Ensign and the Town-Clerk—The Reverend Fell Akehurst—An Imaginary Address of his to the Countess of Bessborough, by Lord John Town-shend—Lines by the same Nobleman to the Memory of his Daughter—The Foreign Grave—Lord John Townshend's Death.

No man better deserves a passing biographical notice than the late Charles Sturt, formerly M.P. for Brid-port, for he was one of the most open-hearted, gene-rous, and charitable men of his day, and many were the striking incidents in his life. His large fortune enabled him to indulge such a disposition without restraint; and in the town he represented he was idolised by all classes,—more especially, however, by the blue-jackets, who would have made Bridport a most uncomfortable abiding-place to any one who said anything against him. These men looked upon him as one of themselves, for he was devotedly fond of yachting, which, from his island-castle of Brownsea, he had every opportunity of enjoying; but the adora-tion in which he was held by the sailors of the town and coast rested not only on his love of that pursuit, but the great personal courage he displayed in his impetuous desire to do good ;—he was, indeed, always "in the van," and frequently at the risk of his own life.

On the 1st of February 1799, the *Bee*, bound for the West Indies, went on shore on the sands at Poole, the wind being at east, and blowing a tremendous gale, with heavy snow. The boats of the *Tickler*, gun-brig, went off to her assistance ; they failed, however, in their attempts to reach her, and she was left to her fate ; but, in the course of the day, the crew were rescued by Charles Sturt, after having been, with his men, twice thrown from his boat into the breakers.

Eighteen months after this exploit, being out in his cutter about two leagues from shore, and sailing against Mr. Weld's yacht, off Lulworth Castle, he observed that his own boat towing astern retarded her progress, and ordered a boy to take her ashore. The sea running very high, the lad declined, as did also the men ; when Mr. Sturt, feeling it then a point of honour, immediately jumped into her : at this instant the rope gave way, and, by the force of the wind and receding tide, he was drifted to sea ; soon after which the boat upset. In this perilous situation his presence of mind did not forsake him : he regained, by swimming, his station on the keel, and pulled off all his clothes except his trousers. It was after one of the many desperate struggles that he made of the same kind, that, giving up all for lost, he wrote with a pencil on a slip of paper, which he put in his watch-case, the following words, " Charles Sturt, Brownsea, to his beloved wife," and fastened the watch to his trousers.

Shortly after, and almost by a miracle, a mate of a transport, three miles to windward, the last of several that had passed, happened to observe him, and four resolute fellows immediately embarked in a boat to his assistance ; but as there was a heavy sea running, and they could only see him occasionally, it was not till after a hard pull of nearly two hours that they reached him. Poor Sturt was all but exhausted, and on the eve of relinquishing his failing hold upon the boat, when his preservers took him into theirs : unable to articulate his thanks, he lifted his hands to Heaven, and instantaneously burst into a flood of tears. Mr. Sturt was one of those who, after the short peace of Amiens, and in violation of the acknow-ledged laws of nations, were detained prisoners in France, from which country he escaped by his own energy and enterprise.

In politics he was a Whig, and he seconded some of the late lamented Sir Francis Burdett's early motions in the House of Commons : in debate he was most vehement, and not very discreet. When Mr. Whitbread moved for a committee to inquire into the conduct of ministers respecting the French inva-sion of Ireland, his abuse of the Treasurer of the Navy was most copious. " 'The whole statement of the security of Ireland made by the honourable gentleman (Mr. Dundas)," said Mr. Sturt, "is a *mis*-statement; he hoped in God he would not have much longer the direction of naval or any other affairs. He might wriggle, and grin " (Mr. Dundas shewing symptoms of uneasiness), " and twist, and toss his head about, as much as he pleased, but he hoped it would soon be twisted somewhere else."

The Sturts were not only a gallant but a merry race, and a most laughable anecdote is told of a relation of the member's, I believe a brother, who was in the army. This young gentleman, when an ensign in the —— Regiment, was quartered at Colchester, the town-clerk of which place, a Mr. S——, was a particularly thrifty attorney, who, in the pride of his heart, had given out, not by the bellman, but next to it, that he could, would, and should give the two Misses S—— the sum of twenty thousand pounds each on their wedding-day. This want of caution, into which his vanity had betrayed him, made it necessary, as he fancied, to exclude the officers of the garrison from all participation in his hospitalities; and his extreme discretion naturally became the subject of many a joke and discussion amongst them.

In one of these mess-room gossips young Sturt, to the amazement of his companions, offered a bet that he would dine with the unapproachable treasures at their papa's own table, at a dinner-party for which they all knew that invitations had just been sent out. Of course the bet was quickly taken, and, on the day in question, young Sturt walked up to the attorney's door precisely at the dinner hour, and begged that he might see Mr. S—— on most urgent business. He was immediately admitted, for that gentleman had no idea of losing a client, though in a red coat; but he was not a little astonished when the officer gravely informed him that he was the bearer of intelligence that would save him ten thousand pounds. At this juncture, however, the dinner was announced, and Sturt, with well-feigned regret, was on the point of retiring, saying that he would call the next morning, when the bewildered lawyer, fearful of neglecting his guests, perhaps old clients, and yet distressed at the idea of losing his particulars, became totally forgetful of the dangerous chance to which he exposed the Misses S——, and pressed him to join the party. This, after proper hesitation, the ensign consented to do, and taking good care to place himself next to the forbidden fruit, made fierce love to the youngest lady and her father's oldest port during the repast.

No sooner was this over, and the gentlemen on their way to the drawing-room, than Mr. S——, now in a perfect fever, hurried the young gentleman into his private room, the door of which was scarcely closed when he exclaimed, "Well, Mr. Sturt, how can you possibly save me ten thousand pounds?" "Why, sir," said the gallant five-and-threepence (sad odds in favour of six-and-eightpence), "they say in the town that you will, on their marriage, give your daughters twenty thousand pounds apiece; now, Mr. S——, I will take either of them with ten." Tradition has not

preserved the indignant town-clerk's reply, but Sturt is
said to have lost no time in returning to the barracks
and claiming the bet. Charles Sturt, of Brownsea,
married Lady Anne Ashley, daughter of Anthony,
fourth Earl of Shaftesbury, and died May 12, 1812.

But to return from this long digression to Lord
John. To judge by the succeeding verses, it was not
unusual for him to amuse himself and his friends with
the real or imaginary flirtations of his acquaintances.
In this pastime it is highly probable that he received
every encouragement from the witty and beautiful
"rival sisters," and it is to the effect that Lady
Bessborough's transcendent charms had upon the fiery
temperament of the gentleman, in whose name he
addressed the following lines to her, that we owe this
original and extraordinary squib. In those days
there was a race of clergymen, now happily extinct,
whose unclerical habits and language were open to the
most serious animadversions from those who respected
their calling; and it is not, therefore, very surprising
if they occasionally fell under the satirical lash of a
witty man of the world, who, in all probability, would
never have exercised it upon a worthy member of the
profession. If the leading features of this pasquinade
be true, Lord John's victim had little to complain of;
still the verses would not have been introduced here
if the author had not ascertained that the reverend
gentleman, who died at Ely in 1803, left no child or
near relation to whom the publication of them would
have given pain.

On the Reverend Pell Akehurst, Rector of Buckland,
   Herts. ; and addressed to the Countess of Bessborough.

Lord John Townshend.

" Behold the fatal hour approach,—
Adieu ! the destined dilly's come ;
D——d be the dilly, curst the coach !
The coachman curst that drives me home !
And must I live,—oh, d—n the life !—
Live without you, and with my wife.
But who, my Lady, who can tell,
If you will ever think of Pell ?

Still shall I trace in dreams my fair
To operas, plays, assemblies, balls ;
How this Lord flies to find your chair,
How t'other for your footman calls.
I start, I waken at the sound,
While fancied flambeaux blaze around—
But who, my Lady, who can tell,
If you will ever think of Pell ?

When Sunday's summons claims the priest,
Far from his flock the wretch shall stray,
Where foot of man, nor foot of beast,
Or guides his step, or marks his way.
There lost, to woods and wilds he sighs ;
Here d—ns his blood, and bl—s his eyes !
But who, my Lady, who can tell,
If you will ever think of Pell ?

By verdant Jewin's silver streams,
Oft shall my listless length recline ;
While pensive memory fondly dreams,
A thousand joys that once were mine.
Tears, such as devils weep, shall flow,
With oaths that none but parsons know.
But who, my Lady, who can tell,
If you will ever think of Pell ?

Here, breathed I many an ardent vow,
Here, as you chanced—blest chance !—to pass
I said with a pathetic bow [1]—
'Miladi, voulez vous le bras ?'
Here, wooed your hand with gentle squeeze,
Here, popp'd down plump upon my knees
But who, my Lady, who can tell,
If you will ever think of Pell ?

Lo ! at your toilet as you sit,
Lordlings and embryo statesmen wait ;
There love, and politics, and wit,
In motley coterie debate !
While these young dogs, and millions more
Day after day besiege your door,
Ah ! who, my Lady, who can tell,
If you will ever think of Pell?

Think in my breast what wild despair,
What rash tumultuous passions rise !
Think of your glossy auburn hair,
Your pearly teeth, your hazel eyes !
Think how this barbarous last adieu,
Robs me of peace, of life, of you !
Think—think, but I'll be d—n'd to hell,
If you will ever think of Pell."

Such are the amusing evidences of Lord John Townshend's wit and humour that I found in Brummell's album, which are characterised by a spirit of playful rather than malignant satire. In the heyday of youth, and even in manhood, when engaged in the turmoil of politics, and surrounded by the excitements of that brilliant society by which he was courted and

---

[1] Probably Lord John was thinking of Tickell's description of him, already alluded to in this chapter.

admired, he had little time, or perhaps disposition, for reflection ; and the last preceding stanzas were no doubt written at the earlier period. But a strong contrast to them is presented in the next and last example of his poetical talent, and, greatly is the estimate that we should have formed of his character, elevated by the impression, that these lines leave upon the reader's mind ; they evince, not only how deep and sincere were his parental feelings, but also those religious ones, which, as he himself observes, were " to cheer his closing day." In the evening of life, Lord John Townshend was visited by several heavy domestic trials, having lost three children ; one of them was the godson of his friend Charles Fox, and named after him. The first of these afflictions was the death of a favourite daughter, and this melancholy event he thus feelingly records :—

" To the memory of Georgiana Isabella Townshend, who died on the 17th of September 1811, in the twenty-first year of her age.

BY HER FATHER.

" Oh ! gone for ever—loved, lamented child !
So young, so good, so innocent and mild,
With winning manners, beauty, genius, sense,
Fond filial love, and sweet benevolence ;
The softest, kindest heart, yet firmest mind ;
In sickness patient, and in death resign'd ;
Never, oh ! never yet a fairer bloom
Of opening virtues found an early tomb !
How hard thy trials, how severe thy woes,
She, she alone, thy sorrowing mother knows,

Who, three long years, with sad foreboding heart,
Bankrupt of every hope from human art,
Still wept and watch'd, and still to Heaven for aid,
Her fruitless vows with meek devotion paid.
But thou, pure spirit ! fled to endless rest,
Dear child ! my heart—Dear Bella ! thou art blest.
And oh ! the thought that we again may meet !
Oh ! not another gleam of hope so sweet
Dawns on thy father's breast with welcome ray,
To soothe his grief, and cheer his closing day. "

It was after reading this natural and affecting epitaph that the author, deeply impressed by its beauty, though unskilled in verse, wrote the following lines ; they have no poetical merit, but may meet with charitable criticism from the many, and interest the sympathies of some, who have passed through the same ordeal as himself. They commemorate the death of Edgar, who was born at Odessa, in South Russia, and died there suddenly on the 7th of March 1840.

THE FOREIGN GRAVE.

" Traveller, why shed the tear ?—the flowing sails
Are spread, and fill'd by favouring gales !
Why sad and pensive thus, when, high and bright,
Old England's cliffs rise proudly on your sight ?
When all around is gaiety and mirth,
Why listless view the land that gave you birth ?

   .   .   .   .

The Traveller paused—then on his friend, his bride,
He threw an earnest glance, and thus replied :—
' Stranger, think not that with regret I view
Those headlands bold—to England I am true !
On mouldering Rome I've gazed with deep delight,
On Marathon look'd down from dark Pentelic's height ;

And wandering on with ardour unsubdued,
Symplegades I pass'd, and Euxine rude ;
But not fair Hellas, with her southern smile,
Compares with yonder gem—our sea-girt isle.
To me that bay, that crag and inlet deep,
Are old familiar friends, yet still I weep ;
For as we journey'd, full of hope and joy,
Death cross'd our cloudless path—we lost our boy !
With aching heart, his beauteous frame I bore
To the wild steppe on bleak Odessa's shore ;
And there, where in the field of death is seen
A small enclosure, with its gate of green,
I laid him down : it was the place of rest
Of friends, who in that land I loved the best.
I look'd into the grave, the snow had drifted there ;
Oh ! what a winding-sheet for one so fair !
Though from his lips no word our ears could greet,
His glance was language, and his smile was sweet.
When last I saw his tranquil little face,
'Twas nestled in his mother's fond embrace ;
So warm, so rosy, cast in such a mould !
Now wreathed in snow, inanimate and cold.
In foreign accents rose the burial hymn ;
My eyes were fill'd—ay to the very brim—
No simple floweret decks that infant's tomb,
Nature denies the daisy there to bloom ;
But near the wall a small acacia grows,
Which o'er the grave a transient shadow throws.
No sculptured marble decorates the spot—
Think you that cherub-boy is then forgot?
Oh no ! so long as life and sense are ours,
His loss will tinge with gloom our gayest hours ;
Tombs must, like man, decay ; the foaming wave
May, in some ages hence, that churchyard lave ;
Perhaps its mounds invade, and with rude hand
Sweep every trace away, and leave a sand——
Stranger ! 'tis for my child these tears I shed ;
Our hearts are on the Euxine with the Dead !'"

Towards the close of his life, Lord John Townshend spent much of his time at Brighton, where he was greatly respected, and received many and marked attentions from his late Majesty. He died on the 25th of February 1833, in the seventy-seventh year of his age.

CHAPTER XVII.

*Estimation in which¦ Brummell was held by Clever Men—The Poet
Crabbe's Opinion of him—The Butterfly's Funeral—Brummell the
Author of it—Julia Storer—The Beau's Verses on her Child—An
Anecdote from the Clubs of London—A Rencontre between Sheridan
and Brummell—Sheridan's Fugitive Poetry—Lines Addressed to the
Countess of Bessborough—Tom Sheridan—The Loss of the Saldanha
Frigate—His Stanzas on the Event—Lines to Julia.*

THAT Brummell possessed a refined taste, not merely
in dress and manners, but on subjects more worthy of
his intellect, is proved by his being admitted on
intimate terms to the society of such women as the
late Duchesses of Devonshire and Rutland; and men
whose pursuits were of a much higher order than
those of the idlers of Watier's, or the *flaneurs* of Bond
Street and St. James's.   Had he indeed been nothing
better than an elegant automaton, he would never have
acquired the influence that he decidedly obtained; he
would not have enjoyed the society of clever men,
neither would they have thought it worth their while
to bestow a word upon him, even in their moments
of relaxation.—But the reverse was the case: his
acquaintance was not limited to men of fashion only;
it comprised a great portion of the most intellectual

men of his time, and at what period of our history was there such a constellation of genii ?

His acquirements, of which I have already spoken, were sufficient to make him a most delightful accession to any society; his reading, though desultory, was extensive, and therefore he could always, in one way or other, take a respectable, if not a leading part in conversation ;—that he showed admirable tact in adapting it to the taste of those in whose society he might happen to be, appears by the testimony of men very superior to himself. In the Memoirs of the amiable Crabbe, his son observes, that his father, when visiting at Belvoir, "was particularly pleased and amused with the conversation of the celebrated Beau Brummell." The *Quarterly Review*, also, the Medo-Persianic lawgiver of literature, and the grindstone of mental reputations, actually acknowledged that he had talent ; though it condemned him severely, and justly, for not having employed it in a more sensible and useful manner.

Of his poetry, the following are specimens. The first, The Butterfly's Funeral, does not, it is true, possess the originality of Roscoe, or Mrs. Dorset, but it is an admirable effort in the same style as their poems, to which Brummell subsequently alludes. Though familiar to, and the delight of every child, these lines have hitherto been published under feigned initials, of which " B," however, was the last letter ; but they have never been attributed to him. Mr. John Wallis, who, in 1804, first brought out this trifle, and printed three thousand copies of it, which were speedily sold, says, in his reply to my inquiry on the subject, " I cannot recollect whether I knew at the time who was the author of The Butterfly's Funeral; it is, however, very likely I may have received it direct from Mr. Brummell, for I knew, and was in the habit of seeing him, and other conspicuous characters about town, at the time I published that poem."

Brummell sent these verses to a lady at Caen, and I subjoin the following extract from the letter that accompanied them. " But to change," he says, speaking of his miseries, " this *larmoyant* egotistical strain, I will transcribe you some verses that I have omitted in my album—they are not of the gayest subject; but never mind ! they were written at the period when The Peacock at Home,[1] The Butterfly's Ball,[2] and other trifling but meritorious poetical things of the same description, were in vogue with all the world in London : the Butterfly's Funeral was then commended by good-natured friends, and, as probably you never read it, should you like it, it may meet with the same charitable eulogy from you."

THE BUTTERFLY'S FUNERAL.

" Oh ye ! who so lately were blythesome and gay,
    At the Butterfly's banquet carousing away ;

---

[1] The Peacock at Home was written by Mrs. Dorset, a sister of Charlotte Smith.

[2] The Butterfly's Ball and Grasshopper's Feast was written by W. Roscoe, Esq., for his children, and set to music by order of their Majesties for the Princess Mary, afterwards Duchess of Gloucester.

Your feasts and your revels of pleasure are fled,
For the soul of the banquet, the Butterfly's dead !

No longer the Flies and the Emmets advance,
To join with their friend in the Grasshopper's dance ;
For see his thin form o'er the favourite bend,
And the Grasshopper mourns for the loss of his friend.

And hark ! to the funeral dirge of the Bee,
And the Beetle, who follows as solemn as he ;
And see where so mournful the green rushes wave,
The Mole is preparing the Butterfly's grave.

The Dormouse attended, but cold and forlorn,
And the Gnat slowly winded his shrill little horn ;
And the Moth, who was grieved for the loss of a sister,
Bent over the body and silently kiss'd her.

The corse was embalm'd at the set of the sun,
And enclosed in a case which the Silk-worm had spun ;
By the help of the Hornet the coffin was laid
On a bier out of myrtle and jessamine made.

In weepers and scarves came the Butterflies all,
And six of their number supported the pall ;
And the Spider came there, in his mourning so black,
But the fire of the Glowworm soon frighten'd him back.

The Grub left his nutshell, to join in the throng,
And slowly led with him the Bookworm along ;
Who wept his poor neighbour's unfortunate doom,
And wrote these few lines, to be placed on her tomb :—

EPITAPH.

At this solemn spot, where the green rushes wave,
Here sadly we bent o'er the Butterfly's grave ;
'Twas here we to beauty our obsequies paid,
And hallow'd the mound which her ashes had made.

And here shall the daisy and violet blow,
And the lily discover her bosom of snow ;
While under the leaf, in the evenings of spring,
Still mourning his friend, shall the Grasshopper sing."

The succeeding stanzas were also in the album,
and Brummell asserts that they are his likewise; but
a gentleman well read in the fugitive poetry of the
last and present century, is not of that opinion, and
thinks they have been published : he referred me to
the collections of Dodsley, Nicholls, and Pearch, in
which, however, I could not find them. It might be
supposed that Brummell would scarcely have felt
sufficient interest in the subject, to take up his pen
either to transcribe or compose them ; but whether
he wrote them or not, if he only applied them to the
circumstance to which they refer, he showed some
feeling, and very good taste. He told the lady to
whom he sent a copy, that he wrote them in 1806 for
Julia Storer, whose unfortunate history I shall pass
over in silence ;—she died a few years after.

" Unhappy child of indiscretion,
     Poor slumberer on a breast forlorn !
Pledge and reproof of past transgression,
     Dear, though unwelcome to be born.

For thee, a suppliant wish addressing
     To Heaven, thy mother fain would dare :
But conscious blushes stain the blessing,
     And sighs suppress my broken prayer :

Yet, spite of these, my mind unshaken,
     In parent duty turns to thee ;
Though long repented, ne'er forsaken,
     Thy days shall loved and guarded be !

And though to rank and place a stranger
    Thy life an humble course must run ;
Still shalt thou learn to fly the danger
    Which I, too late, have learnt to shun.

And, lest the injurious world upbraid thee,
    For mine, or for thy father's ill ;
A nameless mother still shall aid thee—
    A hand unseen protect thee still.

Meanwhile, in these sequester'd valleys
    Still shalt thou rest in calm content ;
For innocence may smile at malice,
    And thou,—oh ! thou art innocent !"

But, amongst all Brummell's friends, none contributed so largely as the Sheridan family to enrich his collection of poetry ; there being in it three sets of stanzas by Mrs. Sheridan, two by Tom, and seventeen by Richard Brinsley. The following anecdote, however, taken from a work entitled, " The Clubs of London," [1] is scarcely consistent with the friendly terms on which he and Sheridan appear to have been, as shown by that paragraph of Brummell's letter, in which he mentions Sheridan as " one of those who, in other and happier days, gave him their minor productions before they had assumed any other form than that of manuscript." This author says, that " the wit, meeting Brummell one day near Charing Cross, and perceiving that he appeared anxious to avoid him,

---

[1] This is not the well-known work of the late John Timbs, "Club Life in London," which was published more than twenty years after the first edition of "The Life of Beau Brummell" had appeared.

accosted him thus : 'Ah ! Brummell, my fine fellow, where have you been at this time of day ?'

"The Prince of dandies was at first rather non-plussed, but at length drawled out, 'Sherry, my dear boy, don't mention that you saw me in this filthy part of the town ; but perhaps I am rather severe, for his Grace of Northumberland resides somewhere about this spot, if I don't mistake. The fact is, my dear boy, I have been in the d-a-mn'd City—to the Bank : I wish they would remove it to the West End, for re-al-ly it is quite a bore to go to such a place ; more particularly as one cannot be seen in one's own equipage beyond Somerset House, and the hackney coaches are not fit for a chimney-sweeper to ride in. Yes, my dear Sherry, you may note the circumstance down in your me-mo-randum-book, as a very remark-able one, that on the twentieth day of March, in the year of our Lord eighteen hundred and three, you descried me travelling from the east end of the town like a common citizen, who had left his counting-house for the day, in order to dine with his upstart wife and daughters at their vulgar residence in Brunswick Square.' When Brummell had concluded this affected rhapsody, Sheridan said—

"'Nay, my good fellow, travelling from the east ! after all, that is surely impossible ; you must be joking.'

"'Why, my dear boy, why?' demanded Brummell.

"'Because the *wise* men came from the east,' replied Sheridan.

" ' So then, s-a-r,' exclaimed the fop, ' you think me a fool, do you ? '

" ' By no means,' answered Sheridan, turning away, ' but I know you to be one, and so, good morning.'

" Brummell, like the equestrian statue just opposite to him, was struck dumb and motionless for a few seconds : at length he vociferated, ' I tell you what, my friend Sherry, I shall cut you for this impertinence, depend on't; I mean to send the Prince to Coventry for the next twelve months, and you shall accompany him.' Sheridan laughed heartily at the idea of being put under Brummell's imperial ban, and to the great amusement of the fellow of his excommunication announced to him the woful tidings the same evening."

That the first answer was really given by Brummell to some jocular remark of Sheridan's, as mentioned by the author of this work, is very possible ; but there are circumstances in the details of the narrative which cast a doubt on the genuineness of the whole story. The "dear boying," and "dear Sherrying," are not like the Beau ; nor did he ever drawl out his words, or "vociferate," in the manner here described ; and though Brummell was not able to cope with Sheridan's wit, he would never have been struck dumb and motionless (by-the-bye, this is the first time I ever saw it intimated that this statue once possessed the powers of speech and motion), or have been so simple as to place himself in a position to be called a fool ; neither is it at all credible that the orator would have made such a vulgar speech, more particularly without the slightest provocation.

The principal part of the poetical trifles that Sheridan sent to Brummell have been already published; but the following interesting fragments of the versatile genius of that clever man have not, I think, met the public eye.

R. B. SHERIDAN.

" The poorest peasant of the poorest soil,
 The child of poverty, and heir to toil,
 Early from radiant Love's impartial light,
 Steals one small spark to cheer his world of night.
 Dear spark ! that oft through Winter's chilling woes,
 Is all the warmth his little cottage knows.
 The wandering tar, who not for years has prest,
 The widow'd partner of his day of rest ;
 On the cold deck, far from her arms removed,
 Still hums the ditty which his Susan loved.
 The soldier, fairly proud of wounds and toil,
 Pants for the triumph of his Nancy's smile :
 But ere the battle, should he hear her cries,
 The lover trembles and the hero dies.
 That heart, by war and honour steel'd to fear,
 Droops at a sigh, and sickens at a tear."

TO THE COUNTESS OF BESSBOROUGH.

" When memory, chill'd by absence, shall decay,
 And love's first warm impression fade away,
 Oh ! may this sketch, with more than mimic art,
 Recall the living likeness to your heart ;
 Revive affection, threatening to decline,
 And while it pleads my faith, recover thine."

ON FEMALE INFLUENCE.

" In female hearts, did sense and merit rule,
 The lover's mind would ask no other school ;

Shamed into sense, the scholars of your eyes,
Our beaux from gallantry would soon be wise ;
Would gladly light, their homage to improve,
The lamp of knowledge at the torch of love."

TO ——.

" Dear object of my late and early prayer,
Source of my joy, and solace of my care,
Whose gentle friendship such a charm can give,
As makes me wish, and tells me how to live ;
To thee the Muse with grateful hand would bring,
These first fair flowers of the doubtful Spring.
Oh, may they, fearless of the varying sky,
Bloom on thy breast, and smile beneath thine eye,
In fairer lights their vivid blue display,
And sweeter breathe their little lives away."

TO ——.

" The stricken deer that in his velvet side,
    Feels at each step the trembling arrow play,
In shades of thickest covert loves to hide,
    And from the cruel hunter speeds away.—
But I, more wounded than the stricken deer,
    Scarce wish from my destroyer's aim to fly—
I weep, but 'tis, alas ! too soft a tear,
    And e'en my groans are mingled with a sigh."[1]

ON A CHILD.

" In some rude spot where vulgar herbage grows,
    If chance a violet rear its purple head,
The careful gardener moves it ere it blows.
    To thrive and flourish in a nobler bed.
        Such was thy fate, dear child !
        Thy opening such !

---

[1] See Pope's lines on his love for Lady Mary Wortley Montague.

Pre-eminence in early bloom was shown ;
For earth too good, perhaps,
And loved too much—
Heaven saw, and mark'd thee for its own." [1]

DELUSION, PHANTOM, AND FICTION.

" In Britain's sad hour of grief and contention,
The three new estates fairly met in convention ;
'Twas to help the poor country's distracted condition
And of royal authority make a partition.
Delusion's attorney, lest things might grow worse,
Laid claim to his houschold, his peers, and his purse :
'You're right,' exclaim'd Phantom, 'I'll serve you with zeal,
But, remember, I'm keeper of him and his seal.'
Quoth Fiction, 'My object with yours quite accords ;
So I rule the proceedings of Commons and Lords ;'
The physicians all said, the decision was fair ;
But old Anarchy swore he'd put in for his share."

The next stanzas are by Tom Sheridan, whose
name, alas ! at the moment I am writing, excites the
most melancholy reflections ; for death has recently
dealt severely indeed with his kindred. His brother,
the last of his own generation, died lately ; and in the
same newspaper was announced the death of poor
Frank, his son, the gayest, the wittiest, and the idlest
of pleasure-loving beings ; he also " has shuffled off
this mortal coil," and in a foreign country. Every
one, as I have often seen, did their best to spoil him ;
therefore it was not extraordinary that he had many
foibles ; but there was a large balance of generous
qualities in his character, which, as he was his own

---

[1] This seems a reminiscence of Mallet's ballad " Edwin and Emma,"
in which occurs the line, " Heaven saw and marked her for its own."

enemy, and never other people's, will not fail to out-
weigh the remembrance of his faults and infirmities.
Both father and son died abroad; the former, at the
Cape of Good Hope, on the 12th of September 1817;
the latter, at the Mauritius, in the autumn of 1843.

Both of these pieces of poetry, by Tom Sheridan,
who had much of the convivial wit of his father, are
of a far more original character than any verses that
Richard Brinsley ever composed. The first was
written shortly after the wreck of the *Saldanha* frigate,
commanded by the Honourable William Pakenham,
brother of the second Earl of Longford, who, with his
officers and the whole of the ship's company, amount-
ing to three hundred men, were lost off the coast of
Ireland, on the night of the 4th of December 1811.
The *Saldanha* was a new frigate, one of the finest in
the navy, and her commander, a rising officer of the
highest character, was only in his twenty-ninth year.
This dreadful catastrophe is thus recorded in the
Annual Register :—

" RATHMILTON, *December the 6th.*—His Majesty's
ship, *Saldanha*, Captain the Honourable William
Pakenham, sailed from Cork on the 19th of November, to relieve H.M. ship *Endymion*, off Lough Swilly;
and having reached that harbour, she, with the
Endymion and *Talbot*, sailed on the 30th inst., with
an intention, it is said, of proceeding to the westward;
on the 3rd of December it blew very hard from the
north-west; the wind continued to increase till the
4th, and in the evening and night of that day, it blew

the most dreadful hurricane that the inhabitants of this part of the country ever recollected. At about ten o'clock at night, through the darkness and the storm, a light was seen from the signal-towers, passing rapidly up the harbour, the gale then blowing right in. This light, it was supposed, was on board the *Saldanha ;* but this is only conjecture ; for, when the daylight discovered the ship a complete wreck in Ballyna Stokerbay, on the west side of the harbour, every soul on board had already perished, and all knowledge of the circumstances of her calamitous loss thus perished with her." The bodies of Captain Pakenham and two hundred of the crew were washed ashore, and the only living thing that escaped on this dreadful occasion is said to have been a parrot, belonging to one of the officers.

THE LOSS OF THE *SALDANHA*.

T. SHERIDAN.

" ' Britannia rules the waves :'
    Heard'st thou that dreadful roar ?
    Hark ! 'tis bellow'd from the caves
    Where Lough Swilly's billow raves,
    And three hundred British graves
        Taint the shore.

No voice of life was there,
    'Tis the dead that raise the cry ;—
The dead, who heard no prayer,
    As they sunk in wild despair,
Chaunting in scorn that boastful air,
        Where they lie.

' Rule Britannia,' sung the crew,
　When the stout *Saldanha* sail'd ;
And her colours, as they flew,
　Flung the warrior-cross to view,
Which, in battle, to subdue
　　　　　　Ne'er had fail'd.

Bright rose the laughing morn,
　That morn that seal'd her doom ;—
Dark and sad is her return,
　And the storm-lights faintly burn,
As they toss upon her stern,
　　　　　　'Mid the gloom.

From the lonely beacon height,
　As the watchmen gazed around,
They saw their flashing light
　Drive swift athwart the night ;
Yet the wind was fair, and right
　　　　　　For the Sound.

But no mortal power shall now
　That crew and vessel save ;
They are shrouded as they go
　In a hurricane of snow—
And the track beneath her prow
　　　　　　Is their grave.

There are spirits of the deep,
　Who, when the warrant's given,
Rise raging from their sleep
　On a rock or mountain steep,
Or 'mid thunder clouds, that keep
　　　　　　The wrath of Heaven.

High the eddying mists are whirl'd,
　As they near their giant forms ;
See their tempest flags unfurl'd !
　Fierce they sweep the prostrate world ;
And the withering lightning's hurl'd
　　　　　　Through the storm.

O'er Swilly's rocks they soar,
　　Commission'd watch to keep ;
Down, down with thundering roar
　　The exulting demons pour—
The *Saldanha* floats no more
　　　　　　On the deep !

The dreadful hest is past,
　　All is silent as the grave,
One shriek is first and last—
　　Scarce a death-sob drank the blast,
As sunk the quivering mast
　　　　　　'Neath the wave.

' Britannia rules the waves ; '
　　Oh vain and impious boast !
Go, mark, presumptuous slaves,
　　Where He who sinks or saves,
Scars the sands with countless graves,
　　　　　　Round your coast."

The following are on a very different theme, and
in striking contrast to the preceding.

TO JULIA.

" Since you will needs my heart possess,
Julia, 'tis just I first confess
　　The faults to which 'tis given ;
It is much more to change inclined
Than restless seas or raging wind,
　　Or aught that's under Heaven.

Nor will I hide from you the truth,
It has been from its very youth
　　A most egregious ranger ;
And, since from me it oft has fled,
With whom it was both born and bred,
　　'Twill scarce stay with a stranger.

The black, the fair, the gay, the sad,
It is so very, very mad,
   With one kind look can win it ;
By nature 'tis so prone to rove,
'Twill quit success, for change, in love,
   And what's more, glories in it.

And now, if you dare be so bold,
After the truths that I have told,
   To like this arrant rover ;
Be not displeased, if I confess
I think the heart within *your* breast
   Will prove just such another."

CHAPTER XVIII.

Other Contributors to Brummell's Scrap Book—Lord Melbourne—His Lines on the Bust of Fox—The Dream—Translation of an Ode from Anacreon—The Honourable George Lamb—The Robber's Good-Night—R. Payne Knight—The Yellow Leaf—George Canning—His Squib on Mr. Whitbread's Speech at the Impeachment of Lord Melville—The Duchess of Gordon's Salute—Mrs. O'Neill— Stanzas by that Lady.

AMONGST the long list of distinguished persons who sent *vers de société* to Brummell, Lady Dacre, Lady Granville, and Lord Melbourne, are the only three individuals who now survive, and consequently the only persons to whom it was necessary to apply for permission to publish these evidences of their taste and accomplishments.[1]   The reply that I received from Lord Melbourne was couched in terms of amiable circumspection, and perfectly in accordance with his known good-nature; he says, "I can have no objection to your inserting any poetry of mine in your intended work, which you think may add to its interest, provided there be in it nothing discreditable to the writer, nor injurious to the feelings of others; on

---

[1] None of these "distinguished persons" is alive at the time (1885) this new edition is published.

both of which points, you will exercise a sound discretion." No objections of this nature can possibly
be urged against the first, or the three succeeding
trifles from his lordship's pen : they were probably
written very early in life, and had been the elegant
occupation of leisure hours passed, in reality, by the
side of the tranquil Cam ; but, in imagination, repos-
ing on the banks of some streamlet wild in the classic
island of Cythera. His lordship had, however, even
at this time, not only distinguished himself by his
classical, but by other and more solid attainments ;
and perhaps, the most flattering testimony of this was
given by Fox, when he made his celebrated speech
on the death of his friend the Duke of Bedford—one of
the finest declamations of the heart ever made within
the walls of the House of Commons. On that memorable occasion, he finished his painful task by introducing the following passage from the Essay of William
Lamb, " Sur l'Avancement Progressif de l'Esprit
Humain ; " recited at the University of Cambridge in
December 1798 : " Le crime n'est un fléau que pour
le temps où le succès le couronne, tandis que la vertu,
soit qu'elle triomphe soit qu'on la persécute, est un
bienfait du ciel, non seulement pour l'âge ou nous
vivons, mais pour la postérité la plus reculée ; elle
sert au bonheur des hommes, dans le moment présent
par ses actions, et dans l'avenir par ses exemples."
Lord Melbourne's admiration for this great, though
unsuccessful, statesman, is powerfully and simply expressed in the following apostrophe to his bust.

ON THE BUST OF CHARLES JAMES FOX.

" Live, marble, live ! for thine's a sacred trust,
The patriot's name that speaks a noble mind ;
Live, that our sons may stand before thy bust,
And hail the benefactor of mankind !
This was the man, who, 'midst the tempest's rage,
A mark of safety to the nation stood ;
Warn'd with prophetic voice a servile age,
And strove to quench the ruthless thirst for blood.
This was the man, whose ever deathless name
Recalls his generous life's illustrious scenes ;
To bless his fellow-creatures was his aim—
And universal liberty his means ! "

The three succeeding pieces were also from his lordship's pen.

THE DREAM.

" Hide, Sun, thy head ! delay thy light,
And yield to Love's befriending night
    Some portion of thy sway ;
I would not change the airy form,
Which seems to meet me kind and warm,
    For all the blaze of day.

In vain I sue—stern Fate denies :
My slumbers break, the Vision flies,
    I lose my Laura's charms ;
That taper waist, that bosom fair,
Dissolving into empty air,
    Eludes my eager arms.

No wretch, his day of respite done,
Who sees his last uprising sun
    And only wakes to die,

Curses the light with so much pain,
And weeps, and sighs to sleep again,
  So ardently as I.

Invidious light! my hated bane,
Why rudely break the ideal chain
  On which my raptures hung?
I saw sweet Laura's angel grace,
My eyes were fix'd upon her face,
  My soul upon her tongue.

Her rosy lips I seemed to press,
Nor seemed the maid my fond caress
  By frowns to disapprove;
I heard her voice so sweet, so clear,
Sound music to my ravish'd ear,
  For it express'd her love.

Smile, then, sweet Laura! let me find,
For once, reality as kind
  As golden visions seem;
For it has been my lot to rue,
That all my sorrows still were true,
  And all my joys a dream."

The following ode was translated by a Mr. Shepherd
—see the "Poetical Register" for 1810—or rather do
not see it, for the translation is sadly inferior.

TRANSLATION FROM ANACREON,

WHO CALLS UPON SOME EMINENT ARTIST TO PAINT HIS MISTRESS.

Αγε, ζωγραφων αριστε·
γράφε,ʹζωγράφων αριστε.

"Come, Painter, who with skilful hand
 Canst rival even Nature's art;

Come, Painter, draw, as I command,
   The absent mistress of my heart.

Paint first each soft and jetty tress,
   With which her graceful head is crown'd ;
If colours can so much express,
   Oh ! paint them breathing odours round.

Above her cheek, full, lovely, fair,
   Where modest blushes reddening glow,
Beneath her mildly curling hair,
   Describe with skill her ivory brow.

Ah ! how to imitate her face
   Thy chiefest science will be tried ;
Between her brows the middle space
   Nor quite confound nor quite divide.

Here let the eyelid's lash be shown ;
   Here let her semblance bear complete,
Dark arching eyebrows like her own,
   Which meeting, scarcely seem to meet.

But, Painter, do not here forget
   To give her eye its native flame,
Azure, Minerva-like, and yet,
   As melting as the Paphian dame.

Her nose and cheek then fashion well—
   That white as milk, and roseate this :
Her lips, like soft Persuasion's swell,
   Pouting and challenging the kiss.

Beneath her chin, where dimples play,
   About her neck of Parian stone,
Let all the Loves and Graces stray ;
   That happy spot is all their own.

But oh ! those beauties of my fair,
   Which I alone must e'er reveal,
Come, Painter, with the strictest care
   Beneath the purple robe conceal.

Yet sometimes let the skin of snow
  Through the thin garment's covering shine,
And faintly tell what beauties glow
  Unseen by any eyes but mine.

Enough, enough ! upon my sight
  Her charms with dazzling lustre break ;
She seems to breathe ! with fond delight
  I pause, for she ere long will speak."

―――――――――

" Come, Painter, Love demands thy care,
  Thy strongest, brightest powers command,
Thy most unfading lines prepare,
  Thy finest eye, and happiest hand.
For though I oft have seen to grow,
  Beneath thy touch, the mimic face ;
Have seen thy magic pencil throw
  Upon the canvas living grace ;
This task must e'en thy labour foil,
  Unequal all thy skill must prove ;
This task will mock thy utmost toil,
  I think thou canst not paint my Love.
Thy pencil—thine alone—may reach
  The charms that fav'ring beauty gave,
And thou, like her, perhaps, may'st teach
  The cheek to blush, the hair to wave ;—
But ah ! a lover more requires
  Than waving hair, and blushing cheeks ;
He asks the idea his flame inspires,
  The form that lives, the face that speaks :
He asks that brow that teems with sense,
  The feature with expression fraught ;
The eye that beams intelligence,
  The pregnant glance, and silent thought.
He asks that lip that seems to swell
  With love it does not dare reveal ;
He asks that eye that fears to tell
  The pleasing tale it can't conceal.

> Oh ! couldst thou trace the gentle heart,
> As in her features it is shown !—
> But here, unpractised in thy art—
> That charm, my Love, is thine alone ! "

There were two or three other fragments of Lord Melbourne's poetry ; and one of them, written in his brother's pocket-book, after Mr. Lamb had recovered from a dangerous illness, offers a pleasing testimony of the friendship that existed between them. This gentleman, well known to the world as the author of a translation of Catullus, appears also to have added several pieces of his composition to Brummell's collection ; and the following very original song is the happiest effort amongst them. At the period of his death, which took place in London on the 23rd of January 1834, in the forty-ninth year of his age, Mr. Lamb was Under Secretary of State for the Home Department.

THE ROBBER'S GOOD-NIGHT.

GEORGE LAMB.

> " The goblet is empty, and toll'd are the chimes,
> Sleep hides from mankind both its sorrows and crimes ;
> And, in quiet repose till the dawning of day,
> The guilty and honest, the wretched and gay.
>
> The guilty can sleep, though terrific, 'tis said,
> The dreams and the ghosts that encircle their bed ;
> But he who a victim's last curses can bear,
> Will not shrink from the bodiless spectres of air.
>
> The wretched can sleep, for the bosom is worn,
> The heart has grown dull with the weight it has borne ;

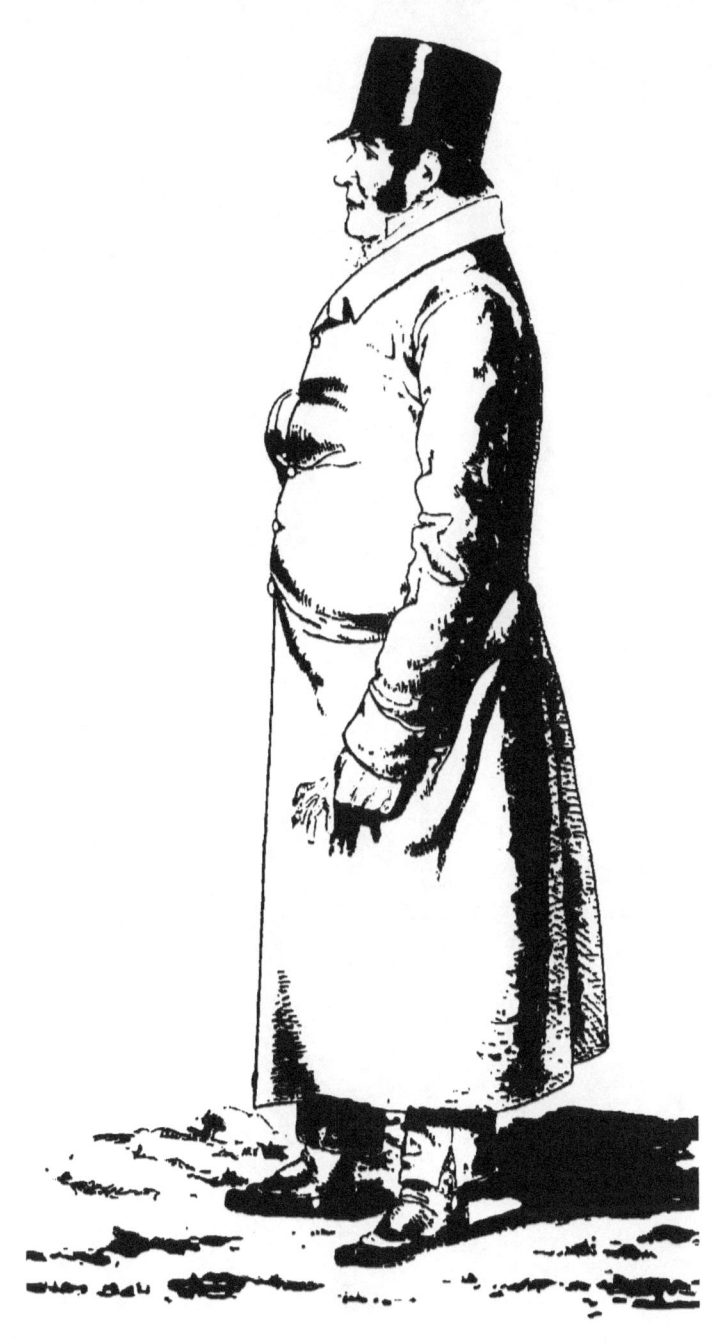

The Honble George Lamb

More sweet are the visions in slumber that live,
Than the mournful realities daylight can give.

Yes ! the goblet is drain'd, and its floods in their course
Have drown'd all reflection, regret, and remorse ;
And shall spread o'er my pallet as tranquil a rest,
As the moralist paints on the couch of the blest."

There were likewise the following verses by Payne
Knight, the author of "Taste," and one of the most
eminent Greek scholars of his day. At his death,
which took place at his house in Soho Square, on the
28th of April 1834, he bequeathed his collection of
medals, drawings, and bronzes, worth more than thirty
thousand pounds, to the British Museum. Amongst
the drawings was a volume of Claude's, for which Mr.
Knight gave sixteen hundred pounds to a person,
who, a few days before, had purchased it for three
pounds !

THE YELLOW LEAF.

R. P. KNIGHT.

" Round flew the bowl, the laugh rose high,
Whilst summer's richest canopy,
The wedded boughs of emerald dye,
      Was all our shade.

So soft the air, so gay the plain,
Though August's moon was in her wane,
We said that summer's verdant reign
      Would never cease.

High rose the laugh, the transports swell,
When sudden, potent as a spell,
Detach'd by no rude zephyr, fell
      One yellow leaf !

The mirth was hush'd, the songsters' lays
Broke short ; and each in solemn gaze
Hung on the leaf, nor dared to raise
            A timorous eye ;

Each fear'd, upon the other's face
His own sad feelings writ, to trace,
As the pale emblem spoke the race
            Of summer run.

It seem'd some fairy, throned in air,
Had mark'd our bliss, and pausing there,
Dismiss'd a monitor to bear
            Truth to each heart,

To tell us that the scene might glow,
But soon should change in cheerless snow,
To tell us that our bliss should know
            An autumn too.

That joys but coming sorrow speak,
As calms precede the tempest bleak,
That death his surest victim's cheek
            With roses paints.

Yes, in that moment, on that day,
Reflection stole my smiles away ;
And, like him, weeping to survey
            His myriad bands,

Methought, ere many a year goes round,
Few may, of us, who on this ground
Now gaily revel, few be found
            To meet again.

The young before the old may go ;
And he who bids this measure flow
May fall, perhaps, the first, to show
            This moral true."

I will close this chapter with the following lines of
George Canning's and some by Mrs. O'Neill, also from
the scrap-book : the former do not certainly impair
the force and truth of Mr. Lockhart's remark on his
satirical powers. "No man," he says, "ever possessed a gayer wit in society than he did ; his lash
fetched away both skin and flesh, and would have
penetrated the hide of a rhinoceros :" it would indeed
have penetrated the hide of that animal, and tanned.
I have not found these lines amongst Canning's published poems. They were written on Mr. Whitbread's
speech at the opening of the impeachment of Viscount
Melville in 1805, of which trial Chief Baron Thompson
observed, that he had "heard of an 'impeachment of
waste,' but that these proceedings were, in his humble
opinion, a waste of impeachment." Many were the
droll stories that the amiable old judge had to tell
of this trial, and that of the famous one of Warren
Hastings ; at which he used to assure his delighted
listeners, the juniors of the bar, that his Brother
Gould, when proceeding with great solemnity to take
his place at the spot appointed for the judges, sat
down on one of the heralds,—who was so disguised
by his tabard, that he mistook him for a state chair !

GEORGE CANNING.

"I'm like Archimedes for science and skill,
I'm like a young princess that went up a hill ;
And, to interest the hearts of the fair, be it said,
I'm like a young lady just bringing to bed.

Would you know why th' eleventh of June I remember,
Much better than April, or March, or November ?
'Twas because on that day ('tis with pride I assure ye)
My sainted progenitor took to his Brewery.
That morn he began his first brewing of beer,
That evening commenced his connubial career :
On that day he died, having finished his summing,
And the angels cried, 'Look! here's old Whitbread a-coming.'
So that day I hail with a smile and a sigh,
For his beer with an E, and his bier with an I.
And on that day each year, in the hottest of weather,
The whole Whitbread family feast altogether.
My Lords, while the beams of this hall shall support
The roof which o'ershades this respectable court
(Where Hastings was tried for oppressing the Hindoos),
While the beams of the sun shall shine in at the windows,
My name shall shine bright, as my father's now shines,
Emblazon'd on Journals, as his is on Signs."

A most extraordinary and touching circumstance
closed the proceedings of this trial, which, however it
may have flattered Lord Melville, did not perhaps
afford him such unalloyed gratification as it did amusement to his brother peers.   It is said that when his
acquittal was pronounced, the eccentric Duchess of
Gordon, his countrywoman, rose from her seat, and
with a warmth of feeling, which made every particular
hair of his lordship's ermine stand on end, rushed
forward and kissed him !—exclaiming, in no very
subdued tone, "Weel, my lord, I'm very glad to see
that we have at least one honest mon in this hoose."

Henrietta Boyle, the authoress of the amusing
verses that conclude this chapter, born in 1758, was

the only daughter of Charles, Viscount Dungarvon, eldest son of John, fifth Earl of Cork. On the 18th of October 1777, she married John O'Neil, Esq., of Shanes Castle, near Antrim, in the streets of which town he was cruelly and brutally piked by the rebels in 1798.

Mrs. O'Neill.

" Ere raging seas between us roll,
Oh come and soothe my tortured soul !
    Return once more to me ;
Come, and each anxious fear remove,
Speak peace, and tell me that you love,
    And bid me live for thee.

Come, and my wayward fancy cheat,
Persuade me by some dear deceit
    That long I shall not mourn ;
Calm all my woes, subdue my sighs,
By some sweet lawful perjuries,
    And be for once forsworn.

Swear, that ere three eternal weeks,
You'll kiss the tear from off my cheeks,
    Though you mean twice the time ;
Swear, that for worlds you would not be.
Another day or hour from me,—
    Love will absolve the crime."

Mrs. O'Neill died on the 3rd of September 1793, and her husband was created a peer on the 30th of November following. This accomplished lady wrote some interesting poetry, amongst which, under the name of Geraldine Verney, was an Ode to the Poppy, originally printed in her friend Charlotte Smith's novel of " Desmond," and subsequently in the Rev. A. Dyce's " Specimens of British Poetesses."

CHAPTER XIX.

"Wales, ring the bell"—The Real Delinquent—Brummell's Quarrel with the Prince of Wales—Causes that Led to it—Ben and Benina —Mrs. Fitzherbert—The Beau's Impudence—" Who's your Fat Friend ? "—Brummell's Intimacy with the Duke of York—Letters from the Duchess to Brummell—Her great Partiality for Dogs— Fête at Oatlands—The Duke's Reply to his Servant—A Pastoral Dialogue by R. B. Sheridan—The Right Honourable George Rose.

NOTWITHSTANDING the great disparity of rank, the intimacy that was formed between Brummell and the Prince of Wales continued for some years uninterrupted. He was a constant guest at Carlton House, and was distinguished by many marks, never pecuniary ones, of his royal friend's partiality for him. At length however a rupture took place, but it was not caused by the circumstance to which it is usually attributed. The story of "Wales, ring the bell!" was always denied by Brummell: indeed he seemed indignant at its being generally credited; and I have heard him, in explanation of the subject, say, "I was on such intimate terms with the Prince, that if we had been alone I could have asked him to ring the bell without offence ; but with a third person in the room I should never have done so ; I knew the Regent too well."

The vulgar impudence of the action itself, without Brummell's denial of it, makes the anecdote extremely improbable ; and he was also too good a judge of his own interests, to run the risk of being turned out of the Prince's society for the mere fun of enacting such a piece of tomfoolery.

Another version of the story is, that one evening, when Brummell and Lord Moira were engaged in earnest conversation at Carlton House, the Prince requested the former to ring the bell, and that he replied without reflection, " Your Royal Highness is close to it ; " upon which the Prince rang the bell and ordered his friend's carriage, but that Lord Moira's intervention caused the unintentional liberty to be overlooked.

This act of folly has, and I believe with more truth, been attributed to a young relation of Captain, after-wards Admiral Payne's,[1] and under circumstances far more creditable to the Prince's good taste and good feeling. Admiral Payne, a wit and *bon vivant*, was comptroller of the household ; and owing to the position he occupied, and his intimacy with the Prince, this lad, a midshipman in the navy, was sometimes asked to dine at Carlton House. Of course, boy-like, he boasted of the honour in the cock-pit ; and one day, when rallied by his companions on the extremely

---

[1] John Willett Payne was a Rear Admiral of the Red, Vice Admiral of the coasts of Devonshire and Cornwall, Treasurer of Greenwich Hospital, and Lord Warden of the Stannaries ; he died on the 17th of November 1803.

easy terms that he represented himself to be upon with his royal friend, he made a bet, that, the next time he dined with the Prince, he would tell him to ring the bell. A few days after he was again invited to Carlton House, and having primed himself with champagne, actually did ask the Regent to ring the bell. His Royal Highness immediately complied, and when the page in waiting, or some other subordinate, made his appearance, said good-humouredly, "Put that drunken boy to bed."

Brummell, as well as his friends, attributed his quarrel with the Prince of Wales to a series of sarcastic remarks, in which he had indulged at the expense of Mrs. Fitzherbert; indiscretions that he was led into by foolishly espousing the part of a noble lady, her rival; but his talent for ridicule once enlisted in her cause, he did not spare even the Prince himself. There was at that time a burly porter at Carlton House, nicknamed "Big Ben," who was so tall that he could look over the gates, and as the Regent was then increasing in size, Brummell often designated the master, by the appellation of the servant —and Mrs. Fitzherbert, by that of "Benina."[1] It is also said, that he annoyed her by various remarks of the same kind; and that, when desired by the Regent at a ball at Lady Jersey's to call her carriage, he obeyed, but in doing so, substituted the word *mistress* for the usual one of Mrs., and laid a strong emphasis on the insulting epithet. If this anecdote is true, no

[1] See Vol. II., Appendix.

wonder that when it came to the lady's ears, as well
as the Prince's, with the allusions to their *embonpoint*
(upon which subject they were, as people frequently
are, extremely sensitive), such ill-timed jokes were
resented ; and that Brummell was dismissed :—he
always, however, considered that the continuation of
the Regent's anger was owing to Mrs. Fitzherbert,
whose absurd vanity in identifying herself with the
Crown of England—for it was that or nothing—made
her peculiarly unforgiving on this subject ; and her
dislike to Fox renders it probable that Brummell's
opinion was correct. Moore, however, in a parody on
a celebrated letter from the Prince Regent to the
Duke of York, on the 13th of February 1812, gives
the former the credit of all the indignation against
Brummell, and adduces another well-known *mot* of
the Beau's as the reason of it.

" Neither have I resentments, nor wish there should come ill
   To mortal, except, now I think on't, Beau Brummell ;
   Who threatened last year, in a superfine passion,
   To cut me, and bring the old King into fashion."

But, whatever the causes of offence may have been
that led to the quarrel, the Beau treated the affair
with his usual assurance ; and waging war upon his
royal adversary, assailed him with ridicule in all
quarters, and affected to say, that he had himself cut
the connection : it was in this spirit, no doubt, that
he said to Colonel McMahon, "I made him what he
is, and I can unmake him." Of course, after this
break, the Regent determined to take advantage of

the first opportunity that occurred, of showing the
world that he was no longer anxious to continue the
acquaintance. An occasion for his so doing presented
itself not long after in a morning walk, when the
Prince, leaning on Lord Moira's arm, met Brummell
and Lord Alvanley, coming in the opposite direction,
and, probably with the intention of making the cut
more evident, His Royal Highness stopped and spoke
to his Lordship, without noticing the Beau—little
thinking that he would resent it ; great therefore must
have been his surprise and annoyance, as each party
turned to continue their promenade, to hear him say
in a distinct tone, expressive of complete ignorance of
his person, " Alvanley, who's your fat friend ? "[1]   But
Brummell was sometimes in a humour to adduce other
reasons than the right one for the *fracas* which led
to his final rupture with the Regent, and the favourite
fiction that he then palmed upon his most eager
listeners was, that they had been rivals in a love
affair, in which the Prince was of course the unsuccessful suitor.

When Brummell found that His Royal Highness
had really closed the doors of Carlton House against
him, he cultivated with greater assiduity the friendship that had always existed between himself and the
Duke of York, who was never known, in good or ill
report, to desert a friend ; and his conduct, and that
of the Duchess, to the Beau in his exile, were striking instances of the steadiness and sincerity of their

[1] See Vol. II., Appendix.

friendship. "The Duchess," says Mr. Raikes, "was a person of excellent taste, and a very nice discriminator of good breeding and manners, and the regard which that Princess entertained for Brummell was highly creditable to him. It may, indeed, be said in favour of the manners of that day, that Her Royal Highness often remarked how superior they were to the tone of those that existed at the period of her marriage, when the Duke was surrounded by a set of *roués* who seemed to glory in their excesses, and showed a great want of refinement and courtesy in women's society. At the time Brummell visited at Oatlands, England had been for many years without a Court, and the limited circle that surrounded the Duke and Duchess of York, though differing scarcely from that of a private family, rendered it the only royal residence that was the scene of constant hospitality ; and it might have been appropriately termed a little Court, in which the affability on the one side, and the affectionate defer-ence on the other, were equally remarkable. Here used to assemble, at the end of the week, Brummell, and all the most agreeable men of the day, intimately acquainted with each other, and sincerely attached to their royal host and hostess."

I am ignorant of the precise dates at which the two following notes from the Duchess to Brummell were written ; but they were copied by myself from her autograph, and are inserted as a proof that he must have stood high in her esteem, and that she corresponded with, and received him, on the most

intimate footing. The first was written to acknow-
ledge the receipt of a note announcing the loss of a
lottery-ticket, which they had purchased together : the
paragraph alluding to the chances of his future life is
happily expressed, and the sincerity of the concluding sentence was fully proved in after-years, by her
generous conduct towards him when she had the pain
of seeing that her good wishes turned out unavailing.

"OATLANDS, *ce* 20 *Septembre*.

"Vous avez une manière si aimable d'annoncer les
plus mauvaises nouvelles, qu'elles perdent par là de
leur désagrémens ; je ne puis cependant que m'affliger
avec vous de la perte de tous nos beaux projets de
fête, qui s'évanouissent avec la perte de notre billet de
loterie, dont je vous acquitte la dette ci-joint, en y
joignant les vœux les plus sincères que ceci puisse
être le dernier mauvais tour que la Fortune puisse
vous jouer, et que dans toutes les autres circonstances
de votre vie, elle puisse toujours vous être favorable.
Ce sera me rendre justice que de vous persuader que
personne ne peut s'intéresser plus sincèrement à votre
bonheur et à tout ce qui vous concerne.

"Je n'ai rien à vous dire de ma solitude qui puisse
exciter votre curiosité, n'y ayant vu personne *de ceux
qui vous* intéressent depuis votre départ. J'espère que
vous reviendrez bientôt dans ces contrées, et qu'il me
sera permis de vous réitérer moi-même ici les assur-
ances de l'amitié sincère et de la considération parfaite
avec laquelle je suis.—Votre toute affectionnée amie et
servante,   F."

The next note from Her Royal Highness was to thank him for remembering her fête-day, and sending her a beautiful little dog, which Brummell, with his usual good taste, had selected for his present in preference to anything else, knowing the passion his royal friend had for that animal. Her Royal Highness is said to have had at one time upwards of one hundred dogs at Oatlands, and she sometimes erected monuments over her special favourites; they are grouped round a fountain in the grounds in front of a grotto, to which, during the summer months, she frequently retired with her work or a book. It is, I believe, near this spot that the inhabitants of the parish in which Oatlands is situated erected a monument to the memory of this amiable woman, to which the humblest amongst the parishioners spontaneously requested permission to contribute their mite.

"WINDSOR, *ce neuf de Mai.*

"On ne saurait être plus sensible que je le suis au souvenir obligeant que vous avez bien voulu me donner au jour de ma fête, et au charmant cadeau que le Duc m'a remis de votre part. Recevez mes remercimens les plus sincères pour ce joli petit *chien,* c'est l'emblême de la *Fidélité;* j'aime à me flatter qu'elle sera celui de la continuation de notre amitié, à laquelle je vous assure que j'attache le plus grand prix.

"J'ai une toux de *cimetière* qui menace ruine; si elle ne m'a pas mis sous terre avant le commencement du mois prochain, je compte me rendre à Londres, dans ce temps-là, et un des motifs qui me fait envisager avec le plus de plaisir ce séjour est qu'il me procurera l'avantage de vous y rencontrer et de pouvoir vous réitérer moi-même combien je suis. — Votre toute affectionnée amie et servante,   F."

Though the parties at Oatlands were generally, as I have before remarked, of a very unostentatious character, the Duchess's birthday was sometimes celebrated with great splendour, particularly the one of 1811, of which I have heard Brummell speak. The King and Princesses were present, and, after they left, the park-gates were thrown open to the public, consisting principally of the tenants and labourers in the neighbourhood, who assembled in the lower part of the house. Here tables were laid out with refreshments, which were soon cleared; and the punch, six quarts of which were placed upon each, having freely circulated, at nine dancing commenced, the Duchess leading off the first dance, called the Labyrinth, with Colonel, now General, Upton.

It was by these unaffected examples of hospitality that the Duke endeared himself to high and low about him; and the numerous instances on record of his generous disposition, more particularly when in command of the army, and his unvarying anxiety to promote the comfort of the most subordinate member of it, have rendered his memory dear to the service, and completely effaced the recollection of his failings. Very many are the anecdotes related of the unpre-

H.R.H.The Duke of York.

meditated proofs of his kindness of heart, and ready consideration for his inferiors in station; but every soldier should know the following one,—and every insolent lackey too. The Duke was on the point of mounting his horse one day at Oatlands, to take a ride, when, observing a poor woman slowly retreating from the door, he enquired of the servant who she was? The fellow flippantly replied, "Nobody, your Royal Highness, but a soldier's wife, a-begging." "And, pray, sir," said the Duke indignantly, "what is your mistress?" It is needless to add, the poor woman was relieved.

In Brummell's album are several interesting souvenirs of his visits at Oatlands, written by Sheridan and Lord Erskine, who very likely gave them to him as having also been a guest on the occasions to which they refer. They are pleasing instances of the cheerful and friendly feeling that existed amongst those who enjoyed the Duke's hospitality; and it was probably after one of these brilliant and agreeable parties, that Sheridan wrote the following admirable and good-humoured quiz upon Erskine, which, though satirical, is much too harmlessly witty to have offended the ex-Chancellor. There was no date attached to it, but it was evidently written after that nobleman resigned the seals, and previously to May 1812, as Mr. Perceval, who is mentioned in it, was assassinated in the lobby of the House of Commons on the 11th of that month.

THE EAGLE AND THE WREN,

OR,

THOMAS AND RICHARD.
(*Erskine.*)   (*Sheridan.*)

A PASTORAL DIALOGUE.

R. B. SHERIDAN.

Where Oatlands' lofty bank, in sylvan pride,
Looks o'er the Thames and the fair prospect wide,
There is the spot where once two shepherds stood,
Safe from the river's fast-encroaching flood ;
Fictitious shepherds, true, and eke 'tis truth,
Swains not exactly in the bloom of youth ;
Yet both had skill to talk, and verse could scan,
And now in measured rhyme their converse ran ;
While Thomas clear'd his pipe, sly Richard thus began :—

RICHARD.

How could'st thou, Thomas, at the festive board,
Admitted guest of Oatlands' royal lord,
Decline the challenge which I gave to thee
To break a lance in sportive poesy ?
Thou know'st, ere now we've tried the gay dispute,
Unvanquish'd then, how could'st thou now be mute ?
Unstudied verse might royal care beguile,
And raise on listening beauty's cheek a favouring smile.

THOMAS.

Friend Richard, well I saw your treacherous aim.
You sought to triumph, and bring me to shame ;
To make a boast in royal beauty's eyes
You dared the contest, and you hoped the prize ;

By nature dull, by art a rhymer made,
Verse your profession, poetry your trade.
I, bred to nobler purposes, disdain
A puny contest with the scribbling train ;
And though I sometimes condescend to rhyme,
When humour prompts, and business grants me time,
I never publish—do you ask the cause?
I'm quite contented with my own applause.

RICHARD.

Nay, Thomas, hold ! for now, by Heaven, you wrong
The taste of friendship, and thy power of song ;
For who has read a line that bears thy name,
Which, though withheld by thee from vulgar fame,
Taste would disown, or genius fail to claim?

THOMAS.

Thy praise, dear Richard, is no doubt sincere,
But justest praise may yet be bought too dear ;
Practised in jingling verse, you know your power,
I, the chance poet of an idle hour,
With thee in verse will battle, when George Rose [1]
Shall hate employment, and demand repose ;

---

[1] The Right Honourable George Rose, son of the Rev. David Rose,
of Lethnet, and descended by his father from an ancient family in
Nairnshire, was born on the 17th of June 1744. At the early age of
four years he was brought to England, where he was educated, and
rose to distinction entirely through his own exertions. One of the
first patrons of this leviathan of industry was Brummell's father, who
from his position in the Treasury was of great service to him in for-
warding his interests. The following is an epitome of his lucrative
and honorary occupations. In 1767, he took a principal share in the
publication of the Journals and Records of Parliament, from the
earliest period : in 1772, he was appointed to the Keepership of
Records in the ancient Treasury at Westminster : in 1776, he was
appointed Secretary to the Board of Taxes : in 1782, he was named
Secretary to the Treasury under Lord Shelburne, and Pitt ; was re-

When Trotter [1] shall the prince of lies outfib,
And Spencer Perceval [2] shall challenge Cribb ;
An eagle you, from your own wing your pen
You draw—then bravely challenge a poor wren !

RICHARD.

Nay, Thomas, sure this flattery's unfit,
Or wish you irony to pass for wit ?

---

moved on the change of Government in the spring of 1783, and re-
appointed under Pitt in the December following. In this year he
also obtained a reversionary grant of the office of Clerk of Parliament.
In 1784, he was elected M.P. for Launceston, and in 1788 he vacated
that seat, on succeeding to the above-mentioned office, and was returned M.P. for Lymington. In 1790, he sat for Christchurch. In
1801, he resigned his Secretaryship of the Treasury, and in 1804, on
Mr. Pitt's return to power, was appointed Joint Paymaster-General of
the Forces, and Vice-President of the Committee of Privy-Council for
the Affairs of Trade, which he retained till the death of that Minister.
In 1807, under the Duke of Portland, he was appointed Treasurer of
the Navy, and re-appointed Vice-President of the Board of Trade.
He was likewise a Privy-Councillor, Trustee of the British and
Hunterian Museums, an Elder Brother of the Trinity House, Deputy
Warden of the New Forest, and one of the Verderers of the same.
Under these circumstances it is wonderful the Honourable Gentleman
did not "demand repose." Sir George Rose died at his seat, Cuffnells,
near Lyndhurst, on the 13th of January 1818, in the seventy-fourth
year of his age.

[1] John Barnard Trotter, Esq., Private Secretary to C. J. Fox, of
whose life and career he published a very strange account. This work
drew forth some strong animadversions from different writers, and
among the rest, Dr. Moseley, who decidedly contradicted the author
with respect to the medical treatment of the illustrious statesman. It
is probably to Mr. Trotter's book that Sheridan alludes, and to the
proverbial saying, " He lies like the d——l."

[2] A specimen of Sheridan's drollery ; for this unfortunate gentleman
was particularly thin, and slightly formed, and not exactly the person
who might be expected to throw down his glove to the Champion of
England.

Your simile forego,—I dared the test,
Not who was strongest, but whose muse was best ;
To cover your retreat retract your theme,
Who hears an eagle's voice must hear a scream ;
Quick then, dear Tom, some new allusion bring,
Till wrens bear thunderbolts, and eagles sing.

THOMAS.

By heavens ! I do my lofty spirit wrong,
To grate this jarring pipe with thee so long :
Hast thou not known me in my hour of pride,
When at the bar I led the legal tide?
Who could more surely, by each trick and fudge,
Humbug the jury, or browbeat the judge?
How many patriots [1] has my fluent tongue
Lifted to glory, who had else been hung !
While, advocating freedom's sacred cause,
I won the mob, and gain'd each jail's applause—
Proving the right of treason to upset the laws.

RICHARD.

Nay, not so warm, my dearest Thomas, pray.
I grant your merit, and grant all you say ;
Thou hast indeed saved many of the gang,
Who in return would gladly see thee hang.

THOMAS.

Richard, I scorn thy taunts and wiliest sneers ;
The merit's mine, the ingratitude is theirs.
But, grant my labours no due thanks obtain'd,
Can you forget the higher post I gain'd ?
Must I remind you of the seal I bore,

---

[1] Lord Erskine defended Lord George Gordon, Horne Tooke,
Hardy, and Thelwall.

The wig and golden tassell'd robe I wore,
The flowing train behind, and broider'd purse before?
Now, by these glorious honours, which again
I surely shall possess—(though God knows when),
In verse with thee I never will contend,
Unless I choose the theme   .   .

RICHARD.

.   . .   Agreed, my friend.

THOMAS.

Then will I sing to our great Master's praise.

.   .   .   .

CHAPTER XX.

A Dinner Party at Oatlands—Lord Erskine's description of it in Verse
—The Company present—Colonel ¿Armstrong—The Honourable
William Spencer—Monk Lewis—Kangaroo Cooke—Lady Anne
Culling Smith—Miss Fitzroy—Colonel de Lancey Barclay—
Brummell—Le Chevalier Cainea—Lord Erskine's Childhood—One
of his Letters written from School—Goes to Sea in the " Tartar"—
Letter to Lord Cardcross from Jamaica.

THIS challenge of Sheridan's seems to have had its
effect upon Lord Erskine on the 31st of December
1812, on which day, in compliance with the good old
custom of seeing the Old year out and the New year
in, a dinner party was given at Oatlands ; and this he
afterwards described in the following lively and agreeable manner.

LORD ERSKINE.

" The fair Princess[1] sat first, far the highest in place,
But her rank in eclipse by good-nature and grace—
Her manners no court upon earth could bestow,
To the best of all hearts their perfection they owe ;

---

[1] Her Royal Highness Frederica Charlotte Ulrica Catharina, Princess Royal of Prussia, married to the Duke of York, on the 29th of
September 1791, and died at Oatlands, on the 6th of August 1820,
in the fifty-fourth year of her age.

And her converse, so pleasant, so keen, so refined,
No reading could give—its bright source is the mind ;
Her elegant form gives a life to the whole ;
Coalition complete of the body and soul.
Next, Armstrong[1] was seated ; on Armstrong depend,
For wit as companion, for truth as a friend ;
As a man of the world he's completely at ease,
No effort he makes to amuse or to please ;
Yet is sure to do both, with his manners so quiet,
Sliding in better things than many who try it.
To Armstrong next sat, my friend William Spencer ;[2]
Why Spencers such poets are, I would fain ken, sir ;
I hate all monopolies—never was seen
Such a fuss as we had, with the famed ' Faerie Queen.'
Ere England had numbers, this bard took the lead,
And wrote like an angel when few men could read.
Thus centuries pass'd ; and now when Old Time
Has exalted our language, and fashion'd our rhyme,
William Spencer runs in, other poets before,
To witch us as Edmund has witch'd us of yore ;
And yet not content with this talent divine,
Whenever he *speaks*, he must sparkle and shine.

---

[1] Lieut. Colonel James Armstrong, originally in the Tenth Foot, and subsequently in the Ceylon and 50th Regiments, was at this time an aide-de-camp of the Duke of York's. He died on the 15th of August 1828.

[2] "Polished William Spencer, the Poet of society," as he was usually called, was the second son of Lord Charles Spencer, by the Honourable Mary Beauclerk, daughter of Lord Vere, and sister of Aubrey, fifth Duke of St. Albans. The first of Mr. Spencer's Poetical Works, and published in 1790, was a translation of Bürger's Leonora, embellished by his aunt Lady Diana, the wife of Topham Beauclerk, a great macaroni in his day. Subsequently to this, he wrote a Drama called Urania, or the Illuminé ; it was performed at Drury Lane, with some applause, and his friend Lord John Townshend wrote the prologue. In 1811, he published a collection of Poems which were dedicated to Sarah, Lady Jersey. This accomplished gentleman, one of the most agreeable dining-out men of his day, died at Paris, on the 23rd of October 1834.

But to make such a picture as friendship would draw,
You must lend me, dear Spencer, your pen or your jaw—
Each a capital prize to a man of the law.
‘ Other poets,’ cried Lewis,[1] who sat next beside,
‘ Who shoulder us thus, may all evils betide !’

---

[1] Matthew Gregory Lewis, born in London in 1773, was the son of
a large West Indian proprietor, at one time Under Secretary at War.
Educated at Westminster, he afterwards travelled on the Continent,
and remained some time in Germany, where he imbibed that excessive
love of the marvellous, which he afterwards displayed in his works ;
exhibiting all the fantastic vagaries of his Teutonic models, in addition
to the wildness, originality, and license of his own ideas. He had
talent, but it was of an illegitimate and unhealthy description ; and
his novel and nickname, “ The Monk,” by which he acquired an infamous
notoriety, and which on account of its licentiousness was very popular
with a certain class, will be a lasting monument of his depraved taste
—lasting, because society will never be without readers who delight
in works of that character ; and in this respect he lives for posterity,
a posterity of demireps and courtesans, inexperienced youth and
debauchees. Mr. Lewis was a senator, as well as a novelist ; but
seldom took part in the business of the house, and never made a figure
in it. The notoriety that he succeeded in obtaining by his works, a
superficial skill in poetry, and great conversational powers, his wealth
and the letters M.P., enabled him to insinuate himself into the society
of people of rank. He was a constant visitor of the Princess of Wales
at Kensington House, and, as seen by this poem, an occasional one at
Oatlands ; where he made himself agreeable to Her Royal Highness,
by writing elegies and epitaphs on the death of her dogs, and possibly
birthday odes when they were living. In the periodicals of the day,
and particularly in a satirical poem, published in 1802, Mr. Lewis and
his works are severely criticised, and the author concludes his censures
with these two lines :—

“ That the man who to talent makes any pretence
Should write not at all, or should write common sense.”

In fairness, however, it ought to be mentioned, that his friend Mr.
Galt says, in the “ Diary illustrative of the Times of George the Fourth ”
that he possessed generous and noble feelings, and talents of a very
high description. Lord Byron, another intimate friend of his, observes,

But Lewis all earthly approach may defy ;
As a canonised monk he may mount to the sky ;
No, no, we can't spare his original brain,
Which has led us so often in Fancy's fair train ;
The scenes that surround us so dully the same,
Who shifts with his genius well merits his fame.
Next to Lewis there sat, would you wish to know who ?
I will tell you—my worthy good friend Kangaroo ; [1]
He who goes by a name by parents not given,
Depend on't is one highly favour'd by Heaven ;

---

that he was a "*good* man, a clever man, but a bore. My only revenge or consolation used to be setting him by the ears with some vivacious person who hated bores—especially Madame de Staël, or Hobhouse, for example. But I liked Lewis, he was the jewel of a man, had he been better set ; I don't mean *personally*, but less *tiresome*, for he was tedious, as well as contradictory, to everything, and everybody. Poor fellow ! he died a martyr to his new riches—of a second visit to Jamaica.

> ‘ I'd give the lands of Deloraine,
> Dark Musgrave were alive again.’

That is—

> ‘ I would give many a sugar-cane
> Mat Lewis were alive again !’ ”

But it is not easy to reconcile these opinions with the spirit of Mr. Lewis's works, which deliberately tend to debase the human heart, always sufficiently prone to error and infirmity. The most correct view of the Monk's character appears to have been taken by Madame de Staël, who wittily and piquantly remarked, that he was not only "*inférieur, mais très inférieur*."—Mr. Lewis died at sea in 1818.

[1] Major-General Henry Frederick Cooke, C.B. and K.C.H., commonly called Kang-Cooke—a portrait of whom, under that sobriquet, is to be found in Dighton's caricatures, was at this time a captain and lieutenant-colonel in the Coldstream, and aide-de-camp to the Duke of York. Various rumours have been circulated to account for his name having been thus humorously associated with the mammalia of New Holland. One is that he let loose a cage full of these animals at Pidcock's menagerie ; another, that on being asked by his old patron, the Duke of York, how he fared in the Peninsula, replied that he

The friend whom we love we mould at our pleasure,
And count on his temper, the best of all treasure ;
Since in spite of the misanthrope's sullen pretence,
Good-nature is still the companion of sense.
Thus take the world o'er, you will find very few
Who have more of sound brains than this same Kangaroo ;
And as for his person, his breeding, and taste,
They speak for themselves, so I pass on in haste.
By this Colonel sat one, in gay circles well known,
Yet, who see him in rounds of amusement alone,
Know little about him—they see him at ease,
A high man of fashion, with talents to please ;
But believe me, in London to rise to the top,
Like Brummell (since London discarded the fop [1]),
You must know all that's known to the highest in place,
And possess the rare gift to give knowledge a grace.
But why should the muse, his acquirements to show,
Fly to commonplace truths which the vulgar well know?
Since the brighter the emerald the duchess now wears,
The higher of course is the polish it bears.
Oh what shall I write ? next him sat Lady Anne,[2]
How shall I describe her ? describe her who can.
When I think on her face ev'ry thought's at an end ;
And my numbers must flow as their chances may send,—
Her eye, full of fire, passes through to the heart,
As Wellington sees through his ranks at a dart ;
But a truce is soon put to this turbulent pother,
By the chain-shot of wife tied together with mother ;
Each beauty-bred wish she's for ever annulling,

"could get nothing to eat but kangaroo." General Cooke died on the
10th of March 1837, at Harefield Park. He was the last surviving
brother of Lieutenant-General Sir George Cooke, K.C.B.

[1] Probably some *passé* dandy about town.

[2] This lady was the only daughter of Garrett Wellesley, second
Lord Mornington, and sister of the late Marquis Wellesley. Her
ladyship was born on the 13th of March 1768, married first, Henry
Fitzroy, third son of Charles, Lord Southampton, and subsequently,
on the 9th of August 1799, Culling Charles Smith, Esq.

All lost in her daughters, and Frederick,[1] and Culling.[2]
Well, I thought myself safe, and that nought could annoy
One pass'd through this furnace,—but Madame Fitzroy ![3]
A plague on such king-craft, renew'd the temptation,
With beauty new hatch'd in the fifth generation.
Ah Stuarts ! I feel in the depth of my soul,
The madness that led ye from loyal control ;
The child of your blood, I renounce your command,
The people's free Brunswicks shall reign in this land ;
Yet still, like a traitor, my fair Caroline,
Your subject I live, as *your* right is divine.
Halt, blundering muse, to the right-about face,
You have pass'd over Barclay,[4] go back to his place ;

---

[1] Frederick William Culling Smith, only son of Culling Charles Smith, Esq., and Lady Anne, and a godson of the Duke of York. On the 18th of January, 1820, he was appointed to an ensigncy in the Coldstream Regiment of Guards, and subsequently obtained a troop in the Blues, in which corps he remained till 1826, when he received an unattached majority, and afterwards joined the 80th Regiment. To the deep regret of his family and friends, Major Smith died at Malta, on the 19th of June 1828, in the twenty-seventh year of his age.

[2] Culling Charles Smith, Esq., father of the above, and son of Charles Smith, Esq., Governor of Madras, who was a younger brother of Culling, the first baronet of that family.

[3] Anne Caroline, daughter of Henry Fitzroy, third son of Charles, Lord Southampton, and Lady Anne Wellesley, afterwards Lady Anne Culling Smith. Henry Fitzroy's father was a great-grandson of Henry Fitzroy, first Duke of Grafton, and, through him, descended from the unfortunate House of Stuart—his Grace having been the illegitimate child of Barbara Villiers, Duchess of Cleveland, by Charles the Second. The cleverness with which Lord Erskine maintains his political principles, and at the same time indulges his gallantry, is very amusing. Miss Fitzroy died on the 16th of December 1835.

[4] De Lancey Barclay, C.B., another aide-de-camp of the Duke of York's, and one of the most popular men in the army. He was at this time in the Royal Corsican Rangers, and died very suddenly of a cold, caught by travelling too lightly clad on the top of a coach. Colonel Barclay was in the Guards at Waterloo ; and, at the period of his death, which took place on the 28th of March 1826, he was one of the aides-de-camp to George the Fourth.

You sure must have seen him, so handsome, so tall,
A straighter has never sprung up since the Fall ;
Better fashion'd without, nor freer within
From malignant ill-nature's original sin.
Him famed in our armies one day we shall see,
Though a Barclay, a Quaker he never will be.
What sounds melt on air ? sure I'm raised to the skies !
What harmony swells on the senses and dies ?
Then rises again and pulls at the heart
With strong chords of Nature, made stronger by art.
Can this be a dream ? No, La Cainea[1] appears ;
The music I thought must be his, or the spheres'.
What again ? have the fairies encircled me round,
And carried me off to their spell-bedew'd ground ?
Do I hear Catalani, or is it a thrush,
In spite of the winter, that sings from his bush ?
No ; those beautiful sounds so novel, so true,
Discover their author ; yes, Mercer,[2] 'tis you :
Yet think not their notes which yet dwell on the ear,
Are all we enjoy when their sources are here.
No—they heighten their value in these social hours
By taking their parts in the mind's higher powers :
Miss Muse, you seem tired, but remuster your pith,
For, next, sat the man of my heart, Culling Smith.
His friendship I've tried, and for ever have found
His soul as sincere as his judgment is sound ;
To look at him now, so sprightly, so gay,
As airy and light as a bird on the spray,

---

[1] Le Chevalier Cainea, a celebrated amateur Italian singer, who resided in England for several years at the commencement of the present century. He was a frequent guest of the first families in the country, as well as at the Duke of York's. His voice was a beautiful tenor, and his style of chamber-singing replete with taste and feeling.

[2] A gentleman who moved in this circle of society, also an excellent singer.

You would think him but made for the joys of the table,
And that all we have heard of grave parts was a fable—
But let Downing Street tell, which has seen him so late,
Alas ! snatch'd away by a too-fickle fate,
How he showed himself form'd for the business of state ;
Quick, active, intelligent, full of resource,
In manner all mildness, in matter all force.[1]
Tom Erskine sat last—sailor, soldier, and lawyer,
A cross, beyond doubt, between the de'il and old Sawyer ;[2]
He tried all the tricks of the old common law,
Till to Chancery sent, which can cure every flaw :
So merrily, merrily, let him live now,
With the planters of trees and the holders of plough."

By two autograph letters of Lord Erskine's now in
my possession, the first of which was written when
he was only twelve years of age, it appears that he
was at school at St. Andrews ; and as trifling circumstances connected with the childhood of such a distinguished man cannot fail to interest the reader, I have
given the letters a place here. Their introduction
is the less abrupt, as they will in some measure
illustrate the allusion made to his own life in the
words "sailor, soldier, and lawyer ;" for a paragraph
in the first seems to account for the early predi-

[1] The allusion which Lord Erskine here makes to the part Mr.
Culling Smith took in public life, refers to the period when he was
Under Secretary of State to his brother-in-law, the late Marquis
Wellesley, at the time Minister of Foreign Affairs.

[2] Sir Robert Sawyer was Attorney-General in the reign of Charles
the Second. When the attack was made on the Charter of the City
of London, ballads were sung about the streets comparing him to the
devil. His daughter and heiress married Thomas, eighth Earl of
Pembroke, and by him had issue Henry, the ninth Earl. She died
in 1706.

lection he displayed for a seafaring life; this was probably acquired in his visits to the captains of the Norway galliots that he speaks of, or in his walks about the quays of the good city of St. Andrews.

/

ST. ANDREWS, *August* 11, 1762.

" MY DEAR BROTHER,[1]—I received your letter, and it gave me great joy to hear that you were in health, which I hope will always continue. I saw in the papers that you have got a new cousin, by your commander, Major Seton,[2] marrying Miss Murray, of Abercarney. I am in my second month at the dancing-school; I have learned Shantrews and the single hornpipe, and I am just now learning the double hornpipe. Our school has the vacation just now : we got them on the 4th day of August, and all the boys that live in the country have gone home. There is a pretty large Norway ship in the harbour : the captain took Harry[3] and me into the cabin, and entertained us with French claret, Danish bisket, and

---

[1] David Stewart, Lord Cardross, Lord Erskine's eldest brother, afterwards eleventh Earl of Buchan. His Lordship was at this time a Lieutenant in the Thirty-second Regiment, which he joined as Ensign on the 2nd of August 1761. He retired from the army in 1763, and died in 1829. ''Lord Buchan's political career," says Sir Egerton Brydges, "commenced under the patronage of the great Earl of Chatham, in the diplomatic department; but he passed the larger portion of his life in literary retirement, cultivating the muses, and occasionally laying before the public the fruits of his acquirements."

[2] Also in the Thirty-second Regiment, and afterwards Lieut.-Colonel.

[3] The Hon. Henry Erskine, the celebrated advocate, and an elder brother of Lord Erskine.

smoak't salmon; and the captain was up in the town seeing papa to-day. He intended to go out that day or the next, if the wind was favourable; but he had not water enough to carry him out. He is to sail on Friday, because the stream is great.

"Yesterday I saw Captain Sutherland, a nephew of Lord Duffus[1] his lady, who has a lieutenant's commission in Lord Sutherland's militia, exercise his party of Highlanders, which I liked very well to see. In the time of the vacation Harry and me writes themes, reads Livie and French with Mr. Douglas between ten and eleven. Papa made me a present of a ring-dial, which I'm very fond of, for it tells me what o'clock it is very exactly. You bid me, in your letter, write you when I had nothing better to do; but I assure you I think I cannot employ myself better than to write to you, which I shall take care to do very often.

"Adieu, my dear brother, and believe me to be, with great affection, yours,

"THOMAS ERSKINE."

In this letter, which is a correct copy of the original, a martial spirit is also observable, and the future sailor and soldier alike peep forth : the note

[1] Eric Sutherland, called Lord Duffus by courtesy, being the son of Kenneth, third Baron Duffus, a distinguished naval officer, who was attainted after the rebellion in 1715. Eric died in 1768, having failed to reverse his father's attainder. He married his cousin, Elizabeth, daughter of Sir James Dunbar, of Hempriggs. The title was restored in 1826.

is written very neatly with lines, and in a plain
schoolboy's hand, and considering the age of the
embryo Chancellor of England, the mistakes of ortho-
graphy and grammar are not to be complained of;
there was, however, very little or no punctuation, a
point on which Mr. Douglas, probably, did not care
to weary his spirited and clever pupil. Two years
after this capital specimen of his epistolary powers
was written, young Erskine went to sea in the
Tartar, with Commodore Sir John Lindsay,[1] which
was ordered in the first instance to Pensacola, in the
Gulf of Mexico, and subsequently to Jamaica, from
whence the following letter was despatched to his
brother :—

" KINGSTON IN JAMAICA, *July* 1764."

" MY DEAREST CARDROSS,—I wrote to you about
ten days ago, giving you some small account of what
I had seen here. I am still with Dr. Butt, but
shall sail now in about ten days ; he is appointed .
Physician General to the Militia of the Island of
Jamaica, by his Excellency Governor Lyttleton,[2]
whom I waited upon at Spanish Town, along with
the doctor, some days ago. He is a very affable

---

[1] Sir John Lindsay, K.B., died at Marlborough House, on his way
to Bath, June the 4th, 1778, aged fifty-one years.

[2] Sir William Henry Lyttleton, elevated to the Peerage of Ireland,
in July 1776, by the title of Baron Westcote, and afterwards to that of
England by that of Lord Lyttleton, which title had expired with his
nephew and predecessor. His Lordship was Governor of South
Carolina in 1755, of Jamaica in 1760, and Envoy Extraordinary and
Minister Plenipotentiary to the Court of Portugal, in 1776. Lord
Lyttleton died in September 1808.

and agreeable man, as I ever saw, and one of great
learning. The longer I stay in the West Indies, I
find the country more healthful, and the climate more
agreeable ; I could not help smiling when Mama
mentioned in her letter, how much reason you had
to be thankful, that you gave up your commission,
or you would have gone to the most wretched climate
on the earth. I don't know indeed, as to the rest
of the West Indian Islands, but sure I am, if you had
come here you would have no reason to repent it.
To be sure, to stay here too long, might weaken
a constitution, though hardly that ; but to stay here
some time is extremely serviceable. As for me, I
have great reasons to like the West Indies ; I have
never had an hour's sickness in them, never enjoyed
better spirits, and found in them so good a friend as
ever I desired to meet with, as I mentioned in my
last letter. She supplies the place of mother when
at a distance from all my relations, and behaves to
me in every respect better than many relatives, whom,
from their kindred to my parents, ought to do ; that
is a great advantage, especially when one is in a
foreign country.

"I suppose you will by this time be thinking of
going abroad, as it draws near the time you intended
going : I suppose you will go first to Italy. Remember to write to me from these places ; you will have
many opportunities when you are in Portugal, or
Spain, as they have great trade with the West Indies ;
so that I expect you won't forget the poor Pots, for I

assure you, he always dearly remembers his own Cowly.

" I begin now to draw indifferently : I am studying Botany with Doctor Butt, so I will bring you home drawings of all the curious plants, &c., &c., and everything that I see. I have sent Mama home a land turtle, to walk about Walcot garden ; it is very pretty, particularly its back, which is all divided into square lozenges, and the shell is as hard as a coat of mail. If you have got anything that you wish to send me, you need only direct it to Dr. Butt in the same manner you direct letters, and put it into a merchantman bound for the West Indies, and it can't fail coming safe. Doctor Butt desires his best compliments to you, and will be obliged to you, if you will send him out such a profile of you as you copied from Mr. Hoar's. Pray give my compliments to all, and know and believe me to be, my dear Cardross,

" Your affectionate brother,

" THOMAS ERSKINE."

Both these letters evince an affectionate, studious, and active disposition, and, from the young sailor's having been made an acting-lieutenant by Sir John Lindsay, it is only reasonable to suppose that he did not abandon his profession on account of either inefficiency or insubordination : this decided step was, however, taken by Erskine soon after Sir John was relieved by Commodore Johnson, and the cause which led to it was said to be the harsh conduct of his new commander.

CHAPTER XXI.

*Lord Erskine Enters the Army—His Slow Promotion—Leaves the Service
—Enters at Cambridge—His great Admiration and Friendship
for Fox—Lines written by him at Oatlands on receiving from the
Duchess of York a Lock of that Statesman's Hair—Lord Byron—
Two Fragments of his Unpublished Poetry—Stanzas on the Murder
of Mr. Weir, by the Rev. J. Mitford—The Younger Brother's Claim
—Les Mille Colonnes—Epigrams.*

AFTER his return home, young Erskine tried the sister
service, and on the 1st of September 1768 obtained
an Ensign's commission in the second battalion of the
First, or Royal Regiment of Foot, most of the officers
of which corps, as well as the Colonel, John Duke of
Argyle, were his countrymen.   In this regiment he
remained seven years, having been promoted in 1770,
at the early age of twenty, to the rank of Benedict,
and to a licutenancy on the 21st of April 1773.

It was possibly this slow promotion which induced
Lieutenant Erskine to quit the army two years after,
added to the encomiums that his talents elicited from
clever and intellectual men ; which possibly encouraged
the idea, that he might distinguish himself in an arena
more suited to his genius.   Dr. Johnson, when on his
tour in Scotland, and at the time sixty-three years of

age, dined at Sir Alexander Macdonald's, where, as
Boswell says, "was a young officer in the regimentals
of the Scots Royals, who talked with a vivacity,
fluency, and precision so uncommon, that he attracted
particular attention; he proved to be the Honourable
T. Erskine, youngest brother to the Earl of Buchan,
who has risen into such brilliant reputation at the bar
of Westminster Hall. Erskine told us," says Boswell,
"that when he was in the island of Minorca, he not
only read prayers, but preached two sermons to the
regiment;" on which Mr. Croker observes, "Lord
Erskine was fond of this anecdote; he told it to me
the first time that I had the honour of being in his
company, and often repeated it, with an observation
that he had been a sailor and a soldier, was a lawyer
and a parson; the latter he affected to think the
greatest of his efforts, and to support that opinion
would quote the prayer for the clergy in the Liturgy,
from the expression of which he would (in no commendable spirit of jocularity) infer, that the enlighten-
ing them was one of the greatest marvels 'which
could be worked.'"

This anecdote completes the illustration of the line,

"Tom Erskine sat last—sailor, soldier, and lawyer,"

with the addition of another profession; and as Lord
Erskine, in his letter to his brother, says that he
"studied botany with Dr. Butt, the Physician-
General," it is not impossible that he practised under
him, and took a degree. This would establish his

credit to a very extraordinary claim—that of having belonged to all the "liberal professions," and would account very satisfactorily for his having so heartily espoused the Whig cause.

After retiring from the army, Mr. Erskine went to Cambridge, and was called to the bar in 1778; in 1783 he was made King's Counsel, and in 1806 appointed Lord-Chancellor. The change of his uniform for a silk gown did not, however, annihilate his military feelings, for during the war he was Colonel of the Law Association Volunteers; and it was while in command of this distinguished corps, at a review in Hyde Park, that he gave one of the many amusing proofs of his talent for repartee. It was the King's birthday, and the royal cavalcade having passed down the line, the Duke of Cambridge fell back and spoke to Erskine, saying, "How well your corps behaves! are they all lawyers?" "Yes, sir," he replied; "and some of them very good lawyers too." "And good soldiers," said the Duke; "for how silent they are!" "Yes," said Erskine; "but does your Royal Highness recollect that we have no pay?"

Lord Erskine had not lost his military spirit at the age of sixty-five, for, in one of his letters, written from the Continent in July 1815, he observes, "As soon as I return you shall have an account of my tour with the army in France, and going with it to Paris: we shall have peace at last." "Neither Lord Erskine's conversation," writes Mr. Croker, "(though, even to the last, remarkable for fluency and vivacity)

nor his parliamentary speeches, ever bore any proportion to the extraordinary force of his forensic
eloquence. Those who only knew him in private, or
in the House of Commons, had some difficulty in
believing the effect he produced at the bar. During
the last few years of his life his conduct was eccentric,
and justified a suspicion, and even a hope, that his
understanding was impaired." Eccentric he certainly
was towards the close of his life. A friend of mine
met him one afternoon walking in the Park, accompanied by his little dog (that, with reverential feeling,
he had christened after the great orator of his party),
and asked him what had been going on in the House
of Lords the night before? when he replied, "Oh, it
was all G—d d—n butter and Ireland. Fox, Fox,"
he continued, as he walked on, whistling to his four-
footed representative of Charles James, " Fox, Fox,"
&c. Lord Erskine's attachment to the memory of his
friend was very great, and the following lines, also in
the Beau's collection, were written by him, at Oatlands, on receiving a lock of his hair from Her Royal
Highness the Duchess of York :—

> "Could reliques, as at Rome they show,
> Work miracles on earth below,
> This hallow'd little lock of hair
> Might soothe the patriot's anxious care ;
> Might, to St. Stephen's chapel brought,
> Inspire each noble, virtuous thought
> With which its echoing benches rung,
> Whilst thunders roll'd o'er Fox's tongue ;—
> Alas ! alas ! the vision's vain !
> From the dark grave none come again.

That spirits wait on human weal
Is but the dream of holy zeal ;
Yet, not for that less dear should be
Whate'er may lift my mind to thee ; —
And this shall tell beyond the grave,
The head that bore, the hand that gave !"

It is singular, considering the number of witty but
briefless barristers, which either an increase in the
population and therefore in their own numbers, or a
disinclination to employ them, has left in the enjoy-
ment of learned leisure, that not one of them should
have amused himself and others with the biography
of their great model, and collected the *jeux d'esprit*,
impromptus, and other memorials of his humour and
talent, with which he used to " humbug the jury, and
browbeat the judge."   The description of the dinner-
party at the Duke of York's is an interesting specimen
of the light and lively spirit which, at sixty-two years
of age, animated this great advocate's leisure hours,
after his retirement from public life.   His egotism,
which has so often been complained of by his contemporaries, and which has been alluded to by
Sheridan in " The Eagle and the Wren,"

" I'm quite contented with my own applause,"

is certainly not perceptible in that poem.   Lord
Erskine seems to have been amiably occupied in
selecting topics for praise in others, instead of extort-
ing their admiration for himself, which he is represented by Lord Byron to have done, to a most unpleasant degree, in the summer of the very same

year. They were dining together at Middleton, Lord
Jersey's, and, in Byron's words, "amongst a goodly
company of lords, ladies, and wits, &c., there was
. . . ., Erskine too! Erskine was there, good, but
intolerable. He jested, he talked, he did everything
admirably, but then he would be applauded for the
same thing twice over; he would read his own
verses, his own paragraph, and tell his own story
again and again, and then the ' Trial by Jury,' I
almost wished it abolished—for I sat next to him at
dinner. As I had read his published speeches, there
was no occasion to repeat them to me." Lord Byron,
who was only twenty-five years of age when he made
this flippant remark, appears to have dwelt frequently
and severely upon this point of Lord Erskine's character, for he says—" March 6th, 1814. On that day
I dined with Rogers : Sheridan told a very good story
of himself and Mademoiselle Recamier's handkerchief:
—Erskine, a few stories of himself." If Lord Erskine
was vain, which appears to be universally admitted,
he had at least good grounds for being so ; though
not on account of his poetry—very nearly all that
Lord Byron had to be proud of; and this he was, as
Lucifer himself : had he lived to Counsellor Ego's age,
he might possibly have talked over Childe Harold
and The Corsair till his hearers were sick of listening
to him. In his youth the noble Poet was certainly
not deficient in anxiety for praise, as his actions,
and talented lampoon upon better men than himself,
though not such clever poets, fully attest. Brummell

was very intimate with Lord Byron: he not only speaks of him in the letter which accompanied his album, when he presented it to his young friend, but also in another, given towards the close of this memoir. In that, he alluded to a correspondence that existed between them " in our familiar days ; " and as the two following pieces of his Lordship's poetry, taken from the album, are not printed in the latest edition of his works, I venture to hope that they have never been published.

TO ONE WHO PROMISED ON A LOCK OF HAIR.

LORD BYRON.

" Vow not at all, but if thou must,
Oh ! be it by some slender token :
Since pious pledge, and plighted trust,
And holiest ties, too oft are broken.
Then by this dearest trifle swear,
And if thou lov'st as I would have thee,
This votive ringlet's tenderest hair
Will bind thy heart to that I gave thee."

TO ———.

LORD BYRON.

" Go — ! triumph securely—the treacherous vow
Thou hast broken, I keep but too painfully now ;
But never again shalt thou be to my heart
What thou wert—what I fear for a moment thou art :
To see thee—to love thee—what heart could do more ?
To love thee—to lose thee, 'twere vain to deplore !
Ashamed of my weakness, however beguiled,
I shall bear like a man what I feel like a child.
If a frown cloud my brow, yet it lours not on thee ;
If my heart should seem heavy, at least it is free :

But thou, in the pride of new conquest elate,
Alas ! even envy shall feel for thy fate.—
For the first step of error none e'er could recall,
And the woman once fallen for ever must fall ;
Pursue to the last the career she begun,
And be false unto many, as faithless to one ;
And they who have loved thee will leave thee to mourn,
And they who have hated will laugh thee to scorn ;
And he who adored thee—must weep to foretell
The pangs which will punish thy falsehood too well."

The following stanzas, certainly possessing as much originality as any that have yet been given, were the last that Brummell inscribed in his common-place book. They must have struck his fancy much, for it was evident, by the carelessness of the writing compared with every other piece in the book, that he had long ceased to make any additions to it. In them the author apostrophises the bird of night, on the subject of Weir's murder, by the cold-blooded villain Thurtell, in Gill's Hill Lane, near Elstree, Herts, on the evening of the 24th of October 1824. The principal features of this notorious crime are dexterously introduced, and the reader may fancy the feathered witness of it, one of the owls in Der Frei-schutz, who, with dilated eye and waving wings, relates the dark horrors he beheld.

ON WEIR'S MURDER.

Rev. J. Mitford.

" Owl ! that lovest the boding sky !
    In the murky air
    What saw'st thou there ?
For I heard through the fog thy screaming cry.

' The maple's head
Was growing red,
And red were the wings of the autumn sky ;
But a redder gleam
Rose from the stream
That dabbled my feet as I glided by ! '

Owl ! that lovest the stormy sky !
Speak ! oh speak !
What crimsoned thy beak,
And hung on the lids of thy staring eye ?
' ''Twas blood, 'twas blood !
And it rose like a flood,
And for this I screamed as I glided by ! '

Owl ! that lovest the midnight sky !
Again, again,
Where are the twain ?
' Look ! while the moon is hurrying by :—
In the thicket's shade
The one is laid,
You may see through the boughs his moveless eye.

Owl ! that lovest the moonless sky !
A step beyond,
From the silent pond,
There rose a low and a moaning cry ;
On the water's edge,
Through the trampled sedge,
A bubble burst, and it gurgled by :
My eyes were dim,
But I looked from the brim,
And I saw in the weeds a dead man lie !

Owl ! that lovest the darken'd sky !
Where the casements blaze
With the faggots raise,

Look ! oh look ! what seest thou there ?
    Owl ! what's this ?
    That snort and hiss !
And why do thy feathers shiver and stare ?
    ' 'Tis he, 'tis he !
    He sits mid the three,
And a breathless woman is on the stair ! '

Owl ! that lovest the cloudy sky !
    Where clank the chains
    Through the prison panes—
What there thou hearest tell to me :
    ' In her midnight dream,
    'Tis a woman's scream,
And she calls on one—on one of the three.'
    Look in once more
    Through the grated door—
' 'Tis a soul that prays in agony.'

Owl ! that hatest the morning sky !
    On thy pinions grey
    Away ! away !
I must pray in charity,
    From midnight chime
    To morning prime,—
Miserere, Domine ! "

Thurtell's victim was buried in the churchyard of the village of Elstree, a little off the road from London to St. Alban's, and in the chancel of the church are also the remains of Miss Reay, the unfortunate mistress of Lord Sandwich, the circumstances of whose violent death have already been mentioned. The talented author of these lines gave me permission to insert them here, and to that gentleman, Mr. Leigh Hunt, and the Rev. A. Dyce, I am indebted for much kind and valuable assistance, in my endeavours to ascertain what portions of the poetry in Brummell's album had already been published. This has, I trust, together with my own researches, protected me from the error of publishing, as a novelty, what has been printed before,—a remark which I hope will also apply correctly to the remaining little pieces and epigrams : they were entered anonymously, and with the exception of the epigrams, may or may not be, what he designates in his note, as some of his own "namby-pamby productions ; " if so, the following was probably written at Calais or Caen.

TO MISS F——.

"Though such unbounded love you swear,
  'Tis only art I see ;
Can I believe that one so fair
  Should ever dote on me ?

Say that you hate, and freely show
  That age displeases youth,
And I may love you when I know
  That you can speak the truth."

THE YOUNGER BROTHER'S CLAIM.

"Whene'er in rapturous praise I speak
Of Susan's eye, of Susan's cheek,
    And own my ardent flame ;
They tell me that I praise in vain,
For Susan proudly will disdain
    A *younger* brother's claim.

Yet my fond heart will not resign
The hope it form'd to call her mine.
        When first my eyes beheld her ;
I still believe my Bible true,
For there 'tis clearly proved that you,
        Susannah, hate an Elder."

LES MILLE COLONNES.

" Boast, Versailles, thy hundred fountains ;
    Paris, boast thy marble domes ;
Jove may take thine air-built mountains,
    Pluto take thy catacombs.

Place Vendôme let Mars arouse, and
    Raise one column o'er War's throne ;
Cupid elsewhere builds a thousand,
    Vivent ! ah, vivent les Mille Colonnes.

English, French, there throng together
    Round a dame too fair to view ;
Who with glove of white kid leather,
    Rings a bell of or-molu.

Prince Eugene's Italian throne is
    Hers, her smile confers the ton ;
Men who once preferr'd Tortoni's,
    Now frequent les Mille Colonnes.

Pallas wove her Mechlin laces,
    Amphitrite strung her pearls,
Iris tinged that face of faces,
    Flora dressed those towering curls.

But the Queen of love and joy, all
    Heaven forsook, her azure zone,
Casting in the Palais Royal,
    Round la dame des Mille Colonnes.

As the dog of Nile when drinking
  Coy the alligator shuns,
Quaffs the stream with terror shrinking,
  Runs and laps, and laps and runs ;

Dread, fond youths, this Gallic Circe,
  Sip your demi-tasse alone :
Love and Beauty know no mercy,
  Fly ! ah, fly ! les Mille Colonnes !" [1]

ON THE COLLAR OF A LADY'S DOG.

" Je ne promets point de largesse
  A quiconque me trouvera :
Qui me ramène à ma maitresse,
  Pour récompense——il la verra."

EPIGRAMS.

" Certain rimeur, qui jamais ne repose,
  Me dit hier arrogamment
Qu'il ne sait point écrire en prose ;
  Lisez ses vers—vous verrez comme il ment."

Well known, but worthy of a reprint :—

D'UNE FEMME PAR SON MARI.

" Ci-gît ma femme ; ah ! qu'elle est bien
  Pour son repos, et pour le mien ! ! "

" Here lies my wife. Oh ! let her lie :
  She's happy now, and so am I ! "

---

[1] The Café des Mille Colonnes in Paris was visited by many people of fashion from 1814 to 1824, chiefly on account of the proprietor's handsome wife, Madame Romain, surnamed *la belle limonadière*, who sat behind the counter on a throne, which had formerly belonged to Eugène Beauharnais, when viceroy of Italy. The "towering curls" refer to her peculiar headdress ; her portrait can be seen in the tenth chapter of V. Fournel's *Les Rues du Vieux Paris*, Paris, 1879. Madame Romain, a few years after the death of her very plain-looking and one-armed husband, retired to a convent, where she died.

CHAPTER XXII.

Brummell at the Clubs—Watier's—Lord Byron and the Dandies—The Ball at the Argyle—Brummell one of the Four Gentlemen who gave it —The Regent goes to it—The Beau's Run of Good Luck at Hazard— Alderman Combe and Brummell—Tom Sheridan and Brummell —High Play at Watier's—Brummell's Continued Losses—His Friend's Good-natured Attempt to Save Him—Ill Success of his Scheme—Dick the Dandy-killer—A New Way to Pay Old Debts— The Sixpence with a Hole in it—The Storm Gathering.

At the commencement of Brummell's career, he was generally with the Prince or his great friends, and but seldom at the clubs; so seldom, indeed, that one of his chums in the Tenth told me that he rarely met him at them. He did not at this period require strong excitements, like his friends Sheridan and Fox, and men of similar dispositions; to them the clubs were like night taverns, to which they retired for amusement, after undergoing the terrible sufferings of politicians wisely condemned by the country to legislate for it till midnight. Deep potations, blade-bones of mutton, and the music of the dice-box he had, at this time, the good sense to eschew: 'tis true he dropped in occasionally upon their orgies, *pour se dévaliser l'esprit,* and to enjoy the jokes of others, but not to steep his own intellects in wine. After his quarrel with the Prince, he was a great deal more at the clubs, particularly Watier's,[1] which was at the corner of Bolton Street, and extremely select; this club was established by a person of that name, with a committee of gentlemen, Brummell being one of its principal supporters. It is thus alluded to by Lord Byron, who calls it the "Dandy Club," and he speaks of Lord Alvanley, Brummell, Mildmay, and Pierrepoint, as the four chiefs.

"I liked the Dandies," says the noble Poet; "they were all very civil to me, although in general they disliked literary people, and persecuted and mystified Madame de Staël, Lewis, Horace Twiss, and the like, most damnably. They persuaded Madame de Staël

[1] Brummell was also a member of Brookes's; he was proposed by Mr. Fawkener, on the 2nd of April 1799, and *declined*, as it is delicately expressed in the ledger of the club, in May 1816. In the July number of the *Edinburgh Review* 1844 appeared an article on John Heneage Jesse's "George Selwyn and his Contemporaries," in which it is stated that, "Watier's Club in Piccadilly was the resort of the Macao players. It was kept by an old *maître d'hôtel* of George the Fourth, a character in his way, who took a just pride in the cookery and wines of the establishment. All the brilliant stars of fashion (and fashion was power then) frequented it, with Brummell for their sun. Poor Brummell dead, in misery and idiocy at Caen! and I remember him in all his glory, cutting his jokes after the Opera at White's in a black velvet greatcoat and a cocked hat on his well-powdered hair. Nearly the same turn of reflection is suggested, on gaming, as we run over the names of his associates. Almost all of these were ruined, three out of four irretrievably. Indeed it was the forced expatriation of its supporters that caused Watier's to be broken up. During the same period, from 1810 to 1813 or thereabouts, there was a great deal of high play at White's and Brookes's, particularly whist. At Brookes's figured some remarkable characters, such as Tippoo Smith, Colonel Aubrey, and a nobleman who was called "le Wellington des joueurs."

that A——— had a hundred thousand a year, &c., &c., till she praised him to his face for his beauty, and made a set at him for —, and a hundred fooleries besides. The truth is, that though I gave up the business early, I had a tinge of Dandyism in my minority, and probably retained enough of it to conciliate the great ones, at five-and-twenty. I had gamed and drunk, and taken my degrees in most dissipations, and having no pedantry, and not being overbearing, we ran on quietly together. I knew them all, more or less, and they made me a member of Watier's (a superb club at that time), being, as I take it, the only literary man, except two others (both men of the world), Moore and Spencer, in it. Our masquerade was a grand one, so was the Dandy ball too."

This memorable fête was given at the Argyle Rooms in July 1813, by the four gentlemen already mentioned, after winning a very considerable sum one evening at hazard. Elated with their run of good luck, they very gallantly determined to give a fancy ball, one that would astonish their friends : a serious question, however, arose among them, whether they should or should not invite the Prince, who had previously quarrelled with Brummell and Sir Henry Mildmay ; but after a long, loyal, and solemn discussion on this most important subject, Brummell very properly laid aside his own feelings, and it was agreed that Mr. Pierrepoint should sound the Regent, and ascertain if he would like to accept the invitation. The Prince immediately intimated, and with some

eagerness, his desire to be invited, and he accordingly
was so, in the names of all the four votaries of Terpsi-
chore; and on the night in question my informant
went early, with a few others, in order that they
might get well placed, for the purpose of witnessing
the manner in which His Royal Highness would
notice Brummell and Sir Henry.

When the Prince arrived he made one of his stately
bows to Lord Alvanley and Mr. Pierrepoint, and shook
each of them cordially by the hand; but of the other
two gentlemen he took no notice whatever, nor would
he even appear to know that they were present. The
consequence was, that when the Regent retired, Brummell, justly incensed at the insult thus publicly and
designedly put upon him, would not attend him to his
carriage : this the Prince did not fail to observe, and
the next day, when speaking of the circumstance,
said, "Had Brummell taken the cut I gave him
good-humouredly, I would have renewed my intimacy
with him," which, in conformity with the feeling thus
expressed, he never afterwards did.   This anecdote is
in strong contrast to the general opinion, that the Prince
was the most finished gentleman of his day.   Surely it
was undignified on his part, to take advantage of his
rank, and cut his old companion when he was actually
his guest, and certain that he could not retaliate.[1]

When Brummell first commenced play, he was very
successful, the case with nine men out of ten, and on
one occasion he won six-and-twenty thousand pounds

[1] See Vol. II., Appendix.

—pretty high play for a man whose patrimony did not much exceed that sum. His friends after this lucky hit strongly recommended him to buy an annuity ; but he either refused to adopt the suggestion, or neglected to act with sufficient promptitude upon their advice, and a few nights after he lost it all again. The following is an example of his success and of his impudence, and also the rather unusual circumstance of his getting the worst of a joke. The loser was the late Alderman Combe, also a great gamester, and who, though unsuccessful in this instance, made, it is said, as much money by his dexterity at play as he did by brewing. One evening while he filled the office of Lord Mayor of London, he was busily engaged at a full Hazard-table at Brookes's, where the wit and the dice-box circulated together with great glee, and where Brummell was also one of the party : " Come, Mash-tub," said the Beau, who was the castor, " what do you set ? " " Twenty-five guineas," answered the Alderman. " Well, then, have at the Mayor's pony [1] only, and seven's the main," replied Brummell ; and he continued to throw until he drove home the Brewer's twelve ponies running ; he then rose from his chair, and, making him a low bow whilst pocketing the cash, exclaimed ; " Thank you, Alderman ; in future I shall never drink any porter but yours." " I wish, sir," said Combe, " that every other blackguard in London would tell me the same." [2]

[1] In gaming slang, a pony means twenty-five guineas.
[2] *New Monthly Magazine.*

" During the height of his prosperity," says Tom
Raikes in his Journal, " I remember him coming in
one night after the Opera to Watier's and finding the
Macao [1] table full, one place at which was occupied by
Tom Sheridan, who was never in the habit of playing,
but having dined freely, had dropped in to the Club,
and was trying to catch the smiles of fortune by risk-
ing a few pounds which he could ill afford to lose.
Brummell proposed to him to give up his place and
go shares in his deal ; and adding to the ten pounds
which Tom had in counters before him £200 for himself, took the cards.   He dealt with his usual success,
and in less than ten minutes won £1500; he
then stopped, made a fair division, and giving £750
to Sheridan, said to him : ' There, Tom, go home and
give your wife and brats a supper, and never play
again.'   I mention the anecdote as characteristic of
the times, the set, and of a spirit of liberality in
Brummell."

The reaction, however, came at last ; the stakes
were too high, and the purses of his companions too
long, for him to stand against any continued run of
bad luck ; indeed, the play at Watier's, which was very
deep, eventually ruined the club, as well as Brummell
and several other members of it ; a certain Baronet
now living is asserted to have lost ten thousand
pounds there at *écarté*, at one sitting : but play ran
high at all the clubs ; " Pay fifteen hundred pounds to
Lord ☆ ☆ ☆," said the late Marquis of H——— one night

---

[1] Macao was a game of cards, somewhat resembling *vingt-et-un.*

Mr Thomas Raikes

to the croupier, at White's—it was for one rubber of
whist. "It should, however, be remarked," added the
member of this club who mentioned the circumstance
to me, "the order was more often given by the noble
Marquis's adversary." The influx of foreigners, in the
years 1814 and 1815, greatly contributed to increase
the taste for play at this period, and the celebrity
gained by Blucher, at the baths of Pyrmont, did not
desert him in London. Gay and gallant Guardsmen
too, fresh from their late achievements in the field,
and tired of "roughing it on a beefsteak and a bottle
of port," were eagerly bent on indemnifying themselves for the hardships they had undergone;
Almacks and the Clubs were burning to receive them,
the women were all crazy to have them in their
drawing-rooms, and they lost no time in making love,
as ardently as they had made war; or in losing their
back pay, that had accumulated by a disease under
which the army in Spain had frequently and severely
suffered—an affection of the military chest. Elder
brothers, who unfortunately did not fight, were immediately laid under contribution; at least all those who
were able and willing to honour the heroes and their
cheques; and these new levies, or a portion of them,
also found their way to the board of green cloth. The
season of 1814 saw Brummell a winner, and a loser
likewise, and this time he lost not only his winnings,
but "an unfortunate ten thousand pounds," which, when
relating the circumstance to a friend many years afterwards, he said, was all that remained at his banker's.

One night, the fifth of a most relentless run of ill luck, his friend Pemberton Mills heard him exclaim that he had lost every shilling, and only wished some one would bind him never to play again ;—" I will," said Mills, and taking out a ten-pound note he offered it to Brummell, on condition that he should forfeit a thousand, if he played at White's within a month from that evening. The Beau took it, and for a few days discontinued coming to the club; but about a fortnight after, Mills, happening to go in, saw him hard at work : of course the thousand pounds were forfeited ; but his friend, instead of claiming it, merely went up to him, and touching him gently on the shoulder said, " Well, Brummell, you may at least give me back the ten pounds you had the other night."

He was at last completely beggared, though for some time he continued to hold on by the help of funds raised on the mutual security of himself and his friends, some of whom were not in a much more flourishing condition than himself; their names how- ever, and still more their expectations, lent a charm to their bills, in the eyes of the usurers, and money was procured—of course at ruinous interest. It is said, that some unpleasant circumstances, connected with the division of one of these loans, occasioned the Beau's expatriation, and that a personal altercation took place between Brummell and a certain Mr. M——, when that gentleman accused him of taking the lion's share.

The author will not undertake to say to whom, or

to what extent, culpability is to be attached in this
affair : Brummell might have hoped that a turn of luck
would enable him to retrieve his losses, and repay
those of whom he had borrowed ; and as to the
punctuality attending the payment of play-debts at
White's and Brookes's, it does not appear that a want
of it was at all unusual,—that is, if we are to judge
by the letters of Sheridan, Fitzpatrick, and others.
The impossibility, however, of settling this quarrel,
is assigned by Lord Byron as the reason which led to
Brummell's departure from England. " When Brummell," says his Lordship, " was obliged by that affair
of poor M——, who thence acquired the name of
Dick the Dandy-killer (it was about money, and debt,
and all that), to retire to France," &c., &c. Certain it
is that he was well acquainted with the money-lenders,
for several of these parchments emerged from their
obscurity during Brummell's sojourn at Calais. Some
of these bonds were drawn by Lord C——, the
Marquis of ——, and George Bryan Brummell, and,
as fragments of them were occasionally sent to one of
his friends there, to mix his snuff in, it may be presumed that at least a few of these proofs of mutual
love and affection had been redeemed ; but there is
also every reason for supposing that, in similar trans-
actions, several of his obligations were left unfulfilled :
those who were parties to them suffered of course by
his departure, and I believe no one more so than
Lord R—— M——.

Among the numerous anecdotes with which he has

been charged, is one which applies specially to his indifference on these matters. According to this *on dit*, Brummell once consented to borrow five hundred pounds of an individual who, from his position in society, had some difficulty in getting introduced into the world of fashion, and who hoped that his assistance in the emergency referred to, would secure him, through the Beau's influence, the much-desired honour: it did so, but not exactly in the manner that he expected, for, when in Brummell's decadence his applications for payment became frequent, and of course annoying, the falling meteor at last replied, that he had already paid him : " Paid me," said Mr. ――. " When ? " " When ? " re - echoed Brummell, with assumed indignation, " why, when I was standing at the window at White's, and said as you passed—Ah, how do you do, Jemmy ? " But verily " there is a tide in the affairs of men," particularly in such men, and it was a neap one with him : Fortune, who had been his housekeeper so long, now fairly gave him warning ; it was useless calling for fresh cards, the game was up. Yet, great as his extravagance was, it was play that completed his ruin ; had he refrained from gaming, he might have lived all his life on the sunny side of St. James's Street ! and been buried by the side of his respectable ancestor, in the churchyard of that parish, instead of wearing away a monotonous existence upon the charity of his friends, in pacing the dirty streets of a continental town.

Brummell had a very odd way of accounting for

the sad change which took place in his affairs at this time. " He used," observes one of his friends at Caen, " when talking about his altered circumstances, to say, that up to a particular period of his life everything prospered with him, and that he attributed this good luck to the possession of a certain silver sixpence, with a hole in it, which somebody had given him years before, with an injunction to take good care of it, as everything would go well with him so long as he did, and *vice versa*, if he happened to lose it. The promised prosperity attended him for many years, whilst he held the sixpence fast ; but having at length, in an evil hour, unfortunately given it by mistake to a hackney-coachman, a complete reverse of his previous good fortune took place, and one disastrous occurrence succeeded to another, till actual ruin overtook him at last, and obliged him to expatriate himself. On my asking him why he did not advertise, and offer a reward for the lost treasure, he said, ' I did, and twenty people came with sixpences having holes in them to obtain the promised reward, but mine was not amongst them.' ' And you never afterwards,' said I, ' ascertained what became of it ? ' ' Oh yes !' he replied, ' no doubt that rascal Rothschild, or some of his set, got hold of it.' If you think the foregoing *plaisanterie* worth inserting, do so ; I can vouch for its authenticity, as it occurred in conversation with myself. Whatever poor Brummell's superstitious tendencies may have generally been, he had unquestionably a superstitious veneration for his lost sixpence." But to continue : a cloud also had for some time been gathering over his fame as well as his fortunes ; the *prestige* of his name was going, and his fiat no longer regarded ; public events had eclipsed him, and the ladies of the *beau monde* were far more interested in hero-worship, or in procuring a hair from the tail of Platoff's horse, than securing the good opinion of the once all-powerful dictator. Brummell and Buonaparte, who had hitherto divided the attention of the world, fell almost together ; the former being doomed to the mortification of seeing his share bestowed on the sea-fight in the Serpentine, the Chinese Pagoda, and Oldenburg hats, and his cleanliness forgotten in that of the fierce sons of the Don.

CHAPTER XXIII.

Symptoms of a Move—Brummell's Epistle to his Friend Scrope Davis—
The Wit's Laconic Reply—His Extraordinary Penchant at College—
Brummell Cuts his Cable, and Comes to an Anchor at Calais—The
Author passes through that Town—Boxing, Gouging, and the
Savatte—The Table d' Hôte at the Royal—The Mysterious Stranger—
A Walk on the Market-Place—English Refugees—Various Reasons
for Expatriation.

AT length the pressing solicitations of the Dandy-
killer made London—London, in the height of the
season—positively unpleasant to the unfortunate
Antonio, who would perhaps have given a pound
of flesh, ay, and perhaps more, to have averted the
crisis; but his creditor was no Shylock, and ducats
there were none, so there was but one alternative
left, and on the 16th of May, 1816, he suddenly retired from the stage on which he had played such a
conspicuous part. On this eventful Thursday, he
dined off a cold fowl and a bottle of claret, which was
sent him from Watier's, and it is said that only a few
hours before he took wing, he wrote the following
laconic note to one of his *intimes :—*

" MY DEAR SCROPE,—Lend me two hundred pounds;
the banks are shut, and all my money is in the three

per cents. It shall be repaid to-morrow morning.
Yours,   GEORGE BRUMMELL."

His friend, very probably thinking that he was
hard up, immediately sent him this equally laconic
reply :—

" MY DEAR GEORGE,—'Tis very unfortunate ; but all
my money is in the three per cents.—Yours,

"S. DAVIES." [1]

" Scrope Davies," says Lord Byron, " is a wit, and
a man of the world, and feels as much as such a
character can do."   In this respect the resemblance
between the two friends was sufficiently strong, and,
if the anecdote is true, the answer could scarcely have
occasioned Brummell any surprise.   But he was not
a man to moralise upon it, or soliloquise in front of
his club or the houses of his friends, those houses in
which he had been so often a welcome guest ; though,
as he passed them this evening for the last time, the
future must have pressed itself upon his mind, with a

---

[1] A clergyman, a friend of mine, told me that he was once roused
from his slumbers in the dead of the night by a violent knocking at his
bed-room door, and a shrill female voice, calling out in accents of
terror, " Sir, sir, Mary's a beginning to cut her throat," another Abigail
of the establishment.   I allude to the circumstance, as an introduction
to an anecdote told of Scrope Davies, who, when at Cambridge, is said
to have cut his, after every Newmarket meeting ; indeed so frequently
did he amuse himself in this way, that on one occasion the medical
man who was sent for refused to hurry when he heard it was Scrope's
throat that he was required to sew up, saying, " There is no danger of
him, I have done that six times already."

very cheerless and unpromising aspect. On the night that he left London, the Beau was seen as usual at the Opera, but he left early, and, without returning to his lodgings, stepped into a chaise which had been procured for him by a noble friend, and met his own carriage a short distance from town. Travelling all night as fast as four post-horses and liberal donations could enable him, the morning of the 17th dawned on him at Dover, and immediately on his arrival there, he hired a small vessel, put his carriage on board, and was landed in a few hours on the other side. By this time, the West End had awoke and missed him ; particularly his tradesmen and his enemies, both of whom had long scores against him.

All sorts of reports were in circulation at the time Brummell disappeared. Thus in the " Diary of a Diplomatist " [1] we find it stated, on May 21, 1816, " The respectable fraternity of legs in high life are thrown into a state of extreme consternation by the disappearance of Beau Brummell, a friend of the Prince Regent, with £40,000, the whole of which he is said to have fraudulently obtained. He absconded on Saturday last." And on May 24, two o'clock P.M. : " Beau Brummell's deficiencies amount to a still greater sum than I mentioned G—— told me an hour ago that he borrowed the money in the way of acceptances from the Duke of Rutland, Lords Charles and John Manners, &c. The Marquis of Worcester stood the flat for £7000. Brummell's private debts are very considerable, he

[1] *New Monthly Magazine*, November 18, 1846.

has even bilked ——— ; Long Wellesley says he is in Picardy."

In much less haste, and happily with a very different object in view, I took my departure for France in the spring of 1842. Calais lay in my route, and, in the few days I remained there, I collected the little that was remembered of the Beau's history during his long residence in that sanctuary of English debtors. The absurd privileges of by-gone times, which were so long left untouched by corrupt Governments, are now falling rapidly before the power of public opinion ; and perhaps no greater proof of the desire to promote the interests of honest men has been given in the treaties with foreign powers of late years, than that clause which has opened the shores of America to the righteous claims of justice. To her demands " la Grande Nation " is still deaf, but though it may be an Utopian idea to suppose that any particular creed of the Christian religion will ever be universal, we may at least hope that this, the greatest of its attributes, will at some period be recognised by all mankind : with us the principle of leaving the course of justice free has long been recognised, and the last remnant of a contrary character was destroyed, when the privileges of the Isle of Man were abrogated. While the rogue has been thus defeated in his plans of emigration, greater facilities for arranging his difficulties, and a greater share of personal liberty, have been afforded to the honest debtor : for the protection of such men, no country

can show a more humane code of laws than England.[1]

If there was any one on board the *Belfast* abscond-
ing from them, or his creditors, the slow rate at which
we made our way down the river, against the still
flowing tide, must have given him some qualms, even
while we were in smooth water, for a silver oar might
easily have overtaken us before we reached Grave-
send. Old Father Thames is always a stirring sight
to an Englishman, but the Pool was nearly clear of
shipping, owing to the lengthened set-in of westerly
winds : and not even a barge was run down, or a
wherry swamped, to enliven the tedium of looking at
the sedgy banks of the Essex shore. Tired of nature,
I turned to my steaming companions ; but with
them, alas! all was unprofitable as on *terra firma :*
they were as taciturn as Englishmen, when strangers,
and dependent entirely on each other for amusement,
usually are ; and the only sociable creature on board
was Boatswain, the captain's Newfoundland dog,
whose good opinion I soon secured with a biscuit : it
would have been difficult to say how long it would
have taken me to secure that of my companions. It
was night when we reached our destination, but there
was still light enough to see that the "juste milieu"
authorities had grubbed up the plate on the pier that
marked the spot on which Louis the Eighteenth

"Set the first of his own dear legitimate feet"—

---

[1] On the 13th of February of the year 1843, a Convention was
signed between England and France, for the mutual surrender in
certain cases of persons fugitive from justice.

his left foot : unfortunate omen ! when he returned from his exile. Everything else wore the same aspect here as on a previous visit, when, to prevent me from introducing the cholera, I was obliged to submit to a quarantine of three days, in company with a Spanish courier, as highly seasoned with garlic as any *olla podrida* that he had ever eaten. A villanous place near Fort Rouge was the one appointed for our purification ; whether that happy consummation was ever obtained by my companion in this world, I will not undertake to say positively—in purgatory it might have been just possible. The morning after my arrival I took a stroll on the ramparts, and found Hogarth's Gate looking not a day older; the fish-women and their skate not a whit more handsome; they—the women, not the skate—still wearing huge gold earrings, and blue-and-red worsted stockings and petticoats. The habits of the people, at any rate those of the lower orders, appeared to have remained as unchanged as their costume ; and it still happens that a Frenchman may be seen to bite his friend's nose off on the Grande Place, in the squabbles that take place on a market-day, or beat his head in with his *sabot* after he has got him down.

Boxing may be termed a noble science, though the exhibitions in the prize-ring of late years have led many to think it otherwise ; as the lion does not yet lie down with the lamb, nor is likely to do so for some time to come, the utility of " the noble art of self-defence " must be acknowledged—in so far as it restrains all unfair and savage propensities, when men will not settle a quarrel without proceeding to blows. What will its enemies say to the execrable American practice of gouging? or the disgusting mode of fighting, indulged in by our neighbours, called the "savatte"? It was, probably, a detestation of these, or other brutalities, and a conviction of the necessity of maintaining in the more humble classes what is natural to every Englishman, a love of fair play, that induced such men as the late Duke of York, many noblemen of high rank, and others, to countenance the prize-ring by their presence.

Calais has great attractions in the eyes of a "Levanter," but, I imagine, in his only : he sleeps securely within its walls, and does not dream of those which might have held him within their stern embrace in his own country. With all its disagreeables of "canaux et canaille," and its deficiencies of all sorts, there is one fact which must recommend Calais, not only to the debtor, but to every Englishman, above all the towns in

"The vine-covered hills and gay regions of France "—

it is the nearest to Shakespeare's Cliff in that country of England, which the Beau, in the amusing quintessence of his refinement, always spoke of as "Albion."

Various are the shades of guilt or necessity that have made it expedient for so many of our countrymen to expatriate themselves to this uninteresting place, and to give a detailed account of the reasons

which have induced the greater portion of the English
residents to cross the Channel would, indeed, be a
work of labour, and invidious as well as useless ; but,
without concerning oneself upon the subject, it was
impossible to take a morning walk and not meet some
of them loitering about the streets, and hearing of
their various misdemeanours.

The "table-d'hôte," at the Royal, introduced me
to a countryman, who was, I firmly believed, an
unfortunate *échappé* of some sort, but what I could
not divine ; and such a surmise was not uncharitable
at Calais, where a " table-d'hôte " is scarcely *en règle*
without one.

The stranger sat opposite to me, and I saw at the
first glance that he was not a debtor ; or, if so, not
a *chevalier d'industrie*, or a ruined man about town ;
he was too well dressed to be either ; moreover, his
countenance had not the slightest characteristic of
the genus Diddler. His face was one of those faces
which the French call *impassible*, and looked as if it
had never been ruffled since his last flagellation at
school, some fifty years before. I allude only to his
nose and mouth, for his eyes were concealed by a
pair of dark-green goggles, which defied all speculation as to the shape or colour of the features behind
them. During the repast he ate but little, and spoke
less ; and I observed that he appeared very uneasy
and fidgety whenever the door was opened by the
servants on entering the *salle.* Once, too, during
dinner, he removed his spectacles, and then I saw

that his eyes were as strong as the bull's-eyes in a
ship's deck: indeed, I felt from this moment certain
that they were put on as a disguise. While specu-
lating, however, in my own mind what this mysterious
elderly gentleman could be, or why, with such eyes,
he wore goggles, the dinner concluded—and as I was
sipping the remainder of my Bordeaux and watching
the assiduous manner in which he continued chopping
up his apple-parings, the waiter came in and announced
the arrival of the English mail. Ah! how strangely
was the stout gentleman agitated at this intelligence!
how he chopped away! I could hear him breathing
as loud as the beast in Sinbad's cave; and his complexion, from being the colour of the *vin ordinaire*
before him, became as white as the table-cloth—
indeed, whiter, for that was, as usual at every "table-
d'hote," anything but white. "Are you unwell, sir?"
said I across the table. "No, sir, thank you,"
replied the stranger hesitatingly; and, while he was
yet speaking, the *garçon* again entered with a bundle
of English newspapers. The forced calmness of his
demeanour now forsook him altogether; off went his
goggles, and, before the papers were well out of the
waiter's hands, he seized one of them. How he
trembled as he tore away the envelope!—how he
buried his eyes in the type! He seemed to throw
each into a different column, to skim it the quicker—
down the middle and up again; his organs of vision
were fairly dancing a country-dance. At length the
Times was scanned, was searched in every part, and,

having terminated his examination, he, to my surprise, threw it down, quite careless of the general contents.

The suspicious goggles were then replaced, and monosyllables came slowly from between his half-closed lips—" Oh ! ha ! very odd !" and then a groan, and then a pause,—and then a " Not yet," like the thief in Ali Baba ; and the good man threw himself back in his chair with a most hopeless expression of countenance. Very soon after he left the room, and my compassion being increased rather than diminished, I followed him out into the court-yard of the hotel, and approached him. " You appeared anxious to see the paper, sir," said I, " was there any news ? " " Nothing particular," replied the stout gentleman ; " funds wonderfully high — wonderfully high ; ninety-three, sir, ninety-three ; but it is a mere flash in the pan. Peel must go out." How I happened to fix upon the subject I know not, but my next inquiry was, whether the election petitions were concluded. He started, as if I had been a rattlesnake ; and, struggling to gain composure for his answer, another " Not yet " came from his rotundity in thick and laboured accents. In a few minutes he was confidential, and I was informed why he was domiciled in Calais. " Sir, you see before you a most unfortunate individual ; but let me ask you first of all whether you are a Whig ? " " No, sir," said I, " I am not now, they are extinct." " Well, sir, Whig or Tor "—I frowned—" Conservative I mean,—no offence, sir,—I hope no offence, but cannot you feel for a man in my situation ? " " That

I can," I replied; "but pray what is your situation? are you in debt, sir?" "In debt! no, sir;" and the gentleman looked dreadfully shocked at the imputation,—the green spectacles rose at least half an inch. "Why then here?" I continued. "Ah, sir! you may well inquire why I, one of the first merchants in Liverpool, am living in this froghole of a place. I hate the French, sir, and thank Heaven I do not speak a word of their language : the fact is,"—and the old man sunk his voice to a whisper, and looked anxiously round the court,—"the fact is, sir, I am here to get out of the way, sir—out of the way of a Speaker's warrant." Then came all the details of the election, how the Tory member bribed, and how the affable Lady Anne had induced him to administer to the necessity of the electors on the other side; and finally, what a martyr he was to the cause.

A month in Calais, away from his wife and children, and his coal fire and bottle of port, to say nothing of his ledgers, had however worked a miracle with the enthusiastic reformer, and most solemnly did he swear never to have anything more to do with elections or Lady Annes again. "Sir, they may return who they like for me in future;" and as the exiled merchant said this we reached the Grande Place. There he drew my attention to several Englishmen who were promenading up and down, and pointed out certain individuals amongst them who had acquired an unenviable notoriety in England. "That person crossing the square," said my informant, "is Mr. R——o, who

figured in the Exchequer Bill affair; that one moving
off through the crowd is Mr. M——, a forger in
another line; and that dissipated-looking fellow crossing to the Hotel de Ville, at one time drove his four-
in-hand, and was one of the most wealthy commoners
in England. The only thing he drives now is a hard
bargain, which he does with every tradesman he deals
with." A political refugee was next pointed out as
the ex-radical candidate for Marylebone; and in conversation with him, was a dark-looking, pock-marked,
black - whiskered man in a blue greatcoat and two
yards of red comforter. "Who do you think he
is?" said my cicerone. "I can't imagine; perhaps
a fisherman."

"Oh no! he is an English policeman in disguise,
just come over to arrest three well-known jail-birds,
who have lately committed a burglary with horrible
violence near Nottingham; and, as I live, sir, there go
the rascals—look! near the *café*, in fustian jackets and
corduroys. See how they are laughing at B 64; and
well they may, for do you know the French Government has refused to give the scoundrels up! The
only chance the policeman has is to kidnap them
when they are drunk, and smuggle them on board the
packet; but he has been here a fortnight, and they
have not yet given him an opportunity." "And are
you acquainted with any of the *soi-disant* gentlemen
delinquents?" "Oh no!" replied my now talkative
acquaintance; "I heard their histories from the Englishman who sat on my right at the 'table d'hôte.' He

meets every packet that comes in, and if it arrives in the morning, knows, before I meet him at dinner, the name, height, parentage, and age of half the passengers; their business, both here and at home; whether they are in the army or the fleet, the church or the law; whether they are travelling solely for amusement or escaping from their creditors; or whether they are, like myself, sir, keeping out of the way of a Speaker's warrant. I know your name, sir; your name is Jesse; you are in the army; you live at Brighton; and your age is thirty-two." "And how on earth does he know this?" said I. "Easy enough," replied my acquaintance; "my right-hand neighbour is acquainted with all the *commissionaires*, and sees all the passports when they take them to be *visés*."

A man-monkey, in a cocked hat and red breeches, who had just perched himself on a chair to astonish the natives of the environs (for it was market-day), now commenced "Grenadier, que tu m'affliges!" in tones less human than those of his crazy violin; and, making my bow to the irreproachable and independent elector, I elbowed my way through the crowd, and soon found myself at the door of Mons. Leleux, in the Rue Royale, where Brummell lodged during his residence at Calais.

CHAPTER XXIV.

*Brummell's Lodgings in the Rue Royale—His Good-natured Landlord—
M. Leleux's Regard for Him—Proofs of it—Brummell's Effects Sold
by Auction in London—Copy of Mr. Christie's Bill of Sale—The
Snuff-box that was Destined for the Regent—Brummell Furnishes
his Rooms—His Passion for Buhl Furniture—Ridiculous Extravagance in the Indulgence of it—His Sèvres China—Napoleon
Paper Weight—The Beau's Conundrum Snuff-box.*

M. Leleux's house, originally the old Hotel d'Angleterre,
is on the right-hand side of the street, and but a few
yards from the Hotel de Ville : the two oval frames
that are still seen over what in former days was the
gateway, once encircled portraits of George the Second
and his Queen ; but these *bas reliefs* were destroyed
by the rioters during the popular outbreaks of the
Revolution.   Half-a-dozen doors farther on, is a shop
which has for its sign " Au Pauvre Diable," not an
inappropriate one in the town of Calais.

Pressing down the latch of M. Leleux's door, the
noise of which was the signal for opening another at
the extremity of the shop, I stood in the presence of
the best bookseller in Calais, and one of its most
goodnatured-looking citizens.   His cap, with that old
snipebill-looking peak so commonly seen in France,

and my best André, were immediately raised ; and to
my request that he would assist me in gleaning some
intelligence of the deceased Beau, he acceded with
ready politeness, and with a frank and soldier-like
bearing that I certainly thought smacked not of the
Garde Nationale. In my further intercourse with him
I found that my surmise was correct : it had been
acquired in the tent of Miranda, during the wars of
the South American republics, for M. Leleux was
secretary to that celebrated man. His countenance
lighted up as he spoke of his old lodger ; and, having
opened the trenches of conversation, by taking a large
pinch of snuff, he commenced a kind of recitative of
his sayings and doings, which unfortunately amounted
to very little in the end. " Ah, mon cher Monsieur,"
said the old *militaire,* "je n'ai aucun documens de lui.
Je pourrais cependant vous fournir quelques petits
détails, et cela volontiers. D'abord, c'est moi qui
l'avait bien connu, car quatorze ans il a demeuré dans
cette maison, et je vous ferai voir son appartement ; "
and we ascended the staircase together to the first
floor.

" This, sir," observed M. Leleux, in very good
English, but with a slight accent, " was his drawing-
room, and this one adjoining, his dining-room ; you
see they are front rooms ; his dormitory was on the
other side of the passage. After he had resided with
me about five years, I allowed him to have the rooms
a little to the left of these ; they are approached by
a different staircase : that suite consisted of a dining-

room on the ground-floor, and a drawing-room over
it, and a handsome bedroom at the back. It was at
this time Mr. Brummell's ambition to obtain the office
of consul at Calais, and the gentleman who held it
being then in very bad health, made him rather
sanguine on the point. The expectation, however,
was never fulfilled, for he is still living, and likely to
live ; but being won over by my *locataire's* persuasive
manner, I permitted him to decorate his rooms in
his own way; and though he did it very well, I can
assure you I was not much the richer for the money
he laid out. Mais, Monsieur, le pauvre homme était
si amusant, si amusant, qu'on ne pouvait rien lui
refuser. Sir, I would have kept him for nothing if
he would have stayed : ah ! he certainly was a very
droll fellow."

Our conversation here terminated, and I took my
leave; but on a subsequent visit the old gentleman
showed me over the rooms already alluded to. They
must have been very comfortable : but the black and
white marble pavement of the private entrance, which
Brummell laid down, and the rich crimson paper of
the dining-room, are all that remain as evidence of
his acknowledged taste and extravagance.

I must now "hark back to his burst from London,"
when, in the words of Pope, he bid farewell to the
" dear d—d distracting town," and left the box of
Lady —— with a joke more than usually satirical.
The dogs of the law were quickly on the scent ; but
they no sooner reached Dover than they dropped

their tails discouraged, for Reynard, instead of running to earth, had taken the water, and not a hope
remained of their catching him. On his arrival at
Calais, he took up his temporary abode at Dessin's
hotel, then in the hands of Quillacq, to whom he
sold his carriage : he remained there a short time,
and afterwards hired a set of rooms belonging to the
same proprietor.

When Brummell left London, he was living at
No. 13 Chapel Street, Park Lane, to which house
he had removed from Chesterfield Street some time
before ; it belonged to Mr. Hart, the Duke of Gloucester's steward. The change appears to have been
much for the worse, a mews gracing one side of the
house ; his tradesmen also began to whisper that
he was getting shaky, and would not pay much
longer. By the dinner-service and glass that were
disposed of after he left Chapel Street, it seems that
he occasionally entertained his friends in his new
residence, though he had discarded his cook on
quitting Chesterfield Street. He did not ever replace
him, and found, no doubt, that other people's viands
were much cheaper than his own, and quite as good ;
when by any accident he was thrown upon his own
resources, he managed to content himself with the
best repast Mr. Brookes could provide ;—

> " Liberal Brookes, whose speculative skill
> Was hasty credit and a distant bill."

A few days after his flight, his furniture and
effects were sold at public auction by Mr. Christie ;

the following is a copy of the first page of the book of sale :—

A Catalogue
of
A very choice and valuable assemblage
of
Specimens of the rare old Sèvres Porcelaine,
Articles of Buhl Manufacture,
Curiously Chased Plate,
Library of Books,
Chiefly of French, Italian and English Literature, the best
Editions, and in fine condition.
The admired Drawing of the Refractory School Boy, and others,
exquisitely finished by Holmes, Christall, de Windt,
and Stephanoff.
Three capital double-barrelled Fowling Pieces,
By Manton.
Ten dozen of capital Old Port, sixteen dozen of Claret
(Beauvais), Burgundy, Claret and Still Champagne,
The whole of which have been nine years in bottle in the
Cellar of the Proprietor ;
Also, an
Assortment of Table and other Linen, and some Articles of
neat Furniture ;
The genuine property of
A MAN OF FASHION,
Gone to the Continent :
Which,
By order of the Sheriff of Middlesex !
Will be Sold by Auction
By Mr. Christie,
On the Premises, No. 13 Chapel Street, Park Lane,
On Wednesday, May 22nd, and following Day.

Amongst the articles of Brummell's furniture, were a mahogany-framed sliding cheval dressing glass on castors, with two brass arms for one light each, a medicine chest, and colour box. The drawing-room had a chimney glass, in a carved ebony frame, chintz furniture and Brussels carpet; the back drawing-room had also a chimney glass, book-shelves, and library bookcase. The dinner service consisted of twelve oval dishes, twenty soup-plates, seventy-eight meat ditto, nine wine-coolers, a breakfast service for eight persons, three claret jugs, twelve hock glasses, forty wine ditto, decanters, &c. There were sixteen pairs of sheets, forty huckaback towels, napkins, &c. Amongst the Sèvres china was a pair of oval vases, which sold for nineteen guineas; they were green, with flowers and fruit, and mouldings of burnished gold. A small cup and cover of the same, eighteen pounds. An ewer and basin, mazarine blue and gold ground, richly ornamented with birds and exotics finely painted in compartments, with the name of each specimen upon them; the handle of this ewer was silver gilt, and the lot fetched twenty-six pounds. There were also a variety of chocolate cups and other articles, a clock of Vulliamy's, a letter scale—(no doubt, all his letters were franked)—the design a figure of Cupid, weighing a heart with a brace of doves; this was in or-molu on a black marble plinth. A silver tea-kettle embossed and chased, brought forty-seven pounds. There were only six spoons and four forks—how did they happen to be left behind?

Amongst the books were some good historical works, the Standard Poets, two editions of Shakespeare, his friend Ellis's Specimens of Early English

Metrical Romances, bound in curiously raised calf; the Quarterly and Edinburgh, the Memoirs of de Grammont, Chesterfield's Letters, Berrington's Abelard and Eloisa, and a large collection of novels now forgotten. A family party at dinner, by Holmes, fetched eighty-five guineas. There were also editions of Flaxman's designs for the Iliad, Æschylus, and Bürger's Leonora; a copy of the Musée Français, portraits for the Memoirs of de Grammont, prints by Cipriani and Bartolozzi, a portrait in oils of his father's benefactor, Lord North, and portraits of Nelson, Pitt, the Duke of Rutland, and George the Third. The Beauvais Claret sold for five pounds eight shillings; the Champagne, three pounds five shillings; and the Port, four pounds per dozen.

The sale was attended by many members of the fashionable world, every one being apparently anxious to purchase something; the Duke of York was not there, but he gave orders for some Sèvres china to be bought for him. Purchases were made in this manner by many of his friends. Amongst the company present were Lords Bessborough and Yarmouth, Lady Warburton, Sir Henry Smyth, Sir H. Peyton, Sir W. Burgoyne, Sir T. Stepney, Colonels Sheddon and Cotton, General Phipps, Mr. Massy Dawson, Acland, of the Albany, Mr. Mills, of Park Street, Mr. Tower, and the Rev. — Belli.

The competition for the knick-knacks and articles of *virtù* was very great; amongst them was a very handsome snuff-box, which, on being opened by the auctioneer before it was put up, was found to contain a piece of paper with the following sentence, in Brummell's handwriting, upon it :—"This snuff-box was intended for the Prince Regent, if he had conducted himself with more propriety towards me." The proceeds of the sale amounted to about eleven hundred pounds, and the sum was paid to the Sheriff of Middlesex.

But I must return to Calais. Brummell remained but a few months in M. Quillacq's lodgings, from them he removed to the house of M. Leleux, where he remained till he left for Caen, in the month of September of 1830. He was no sooner in possession of his new apartments, than he set about furnishing them in the most expensive manner ; and five-and-twenty thousand francs, which he took with him, or received shortly after his arrival at Calais, were quickly spent in making himself perfectly comfortable in his new abode. He had quite an old dowager's passion for buhl furniture ; and in the indulgence of this taste, he expended large sums of money. Many of the most *recherché* articles that adorned his *salon* were brought from Paris by a courier, who executed these and other commissions for him, and who gained a profit of thirty thousand francs upon the purchases he made, during the ten or twelve years he was thus employed. This was a large sum ; but Brummell, in his absurd mania for such things, sometimes disbursed half as much in one year. Sometimes a *chef-d'œuvre*, a darling cabinet, did not suit ; it had then to be disposed of, which it was for half the original cost ; at other times, a perfect gem had to be sent back to Paris, of course at his own expense; or perhaps the article was exchanged; in this case his *commissionnaire* profited both as buyer and seller.

At length, having bestowed incalculable pains, and many sleepless nights and anxious days, upon this interesting and important subject, he managed, in spite of his extreme fastidiousness and his poverty, to collect a sufficient quantity of buhl and or-molu to furnish his three rooms in the elegant and costly style of Louis Quatorze; and they would have commanded the approbation of the most *enragé* buhl-furniture-fancier of his former clique. He also squandered large sums in bronzes, japanned screens, and whims of every description. On one side of his drawing-room stood a large cabinet, with brass wire doors; these were kept locked with the most jealous care; for they protected, from the familiar and dangerous inspection of his visitors, a service of extremely beautiful Sèvres china. The designs were most exquisite, and on each plate was represented, in colours chaster than the originals, all the celebrated beauties that held such powerful sway over the courts of Louis the Fourteenth and Fifteenth; and, as they were not few in number, the reader may imagine that his inanimate but elegant harem completely filled his buhl seraglio. These portraits were so charmingly done, that the Beau, in the true spirit of a sultan, used to inform his visitors, that it was "almost profanation even to look at these frail fair ones."

The walls of this room were covered with pictures and prints—a few of the former being from the pencil of a young artist of the town,' who was patronised by the Beau by way of encouragement. Some favourite books, in handsome suits of morocco or silk, reposed on the card-tables ; and, on the circular one in the centre of the apartment, lay a little crowd of valuable snuff-boxes, miniatures, card-cases, paper-weights, and knives, and portfolios, in every variety of gold, enamel, mother-of-pearl, ivory, and tortoise-shell, embossed leather, and embroidered satin. Amongst this collection of expensive trifles were an or-molu greyhound and a *presse-papier* of Sienna marble, surmounted by a small bronze eagle ; the latter was presented to him, as a souvenir, by Monsieur de Montrond, Talleyrand's foreman, and had at one time pressed the despatches and private papers of Napoleon.[1] It is now in the author's possession, and not the less valued for having once belonged to the greatest and bitterest enemy England ever had.

Many amongst the multitude of little *bijoux* that ornamented this table were esteemed by him far beyond their intrinsic value ; some of them were the *cadeaux* of royalty, and, could they have spoken, especially those that were the gift of an amiable woman, whose charitable remembrance of him will be hereafter alluded to, they might have wiled away many of his lonely hours. His passion for snuff-boxes was extreme : he had one which he only could

[1] See Vol. II., chapter XIII.

open, and some friend of his, while he was at Belvoir, tried it with his knife, with the intention, no doubt, of purloining his snuff, which was always excellent. Hearing of the outrage, Brummell said, "Confound the fellow! he takes my snuff-box for an oyster:" but notwithstanding the splendid collection he possessed, and having sent his friend Capel, by permission of the First Lord, to Naples, to procure him a perfect *tabatière*, he actually had one of black shell and gold built at Calais. This he gave to the Duke of B——, in exchange for a bank-note of fifty pounds; in other words, that nobleman consented to receive it that he might with more delicacy present him with that sum—for, though a ruined man, Brummell had not yet been subjected to all the dirty degradations that invariably accompany that character, when his ruin is the result of premeditated folly and unrestrained indulgence. This sketch of the drawing-room would be incomplete if I omitted to mention, that the table-cover on which all his useless elegancies were displayed was worked for him by the Duchess of York, and that his easy-chair was the gift of the same kind friend.

Correctness of taste in everything was decidedly the Beau's forte, and, seated in his *fauteuil*, surrounded by his buhl, paintings, prints, knick-knacks, and the Sèvres portraits of the beautiful La Vallière and her discreet rival, he appeared, amongst the heterogeneous medley of English who subsequently attended his levee, nearly the only living creature in keeping with the room and its details.

CHAPTER XXV.

CONSIDERING the reduced state of his circumstances, the reader will naturally inquire how it happened that Brummell managed to gratify a taste so little in accordance with them ?   The answer is, that though a man of fashion, he had an extraordinary number of good friends; and the sums of money that he must have received from various sources, many of them unknown, attest the fact, that he was, at this time, even too generously assisted.   A clerk of M. de Vos, a Calais banker, called on him one morning to place a large sum in his hands, that had been paid into their bank the day before ; it was stated to me to have been a thousand pounds, but supposing it was only half that amount, it was a large donation. So strict was the incognito preserved, that the fortunate recipient could never trace the gift to the

generous individual who sent it. But in the circle
of those who administered not only to his wants but
to his luxuries (the evil day had not yet come, when
he was to find the utmost difficulty in procuring the
necessaries of life), no one appears to have extended
relief to the expatriated Beau, with more warmth of
feeling or delicacy of manner, than the late Duchess
of York. The "votre toute-affectionnée amie et servante" of more prosperous times, was practically
illustrated towards him to the day of Her Royal
Highness's death. Every year at Christmas some
token of regard was conveyed to him; a purse,
a card-case, or note-keeper, the work of her own
fair hands; Brummell treasured these proofs of the
Duchess's taste and skill, and had several of them
remaining when he was at Caen. These little marks
of her regard, when opened, were never found empty,
and a rustling was always heard within their folds,
which no doubt fell agreeably upon ears now so little
familiar with the sound of bank-notes.

Here is a note she wrote to him when Brummell
had only left his native land about a year, and
when one of her letters addressed to the Beau
had miscarried :—

"Londres, ce 26 April 1817.

"Vous n'avez rien perdu à la lettre qui vous était
destinée, et que Lord Alvanley a consignée aux
flammes ; elle contenait seulement mes remercimens
pour les charmans cadeaux que vous avez eu la bonté

de m'envoyer (dont je me suis parée le soir même de ma petite fête), et mes regrets que vous n'en étiez plus. Ces regrets se renouvellent journellement, et surtout les raisons qui en sont la cause. Croyez que personne ne sent plus la perte de votre société que je le fais ; je n'oublierai jamais les momens agréables que je lui ai dus, et tout ce qui pourrait m'en compenser serait la certitude de votre bonheur pour lequel je ferai (les voeux) les plus sincères comme pour ce qui peut y contribuer le plus efficacement, me flattant que vous conserverez toujours quelque souvenir de votre toute affectionnée amie et servante, F."

But women are ever the most lasting in their attachments, whether of love or friendship, and the conduct of this royal lady is the more meritorious on account of her high rank ; for the opportunities which persons in her exalted station have of witnessing the miseries of human nature are few, and, from ignorance rather than indifference, they frequently are not so much alive to the sufferings of mankind as those who daily witness those sufferings : they bask in the sunshine of perpetual personal comfort, and, while plenty is ever pouring forth her blessings around them, no beggar is allowed to tread the palace courts— poverty is scarcely bold enough to make its appeal to their hearts in person, and language in the form of a petition, however strongly worded, does not truthfully and vividly describe what they seldom or never see.

The Duke of Gloucester also treated Brummell with much kindness and consideration, and when His Royal Highness, in his way through Calais, went down to the packet to embark, Brummell always accompanied him : had he only imbibed a small portion of the Duke's punctuality in the weekly audit of his accounts, he might perhaps have had the satisfaction of one day returning in his company to the opposite shore. He had also a kind friend in John Chamberlayne, Esq., who contributed to his comfort by the payment of a yearly gratuity, which it was his intention to continue in the event of his own decease ; but, becoming afflicted by insanity, he left no will. This was a sad chance for Brummell : he wrote to his representatives on the subject, but the answer was unfavourable ; and it was intimated to him that there was no memorandum to that effect among Mr. Chamberlayne's papers. The Duke of Argyle, though not affluent, seldom forgot to call and assist him with money ; and Lord Alvanley, who never passed his door without doing the same, invariably dined with him ; the dinner, *bien entendu*, being sent from Dessin's at his Lordship's expense.

Many other noblemen and gentlemen at various periods relieved the dull tenor of his life by their visits ; and from each he received substantial proofs of their regard. Among them were the Dukes of Wellington, Rutland, Richmond, Beaufort, and Bedford ; Lords Sefton, Jersey, Willoughby d'Eresby, Craven, Ward, and Stuart de Rothesay. To the

Duke of Gloucester

assistance tendered him by his friends, may of course be added that of his relatives. His principal correspondents were the Duke and Duchess of York, Lord Alvanley, and J. Chamberlayne, Esq.

In the early part of his residence at Calais, he led a very retired life, for he was unable to speak French with fluency, and his mornings and evenings were occupied in perfecting himself in that language : he could not otherwise have entered a French *salon* with any degree of comfort ; the English society he abominated, and frequented it only during the latter part of his stay there, when he had grown less difficult and less exclusive.

Nothing could be more indicative that Brummell had ability and energy, when the occasion suited him to exercise it, than the proficiency he attained in French ; for, as will be seen in the sequel, he made himself master of the language, and could, for an Englishman, write an excellent letter. Byron's anecdote of Scrope Davies, given in Moore's Life of the noble poet, is delightfully incorrect :—" When Brummell retired to France," says his Lordship, " he knew no French, and having obtained a grammar for the purpose of study, our friend Scrope Davies was asked what progress Brummell had made in French ? He responded, that the Beau had been ' stopped, like Buonaparte in Russia, by the *elements.*' "[1] Like many other good things told of Brummell, it is deficient in the desideratum necessary to give it value

[1] See Vol. II., chapter V.

—truth. During the period that the army of occupation remained in France, he enjoyed the society of several of his old friends, who were serving with it, and many others on their way to Paris, which capital was then all alive with the revelry and dissipation of foreigners, and *emigrés* who had been exiled from the Trois Frères, Véry's, and *rouge et noir*, for upwards of twenty years : the chief of our gallant army, also, paid the town some flying visits *en route* to or from England, and I have heard it asserted, without, at this period, noticing his great rival in notoriety; but at length the most good-natured man in all England, the Marquis of ———, effected a reconciliation between them, and, from this time, his Grace never passed Brummell's door without inquiring after him, and sometimes giving him an invitation to dine with him at Dessin's. This was sometimes announced from his carriage, as he went by, for he had not, of course, a minute to spare.

It appears that the late Lord Westmoreland, when passing through Calais, also called on him, and said how happy he should be if he would dine with him that day at three o'clock ! Brummell's answer was truly characteristic :—" Your Lordship is very kind ; but I really could not feed at that early hour ! " " When I first knew Brummell at Eton," said the courteous old gentleman who sent me this anecdote, " we daily dined together at twelve, and fed very heartily ! "

But Brummell, soon after his arrival, had less

distinguished and agreeable visitors than either the Duke or Lord Westmoreland. On one occasion an itinerant communicater of the legal house of Howard and Gibbs tapped softly at his door, with the intention of presenting some law paper for his signature, or consideration : " Come in," said the Beau, deceived by so gentle an application for admittance ; his visitor's head, on a level with the latch, was instantly in the room—his body being cautiously kept in the passage. "Why, you little rascal," screamed the astonished George Bryan Brummell aforesaid, directly he saw him, " are *you* not hung yet ? begone ! " The head obeyed, the door closed, and the little body departed.

His routine of life at Calais was methodical in the extreme ; he rose at nine, breakfasted off *café au lait*, and sat reading the *Morning Chronicle, brochures*, or books (that is, after his Lévizac had been laid aside), till twelve ; precisely at that hour he might be seen in a flowing brocade dressing-gown and velvet cap, like the beret of the olden time, crossing the passage to his bedroom ; and so punctually did he keep to stated hours, that his landlord's " devils " used to exclaim, when he appeared, " Ah ! voilà Monsieur Brummell ; c'est midi," and they immediately struck work, and went to their dinner.

The business of his toilet now commenced, and this occupied a considerable part of two hours : from the time that was completed he held his levee, and sat *en prince* chatting with his friends. If it was

in the summer, he resorted to the open window of
his charming drawing-room, and apostrophised his
acquaintance as they passed. "Brummell!" shouted
one of them to him under his window,—the Beau
looked out,—"have you heard the news?" "No,
what's the matter?" "Why, S——, the banker,
ran off last night." "Well, what of that?" "Why,
I have lost a thousand francs." "Have you? then,
my good fellow, in future take a hint from me, and
always keep your banker in advance." At four
o'clock he stepped into the Rue Royale, as well
turned out as he ever did into St. James's Street,
in the very meridian of his glory. A walk on the
ramparts, or to his garden at the foot of them, killed
the next hour; but he walked more *pour se distraire*
than for exercise, his "long walk," as he termed it,
being out of one gate and in at the other, the two
being about a hundred yards apart. The fact was
that Vick, his terrier, was so afflicted with *embonpoint*,
that even during this short promenade he was obliged
to turn round and wait for her at least a dozen times
before he had accomplished fifty paces. His partiality
for this dog was extreme. Vick was once very ill,
so he sent for two of his friends, learned in the
diseases of the canine race, who, on their arrival,
found her laid upon his bed, and Brummell in great
distress standing by her side. An examination of her
condition having taken place, the two dogopathists
opined that she ought to be bled. "Bled!" said her
master, turning away, "I shall leave the room;

inform me when the operation is over." When poor
Vick died he shed tears, and observed to Mr.
Marshall, in his usual cynical tone, that he had "lost
the only friend he had in the world," meaning, most
likely, in the world of Calais.

Lister has introduced a version of this anecdote in
" Granby," but there is a difference in the dog's name
and species, and the time and place. The scene I
allude to is laid at a nobleman's house in the country,
where he broke up a prolix conversation one morning
by making his poodle perform some laughable tricks,
and directing the attention of the company to the
beauty of his dog. " Come here, Polisson," he said,
" come here and show yourself; is not he magnificent ?
Look at these tufts, I had him shorn by the best
tondeuse in Paris. Lady Harriet, I'll give you her
direction." " Oh thank you ! how handsome he is !
he must be quite a treasure." " Oh ! invaluable :
when Polisson dies I shall steal for him Lord Byron's
epitaph on his Newfoundland dog ; then I shall say,
with my hand on my heart (speaking of my friends),
' I have never had but one, and there he lies,' " pointing to the dog who was stretched upon the hearth-
rug.

Poor Vick was buried, by his special desire, in
Dessin's garden ; and though her master did not
actually put on mourning, he talked seriously of
erecting a monument to her memory. His *salon* was
peremptorily closed against visitors for three days,
and it was several weeks before he permitted any one

to speak of her death. He had subsequently three poodles : the most famous of the trio was called "*Atous*," and had been trained by a soldier of the garrison. This dog was a perfect specimen of canine intelligence, and he turned out for his walk at four, quite as neat as Brummell. His great accomplishment was to take a hot muffin from the plate before the fire, and run round the room offering it to the company ; but poor "*Atous*" also died, and Brummell was again a prey to grief. Like a true cynic, his eye was seldom if ever moistened on hearing of the death of a friend, though a flood of tears was always ready when his dogs died. His poodle was regretted because it was constantly in his presence, and his decease left a blank in the daily routine of his habits and ideas.

But to resume the sketch of his diurnal proceedings. At five o'clock precisely he ascended the staircase to his rooms, and dressed for dinner, which was sent from Dessin's at six : at this meal he washed his œsophagus with a bottle of Dorchester ale, of which he had always a barrel in the house. This showed plainly indeed that he had "fallen from his high estate," and was fain now to treat with rather less contempt than he felt on hearing it—the sarcastic remark of the alderman, for the beverage was at least malt liquor. This potent stuff was followed by a liqueur glass of brandy, which he always took during dinner, and the rear was brought up by a bottle of Bordeaux ; a pretty comfortable refection for a man who lived entirely on the charity of his friends.

It was after one of these niggardly repasts that he is said to have written to the late Lord Sefton that he was "lying on straw, and grinning through the bars of a gaol; eating bran bread, my good fellow, eating bran bread." I will not, however, vouch for the truth of the story. The double X did not take great effect upon his brain; for though not given to excess, he had been well accustomed to a tolerable quantity of wine, to say nothing of Roman punch, into the mysteries of which it has been asserted that he initiated the Prince Regent. One who knew him intimately at Calais, assured me that he had never seen him inebriated but once, and then he was so disgusted with himself that he performed a voluntary penance of solitary confinement for eight days; query, with or without his Dorchester ale? At seven o'clock, or half-past, he went to the theatre, where he had a small box; or in the long warm evenings he retired to his garden, in the summer-house of which (now thrown down) he either read or noted down his recollections of his past career.

CHAPTER XXVI.

SUCH was the general tenor of his life, varied occasionally by a dinner at the consul's, or a visit from
some friend of former years—a few of these stray
birds of fashion would sometimes delay their departure
for two or three days, merely to enjoy a laugh at the
fund of anecdotes with which he was charged; and
one of them, who had a house at Dover, frequently
crossed the water to see him, and always gave him
notice of his intention, desiring that he would have
all in readiness for his party at the Hotel, himself
included.   At these little fêtes, he was always in
good spirits, and as amusing as ever.   One day after
dinner, the elegant Beau, though always on the *qui
vive* that his proceedings should be faultless, upset
a cup of coffee on the cloth.   The bell was rung for
the waiter to remove it, and on his appearing for
that purpose he gave him to understand, with the

most imperturbable gravity, that a young and graceful
lady, the daughter of his friend, had committed this
piece of *gaucherie*. Directly, however, he had left
the room, the real delinquent hastened to apologise
and soften the indignation of the innocent victim, or
at least attempted to do so; adding drolly to a string
of excuses, " You know it would never have done
to let the world know that *I* was guilty of such
awkwardness." This was not very chivalrous; even
if his fair neighbour had really spilt it, it would have
been more goodnatured, if not so entertaining, to
have taken the odium on himself—*mais son égoïsme
régnait partout.*

But, however glad he might be to accept any
invitation that promised to afford him amusement
within the walls of the town, his friends could never
succeed in persuading him to spend one night away
from his own rooms. Lord Alvanley did, I believe,
once prevail upon him to go to Dunkirk, and his
landlord thought that he would at any rate not return
that night; but he was mistaken, for at four o'clock
in the morning, Brummell knocked at the door. The
Beau appeared much flattered and pleased by any
attentions paid him by his itinerant visitors, and
always endeavoured to be more than usually agreeable to them—if that were possible, though he could
not deny himself a joke, if it came into his head. I
remember, said one of his Calais friends, that when
sitting with him one morning, in walked Wellesley
Poole, who had just landed from the Dover packet;

it happened to be a very cold day, and the new
arrival drew his chair close to the fire ; this Brummell
observed, and said, "Why, Wellesley, you appear
cold ! but I am not surprised at it, for you must
have been devilish *hot* in England, or we should
never have seen you here."

It was not till his old friends, Mr. G. C——m,
Sir Arthur F——s, and afterwards Col. D——,
Berkeley Craven, and Henry Berkeley, came and
fixed themselves at Calais, that Brummell entered
at all into the English society of the place, and
then with great discrimination in the choice of his
acquaintances.

But, even in spite of this caution, he sometimes
came in contact with his friends' friends, whose
manners were most disagreeable to him. At one
house at which he visited, the master kept a kind of
fag, a tame animal, who was ready to follow him
anywhere, and eat his dinners. This person was
also kind enough to market for him, go to the post,
or to the stables on a cold night—moreover, he was
obliged to submit to be roasted : not like a former
Lord Chief Justice, at Eton, once only and in earnest,
and as a juvenile martyr to the ardour of his political
opinions, but *à discrétion*, and get no credit for it.
Nature had done little for this convenient creature of
a convenient race, and his parents less ; but, *malgré*
his outlandish bearing, his patron had the bad taste
to permit him to appear in the presence of his company. It happened that on one occasion the Beau

was of the party, and shortly after they had sat down
to dinner, the toady, thrusting out his plate, said, " Mr.
Brummell, I'll trouble you for a potato." There was
never a very large supply of silver at the tables of
the English residents at Calais, and Brummell looked
right and left for a spoon : but there was none, and
he paused at the difficulty ; the toady, however, tired
of holding out his arm, quickly relieved him from
the dilemma by saying in a persuasive tone of voice,
" Oh, take your fork—I'm not particular." " My
dear Berkeley," said the Beau afterwards to his
friend, " how can you ask gentlemen to meet such
people at dinner ? if your horses are ill, pay the
fellow five francs and have done with him."

However, towards the close of his residence at
Calais, he was not so particular whom he dined with.
One day, when walking on the ramparts arm-in-arm
with the late Lord Sefton, they were met by an
extremely vulgar-looking Englishman, who bowed to
Brummell in a very familiar manner. " Sefton," said
the Beau, " what can that fellow mean by bowing to
you ? " " To me ! he is bowing to you, I suppose,
for I know no one in Calais." Soon after, however,
the stranger passed again, and, seizing Brummell by
the arm, said to him in a most frightfully cordial
tone, " Don't forget, Brum, don't forget, goose at
four—goose at four ! " thus betraying the Beau's
engagement to dine with his hospitable but vulgar
friend, an invitation that he thought he had so
cleverly concealed from his refined one. It was

while promenading one day on the pier, and not
long before he left Calais, that an old associate of
his, who had just arrived by the packet from England,
met him unexpectedly in the street, and cordially
shaking hands with him, said, " My dear Brummell, I
am so glad to see you, for we had heard in England
that you were dead; the report, I assure you, was
in very general circulation when I left." " Mere
stock-jobbing, my good fellow, mere stock-jobbing,"
was the Beau's reply.

Like all small towns, whether in England or elsewhere, in which the society is limited, there were in
Calais several male as well as female gossips, whose
only occupation was, to perambulate from house to
house, and retail, at each in succession, all that was
true, and a great deal that was not, that they had
seen or heard, or neither, in their morning walks.
Brummell, as well as many others, was subject to
have everything he said or did carefully discussed, and
often enlarged upon, by such people; and they frequently fastened an ill-natured remark, or perhaps a
good joke, upon him, when he had in fact never heard
either, till he was called upon to contradict the *cancan*
of the day.

This exaggeration was quite unnecessary as regarded him, for his satirical vein and impudence led
him to make a sufficient number of pointed and satur-
nine remarks upon his countrymen, and lay himself
open to retaliation. But Brummell was more particularly severe with those who manifested a disposition

to intrude upon him without due introduction, or who vulgarly affected to be somebody, when their conduct and manners plainly indicated that they had never frequented that class of society to which they assumed to belong. Those who called themselves colonels or captains, without having any claim to the rank, were sure to be objects of his displeasure; retired tuft-hunters, also, and self-important fat gentlemen, were always singled out as targets for his keen and droll remarks. Whenever he was asked whether he knew any character of this kind, or indeed others more agreeable, but not to his mind, his usual reply was, "Know him, my good sir? to be sure I do. The fellow is a rank impostor; I recollect him perfectly, when he was butler at Belvoir." Or, "Don't you remember Jones, who kept the snuff-shop in Bond Street? that's the very man." In the following instance, however, he was called upon, in a very summary manner, to contradict one of his mischievous witticisms.

The sufferer in this case was a military man, who in the Peninsular, or some other war, had had the misfortune to be severely wounded in the face—in fact, to lose the most prominent feature of it. The sarcasm in question at length reached the ears of the injured party, and in consequence the Beau was one morning disturbed, at his breakfast, by a loud knocking at the door; his permission to enter was scarcely given, when the grisly warrior, with indignation in his eyes, and "satisfaction" in his thoughts, stalked

into the room and confronted him. " Pray, sir," said
Brummell, rising from his *fauteuil* " what happy
circumstance has induced you to favour me with such
a very early visit ? "   " Why the fact is, Mr. Brummell," replied the veteran, in a tone of voice which at
once told his aggressor that the circumstance was
anything but a " happy one," and that if his wit did
not speedily get him out of the scrape, his valour
must see him through it ; " the fact is, Mr. Brummell, I have heard that you have been kind enough to
spread a report about the town, affecting my position
in society here, by stating, that I am not a retired
officer, and never held a commission ; and that I am
really nothing more nor less than a retired hatter."
With admirable presence of mind the Beau listened
to this accusation, which was certainly delivered in a
manner savouring more of the camp than St. James's,
and with much gravity thrown into his countenance,
he immediately answered, " I am sorry, very sorry,
that any one should conceive it possible that *I* could
be guilty of such a breach of good manners.   I can
assure you, that there is not a word of truth in the
report."   The captain, perfectly satisfied and delighted
with his reception, now moved towards the door ;
when Brummell followed him to it, and as he was
leaving the room, again affirmed that the report was
false ; " For," said he, " now I think of it, I never
in my life dealt with a hatter without a nose."   It is
probable that the officer was not much pleased with
this unfeeling speech, but he was so taken by surprise

that he made no reply, and beat a retreat immediately. The only notice that Brummell took of the affair was, to express his astonishment the next day that any one should have sent him a "death's head!"

If his wit provoked a quarrel, it, as in this case, generally settled it; for he was by no means a lover of the duello. Some years before this period, the second of a gentleman, who had received instructions to call upon him and demand either satisfaction or an apology, is said to have announced his errand in a very peremptory manner, and concluded his message by saying, that he must apologise in five minutes. "In five minutes, sir!" replied the Beau in a cold sweat, "in five seconds, or in less time, if you prefer it." Brummell attributed his dislike to assignations in defence of his honour to a constitutional tendency to knock under. He was, he said, dearly fond of notoriety, but not of this particular kind. "My dear fellow," observed the Beau to a friend, when conversing on the subject, "perhaps you are not aware of the circumstance, but I am not naturally of an heroic turn. Nevertheless, I once had an affair at Chalk-farm, and a dreadful state I was in, I can tell you; never in my life shall I forget the horrors of the previous night! sleep was out of the question; and I passed it in pacing my room, cursing the cruelly good joke, for which I was on the eve of being torn from Lady —— and Roman punch for ever. The dawn was to me the harbinger of death, not of another day; and yet I almost hailed it with pleasure; but my

second's step upon the stairs soon neutralised the
feeling; and the horrid details, which he carefully ex-
plained to me, annihilated the little courage that had
survived the anxieties of the night.   We now left the
house, and no accident of any kind, no fortunate
upset, occurred, on our way to the place of ren-
dezvous; where we arrived, according to my idea
much too soon, a quarter of an hour before the time
named.

"There was no one on the ground, and each minute
seemed an age, as, in terror and semi-suffocation, I
awaited my opponent's approach.   At length the clock
of a neighbouring church announced that the hour of
appointment had come; how its tones, brought by the
wind across the fields, struck upon my heart!   I felt
like the criminal, when he hears the bell of St.
Sepulchre's for the last time: we now looked in the
direction of town, but there was no appearance of my
antagonist; my military friend kindly hinted that
clocks and watches varied, a fact I was well aware of,
and which I thought he might have spared me the
pleasure of hearing him remark upon; but a second
is always such a 'd—d good-natured friend.'   The
next quarter of an hour passed in awful silence, still
no one appeared, not even in the horizon; my companion whistled, and, confound him! looked much
disappointed; the half-hour struck—still no one; the
third quarter, and at length the hour.   My centurion
of the Coldstream now came up, this time in truth my
friend, and said to me, and I can tell you they were

the sweetest accents that ever fell upon my ear, ' Well, George, I think we may go : ' 'My dear M——, I replied, ' you have taken a load off my mind, let us go immediately ! ' " Brummell was by no means a bad classic, and he no doubt remembered that Horace kept a reputation, though he was not carried home upon his shield ; but though he was certainly no Bayard, there is no reason for asserting that he was another Bob Acres. Still, when he felt a deficiency in such emergencies, he should have applied to his friend, Lord Alvanley, who could have lent him as much courage then, as he did money afterwards, and that was to no trifling extent.

Once, indeed, he showed fight in a most unusual and vigorous manner : it was when the then proprietor of a notorious courtesan called to request him to explain some insult, with which he was said to have regaled the lady, in a morning call that she had made him. High words having ensued between Brummell and this gentleman, he ordered him to leave the room ; but finding that he demurred, the exasperated Beau, like the Bailie Nicol Jarvie, enforced his commands with a red-hot 'poker that was opportunely resting in the fire at the time : in this instance our hero deserved the honour of an ovation, for it was a hundred to one against him, and his opponent was moreover a man of war. If we could muster credulity sufficient to believe the Memoirs of this modern Aspasia, who, singularly enough, has since turned Roman Catholic, she not only held the Beau captive, but in contempt, and this,

too, when he was *Nulli Secundus* in London ; but it
is not astonishing that she affected to do so, for he
must have inspired her with *une jalousie de femme à
femme*—a woman can hardly be expected to forgive a
man for being more elegant than herself.

CHAPTER XXVII.

Brummell's Screen—Destined for the Duchess of York—Description of this Pasticcio—The Six Compartments—The Elephant and Napoleon —Portraits of the Beau's Friends—His Illustrations of their Characters—General Upton—The Marquis of Hertford—Lord Sefton— The Hyæna Tamed by the Muses and the Graces—The Tiger and the French Revolution—Brummell's Satire upon Lord Byron—Price offered for the Screen—M. Leleux's Parrot.

THOUGH Brummell read a great deal, his favourite matinal avocation was working at a large screen, which, when finished, he had destined for the Duchess of York ; but the pleasure of recording, by this present, his sense of her great kindness, was denied him, for Her Royal Highness died before it was completed ; he then laid it aside, and never resumed his labours.

This work of taste and patience is a masterpiece in its way; and had it ever reached Oatlands, many a fair dame and antiquated spinster would have envied its royal owner. The screen measures five feet and a half in height, and, when opened, is rather more than twelve in length ; it is divided into six leaves, and the ground is of green paper. The idea of a general design, with which it was evident Brummell had commenced, seems to have been soon laid aside. The

most prominent features of it are the quadrupeds,
which form the centre of the upper part of each leaf;
these prints are on a scale much larger than the generality of the other drawings.   In the first compartment
is an elephant, the second bears a hyena, the third a
tiger, the fourth a camel, and the fifth a bear.   The
sixth has no animal upon it.   Many of the drawings
which cover the remaining surface of the screen are
coloured : the engravings are in line, mezzotint, or
lithograph, with sketches in chalk, pastel, or pencil ;
in fact, a specimen of every possible variety of the
limner's or engraver's art, if oils be excepted, is to be
found upon it.   It will therefore be easily imagined,
that the general effect produced by such a multitude of
objects of every colour and form, is on the first *coup
d'œil* very confused : but, on a closer inspection, the
attention that has been devoted to arrangement of
almost every part, becomes easily discernible ; each
little pictorial episode, and there are hundreds, is
encircled by wreaths and garlands of flowers of every
description ; the rose predominating, much to the
credit of the paster's taste ; fruit, and emblems in
character with the subject to be illustrated, are also
mingled with the flowers ; to give an exact description
of this glorious piece of fiddle-faddle, the trifling industry of a thoroughly idle man, would be both useless and
tedious. I shall therefore merely attempt a slight sketch,
in the order in which I examined it, commencing with
the first compartment.

On this leaf, as I have before remarked, there is

an elephant, under the neck of which is a full-faced
portrait of Napoleon, who, in this case, is the subject
to be illustrated. By introducing this animal the Beau
intended to express the Emperor's power; but on the
throat of the modern king-maker is a butterfly, intended
to represent another of his attributes, and to neutralise
his greatness. The portrait is encircled by the neck,
shoulder, and trunk of this Chouni;[1] and the edges of
the two drawings, which would otherwise have been
discoverable, are concealed by other attributes, as well
as by fruit and flowers, cut out and arranged with
infinite pains. This plan of concealing the edges was
pursued throughout with as much nicety as a semp-
stress would bestow on the hem of a *chemise d'homme.*
Amongst these emblems, and immediately above the
Emperor's head, is a mortar elevated for firing; from
the mouth of it proceeds a sword, round which a
serpent has entwined itself: a scythe and a flag, with
the Russian eagle on it, are crossed above the sword,
and the trophy is completed by laurel branches over.
the emblem of Time. The trumpet of Fame, and a
port-fire nearly burnt out, are above the Muscovite
colours. The reader can scarcely fail to see the application of these illustrations to Napoleon's history.

Below the elephant, and in the centre of the same
leaf, are grouped four coloured portraits; the one on
the left hand looking outwards is General Upton, next

---

[1] Chunee, the largest elephant ever brought to England, first
appeared in a pantomime at Covent Garden in 1810, was then shown
at Exeter Change—now the Lowther Arcade—and on its becoming
mad, was shot by a detachment of the Guards.

to him are the late Marquis of Hertford and Lord Sefton,
apparently in conversation ; and the fourth (to me an
inconnu) is on their right, and looking towards them.
The general, who has a neck-cloth large enough for
three, and a rounded shirt-collar on the same scale, is
smelling a sprig of jessamine ; a Cupid lolls on his
shoulder, as much at ease as the reading Magdalen at
Dresden, and is killing, not the general, but Time, with
a book, probably Ovid's Art of Love.   On the body
of the gallant officer, who is thus indulging poor Cupid
with a ride a pig-a-back, is pasted an unnatural and
classical-looking landscape, representing a forest in the
distance, with a rocky foreground ; but the principal
subject is a young lady, who having thrown aside her
harp, is caressing the antlers of a wounded stag.   Back
to back with the general is the late Lord Sefton, the de-
fect in whose figure Brummell concealed with a flower,
probably with the intention of showing that he considered his physical infirmities were entirely overbalanced
by his amiable disposition.   This he might well do, for
he was one of his greatest benefactors.   Between his
lordship and the marquis is the head of a very lovely
woman, ornamented, without the slightest necessity, by
a plume of ostrich feathers.   The two peers are so
placed that it is difficult to say out of whose pocket
the divinity is emerging ; most likely that of the latter.
Lord Sefton is in Hessians, and wears a very peculiar
hat.   My Lord of Hertford, whose whiskers look as
if they were made of leopard's skin, is dressed in a
great-coat, and carries a large cane between a pair of

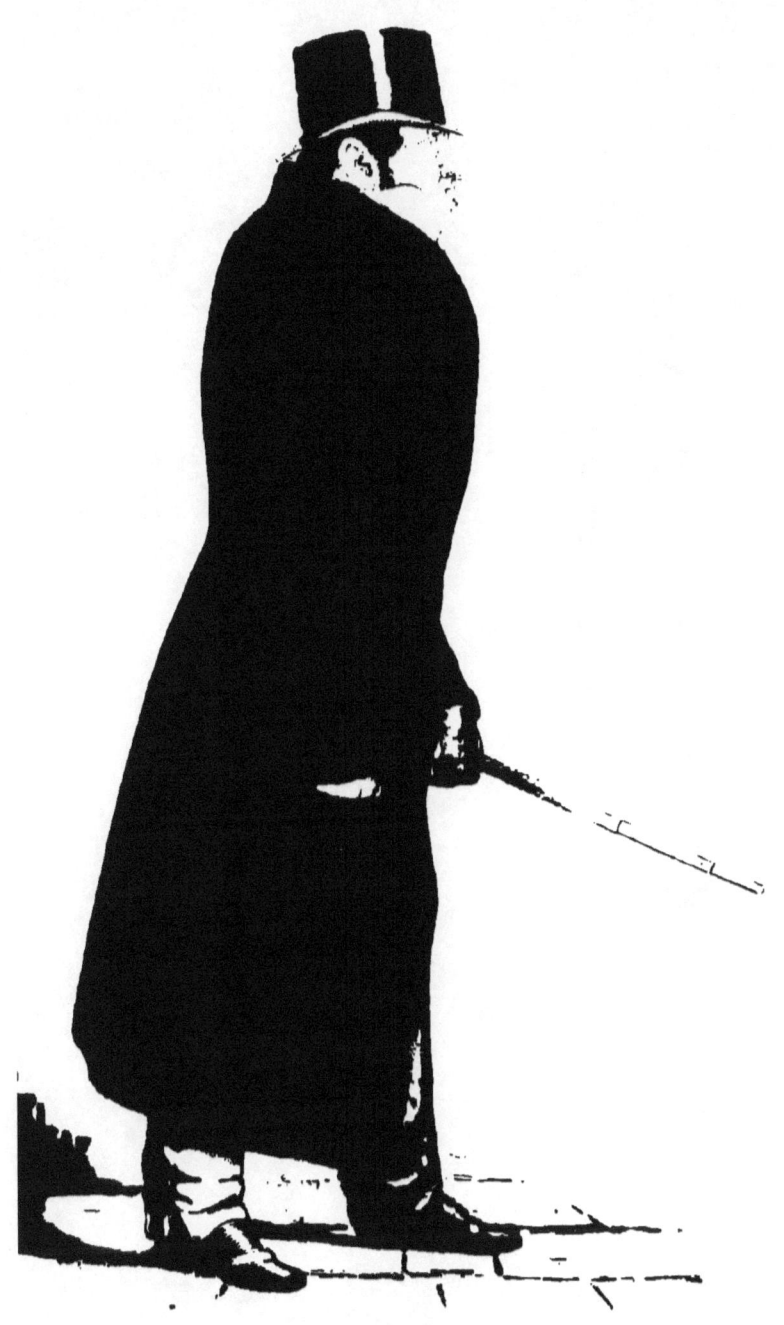

Earl of Sefton

yellow tan gloves, his left hand being inserted, like
Lord Sefton's right, in his pocket behind. His emblems are also highly appropriate and numerous.
First, and in the front, are two Cupids in an azure
cloud, one bearing the hymeneal torch, and the other
a dove, which is looking him amorously in the face.
Cupids, in every variety of position that the *coryphée*
of the grand opera could devise, float around his lordship. They may be literally said to swarm; and
judging by their looks, each of them seems to be laden
with the sweets of a different hive, more luscious than
those of Narbonne or Hymettus. One, much larger
and more saucy-looking than the rest, is standing on
his lordship's shoulder, and rests, with folded arms,
and the domesticated air of a favourite spaniel, upon
his hat. To the right is a charming print, by Bartolozzi or Cipriani, of a young girl attended by the ever-
lasting Cupids ; above her is a little archer shooting
at doves in a palm-tree, and around are Satyrs carrying Bacchantes and Shepherdesses in their arms.
Farther on is a gentleman who sports a pair of yellow
knee-breeches, and is presenting a nest of doves to a
lady in a scarlet-bodied dress. All these subjects
appear to have been *appliqué* with great judgment
in honour of the most noble the late Marquis of
Hertford. The *inconnu*, the last of the quartet, is
the counterpart of a piping bullfinch, and by the emblems that surround him may perhaps have been a
celebrated " fanatico per la musica." These portraits
are from Dighton's caricatures.

The Hyena in the second compartment is represented as being tamed by the Arts, Sciences, and Religion, symbols of which, mingled with the Muses and the Graces, are seen on every side. In the centre of this leaf is a coloured print, taken from a scene in the " Fille mal gardée." There are also various drawings representing historical, mythological, and rural subjects. Amongst the most striking are Telemachus relating his adventures to Calypso, Phaeton driving his car, Time his chariot; a French dragoon at bivouac preparing a fowl for the camp-kettle; a *religieuse* at her devotions; a minuet at a French fair; a gentleman and a shepherdess, whose dog has seized the skirt of her dress, and with an anxious look is endeavouring to detach her from her admirer.

The tiger on the third leaf is surrounded by Cupids, cows, goats, &c., all, with the exception of the first, harmless and peaceful animals. On each side of the royal brute is a coloured print, representing the juvenile amusements of the Dauphin and the Duchesse d'Angoulême. In the one to the right they are playing at soldiers: she is marching in front of her brother and beating a drum, thus indicating the resolute spirit which she afterwards showed : her dog is scampering before her ; and her companion, who is dressed in the national colours, is carrying a flag, on which are inscribed the words *Union, Force.* She has evidently tempted him away from his ninepins to follow her, and these toys are seen behind him scattered on the ground. In the other print they are playing at battledore and shuttlecock, looking very happy and very merry. The ferocious tiger was well chosen to illustrate the period and the subject to which this part of the screen is devoted ; for in this beast of prey are plainly personified the cruelties of the Revolution, and, in the domestic animals, the helplessness of those who suffered by its horrible excesses. The children's ignorance of the nature of the proceedings of which their flag and their tri-coloured sashes were the emblems, and their utter un-consciousness of the anxiety and danger which at that very time surrounded them and all belonging to them, as expressed by their game of battledore and shuttle-cock, is truly characteristic of their years. Such happily is generally the case with children. In the midst of the dreadful hurricane in which the crew of the *Bridgewater* so nearly perished, and when not a ray of hope existed for the safety of a soul on board, where were the little children of one of the passengers, and what were they doing ? Were they frightened at the unusual trembling of the ship, as she staggered under the concussions of each succeeding wave, or sobbing in their mother's arms ? No; at that awful moment they were floating their little paper boats in the water that half filled the cabins. Below these prints are many other Cupids also, but by no means so comfortable as the one on Lord Hertford's shoulder. One poor boy is standing, in a cold wretched night, at the door of a house ; his torch is thrown down in the snow, and his dripping pinions are scarcely covered by a scanty red mantle.   He seems to be a good illustration of the old song, " In the dead of the night," and is apparently singing the insinuating line,

" I've lost my way, ma'am ; do pray let me in."

Near this mischief-maker is another smoking a pipe.

Below the camel, in the fourth compartment, is a man in Cossack trousers : a monkey is sitting on his back, gently exciting his own epidermis : a pensive Cupid is clinging to the coat of the incognito.   Near him is a gentleman with a lady in his arms ; a Cupid is looking up at them, and pointing to a volume of sermons which he holds in his hand : a butterfly has alighted on the cavalier's coat, and not far off is a group of Cupids and satyrs rushing in among bathing nymphs.   There is also a female barber.

The bear in the fifth compartment is stimulating his appetite with a young crocodile : around him are children at play, shepherds, the Graces, Venus, and numerous insects and shells.   Lower down are portraits of Charles Fox, Nelson, Sheridan, the Regent Philip of Orleans, and John Kemble.   Fox has a butterfly near him ; Nelson, Greenwich Hospital ; Sheridan, a Cupid carousing on some straw ; and Kemble, a ladybird on his waistcoat.   Round the arm of a man in Hessians is a green monkey holding a mask, and another monkey is between his legs. There are also likenesses of Lucien Buonaparte, the Princess Charlotte, and the Duke of Cambridge when a young man ; and a little piece representing an old

curé de village trying, but in vain, to thread the needle
of one of his pretty parishioners.

Byron and Napoleon, placed opposite to each other,
occupy the upper centre of the last and sixth leaf:
the former is surrounded with flowers, but has a wasp
on his throat. This to his friend was base ingratitude
on the part of Brummell, for the noble lord spoke of,
and would have pasted him, with more charitable feeling. Kean, as Richard, is the last print I shall notice.
He is below the Emperor, and his neck is ornamented
with two hymeneal torches laid together crosswise by
a true-lover's-knot.

It will be seen by this imperfect description that
to understand fully the wit shown in the arrangement
of all the groups, it is necessary that the observer
should be familiar with the gossip of the day; and
there is little doubt that any of Brummell's contemporaries would, with the greatest ease, recapitulate
the histories attached to each, and explain to his
juniors, circumstances in the arrangement, that to them
are merely unmeaning riddles.

When Brummell left Calais, the screen, according
to his valet's version of the affair, was placed in his
hands as part payment of a debt. Subsequently,
when Sélègue's affairs became deranged, he was
obliged to put it in pawn at an upholsterer's at
Boulogne; and it was at this person's house that I
saw it during my short stay in that town. A nobleman, one of Brummell's former friends, in passing
through, was once anxious to buy it, but the gentle-

man's gentleman valued his master's exertions too
highly, and foolishly asked seven thousand francs for
it, a bargain which his customer very naturally refused.   Since that period, another Englishman offered
two thousand; this, however, was declined; and when
I saw it, the cabinet-maker was fitting it up very
handsomely with a mahogany frame, and intended
sending it to London, where he hoped to realise a
large sum by the sale of it.   This screen must have
been a fertile subject of conversation for Brummell's
privileged visitors, and to them only was it ever
exhibited.   To have heard him while employed in
cutting out, cutting up, and pasting his dearest
friends, and expatiating upon the group that was
under his hands at the time, must have been a treat
indeed.

Having now introduced the reader to the Beau's
buhl, Sèvres, quadrupeds, and screen, I must not omit
to mention a biped that completed his effeminate
establishment.   This was no less a personage than a
stately green-and-yellow parrot, which was very much
attached to him, and, in return, he treated the intelligent bird with great consideration.   Brummell was
never tired of singing his praises and calling the
attention of his visitors to his beauty.   " Is he not a
fine bird ? " he used to say.   " What plumage ! what
a beak and tail !   How solemn he looks !   Stand
here, my good fellow, and examine him : don't you
see a likeness to somebody ?—a traveller, a poet, ay,
and a patriot, too—a man who had the good luck to

be sent to Newgate. Well now, how very obtuse; the likeness don't strike you, I see;" and then placing his visitor in a different position, he would continue thus: "Now, look at him in this point of view —*now* don't you see? how very odd! why, don't you see how like he is to Hobhouse?"

Hobhouse, however, at length got beyond the Board of Control, and was dismissed for malpractices into the court below, his beak being on more friendly terms with the curtains and the buhl furniture than was agreeable to his master, or rather to his master's *locataire*, for he was the property of Mr. Leleux. Whenever an opportunity offered, however, Hobhouse broke loose from his cage, and would fly up to the Beau's windows. For this contumacious conduct he at last got pinioned; but he was an obstinate fellow; and, as he could not take wing, he used to walk upstairs, as well as his namesake or any other visitor, knock at his friend's door, and having obtained admittance, which he never failed to do, did not return to his cage without having received both wine and biscuit. This bird, I believe, came from Hâvre, appropriately termed, by Miss Costello, "the town of parrot."

 END OF VOL. I.

PRINTED BY BALLANTYNE, HANSON AND CO.
EDINBURGH AND LONDON.